CHICKEN OF THE SEA

NEIL BARRY

To Dot,

Remember this version

July 4th 2015

"First things first; I need a diversion"

Neil Barry

July 4 2015

Chicken of the Sea, and its sequels, are fiction, written so as to appear realistic. The reader should note that the books combine real settings, things, and events (to encourage additional reading and research) with fictional characters. The fictional characters are the result of the author's imagination and have no intentional resemblance to people, living or dead. Any resemblance to actual persons is entirely coincidental.

Ordering Information:

Special discounts are available on quantity purchases by schools, associations, and others. For details, contact the publisher at the address above.

ISBN 0996292616

EAN 9780996292610

First Edition, Published April 30, 2015

In Appreciation

The author extends his heartfelt appreciation to his wife, whose exhaustive edits added charm and wit, his daughter, whose great writing skill was motivation to try harder, and his son, who slogged through early drafts and provided insight into the mind of Victor Joshua. To Susan, Kylie, Kathryn, and others who reviewed the manuscript prior to publication, the author offers his sincere gratitude, in particular to those who inspired him to finish the project, who reported discrepancies and errors, and who made helpful suggestions.

To readers,

If you enjoy this book, the author would be very grateful if you encourage your friends and others to read it. Please visit the author's website, neilbarrybooks.com for more information and background about *Chicken of the Sea*, the next book in the series, *Chicken Too*, and *Free Range Chicken*, a work in progress.

Abstract

Victor Joshua Walker's father is an assistant manager of the local supermarket, obsessed with Russian composers and Captain Joshua Slocum, the first man to sail alone around the world 100 years earlier. Much to Victor's dismay, his father has planned a similar journey for his family and is building a boat in the barn next door. After a neighbor's trailer burns to the ground, he launches his boat and they move aboard. After nine years, it still isn't finished; it's the dead of winter; the marina's deserted; the boat is the size of a school bus; and there's no heat! No matter that Victor's father has told everyone he will follow Slocum's route across the northern Atlantic, for seemingly no reason at all, he suddenly decides to head south. No one is happy about spending three years away from home, especially Victor.

Chicken of the Sea is more than a story about dragging three cynical kids around the world. Along with wry humor are the realistic aspects of living aboard a small sailing boat, the hardships of ocean voyages, storms at sea, fascinating foreign cultures, and exotic tropical islands. There are also clues to a past life; burns on Victor's forearms, grandparents who died in a house fire, a missing uncle and aunt, rare Russian Christmas ornaments, first-edition books, a guitar once played by Segovia... If that's not enough, people are following them.

On a desolate island in the southern Bahamas, an old man arrives just in time to save Victor and his younger brother when they encounter a Hammerhead shark. Victor soon discovers that the old man, while a good friend, launders money for a drug cartel, and is as dangerous as the shark. Like the men who have followed the Walkers from Norfolk, Virginia, he's never far away.

In the midst of long days spent at sea, there is murder, kidnapping, a life-threatening appendix operation as the family rounds Cape Horn, and a thrilling conclusion when the Walkers arrive in the Marquesas Islands in the Pacific. Or is it the conclusion when there are so many unanswered questions? *Chicken Too* picks up the story, beginning two weeks later when disaster looms on the horizon...

Contents

Please visit neilbarrybooks.com for background information for many of the places and things in this story.

Chapter 1

I was four when my father stopped shaving. A shadowy haze spread over his face. Within days, fuzz became bristles, slowly turning into a beard that looked out of place. One Sunday before church, he trimmed it with manicure scissors. I watched him peer into the mirror, snipping as if one hair too short would be a disaster. When he finished, a goatee remained—just a mustache and a tuft on his chin.

"I look different, don't I?" he asked.

Except for the beard, he looked the same, but I nodded. He turned to my mother, seeking a second opinion.

"You look different," she confirmed. He seemed pleased until she added, "It needs to be dyed." His beard was light brown, not dark like his hair.

He looked back at me. "Do I look like the Captain?" I nodded again. There was a passing resemblance because of the beard, though not much else that I could see.

Few photos of the Captain survived 100 years. We had one, crinkled and yellow with age. He stared out from a small, gold-edged frame on the living room wall, a mostly bald man with a thick goatee and the hardened features of a ship's master from Nova Scotia. He shared more than a beard with my father. Long before I knew what the words meant, I envisioned the Captain as resourceful, unyielding, and stern, like my father.

The Captain was Joshua Slocum. He was the first person to sail alone around the world, spending three years, two months, and two days away from home. He sailed 46,000 miles by himself, and then wrote a book about it. It had the descriptive, if uninspired title of *Sailing Alone Around the World*. Our copy had a red cloth cover faded to brown, embossed with two seahorses and an anchor, its white lettering almost worn off. It was dated 1900, the first printing in England by Sampson Low, Marston & Company.

My father read to me every night from that book, carefully turning each yellowed page, his voice rising and falling like the waves, harsh in the cold dead of night or whispering like the palms on the shores of Samoa. He stoked my dreams with sailing the mountainous seas off Tierra del Fuego in a howling gale, scarcely outdistancing savages led by the murderous Black Pedro, nearly dying in the surf after running aground, and sailing for 72 days without sight of land.

Every night until I was six, I gorged on my father's tales of the Captain and his voyage from Boston in a small, oyster sloop; and then I tossed and turned and whimpered in my sleep. Sometimes my bed was shamefully soaked when I awoke, yet the bright morning beamed back at me from the mirror, dispelling what I thought to be the consequences of the previous night's epic. I spent my afternoons in a cavernous barn next to our trailer. I played among wood shavings that my father planed from a keel, sweet-smelling, long curls of wood that cushioned my falls; or I hid behind boxes of secondhand tools and white pails of glue to watch him carefully bend strips of wood over frames.

"It's Kauri," he would say with pride, if anyone asked, "from New Zealand. It's worth every penny. There's no better wood for boat building. It's strong, easy to work, and it won't rot under water." The brief lecture seldom varied.

By my ninth birthday, a sturdy yacht with a wide beam and a full keel filled most of the barn. It bore a marked resemblance to the Captain's *Spray* despite modern devices, like a motor.

People chose their words carefully when his boat came up for discussion. The topic surfaced as inevitably as a whale comes up for air. Puzzlement or disapproval lurked behind even polite questions. My mother busied herself during such exchanges. It didn't matter that he kept the barn doors closed; everyone knew he was building a boat; and every kid in my school called me 'Noah Junior.' Shame struggled with anger, but I kept my mouth shut.

+++

Only my grandmother, his mother-in-law, voiced opposition. My parent's fifteenth wedding anniversary was no exception. It was a miserable night in December, the wind ceaselessly battering the roof of her Victorian cottage, the rain drumming behind my father's words, loosened by champagne.

"It won't be long before we leave," he said suddenly.

"Are you seriously proposing to keep them on that boat for three years?" She was elegant and seemed fragile, like the cut crystal glasses that held their champagne.

"We don't have a choice, Sarah."

"There's no need to do this," she continued.

He looked at my brother and sister, both engrossed in the newspaper. His eyes, cold like the Atlantic, rested on me. He said nothing.

She sighed, pushing back a wisp of snow-white hair. "You could leave them with me."

"That isn't possible. Not now."

"Of course it's possible! Possible and sensible," my grandmother snapped.

"I don't know about sensible," he murmured. "Congratulations by the way."

He took the local newspaper from my brother and spread it out on the coffee table. Her photo was on the bottom of the front page, Outstanding Staff Person award from the Richmond School District. She'd intervened in a case of middle-school bullying, going out of her way to prevent it. The article named her three grandchildren, which delighted my brother and sister as much as it appeared to bother my mother. My father hadn't mentioned it until then.

She stared at him. "There's no reason why they can't live here."

"There's always a reason," he said, his face almost hopeful as he glanced back at me.

"It's mad," she said, seeming suddenly tired.

Silence blanketed my grandmother's sitting room. A log's crackle in the fireplace sounded like a gunshot.

My father smiled and touched her shoulder. "Sarah, it's good of you to worry."

After that, we turned with relief to my grandmother's crab bisque, veal and asparagus, and crème brûlée. When the storm ended, we gathered our belongings. My grandmother followed us out to the family van. Branches ripped from the trees covered the yard, and a garbage can rested against the van's front bumper. My father dragged the garbage can back to where it belonged.

"There'll be far worse storms at sea," she remarked in her no-nonsense way. She looked professorial, her wavy hair caught in a tidy bun, prim reading glasses perched on her nose.

"Slocum survived them, and so will we."

"He was a real sea captain," she said factually.

"I built a real boat, Sarah."

"It's tiny, the size of a school bus!"

"A regular school bus is two feet shorter," my little brother added cheerfully.

I hid my smile as my father glared at him. "Seaworthiness isn't a matter of size. The Captain's boat was the same size, and he didn't have today's technology."

If he meant his motor, I'd watched him rebuild the rusty-blue motor he'd salvaged from an abandoned 1985 Ford tractor, learning new cuss words when he tried to start it. After three days, he gave up and called a mechanic.

"Our boat is much safer," he went on. "If we run into a bad storm, we'll heave to or use the sea anchor."

"You can't learn everything from books," I said under my breath. I was almost a teenager, old enough to know not to say it aloud.

"And you won't always be lucky," my grandmother promptly added.

Before my father could reply, my mother interrupted. "Mom, thank you for a lovely meal. We need to go. I'm already late for my shift."

My grandmother waved from the sidewalk as our van pulled away.

We never went home the same way. Sometimes, my father drove on suburban streets and we spied on rich peoples' houses, weaved through the city, or used back roads, so it always took longer get home. However, he was so grumpy he stayed on Parham Road, and took I-64 to Norfolk, Virginia.

+ + +

That night, sirens woke me up, still far away, yet loud enough for me to distinguish between the wails of fire engines and the hee-haw of police cars. Half asleep, I wandered into the living room. Through the front windows, I saw an eerie glow near the entrance to Arcadia Park. Strobe lights lit up the trailers at the end of our lane. Suddenly, the front door flung open. My father stood in the

5

doorway, breathing heavily, a jacket over his pajamas. Something about him terrified me.

"Close the curtains and turn off the lights," he ordered. Mud covered his slippers, yet he stalked across the room, leaving a trail on the carpet and into the kitchen.

"Whose trailer is it?"

"The Masons,'" he snapped before checking the lock on the kitchen door.

My sister sometimes played with the two Mason girls. Their brother, Ryan, was 12, like me. We seldom spoke once he decided I was Noah, Jr. When they moved in, their last name was Mason. Their mom remarried soon after. Her new husband's name was Walker, like ours. He'd lived at Arcadia Park for a month before he painted 'Walker' on his mailbox.

"Are they okay?"

He picked up the telephone and punched in numbers before he turned back, his face as pale as altar marble. "Walker got out. Get Ben and Jessie dressed. Don't leave here, no matter what. Don't open the door to anyone, and keep the lights off."

"Why?"

"Just for once, will you do what you're told?" he barked, hurrying into his bedroom.

I could hear him speaking on the phone, too quietly for me to make out words. He slammed a drawer and returned. Without warning, a roar erupted, rattling the windows, creating a brief and terrible daylight inside our trailer.

"Jesus!" I jumped involuntarily.

The tongue slip went unnoticed. "The van," he muttered to himself on his way out the door. "It was parked next to the trailer."

Mr. Walker had a blue Ford minivan like ours. Our neighbors came out to watch the flames leap into the night sky, the fire raging for an hour against the torrents of water gushing from the firefighters' hoses.

+ + +

The next night began like most nights of the last nine years. My father came in from the barn, stopping to wash his hands at the sink. He was an assistant manager at the local Food King, a 24-hour supermarket two blocks away on South Military Highway. He assigned himself the sunrise shift and devoted the rest of the day to building his boat. He emerged from the barn only when it was time for dinner, thirty minutes before my mother left for the night shift at Norfolk General Hospital.

As usual, he smelled of varnish when he sat down to eat. What we didn't expect came when he put down his fork. "I quit today," he announced.

It wasn't as if he hadn't talked about quitting before. A boat filled the barn, books about navigation and seamanship lay on the table, and boxes with labels like 'compass' and 'windlass' gathered dust in the closets. Like death, you knew it would happen, just not at dinner.

"We're leaving here in two days," he added as if he was saying 'pass the peas.'

"Jessie!" my mother barked. My sister played with her pigtail, oblivious to fingers greasy from chicken. "You said next year, John."

"Don't have a choice, do we?" He leaned across the table. "We ought to leave right now," he whispered to her.

My mother simply nodded. He looked at me. I shifted to avoid his gaze and forked the remains of my dinner into a mush of potato and beans.

"What about Christmas?" I asked.

"Don't worry, Josh. We'll have Christmas on the boat," my mother said quickly.

"Is the boat finished, Daddy?" Jessie asked. She hadn't talked much since the fire.

"Almost."

"Why don't we stay here until it is finished?" I kept my eyes down.

He pushed his chair back and crossed the room to the Captain's photograph. Eye to eye, goatee to goatee. "What we'll save in rent is worth a little inconvenience."

"Inconvenience," my mother repeated, looking at the Captain's picture.

I wondered again whether it troubled my mother that Captain Slocum's first wife had been born Virginia Walker, her married name. I viewed my own name as no particular blessing—Victor Joshua, after the Captain's first son, born on his father's sailing ship, *Constitution*. My brother was Benjamin Aymar, after Slocum's second son. My brother bore little resemblance to his namesake. Benjamin Slocum used a shiny tin can on a string to draw sharks to the stern of the ship so his mother could shoot them with a revolver. My brother read books, all books, any books. They named my sister after Jessie Helena Slocum, who was born in the Philippine Islands. The Captain's fourth child gave his name to our Bengal cat, James Abraham Garfield: 'Jag' for his dark, jaguar spots.

"The sooner we decide what we're taking, the better," our captain continued. Easy for him to say. The only things he would take from Arcadia Park were his boat, his books, his music— hundreds of CDs of Russian composers—and his unwilling crew. "You can take whatever you want if you have space for it. There are two lockers under each berth. The things you want to save we'll leave with your grandmother; the rest goes in the dumpster."

"I'm taking the *Britannica*," Ben announced. "We'll need it for the trip."

"Not that."

There were 32 thick, leather-bound volumes in the 15th edition of the *Encyclopedia Britannica*. Our grandmother had purchased it for Ben at a yard sale for less than the paper was worth. Ben's expertise ended in 1989, the year it was printed. It drove me crazy; however, it was just the way he was.

"You just said we could decide what to take," I reminded my father.

"Not the encyclopedia. It's too heavy."

"I'm taking it, even if I can't take anything else."

He returned Ben's relentless stare. "There's no room for things that aren't essential."

"I'm taking my guitar." I was ready for a confrontation.

My guitar had belonged to his mother. It was old, with rich basses and pure trebles despite a small split in the Brazilian rosewood side. The ebony fingerboard was inlaid with tiny mother-of-pearl flowers. Inside, a label read 'Ignacio Fleta e Hijos, Barcelona, 1961.' Once, when I was tuning it, my father said he'd heard Segovia play it. I didn't believe him.

"I should be thankful it's not my father's Hamburg Steinway," he said.

"He played the piano?" I asked. There was no reply.

+ + +

On Tuesday morning, a huge crane and a long semi-trailer from the Chesapeake Bay Boat Transportation Company pulled up in our street. With all the mud in the yard, it took an hour to get the crane into place, and almost as long to line up the truck and the barn. Meanwhile, my father climbed up a precariously balanced ladder and ripped eight panels of roofing from the barn, sending them crashing to the ground, allowing the crane's cables to pass through and lift his boat into place. From the outside, it looked finished, white with a blue stripe from stem to stern, where he'd painted '*Spray*' in lettering that looked almost happy.

We followed the boat with a wide load warning strapped to the roof of our van. Neighbors waved us on, their bewilderment complete. Eight slow-moving miles later, we arrived at Pearson Brothers boat yard. Another crane lowered the boat into murky water after my mother, with a kind of grim enjoyment, whacked a bottle of cheap champagne against the bow. When Captain Slocum launched his *Spray*, he wrote 'she sat on the water like a swan,' a swan costing $553.62 for materials and 13 months of labor. My father's boat shared the same name, an ugly duck that cost $179,258.27, took nine years to build, and still wasn't finished. I hated it.

Chapter 2

My father, who seemed both excited and exhausted, suggested that we celebrate by eating dinner at a restaurant. His crew went along because the dining area was bright and warm and the food was good. It was dark when we returned to his boat. The wind howled, driving ice crystals that pricked our skin. The air was so cold that it hurt to breathe. Hazardous, black sheets of ice hid in the dark and waited for an unwary foot. We hurried back and forth from the van, carrying our belongings.

Our trailer was vast compared to my father's boat: 38'6" long, 14'1" wide, just high enough inside for him to stand up. The center cabin, or 'salon,' combined kitchen, dining room, living room, navigation area, and bedroom in a space 14 feet square, most of it taken up by a table and seats. There were two beds, which my father insisted on calling 'berths.' Jessie's berth was next to the tiny kitchen. My father called that a 'galley.' There was a spare berth wedged above and behind the table. In the front of the boat was the bow cabin that I would share with my ten-year-old brother, with two narrow berths the size of sleeping bags. Our parents' cabin was in the back of the boat, 'the stern,' behind the engine room. They had their own bathroom. Our 'head' was crammed next to the table—a sink, a commode, and a shower that could fit in a construction site toilet.

The electrical supply came from a series of extension cords joined end to end, stretching from an outlet in the workshop, past rows of boats sitting on blocks, to us. It powered two flickering lights, a dismal glow, yet we gathered like moths around a candle, hoping for warmth.

"There's foam

insulation behind that plywood, the same as our trailer," he volunteered. "One of my better ideas."

We shivered and glared at the varnished plywood that lined the inside of his boat. His insulation made no difference to the temperature. Wearing sweaters and jeans to bed, with extra blankets folded in half, wasn't enough—we were still cold. In the middle of the night, Ben squeezed into my berth where he stayed until early morning; his tossing and turning made me send him away.

"It's cold as hell over here."

I could hear his teeth chattering. "Hell is hot! Go back to sleep."

"You're mean."

I was mean. I didn't care.

The wind, which had shrieked like a ghoul through the night, ended at daybreak when resounding booms from the nearby navy yard took over. Ben and I stayed in bed for an hour. It was too cold to get up. Finally, with nothing else to do, we crawled out of our cabin, clutching blankets around us, making clouds of mist with every breath. In the bathroom, a cup with water left over from brushing my teeth, had frozen solid during the night.

Our first meal aboard was cereal and milk too cold to drink. Without coffee in the morning, my parents seemed unable or unwilling to speak. The noise from the navy yard made the mood worse. Without a word, my father left, returning fifteen minutes later with a kerosene heater borrowed from the boatyard's caretaker. The heat spread out slowly. The smell of kerosene sickened me. My mother had told me more than once that the scars on my arms were from a fall on a heater like that when I was three. I kept a safe distance, while my family huddled around it with blankets over their backs, playing cards until it was warm enough to unpack the boxes and bags we'd carried aboard. All the while, Captain Slocum stared down from the bulkhead overlooking the table, his expression silently critical.

"It's a rite of passage, putting up the mast," my father announced with the arrival of the boatyard crane. His enthusiasm met with silence. "I'll need someone to help," he added. He meant me. The silence continued while my dread dueled with pride at being needed.

"It's tradition to put a coin under the mast step for good luck," he explained. He opened the loose change jar, emptied it on the table, and inspected the coins like a miser. Any money not spent on his boat, he had saved for the trip.

"He better not use pennies. We'll need all the luck we can get," I whispered to Ben, who erupted in giggles.

A mast soon swung from a crane, the chaos of rigging everywhere, each piece with a name: shrouds and stays, which held the mast up; and halyards, which hoisted the sails. I hated them all. By late afternoon, both masts stood on Virginia state quarters. My fingers and toes were numb and my skin matched the boat's blue stripe. Exhausted, we went below. After seeing the clutter of boxes and bags in the cabin, my father disappeared into the engine room; he said to work on the wiring. Ben and I sorted cans of food purchased on sale at Food King and stacked them into compartments in the bilge. Forty cans of chicken noodle and tomato soup filled the smallest compartment, beside it, assorted canned vegetables. We filled another compartment with tuna after identifying each can with a waterproof marker in case the bilge flooded and the labels came off—'T 4/240,' was tuna, the fourth can of 240. My father liked tuna.

+ + +

Christmas Eve sneaked up on us. My father rescued a tree from Food King's outdoor display, a lop-sided, spiky orphan, ridiculously small after he trimmed three feet from the end. It seemed uneasy bearing the antique ornaments that came out of my mother's boxes, enameled bells, glass balls hand-painted with winter scenes, and lacquered wood figures of strange-looking Santa Clauses nested together. They came from my father's side of the family.

The next day, dawn to dusk drizzle matched the mood on his boat. There were few presents under the tree, nothing that couldn't fit in a shoebox, educational board games, books, wet weather gear, and two blue blazers. I poked at a metal button decorated with a tiny anchor and a coil of rope.

"Try them on," my father insisted.

"I'd like to see my boys dressed up," my mother added. "It'll only take a minute."

As Ben and I reluctantly rose to change our clothes, my grandmother arrived. A friend had dropped her off a few blocks away on the way to visit her daughter, a chief petty officer on maternity leave from the Navy. My grandmother brought real presents—a digital camera for my mother, a crate full of craft materials for Jessie, and small laptop computers for Ben and me.

"You've spent too much money," my father protested after we'd opened the last present.

"They'll need computers when they start home school next week." My grandmother continued to help Jessie sort through her paints, pencils, tubes of glue, and colored papers.

"It's not that we don't appreciate it," he went on. "You're spoiling them."

"After everything that's happened, I don't think I'm spoiling them."

"You're not, Mom," my mother said. "You can always get on a plane. There'll be long periods of time when we aren't sailing."

"It'd make more sense if you came with us. There's plenty of room on the *Spray*. You could sleep in the spare berth," my father added.

I jumped on the wagon. "If she slept in our cabin with Jessie she wouldn't have to climb over the dining table."

"It's nice of you to offer, Josh. I'm too old to go traipsing around the world," she choked, looking at me. I felt even more miserable.

"You used to say you'd never be too old to travel, Mom," my mother said.

She dabbed at her eyes. "I'm worried about you, that's all. I want you to send me lots of photos."

"We have a long-range radio so we can contact each other in an emergency," my father said. He jotted down numbers and letters on a scrap of paper. "This is our call sign."

She ignored him when he tried to hand it to her. He poked it inside her handbag.

"Now you've each got a computer, there's no excuse for my boys not to send me email." She turned to my father, holding Jessie's hand tightly in hers. "That way, I'll know you're safe."

The Captain, the *Spray*, or our forthcoming trip, weren't mentioned again, not until my grandmother left for Richmond.

+ + +

We returned to Arcadia Park for the garage sale. Snow was still on the ground in grubby mounds where the sun didn't reach. Nothing remained of the barn, just a rectangle of bare earth to show where I'd spent so much of my childhood, and stacks of concrete blocks, ready to construct foundation walls for more trailers. It was a dreary sight, still better than the Pearson Brothers' boatyard, where stray cats wailed through the night, and deafening bangs came from the navy yard during the day.

With our trailer already sold and another family scheduled to move in within a week, we had to sell everything still inside. Some customers were neighbors, most were strangers, yet all wanted a bargain. They picked apart our possessions, haggled over how much things were worth, and sometimes ridiculed what we owned with 'nothing worth buying.' As my mother pointed out to perk up our spirits, it was better than throwing stuff away. When I couldn't stand it any longer, I went from one trailer to another, saying goodbye. No one said it was the last time we would see each other, yet everyone knew.

The O'Neils lived in a double-wide trailer across the road from us. They were retired and talked endlessly of selling out and moving to Florida. Almost every day, Mr. O'Neil came to chat with my father. When I returned, they were in our kitchen, searching for last minute bargains even as my parents boxed up what hadn't been sold. Mr. O'Neil sauntered over with two chisels and a wooden mallet, although arthritis had turned his hands into claws.

"They're going to turn the Masons' lot into a basketball court," he said to me.

"Ryan would like that."

My father looked up from the box he was packing. "Any news on what caused it?"

"The firemen said their Christmas tree caught on fire."

"I told the police I saw them at Burke's Farm earlier in the day," Mrs. O'Neil said.

"You told the insurance investigator," he corrected. "Least he said he was. He had a fancy car for an insurance investigator. New black Caddy. They cost more than most people make in a year."

She shrugged, not disputing, and sorted through a box full of paperbacks. "They had their tree cut while they waited, so it was fresh, but he wasn't interested. He was more interested in you, John."

My father glanced at me, seeming annoyed that I was there. "Why do you say that?"

"He wanted to know if you'd left a forwarding address," she replied. "He's come back twice to ask if we've seen you." She looked at her husband as though anticipating disapproval.

"He's suspicious because Walker disappeared. Didn't even go to the funeral!"

"He wanted to know what trucking company you used, only I forgot," she went on. "Unpleasant little man. His taste in shirts is awful."

"He's persistent for being so short. I think Josh is taller." Mr. O'Neil winked at me.

"He might think we're related because of the name," my father said, his mood darkening. I could tell from his eyes—they grew distant. He scribbled on the back of a paperback and gave it to Mrs. O'Neil. "If you see him again, send me an email."

"You use email?" I'd never seen him use the family computer except to order boat parts.

He gave me a withering glance. "Make yourself useful and carry stuff out to the van."

A few minutes later, he shepherded Ben and Jessie into the van and took one last look around. Instead of taking the shortest way out of Arcadia Park, he went out the back gate. When my mother asked why, he said the main road into Norfolk was busy at that time of day, yet it still took an hour to drive back to the boatyard.

+ + +

The next morning, it was so cold that even the cats sought shelter from the wind. While we shivered in our berths and waited for the kerosene heater to warm the cabin, my father began his day by making calls on his cell phone.

"We're moving to a marina in Scott Creek, just across the river in Portsmouth," he explained when he finished. "It'll be quieter, and they allow live-aboard boats during winter."

"Do they have hot showers?" My mother never dodged the important things.

For the last five days, bathing had consisted of wiping ourselves down with a cold, damp cloth and replacing our clothes as quickly as possible. It was like camping out, without the tent. The manager of the Pearson Brothers' boatyard offered to let us use the workers' shower. It was filthy, it stank, and the cats were annoying. It was almost as bad as their toilet, which we did use because there was no other choice.

"I didn't ask," he replied shortly. "We'll only be there for a week or two. We can shower at the YMCA if we have to."

His temper went downhill when he tried to crank the engine. There wasn't a sound, not even a click. He turned the key repeatedly, muttering about bad connections. With the heater back at wherever he'd borrowed it from, we shivered while my father and the boatyard workers discussed electrical problems in terms that only they understood. It was just after 10:00 am when he discovered that his expensive, new batteries were flat. He borrowed a fresh battery from the workshop. It took an hour to install. Once connected, the engine started and the boat vibrated around us. Our cheering stopped when the smell of something burning drifted through the cabin, an odor worse than the burned-plastic stench from the kerosene heater. It was easy to imagine what happened when a wooden boat caught on fire.

"It's just paint burning off parts of the engine where it gets hot," the mechanic explained. "It'll stop long before you get to Boston."

"We're not going there now," Ben corrected. "Just across..."

"Ben, haven't you got something to do?" my father interrupted. "He needs to get back to work, and we need to be on our way."

He escorted the mechanic upstairs, and lugged the battery back to the workshop. After a cup of coffee, he announced we were ready to leave. He assigned tasks like a captain preparing his ship for departure. My job was to untie the ropes securing the bow of the boat to the wharf, while my mother took care of the stern.

"The rope's frozen!" I shouted from the dock.

"There are no ropes on a ship. They're lines, sheets, or halyards." He wasn't happy.

He hopped from his boat to the wharf, slipping on a patch of icy wood. He flailed wildly to regain his balance. I snorted back laughter as he stalked up the walkway. He squatted and tried to unfasten the bow line, a solid, yellow mass enclosing a cleat.

"It's cat piss," he growled when he recognized the smell.

He stood up and kicked at the lump. It took a bucket of hot water from the workshop to loosen the line before his boat moved under its own power for the first time. He changed from reverse to forward gear and pushed on the throttle lever. The engine spluttered and cut out.

The wind pushed his boat away from the wharf, towards the busy Elizabeth River. Ben and I stood stiff in our uncomfortable life-jackets, trying to keep out of sight, while my father rushed to the engine room to work on the problem.

As he cussed at Henry Ford, we continued to drift. We were perilously close to rows of warships when he discovered a faulty throttle cable. He rerouted the cable and restarted the engine.

At Portsmouth, a man came down to the dock to give directions after we passed by the marina for a second time. He was Stan, the harbormaster, whose shouting and wild gestures failed to convey the complicated maneuvers needed to enter a space only a few inches wider than the *Spray*. My father grouched as he carried out Stan's directions. Ben and I exchanged glances and hoped his new fenders would save his boat from a bad scrape. Miraculously, he didn't need them.

With the *Spray* safely tied, Stan climbed aboard. His beard was longer than my father's, his hair tied in a pigtail. He wore a plaid shirt under grease-spotted overalls, and despite the temperature, leather sandals.

He looked up the masts. "I haven't seen a gaff-rigged ketch in years. God only knows why…" He surveyed fore and aft, and then he leaned over the side. "You'll be better off running the engine."

His blunt assessment hung in the air.

"I wanted a boat with a lot of room," my father said.

"There's that, and she'll be sturdy in a breeze." Stan added the nod of experience, if appearance was anything to go by. "By and large…" We waited, expecting the worst as he looked about. He nodded again. "She's a first rate ship for being home made."

"Good enough to sail across the Atlantic?"

"She could take you around the world if you wanted, Cap'n."

It was the first compliment paid to the *Spray* by someone who knew about boats. My father's disposition brightened immediately.

The marina was a haven, fresh water filled the boat's storage tanks, and a thick yellow cable provided ample electricity. With the flick of a switch, the lights came on, warm air blew from the heater, and hot showers waited. We dined on baked beans and hot dogs, microwaved one course at a time. We had music too, my father having arranged his CDs by composer in alphabetical order.

"We'll start with this." He held up Alexander Borodin's *Prince Igor*, one of his favorites, a live recording of the St. Petersburg Philharmonic Orchestra. "Borodin was unusual, even for a Russian composer," he spoke as though to himself. "He was the illegitimate son of a prince who became a doctor and a professor of chemistry, and he still found time to write music." He paused until I glanced up. He lifted his wineglass. "To Alexander and Russian genius," he added, squinting at me through the glass before he drank.

Chapter 3

Living on a boat was dreary, like the dank, dark winter. Despite my father's daily 'it won't be long now;' January turned into February. It was too cold to go outside for very long. Maintaining a normal life was impossible in such a small space, despite my father's insistence on routine and his long list of rules. After breakfast, Ben and I tidied the cabin, while my mother and sister washed dishes by hand and dried them with a towel. When we finished, home school took over—four hours of schoolwork, six days a week. Other than not being in a classroom with 30 other kids, nothing had changed except we covered the same material at a much faster rate and constant interruption as my father went from one project to the next.

After home school, my mother slept until dinner, when she left for the night shift at Norfolk General. My father took over our nautical education. 'Boat school' lasted for two hours and began the same way every day with him saying, 'The more you know, the safer you are,' followed by, 'The most important thing is to keep a clear head in an emergency,' as though somehow that was a matter of will. For three weeks, I studied *A Practical Guide to Lifeboat Survival*, a manual that ranged from how to immobilize a broken limb to identifying sharks and stingrays. With survival covered, he filled my head with the theory of sailing and the parts of his boat until I was completely confused. He stopped only when it was time to take me to swim team practice.

During the weekends, we rearranged our belongings to make room for the things that continued to arrive—a big, white capsule that housed a self-inflating, survival raft, a rubber dinghy with foot pump, and six bags of sails. His already crowded boat overflowed with rope, charts, a secondhand outboard motor, anchors, life-jackets, and a yellow life-ring in the shape of a horseshoe.

On February 17, my 13th birthday, he drove to Richmond and brought back my grandmother. In the afternoon, we dragged the sails up the stairs, freeing up space in the aft cabin so he could varnish the woodwork again.

"If it stays like this for a while, I could put up the sails," he mused, looking around the empty, dead calm marina.

He opened a bag and pulled out a sail, like thick, crinkly paper. It filled the cockpit. Head, clew, tack, foot, leech, and luff—every part of the sail had a name. He hoisted the sails high above, and then sat in the cockpit, staring up. Vast, white sheets drooped in the unmoving air, his boat finally looking like a yacht with an outer jib, a staysail, a mainsail, and a mizzen sail.

"We're almost ready to go," he declared when my mother and grandmother came up to see what he'd done.

My grandmother looked at the tangled ropes: furling gear, outhauls, downhauls, sheets, and halyards. "I can see that."

"Success is all in the planning." He turned to my mother. "Which reminds me, first aid kit ready for the worst."

"How bad is the worst?" I asked to provoke him. With burn scars from my wrists to my elbows, imagining the worst was easy for me. Poisonous fish, broken limbs, concussions, food poisoning, drowning, being mauled by a shark; the list was endless.

"Pretty bad." He avoided my grandmother's stare. "You probably should include some surgical packs too, just in case," he said to my mother.

I wanted to scream, 'Mom's a nurse, not a doctor.'

"I'll talk to Bob Whittaker," she said as if medical school and internship weren't important. Doctor Whittaker was in charge of the emergency department of Norfolk General.

When the sails came down again, they didn't go back in the bags. Instead, my father left them in place, furled up with blue covers to keep off the sun, rain, and seagull dung. While there was more room below, his real message was clear; departure was on the horizon.

+ + +

It was three days later when the rain started. It was the same day my brother and sister's passports arrived by registered mail. The rest of our passports had arrived a week earlier in a plain white envelope. My passport might have been secondhand with scrapes on the cover and grubby pages inside. We stayed in the cabin, listening to rain pound overhead. The drips began in the middle of the night, beating an unwelcome staccato in the companionway. My father used a pot to collect it. The next day, another leak started around a porthole and dribbled onto Jessie's berth. He tightened the porthole, muttering about seals. My mother put aside her medical journal when a pool of water suddenly appeared on the table. While I mopped it up with a towel, he traced it up the wall to a hatch.

"We ought to pack up and head to the Caribbean," she said.

Ben and I looked up in surprise. We all knew my father planned to follow Captain Slocum's route from Boston to Westport, Nova Scotia, before sailing across the Atlantic Ocean.

"Why don't we go south?" I chimed in in support.

"We'd have to go due east to reach Europe if we left from here, not south."

"It's too cold to go north at this time of the year," my mother continued in a determined voice. She unrolled his chart on the table, avoiding the water still dripping down.

"It's much faster if we…."

"How long will it take to get to the Azores?" she interrupted, stabbing her finger on a few dots in the middle of the Atlantic, a little closer to Portugal than North America.

He barely looked at the chart. "About two weeks, if we do a hundred miles a day. The same as the Captain."

"It took him 19 days to reach the Azores," I said. Close to three weeks without sight of land! What was he thinking?

My mother took over. "John, we haven't even left the dock and we're leaking like a sieve. I want to begin with an ocean less brutal."

We looked at our father intently.

"You heard Stan say the *Spray* could take us around the world." He didn't wait for her to respond. "When we get to Lisbon, we'll take a bus trip through Spain and Portugal," he said to Ben and me, as if we had a say in what the family did.

"Assuming we're still alive." I took up the cause despite knowing better. "Have you even been sailing before?"

He hesitated. "As soon as it warms up, we'll practice for a few weeks on Chesapeake Bay before we head north."

My mother said nothing as she rolled up his charts.

When the rain eased enough to go outside, he got out his tubes of caulk and the rest of us tidied the *Spray*. After I carried the trash to the dumpster, my mother drove us to the mall, not to shop, to be away from him. He was waiting for us in the parking lot when we returned.

He rubbed his hands to warm them. "All fixed. We'll be sailing tomorrow."

We just stared at him. "On Chesapeake Bay?" I finally asked.

"Water is water," he said. My mother gave me a warning look when he glanced at Stan's office. "I called your mom. She's free this evening."

"I'd rather sit down with a book and a cup of coffee. The kids are tired too."

"When exactly do you plan to leave?" I asked, my voice unnaturally high.

"Don't panic, Josh. There's plenty of time," my mother said, looking at him to confirm it.

"Sarah can drive us back tonight." He turned away, his eyes cold like the mostly empty marina. "We leave in the morning," he said simply.

Long years of waiting were suddenly over. Jessie cringed. She tugged on my mother's arm, blinking tears, too upset to speak.

"What about championships next weekend? I'm seeded third in the 100-yard freestyle," I said. He didn't care.

"I'll take him, John," my mother added before he had a chance to say he was too busy.

"We can't wait that long," he said firmly. He put a hand on her arm. "It won't be any easier a month from now. The kids can phone their friends and let them know. We leave in the morning," he repeated.

"Aren't there a lot of things to finish on the boat?" I asked. Ben just stared at the ground.

"I can do them on the way, Victor."

"It's Josh." I snarled. Only he called me Victor. I hated that name. Resentment swelled inside me. I stalked off, Jessie and Ben following.

"John," my mother began.

His voice dropped. "I just spoke to Stan. We need to leave."

"Why?" I asked, turning around.

"Stan needs the space."

"There's plenty of space," Ben pointed out.

"I've got too much to do to stand around talking," he snapped, yet he stopped to talk with Stan before going back to get his jacket and lock the cabin.

+ + +

My sister threw up during dinner at Carole's Café, where we'd taken my grandmother to say goodbye. That's how Jessie's stomach usually handled tension. My mother and grandmother cleaned it up.

Without pausing in the conversation, my grandmother asked, "What if something important breaks?"

"I'll fix it. There are always a few problems with a new boat."

"Like the toilet not working for more than a week?" I asked.

He turned on me. "It would be a good idea if you kept out of this, Victor."

"Why do you insist on calling him Victor when you know he doesn't like it?"

"Because it's his name, Sarah."

"I've had enough grief," she said, her gaze fixed on me.

My father sighed. "I can't guarantee that something bad won't happen, here or there."

"Leave the children with me. I retire in June."

"Mom, we can't; you know that," my mother said quietly.

"You ought to come too, Sarah," my father added.

My grandmother rubbed her forehead. "I don't need you to take care of me."

He stood up abruptly. "It's getting late. We'd better start back."

Outside, mist shrouded the cars in the parking lot, glowing yellow from the overhead lights. My father stopped, staring at the darkness under the trees at the end of the lot.

"No point in everyone getting wet. I'll fetch the van."

He hurried off, keeping close to the building, holding his jacket over his head to avoid the drizzle. When he pulled up outside the door, we clambered into the van and he pulled away quickly.

"That's rather strange," he muttered to himself.

My mother glanced at him, and then out the side window. She was about to say something when he accelerated out of the driveway and onto the road.

"Has everyone got their seat-belts on?" she asked nervously.

A bus braked hard to avoid us, and the black sedan that tried to follow us out.

At the next intersection, my father turned left, across two lanes of oncoming traffic, into a gas station, where he negotiated a narrow gap between cars at the pumps, turned left, and returned to the intersection. He stared at the rear vision mirror while he waited for the traffic lights to change. He floored the accelerator and turned in front of several cars rushing through the intersection. One of them blared his horn at us.

From behind the back of the minivan, Ben piped up; "Dad used the wrong indicator."

My father seemed not to notice, let alone care. He raced down Patterson Avenue towards downtown Richmond.

I leaned over and whispered to my grandmother, "He's crazy."

I thought she'd agree. Instead, she shook her head and said, "Not all the time."

My sister wailed when we reached the marina. Ben cried too. I was too old to cry. I just buried my face in my grandmother's chest and hugged her until her blouse was wet on my cheek. My mother choked back tears of her own.

"It's not too late to change your mind, Sarah," my father said quietly.

He carried our cat in the big cardboard box from the windlass. It was punched with holes, enough to see that Jag was miserable too.

"I can take care of myself and Jag," my grandmother said tersely. "It's you I worry about."

He put the box on the passenger seat, helped her into the driver's seat, and closed the van door, talking so softly that we couldn't hear. She nodded and dabbed at her cheeks before she drove off.

Chapter 4

We picked at an early breakfast of yesterday's bagels and cream cheese, despite my father's warning that our next meal might not be lunch. Wasting no time, we took turns cleaning up and showering before he disconnected the power and water supply. We went up on deck when Stan came down to say goodbye. Accepting a cup of coffee and one of my mother's freshly baked bran muffins, he offered a few parting words of advice.

"Remember what I said about carrying too much sail. Put your reef in before the wind arrives."

My father nodded wisely. Stan wasn't finished. Between bites of his second muffin, he talked about sea anchors, trailing warps, and the dangers of breaking waves that could flip a boat over.

"She's sturdy, Cap'n, but if she broaches, she might not recover."

"I'll heave to long before that happens." My father held out his hand, impatient to leave. They shook while Stan continued to give advice on surviving disaster.

"If anyone asks about us…" my father interrupted.

"You're following Slocum's route from Boston," Stan finished. "Remember what I said about being safer at sea than trying to enter a port in a storm." With a final swig of coffee, he handed his cup back, said goodbye, and ambled off.

The engine started with a cough and a sputter. It settled down to a reassuring, gurgling idle. My brother and I released the dock lines and climbed aboard. In the morning calm and full tide, the *Spray* rested against the rubber edge of the dock, undaunted by what lay ahead. My father rubbed his chin, perhaps reflecting on why he left his job as assistant store manager, or trying to remember what his books said to do next. He placed the gearbox into reverse. The last time he did that the engine conked out. This time, a tremor passed from bow to stern and his boat began to pull back from the dock. He made slight adjustments to his teak and bronze steering wheel.

"Best get an early start when there's bad weather ahead," Stan called from the end of the dock, where he'd waited in case he was needed.

"Thanks for the warning." My father took a deep breath and let it go in a rush.

I thought it was advice more than warning. With a final wave to Stan, he spun the wheel and the stern began to turn, still moving back.

Jessie hung over the side, gazing into the churning water. "There's something in the water. It's a dead seagull," she murmured.

No one else saw us go. Even my grandmother didn't come to say goodbye. During dinner the night before, she said she would. My mother said seeing us leave must have been more than she could stand.

As my father motored into the river, I stacked the fenders under the cockpit seats. I looked back for the last time. I felt tears in my eyes. Beside me, Jessie clutched the stuffed cat that had taken Jag's place in her lap.

"Do you want to go? I don't," Ben whispered.

I didn't answer. I clenched my fists and resented my father's power to determine my life. Because of him, I lived on a boat—not a house on a street like everyone else, not even a lousy trailer at Arcadia Park. Then, he turned right.

"North is that way." I pointed left.

"We're heading south. I've decided to pick up the Captain's route in South America," he said as if it was his idea all along. My mother said nothing; she clearly approved. As if to change the subject, he suddenly asked me, "When you took the trash out yesterday, did you see anyone in the parking lot?"

"A man asked me whether you'd take $1,000 for the van. I told him I didn't know."

"What was he like?"

"Older than you. He had glasses like Grandma's, oblong ones. He didn't seem that interested in the van. He had a brand new Cadillac."

"That's it?"

"He was kind of wimpy, and he had a creepy smile, like he knew something about me."

"Creepy?" he repeated.

"You know, like a smirk, like he couldn't help it."

"Next time, tell me right away," he said.

+ + +

The river pursued the remnants of Norfolk and Portsmouth. Rusting freighters, barges, and empty, falling-apart wharves replaced rows of immaculate, gray navy ships. We came to a bridge and waited for someone to raise the center span. Henry Ford's tractor motor droned beneath the cockpit floor, the compass moving back and forth as the river narrowed and changed direction. Every time we changed course, there was a new creek. Not one was pretty. The bridges were more interesting. All sorts of bridges: fixed bridges, swing bridges, lift bridges, and bascule bridges, which worked like castle drawbridges. Whenever a bridge blocked the sun, I worried that the masts would hit it, yet miraculously, the structure passed overhead—arches and trusses made of great girders, resting on massive, stone fortresses that stood against the tide. Of all the bridges I'd traveled across, never once had I thought about what was below.

Soon, the river branched and became narrower, as if about to peter out. My father eased back on the throttle, slowing to a crawl to enter the Great Bridge Lock of the Albemarle-Chesapeake Canal, the only lock we would go through to reach Florida. We soon headed off again, my father congratulating himself on a job well done, although all he'd done was steer and stop without hitting the sides of the lock.

We opened our schoolbooks two hours later than usual. Other than that, we might as well have stayed in Portsmouth. The novelty of being underway wore off after traveling miles along a straight, man-made canal. I waded through quadratic equations, catching glimpses of an endless wall of pine trees through the portholes. Eventually, the canal changed direction. The shoreline moved back and forth, interrupted by tiny coves and spurs that suggested the beginnings of creeks. By then, I'd earned a five-minute break. The *Spray* glided along, fanning out ripples from the stern. Despite the steady chug-chug from his reconditioned diesel, egrets and herons pecked along the shore. Fish splashed on the surface. The air was still and fresh, as if spring was just around the next bend.

"Don't you have schoolwork to do?" he said.

+ + +

I'd transitioned from quadratic equations to writing an essay on the elements of tragedy when my father's voice boomed, "All hands on deck."

It was his idea of a joke. With relief, I left my books on the table and headed up the stairs. The waterway had changed again— the shores were at least a mile apart.

He oozed satisfaction. "We'll sail for a while."

We looked around nervously. The nearest vessel was far in the distance. For his inexperienced crew, it still seemed too close. If something broke and a mast crashed down, we'd die.

"Don't you think we should wait a bit?" my mother asked doubtfully.

My sister buried her face in her stuffed cat, communicating with muffled whimpers.

"I think she's going to be sick," I said.

"She'll get over it," my father asserted. "There's only one way to sail and that's to put up the sails, the sooner the better."

"Can we help?" Ben offered. My father mussed up his hair.

"What on earth do you think you're doing?" he asked with a mood shift as quick as it was unwelcome. I glanced around, uncertain that he was speaking to me. "Yes, you! You ought to know better."

I stared back at him until I realized that I was the only one without a life-jacket. In my rush to escape the boredom of schoolwork, I'd forgotten to put one on, breaking the first of his nautical rules. My father began a lecture on safety at sea. He appeared to believe that a lecture's length was inversely proportional to my interest. He concluded his safety harangue with a rash of orders. My mother was to steer a course that kept the wind 'over the bow' while he raised the sails. She looked at him as if he'd told her to sprout wings and fly.

"The bow is the front!" he barked, very annoyed. "I need the wind from the front."

He handed over the steering wheel and sprang into action. He unfastened the cover on the mainsail and moved around the cockpit, releasing lines. He wrapped a halyard around a winch and pulled on the handle. The mainsail rattled up the mast, flapping as it went higher. Overhead, an immense trapezoid of white sail swung back and forth. He continued to pull on ropes and another sail unfurled from the bow. The triangular jib was noisier than the mainsail, flailing wildly. His boat banged and clattered as if shaken by a giant, invisible hand. Down in the cabin, things fell on the floor, yet my father continued to make adjustments to lines and fittings whose names I'd forgotten. He hauled sheets through blocks and cranked them onto winches. When he was back behind the wheel, he steered away from the wind. The flapping stopped. The boat surged, picking up speed.

"It feels like we're flying," Ben shouted, although he'd never been on a plane. My sister clung to her toy cat.

My father turned off the engine. The vibration and fluster disappeared, leaving waves sloshing against the hull. Ben and I looked at each other. He was as surprised as I was. We were actually sailing.

"It's so quiet," my mother said, looking almost happy for the first time in days. She stretched out on the seat and raised her face to the sun.

My father hummed a few bars of Rimsky-Korsakov's *Scheherazade.* He turned to me. "Put on the CD, and while you're below, put your life jacket on."

"How did I know you'd want to play that?" she teased when I started downstairs.

"Masterful orchestration," he claimed. "Just the ticket."

I ignored his lecture on *Scheherazade,* its expression, style, and phrasing; and listened to the waves slapping the *Spray.*

We stayed on deck for the rest of the afternoon, turned toward the half-hearted sun. Everyone was on the lookout for floating debris, other boats, and landmarks like Live Oak Point and Halfway Point. A red Coast Guard helicopter passed overhead, and we waved at the Knotts Island ferry crossing Currituck Sound. At four o'clock, three hours after my father raised the sails, he anchored in Coinjock Bay, North Carolina, his boat peacefully swinging at anchor for the first time. The sun went down accompanied by the calls of waterfowl deep in the marsh. We played seven-card rummy in the cabin, listening to the water lapping against the hull. Unlike Captain Slocum, who ate salt pork and sea biscuits for months at a time, our bellies were full of salad, spaghetti, and meatballs.

After my mother called 'rummy' for the fifth time, my father beckoned me to follow him on deck. He switched off the cockpit light to conserve the batteries. The night had closed in. Not a sound. No cars. No sirens. No planes.

"You think we're only doing this trip because I want to, don't you?" he began from behind me.

"Yes." I replied before thinking

He knelt on the seat next to me, gazing into the darkness. "It's not what you think." He took a deep breath. "I'm counting on you to help me."

"I wanted to help put up the sails today," I reminded him.

"And I appreciated it, but there's a lot you need to learn about being responsible."

For a moment, I thought he was finished. I turned around. His expression said otherwise. I waited for the inevitable lecture.

"I was hard on you about the life-jacket. The rule is there for a reason. If you do the wrong thing, you put another person's safety at risk."

"I can swim better than you can," I argued. "You've said so dozens of times."

Before we left Portsmouth, I spent two hours every day in the YMCA pool, a swim-team kid since I'd turned six. No matter what shampoo I used, chlorine bleached my hair to corn-silk, tinged green and split on the ends. I was a sore thumb in my brown-headed family.

"That's not the point. If you want to assist, you can start by being more responsible." He studied me. "One day you'll understand. You're a lot like me."

"I don't see how." I didn't want to be like him, unhappy and impossible to please. We had nothing in common.

"We're dreamers," he said simply.

The *Spray* rocked gently on a wave that had traveled a long way. The *Spray* was always moving, never still. My father turned and sat beside me, stretching out his legs. Flapping wings and a screech disturbed the reeds.

"My father in law once said our memories determine who we are."

I waited, wondering if that was true for everyone, and who that made me.

"His point was that our memories shape how we see the world. I want your memories to be good ones. Someday, that's all you'll have left."

A fish splashed just a few feet away. Perhaps it was as surprised as I was. I turned, peering down into the dark water; however, it had already gone.

"I won't forget today. It was more fun than I thought it would be," I admitted.

+ + +

The following morning, after NOAA weather radio issued a 'small craft advisory: strong winds gusting to 30 miles per hour with choppy seas,' my father spread a chart out on the table, and mulled over his options. Without consulting his crew, he motored off to find a canal leading to Albemarle Sound, seeming unaware of pellets of hail pinging on the deck. When the wind and rain began, he put on wet weather gear—long, plastic pants and a jacket with a hood—and remained in the cockpit to steer, hunched over the wheel, holding a mug of coffee in one hand. The distant roll of thunder, halyards rattling against the mast, and the steady chug of the motor as it pushed against the wind all but drowned out Rachmaninoff's *Isle of the Dead.* With rain dribbling down his face, he might have been Slocum's ghost.

The worst of the storm passed long before I finished my schoolwork. After reading about sustainability and population growth in social studies, I took a break, put on my wet weather gear and life-jacket, and went upstairs.

"It's a good breeze for sailing," my father announced.

The other side of Albemarle Sound wasn't visible on the horizon. There were white-capped waves as far as the eye could see: no boats, no islands, nothing except waves. I pictured his boat foundering, swamped by waves, all of us drowning.

"You still want to help?" he asked as if he didn't care either way.

'Beats drowning,' I thought to myself. His face was grim, his lips blue from standing for hours in wind and rain. "What do I do?"

"What I tell you."

He called my mother up to steer while he rushed about releasing lines, cranking winches, hauling up the sails. They flapped much louder than before, drowning out his instructions. The *Spray* bucked and tossed from side to side while he put a reef in the mainsail to reduce the sail area, all done swiftly yet carefully, a pleasure to watch under different circumstances.

"Careful of rope burns," he warned before I released one line, and tightened others.

He raised the staysail and partially unfurled the jib. Suddenly, he was back in the cockpit, hauling in the sheets, turning the wheel towards the unseen shore. The sails stopped flapping and the *Spray* came alive. It surged into Albemarle Sound, punching waves that got in the way.

"Where are you off to?" he asked as I began to follow my mother downstairs.

"To finish my schoolwork." World hunger awaited me in the cabin.

"You can finish it later. It's time for gym."

My father's attempts at humor could be as disconcerting as his temper. I returned to the cockpit with a sudden longing to memorize populations of the world's countries in my dry, rocking berth below.

With the wind perpendicular to the direction we were going, the *Spray* skipped along, heeling over in the gusts. He called it a 'beam reach.' Approaching gusts rippled the water, requiring a constant watch for dark patches. That was my job. Sometimes, his boat tilted so much that it was alarming. Ben hated the *Spray's* heel and stayed in the cabin with my queasy mother and sister. Huddled in the cockpit's dry corner, I began to anticipate and lean into the *Spray's* roller-coaster plunges as sheets of spray cascaded from the bow.

In two hours, we traveled 13 miles to South Point. Only then, did my father, who seemed less tired than he had hours earlier, release me to finish the day's social studies, algebra, and a chapter on vertebrates. Four hours later, I emerged from the cabin when the anchor chain rattled into the brackish water of the Alligator River, surrounded by a forest of stunted cypress pines and a smelly swamp.

Chapter 5

Our fifth day dawned cold and gray with thick fog hanging motionless over Broad Creek. No wind disturbed the marsh reeds or the birds brooding in shadowy trees along the shore. My father delayed his usual departure of 7:00 am until he could see where he was going. Without the sun, time hung heavy and damp.

I used the time to review *Spanish for Home-Schoolers* on my laptop. My concentration faltered when Jessie sounded out vocabulary words. Even worse, Ben memorized facts about weather systems, preceding each one with 'you know,' as if I was as interested in cloud formations and air pressure gradients as he was. When I heard my father raise the anchor, I took my laptop upstairs. He stood behind the wheel, steering with one hand while he conducted an imaginary orchestra with the other. He often played *The Nutcracker* when he was by himself. While the Sugar Plum Fairy danced, he plucked notes out of the air.

"Tchaikovsky was your grandfather's favorite composer," he declared before I had a chance to flee the Fairy.

"Is that why you like Borodin?"

He smiled slightly. "Probably. We often argued about it. I never won, of course. Tchaikovsky was the better composer by far," he admitted.

"What did he do? Your father I mean, for a living."

"Isn't Friday a school day for you?"

I knew better than to pursue it. I stretched out on the seat, unfastened three of the four plastic clasps on my life-jacket, and spread a jacket over me to keep off the wind. With my headphones plugged into my laptop, I reviewed spelling and definitions, while practicing my accent by mouthing words. There were worse ways to learn Spanish. On Fridays before recess, my old class sat in a stuffy classroom, its walls covered by tatty travel posters from Mexico. Our teacher, Señorita Gaitán, from Colombia, was beautiful, with dark, curling hair that bounced behind her. She taught Spanish by telling us jokes; we had to translate to get to the punch line. When she laughed, it sounded like singing.

We were passing the Garbacon Shoal marker, jam-packed with seagulls, when a huge powerboat hurtled out of Oriental's harbor. It made so much noise, that I stood up to watch it blast over the water. Spray exploded in the air when it crashed through the wake of a slow-moving fishing trawler. It was loud, long, and low, without any sign of a cabin to break the swept-back lines. Vivid splashes of color from a distance became flames emblazoned down the side, and a name, '*Aquaholic.*'

The boat changed course as it came closer, keeping a safe distance from the marker, where displaced seagulls now shrieked. To get a better look, I stood on the seat. The man behind the wheel reminded me of the animated character who randomly appeared in my Spanish program to provide comic relief—he had the same black, unruly hair and swarthy face of generations who toiled on the land. He glared at us as if we shouldn't be there.

My father shouted 'look out' when the powerboat swept by us. Instantly, the wake struck, heaving the *Spray's* bow into the air. I toppled back, screaming and flailing. He lunged and grabbed my life-jacket, his chest thumping against my back. The wave swept by the stern, thrusting the bow deeply into the trough. My father pulled me away from the open companionway, ripping open my life-jacket. Without a steadying hand on the wheel, the *Spray* slewed wildly, exposing its side to the full force of the next wave. Down below, Jessie shrieked and books and dishes crashed to the floor. Gripping my arm, he pulled me down before the next wave arrived. I slid past the seat and slumped onto the cockpit floor, my computer clutched tightly to my chest. The *Spray* rocked in the turbulent water, clanging and banging.

"God damn idiot nearly rammed us! The whole Neuse River out there and he buzzes us!"

"He could have killed us," I said.

My father turned on me. "He could have killed you! You're lucky you didn't go over the side! And fasten your life-jacket properly! You'd better start doing what you're told. Do you understand me?"

For once, I did. My mother poked her head out the hatch. "What happened?"

"Victor decided to pirouette off the seat."

"No one calls me that, except you!" I yelled, finding a focus for my fear and embarrassment. He took a breath. "I'm sorry, okay?"

"Bloody hell." He turned away with a dismissive shrug.

We rarely heard that, and it was never good.

"I said I'm sorry. What more do you want?"

"I want you to start acting as though you had half a brain."

"John, that's enough," my mother intervened. "Josh, finish your Spanish."

As lectures went, it was over quickly. However, for two days my father and I said barely spoke.

+ + +

Sunday night fell cool and clean as we anchored in a snug cove so shallow that few boats would venture there. Tree branches were lacy against the moon and still water gleamed like a silver platter. In the cockpit, my mother and father sipped red wine from plastic glasses while Ben, Jessie, and I snacked on sunflower seeds.

"Get your guitar," my father said suddenly.

My mother smiled at me; the message was clear—reconciliation was at hand, at least temporarily. We turned in a half-hour later, my father humming *Here Comes the Sun,* the last tune I'd played.

+++

"There's a dolphin outside," Ben announced in my ear the following morning.

I was half-asleep when he dragged away my blanket. Bleary eyed, I stumbled after him to find a cold, leaden dawn. "So where is it, nature boy?" I grumbled.

"It was over there." Ben pointed to the marshes.

Not even a ripple until a gray fin broke the surface near the reeds along the water's edge. I yawned and pulled down the front of the 'I love New York' T-shirt that I used as a nightshirt. Ben had been awake long enough to put on a sweater and jeans.

"You woke me up for that? I'm going back to sleep. If you can touch it, come get me."

As I turned to leave, there was a loud splash next to the boat. We bolted to the other side. The dolphin was sleek, shiny, and blue-gray, barely moving in the water. Its blowhole was a dark void in the back of its head. It rolled over, showing a black, friendly eye. With a flip of its tail, it glided away.

"It's a bottlenose. You can tell by the head."

"Now you're an expert on dolphins?"

"The common variety is called *Tursiops truncatus.*"

"Only you would know that, or care."

He left, muttering to himself. I waited for the dolphin to reappear.

"That T-shirt you're wearing is mine." I hadn't heard my father come up the stairs. He looked around, taking in the dull morning.

"You threw it away. I got it out of the dumpster." I yawned and stretched until a winch wedged into my back. Something or someone was always getting in the way. His boat was too small for five people.

"You should have left it there. It's too big for you," he said. I squared my shoulders and stared, daring him to ask for it back. "What did you say to Ben?"

"Nothing. He's learning Latin now." I was tired of him having the answers when I didn't. For his age, Ben was two grades ahead. I worried about him catching up, and then overtaking me.

Close to the shore, the water exploded. The dolphin thrashed on the surface, and then made a furious lunge sending water high into the air. The difference between life and death was being in the wrong place at the wrong time.

"Grandma's on the phone," Jessie yelled from the cabin. My grandmother called us every other day, never before 8:00 am.

"John, you'd better talk to her." My mother's face was pale. "Stan's dead. She went to the marina yesterday to pick up our mail. She can tell you better than I can." She handed up his cell phone.

He carefully picked his way over the slippery dew-wet deck, all the way to the bow before he stopped, speaking softly.

"What happened?" I asked. It seemed impossible.

"He fell off the dock and hit his head," my mother said. "They think it happened on Wednesday."

We left Portsmouth on Wednesday, February 23rd, six days after my birthday.

Chapter 6

After the long scalloped coast of North Carolina—broad expanses of cloudy water, swampy marshes, and sand hills dotted with holiday homes; we motored along a canal through Myrtle Beach, mile after mile of waterfront mansions, condominiums, and the backsides of strip malls. Waccamaw River was welcome relief from vacationer paradise, a dense forest of bald cypress, loblolly pines, and American white cedar. There were wobbly landings hidden in inlets—rotting pilings leaning out, planks askew, worn out runabouts, and half-submerged barges. A snake as black as the water coiled on a sunlit stump, ignoring frogs lined up along the shore, and the wading birds stepping over turtles half-buried in patches of sugar-white sand.

My father always played his CDs when no other boats were close by. Today, it was Sergei Rachmaninoff's *Third Piano Concerto*. Cold clear notes rushed together in vibrant passion.

"You can hear the Slavic soul," he said, with a far-away look.

Rachmaninoff ended.

"Put your hat on properly, Victor."

"Victor?" I glanced around. "He must be downstairs."

"Why do you wear that thing anyway?"

My New York Yankees cap was old, frayed at the edges and faded beneath the dirt. It was a relic of my father's that I'd found in the back of a closet when we were packing to move out of our trailer. My mother said he used to be a Yankee's fan.

"Because I like it. When were you in New York?"

"Why do you have it on backwards? It doesn't protect you from the sun like that."

45

"The sun isn't that strong. Did you live in New York?"

"It looks stupid, Victor. Turn it around."

I did what he said, turning my cap so that it pointed forward.

"It's beautiful here, isn't it?"

Was he talking to me? I put my book aside. "Very. Where are we stopping tonight?"

There were still a few hours of good light left. We could go another dozen miles and still have time to explore. Ahead, the forest stretched as far as the eye could see.

"Near Brookgreen Gardens. It used to be a rice plantation."

After that, he listened to Rachmaninoff again, scowling at any disruption. I turned my attention to scratching insect bites. With each day warmer than the last, no-see-ums and bloodsucking mosquitoes rose from the wetlands. Repellent smelled and it gave me a rash.

+ + +

Brookgreen Gardens, 9,000 acres of manicured gardens and unruly wilderness, had 500 statues. The next morning, we saw half of them before a bus from a nursing home disgorged its elderly passengers. We headed in the opposite direction, along a gravel pathway to find ponds and splashing fountains, and huge oak trees draped with Spanish moss. From the river terrace, we gazed out over abandoned rice fields and peered into cypress swamps. I dropped back until my family was out of sight, and went exploring by myself, following a path overlooking Brookgreen Creek, a branch of the Waccamaw River.

I stopped to look at a bronze sculpture, a man with deer antlers sprouting from his head. He seemed to be running out of the swamp, his left arm and left leg extended, his right arm and leg lifted and bent at the same angle. One dog leaped on him, another raced beside him, about to jump.

A cane tapping on the brick paving startled me. An old man wielded it. He nudged over a folded sheet of paper with his cane and bent to pick it up with a spotted, papery hand. It was too far away. He slowly straightened.

"I'll get it," I offered, hurrying from the other side of the statue.

He leaned on his stick, not moving, not even when I squatted to pick up the paper for him. His hand shook when he reached for it. A list of sculptors and their works covered both sides.

"Damned awkward pose, even if it is by Paul Manship," he wheezed, tilting his head to look at me. He gestured at the sculpture. "Same age as me. Not too bad for eighty-odd years, eh? You know who it is?"

"It's Actaeon. A goddess turned him into a stag because he saw her without her clothes. His dogs tore him to pieces."

He looked like a professor in saggy brown corduroy pants, a shabby tweed jacket with skinny lapels and leather elbow patches, and a blue-striped tie with a coffee stain. His shoes gleamed glossy brown in the sunlight. "And the goddess?"

"Diana, sir. The Greeks called her 'Artemis.'"

He chuckled, nodding like a bobble-head doll. "Zeus be praised. A boy who knows his Greek mythology."

I grinned. Where was Ben when it was my turn? "My grandmother used to tell me stories."

"And you listened, by the sound of it." He peered at me as if he recognized me, held out his hand, and we shook. His hand was a mottled claw with tobacco-stained fingers. "Have you seen his other sculptures? Diana's by the pond, over there." He waved towards the marsh gardens where the rest of my family had been walking when I made my escape. "When I was your age, kids knew their mythology. The smart ones studied Classics. My wife was one of my students; Greek History, good at it too. She was better at Latin, so she taught it instead."

He startled when a big cigarette boat roared down the meandering river, glimpses of painted flames flashing through the trees. He shook his head. "That'll ruin the fishing for the rest of the day."

"A week ago, we almost capsized because a boat like that came too close."

"I figured you for a water rat."

"We're sailing around the world. Next stop, Australia." I didn't add that we'd traveled only 390 miles.

"I know someone who went to Australia. He caught some whoppers over the years. 'Use little fish to catch big fish,' he'd say," he rambled. "He left right after it happened."

"What happened, sir?"

"Never heard from any of them again. My other daughters visit me, not her. Not even a Christmas card." He coughed from deep in his chest, pulled a handkerchief from his pocket, and wiped his mouth. "Don't ever start smoking, son."

"No sir. I won't."

"I never smoked until Zagarovsky ruined my life." He frowned at me as if trying to make up his mind. He shook his head. "Too many bad memories. It's been nice chatting, but I'd best go before they send the nurses' aides to find me. Look for Diana. It's a good one."

I watched him shuffle along the path, coughing until he was breathless. I went in the opposite direction, towards Diana, wondering who Zagarovsky was.

+ + +

After twelve days, my clothes were dirty and stank of mosquito repellent. My scalp itched as if lice had taken up residence. Jessie's hair was full of tangles. My brother smelled. We needed more than a sponge and a gallon of water to get clean; however, my father dropped the anchor in Duck Creek for the night. No sooner than we went to bed, a severe thunderstorm started. The *Spray* dragged its anchor dangerously close to the shore. By the time he reset the anchor, the worst of the storm had passed. He came downstairs, cussing and soaked to the skin, and used his cell phone to call ahead to a marina in Charleston, South Carolina. He'd had enough too.

The following day, we docked at a marina near the center of town. It had everything we needed: warm showers, a Laundromat, and a courtesy bus to the historic district. It dropped us off at Market Street, where little had changed since the Civil War. For four days, we gorged on ghost stories, wandered down quaint lanes, gazed into shop windows, peered through elaborate iron gates guarding mysterious gardens, and dined on southern take-out. When we boarded the *Spray*, my mother and Jessie settled in the aft cabin to watch TV and my father spread out his chart to plan the next leg of our journey. When I asked if Ben and I could go fishing, he barely nodded.

We took our rods and a handful of leftover shrimp to the end of the pier where the water was deeper. Our shrimp were fried, our hooks were too big, and our know-how was too small. With minnows stealing our bait, we soon gave up.

As we were gathering our things to go, we heard voices across the marina, one voice tense with anger, the other lighter and taunting. Both men spoke Spanish, too rapidly for me to follow. I looked to where the voices came from; no one, just yachts and powerboats lazing against a deserted pier.

The angry voice shouted, "Usted perdió un cubo de esnortiar!"

I didn't know what 'esnortiar' meant. Whatever it was, apparently the other man had lost a bucket of it.

We started back along the dock. Behind the large fly-bridge motor yacht at the end of the pier was a long powerboat. The dock lights cast a yellow glow over it, enough to reveal a blaze of red and yellow flames and '*Aquaholic*' on the side.

Chapter 7

The weather was dismal when we cast off from Charleston—a leaden sky, no wind, and a chilly drizzle. It followed us south. Ben, Jessie, and I stayed in the cabin, four days of missed schoolwork crammed into two. When we reached St. Helena Sound, we put on life-jackets and crowded into the bow to watch dolphins play in the waves as the Spray battled the outgoing tide. The more noise we made, the more the dolphins dove and darted, blowing out waterspouts or rolling onto their sides and swimming with one eye staring up at us. When the show ended, my brother and sister went back to school. My father decided it was time to teach me how to steer. The rain resumed as we headed up Coosaw River towards Beaufort, South Carolina.

"Miserable weather!" He leaned over my shoulder, checking my progress on the chart plotter. "Find a place to anchor. We'll take the rest of the day off." He meant 'work on the boat.' There was always something to do; cleaning and polishing for his family, projects for him.

The shoreline was an impenetrable hedge of gray-green grass, interrupted by the muddy banks of wandering creeks. He pointed to an opening wider than the rest with pockets of trees set well back on either side. I steered towards the first of five piles marking the channel, past crab trap buoys strewn along the river.

"Stay in the middle." He wiped beads of rain from his brow. "Pay attention."

He pointed at a buoy that I'd missed. I squared my shoulders and stared ahead, steering a wavering course against the surging current.

After a mile, the engine suddenly spluttered and stopped. He restarted it and shifted into forward gear. The boat lurched and the engine died. Cursing fishermen and crab pots, he tried again with the same result. The *Spray* began to drift back. He rushed forward to release the anchor.

"The anchor chain is jammed in the friggin' roller," he shouted. "Watch out behind us. I don't want to run aground with the tide going out."

Just as he started work in the bow, noisy chattering made me look over the side. A bottlenose dolphin wagged its head back and forth, looking at me with dark, friendly eyes.

I lay between the cabin and the gunwale, wedged my legs against the railing, and reached down as far as I could and still hold on to the gunwale. Blood ran to my head as I stroked the dolphin's nose. It felt like wet, slick rubber. The water swirled past, yet the dolphin stayed there, nose bumping against my hand until it rolled over, like a puppy wanting a belly rub.

Just below the surface was a yellow buoy, covered with algae, a frayed rope trailing behind. It sank slowly until the dolphin pushed it up again, nudging it closer until it touched my fingers. I didn't notice the splash of the anchor hitting the water and the rattle of its chain.

In seconds, the anchor sank 14 feet and took hold. The *Spray* jerked to a stop, dislodging my legs and catapulting me into the water. I surfaced, spitting out water, the stern of the *Spray* already out of reach.

He was on his way back from the bow when I shouted for help. He looked at the empty cockpit before scrambling over the cabin roof, yelling 'man overboard.' He unfastened the life ring from the railing and hurled it towards me. I grabbed it. The slimy rope from the buoy slid through my other hand until I shoved the buoy through the life ring and held on to both of them. The rope snapped tight, nearly wrenching away the life ring, while the water tried to pull me under. Moments later, a line snaked over my head and dropped onto me.

"Tie it around you," my father bellowed. My mother, Ben and Jessie crowded behind him, their faces pale.

I made a loop around my chest, fumbling to make a knot with one hand while I held on with the other. My father had made me practice tying reef knots, bowlines, and hitches until I could do them with my eyes closed and using one hand. With the knot secured, I let go of the buoy. It disappeared under the swirling water and bumped against my legs. He began to haul me in, straining against the tide. The dolphin stayed next to me, nudging the buoy at me. I took hold of the rope again just before he hoisted me up the side of the boat.

"Are you okay?" He didn't sound angry, just worried. That would change soon enough, I thought.

I gagged, spitting out foul-tasting water. "I think so."

"You aren't going to be sick, are you?" my mother asked.

I shook my head and tried to catch my breath. A muddy stream ran down my front. "The dolphin... I rubbed its tummy."

Ben, the dolphin expert, looked over the side. "Was it a male or a female? Male dolphins have a slit. It's inside for hydrodynamics."

"They're mammals, same as us," my mother said. Jessie met her with a seven-year-old frown.

Before she could ask, my father pointed at the crumpled buoy I clutched to my chest. "What's that?"

"I think it's caught on the *Spray*."

"Good job, except you should've used the boat hook to pick it up."

I thought the smart move was to keep my mouth closed and just nod.

He tugged hard on the rope. "It's wrapped pretty tight." He wiped his hands. "Looks like someone shot it."

There was a hole in the buoy big enough to insert a finger, and a matching hole on the opposite side where a steady stream of filthy water trickled onto my sweater.

"Why would anyone want to shoot it?" I shivered, unable to stop my teeth chattering.

"Stupid people do stupid things."

Perhaps viewing this as the start of a lecture on falling overboard, my mother said, "You'd better warm up before you get hypothermia."

"I don't want water all over the cabin," he snapped. "Take off your clothes first."

I tried to unfasten the plastic clips on my life-jacket; however, my fingers wouldn't work. My shaking grew worse. My father snatched at the clips impatiently until I shoved him away, forcing my fingers to do their job. I stripped off my jeans and tossed them into a sodden pile. When all I had left were my boxers, my mother hustled me below. After I dried off with a towel, wrapped myself in a blanket, and drank a cup of hot chocolate my mother had made, I began to feel better. I put on clean jeans and a sweatshirt and went upstairs. The clouds were breaking up, exposing patches of blue sky. In another hour, it would be a nice day.

My father leaned out as far as he could and poked the boat hook beneath the keel, about where the propeller would be

"Do you think you can untangle it?" I should've known better. I could tell by his frown he wasn't having any success at unwinding the rope.

"Not from up here. The angle's wrong."

I was so surprised by the mildness of his response that I almost didn't notice the shrimp trawler slowly making its way up the river, pushing against the tide, smoke belching from a blackened pipe that poked above a box of a cabin. The bow was high to handle big seas, showing off the name, 'Dataw Lady,' carefully painted, black on white. Elsewhere, the paint was scraped or peeling. When the trawler drew next to the Spray, a leathery face appeared at the cabin window.

"Middle of the channel ain't the best place to anchor." The man's observation came with an infectious grin. "Parrot Creek's pretty, but the tide ain't half so bad up ahead."

The trawler remained abreast, a dozen yards away. Seagulls circled behind the stern, making sweeping approaches before breaking away and screeching loudly.

"I'll keep it in mind for next time," my father replied.

The fisherman laughed. "Your prop's tangled up?"

"With a crab trap, judging by this." My father held up the deflated buoy.

"Looks like a pot. Ain't commercial. Some dumbass playing fisherman more than likely. I bet it ain't got a name. They never do. Happens all the time round here. Reckon you can get it off?"

"I'm thinking I'll have to get in the water to do it."

"Bit cold, and there's too many mussels to beach her. Probably do more damage than it's worth. I can tow you to a good place to set her down if ya'll ain't in no rush."

"We've got time."

My father fastened a thick line from the trawler to the Spray's anchor post and raised the anchor. The trawler churned water into waves, smoke billowing through its cranes and cables as it took the strain. Its destination was Edding Creek, and a wobbly wharf perched on woodpiles covered with barnacles below the high-water mark. Five piles bore pelicans and hand-painted signs—'Matt's Marina', 'Select Shrimp', 'Fabulous Fish,' 'Choice Crabs,' and 'NO OYSTERS', in that order.

The trawler chugged down the creek. At the last moment, the captain signaled for us to go straight ahead before veering away. The *Spray*'s keel dug into the bottom and stopped. The trawler backed up, blowing clouds of smoke, roiling water and mud around the stern.

"Tide's nearly done," he shouted. "Another hour and we can get to your prop. I got a lump of concrete from when they redone the bridge." He pointed to the marsh where a big, gray block hid in the grass. "You might want to tie a line to it and another to the dock. Then, ya'll welcome to visit."

"We'll be over when the lines are out," my father shouted back.

I yelled, "Thanks." It seemed like someone should. My father didn't seem to notice.

We lowered the dinghy into the water and he rowed over to the oyster-encrusted concrete block, dragging the thickest, strongest line we had. He forced a path through the reeds and tied the line to a loop of rusted steel protruding from the block. While he rowed back across the creek, I secured the other end to the biggest winch on that side of the boat. We repeated the process on the other side, attaching that line to the only secure bollard on the wharf. He double-checked everything before the five of us climbed into the dinghy and rowed to the wharf, disturbing the pelicans from their perches. They circled, shrieking and swooping to drive off intruding seagulls.

"They're waiting for a snack," the man said, gutting fish with a long, thin knife. Scales, guts, fish heads, and blood covered a weathered wood table and halfway up his arms. "I'm Matt, by the way."

"John," my father said. "My wife, Virginia. The kids are Victor, Ben, and Jessie." I added a wave.

Each fish took less than a minute, scraping the sides to dislocate scales, some as large as fingernails, making a slit along the belly of the fish, blood and entrails spilling out, rinsing away the mess with the constantly running hose. One fish followed another, some flapping about even after he cut off their heads.

"Matt, what do I owe you for the tow?" my father asked.

Matt looked up, considering the cost while he rinsed off his hands. He pulled a cloth from his back pocket and wiped flecks of fish from his face. "Three bucks."

"Three dollars?" My father expected to be charged hundreds of dollars. He'd worried about it for the duration of the tow.

"I figure it took near a gallon of diesel. Three bucks sounds about right. I ain't in the towing business. If it was me needing a tow, wouldn't ya'll done the same thing?"

"Yes."

"Then we're even, ain't we?" He placed the fish in a plastic crate and flushed off the table. "Might as well have something to drink. We can't do anything till the tide's low."

Matt didn't wait for an answer. Carrying the crate and dripping a steady stream of water, he led the way along the wharf. No sooner than we'd stepped onto land, the pelicans and dozens of seagulls descended onto the table, fighting for leftovers.

The house, like the work shed beside it, was small and built to last against untold storms that swept in from the Atlantic—gray, pitted wood, a metal roof, and tiny windows with shutters bleached white where the paint flaked off. There was, however, a riotous flower garden and six rocking chairs on the verandah.

"Kids are at school," he said, waving at the toys scattered across the yard. "We got twins, me and Helen. A boy and a girl. Travis and Deidre, after Helen's mom, but she's always been Dee to us."

He disappeared with the crate, leaving us to claim the chairs, rocking in the afternoon breeze. The marsh stretched to the horizon, broken by clumps of straggly trees—wax myrtle, yaupon, and cedar. Matt returned, his hands full of frosty soda cans. He handed them out, ignoring my father's claim that we weren't thirsty. He sat down and put his feet up on a woven-cane table.

"Do you catch a lot of fish at this time of year?" Ben asked, always curious.

"Not a lot, Benny. The water's too shallow for fishing, but it's good for shrimp and crabs. You boys ever been crabbing?" Matt asked. Ben and I shook our heads. "When my kids get home, they'll teach you. Bit early in the season, but there should be a few around. Best time is when the tide starts back in." He turned to my mother. "You're welcome to stay for dinner. I'll call Helen to get some sausage and corn after she's picked up the kids. Ya'll never had Frogmore stew, I bet."

"We have, but it was a long time ago. We stayed at Beaufort. I was pregnant with Ben at the time," my mother explained.

My father seemed about to say something. Instead, he put down his soda and looked into the distance.

+ + +

The twins were a month older than Ben, wiry and rugged with straight, dark hair and muddy-green eyes. They looked and sounded the same, yet they squabbled about everything, including the best way to catch crabs. After dropping a chicken neck tied to a string into the water, we used long-handled nets to scoop up 18 crabs. We kept the big ones, enough for the promised Frogmore stew by the time my father and Matt rowed back from the *Spray*. They heaved a white drum covered with barnacles onto the wharf, followed by the crumpled buoy and a long length of tangled rope.

"That ain't no crab trap," Dee drawled, sluggishly Southern like her father.

It was an ordinary, plastic, five-gallon drum, the kind used for paint and chemicals sold in bulk at hardware stores, the kind I hid behind while my father worked in the barn.

"Sure ain't," Travis echoed. It was the first time they'd agreed about anything, other than identifying male and female crabs.

"Heavy enough. Not what you'd expect," Matt added. Black mud covered his arms and legs. He climbed onto the wharf, pushing the drum back so my father could follow him up the ladder. "I'm kind of curious to see what's inside since someone went to the trouble of leaving it in Parrot Creek."

He used a piece of flattened pipe as a lever, working it around the rim to pry off the lid. The drum was empty except for six house bricks and a trickle of water.

The foul smell didn't appear to bother Matt. "Don't make no sense; putting bricks in a bucket, attaching a buoy, then shooting it full of holes."

"Unless what was in there was already taken out."

"You thinking drugs, John? Because that's what I'm thinking." Matt squatted, lifted out the bricks, and picked up something from the bottom. "Go figure."

"What is it, sir?" Ben asked, bending to look.

"Reckon I don't know, Benny. Looks like some kind of nut." Matt shrugged, squashing it between his fingers. "Whatever it is, it don't grow around here." He flipped it over the side of the wharf before Ben could look at it and voice his opinion.

"Do you think it's been in the water for long?" my father said.

Matt stood up, wiping his muddy hands on his overalls. "No telling. Barnacles will grow on anything in a week."

"Should we report it?"

"Report a bucket full of bricks? You'll waste a day waiting for the cops to turn up and say you're crazy. It's up to you, John; but if it was my call, I'd toss it back where it came from."

My father concurred with a nod of his head and went over to the hose to wash off.

Chapter 8

Sunday, in the middle of March, was a mild spring day in South Carolina, with nothing to do except stretch out on the cabin roof and read Rudyard Kipling's *Captains Courageous*. It had a blue cloth cover with a fishing dory stamped in gilt. It was frayed on the edges, and smelled musty, like a flea market book. It bore the same inscription as my father's copy of *Sailing Alone Around the World*: "To Alexander, 'There is nothing impossible to him who will try,' Papa," but dated a year later.

I was dozing off when something blocked the sun. I jerked awake, eye level with my father's belt.

"It's time we got underway." He glanced at the book. "Be careful with that. It's a first edition. "

"The inscription's dated 1937." I turned to the frontispiece to show him. The book was already 40 years old when the inscription was written.

"Same year the movie came out. Spencer Tracy won Best Actor at the Academy Awards for it."

"Who's Alexander?" I should've known better.

He made me wait. "The quote's from Alexander the Great," he replied on his way to the stern.

+ + +

Twenty miles brought us to Beaufort, a postcard pretty town that owed its existence to cotton, rice, and indigo plantations. Shops, banks, and southern-style mansions lined the streets, delighting tourists on the lookout for crafts, antiques, and T-shirts. Next to the bridge was a small park with huge trees shading two cannons that belonged on a pirate ship. We ate lunch there,

61

sandwiches of leftover crab, sharing a big bottle of water, which was cheaper than five small bottles.

Wandering back towards the town center, we were waiting for the lights to change at the busy intersection of Bay St. and Carteret St. when my father snapped, "Let's go!"

Grabbing Ben and Jessie by the hand, he bolted across the street. My mother shoved me to follow him through a gap in the traffic, between a black Cadillac with dark-tinted windows and New York license plates that turned left onto Bay Street, and a delivery truck racing down the bridge ramp to catch the yellow light.

"We should've waited," I sputtered as we reached the other side and the pedestrian light began blinking green.

I was talking to myself. My father propelled Jessie and Ben left and away from the intersection, my mother hurrying to catch them. The Cadillac stopped just past the intersection and a man got out, his clothes matching his car. He stared at me.

"Josh, get here now." My mother's voice was shrill.

I sprinted after my family, down the pedestrian path to the riverside quay. We blew by the playground where my father had promised Jessie she could play, the promise apparently forgotten. We half-jogged to the public dock where the *Spray* waited. Within minutes, we were motoring south again, the mood dark and questioning.

After an hour, my mother broke the silence. "Well, that was good exercise."

I kept my head down and stared at *Captains Courageous*. My father looked behind. Except for a trawler, the waterway was deserted.

My mother also turned to look back. "Who knows?" she murmured with a kind of doubtful hope.

"We do," he said.

I wanted to yell 'Who knows what?' Their sudden aligned closeness shut my mouth as effectively as duct tape. Off the beam, the water tower of the Parris Island Marine Base hovered over the trees like a blue flying saucer. Far in the distance, two sleek jets winged side-by-side, out to sea. I went below.

The next time I took a break from reading, he had taken advantage of the breeze to put up the sails. For an hour, we sailed close-hauled across Port Royal Sound, the sheets winched in and the sails tight as drums. In the gusts, the *Spray* heeled and plunged through choppy waves, sending sheets of wet crystal flying out from the bow. My father played Anatol Liadov's *Festival in Russia*, written for a concert band with energetic folk dances thrown in. He tapped against the wheel while I traveled with Kipling, fascinated by the transformation of Harvey Cheyne on the Grand Banks fishing schooner, *We're Here*.

+ + +

Friday, March 19, brought Savannah and Georgia's swampy rivers and broad sounds, with names that laughed like Teakettle Creek and Doboy Sound. With the 12-mile-long Cumberland Sound ahead, and a steady breeze from astern, my father decided it was time that I learned how to steer under sail. He made sailing look simple; but that was how he approached everything.

"What if I hit something?"

"Stop muttering." He tapped the steering wheel. "No time like now, Victor."

Reluctantly, I put down my book and took his place. He stood behind me. Immediately, the wheel jerked in my hands and his boat started to turn. I pushed it back. The wheel turned again, moving as if alive. I forced it back, using spokes for leverage.

"Pay attention!" he said with forced patience.

"I am." I gripped the wheel with white knuckles. "What exactly do I pay attention to?"

"The sails. The compass. The chart plotter. The wind indicator. The depth sounder. What's ahead."

It struck me as impossible. "Right."

"If I can do it, so can you." As though reading my thoughts, he spoke more quietly. "One thing at a time. There's a sequence; there's a rhythm, a flow to it. Like music. Listen and feel, and let the *Spray* move with the wind."

I relaxed my hands on the wheel and tried to hum '*Let it Be*' in my head, thinking 'sails, compass, what's ahead.' I wanted to ask him who taught him how to waltz with the sea, but as always, I couldn't. The responsibility terrified me. The sails billowed above, exploding with wind. Waves slapped loudly against the bow.

"Watch the gybe," he snapped in my ear, shoving the wheel to port. "When the wind is dead aft, you need to stay on the ball."

I was 'on the ball'; it was the boat that changed course while I was looking at his chart plotter. I held my tongue.

With my hands gripping the wheel and anticipating an outburst from the captain, I negotiated the Kings Bay submarine base. Armed powerboats patrolled constantly. The massive degaussing station gave new meaning to magnetism. For once, I knew more than my brother—like mathematics, physics wasn't Ben's forte.

After an hour, I began to enjoy steering, controlling 36,000 pounds of yacht with only the slightest movements of my hands. He pointed to the southern tip of Cumberland Island. A couple of wild ponies stood among reeds. For some reason, I thought of Borodin and his *In the Steppes of Central Asia*. He smiled back at me. It was a moment I wished could go on forever.

"What do you say, Victor? Time to call it a day?"

With the sails down, I snoozed in the cockpit, my schoolwork done for the day. We motored into Florida, a few miles past Fernandina Beach before we anchored for the night.

Chapter 9

We put out our fenders and readied the dock lines before coming into the St. Augustine municipal marina, jam-packed with yachts and motor cruisers. My father took over the wheel to guide his boat into the last space, wedged between an old-fashioned motor boat and barnacle-covered piles. Too late, he realized the *Spray* was going too fast. He shifted into reverse and shouted 'fend off;' however, I'd already flung myself from the deck to the dock, securing two lines before becoming a human bumper. Having saved his boat from a piling collision, he gave me a nod when he tossed the stern line. It was as close as he came to saying 'good job.'

St. Augustine was the oldest, continually occupied, European settlement in the U.S. The remains of the original Spanish town were scarce—only the Castillo de San Marcos was original, everything else was 'tourist crap' and 'sucker bait,' according to our captain. In the Spanish Quarter, blacksmiths, carpenters, leather workers, and candle makers dressed in period costume and made metal mugs and bent-nail puzzles, belts and handbags, and candles with three wicks apiece, all for sale, but not to us.

A wrought-iron gate set in a brick wall opened to a restaurant garden with a fountain surrounded by flowers, where waiters in tuxedos carried silver trays heaped with Spanish-inspired seafood. The smell was enough to make me linger. I was optimistic—my father had promised us dinner at a restaurant.

He glanced at the menu, a scroll fixed to the wall. "The prices are ridiculous!"

"They have an early-bird special for $16.95," I offered, cautious despite saving his boat from the barnacles.

He looked around at our hopeful faces. My mother raised an eyebrow.

"We'll find someplace less pretentious," he said.

At a brisk pace, he led the way down the street, stopping at a carryout Mexican diner. We picnicked in a waterfront park, the green open space a welcome change from the *Spray's* cluttered dining table. No tuxedos; however, at least we ate something other than tuna fish sandwiches, cheese macaroni, garden salad, and tomato soup.

It was dusk when we returned to the marina and heard the high-pitched sounds of kids playing.

"Mom, can we go see?" Ben asked.

My mother looked at my father, who decided. "Back by eight sharp. Life-jackets on if you play on the docks."

Ben, Jessie, and I followed the sounds. Three kids became six, running up and down the two long docks, going from luxury motor cruiser, to racing yacht, to our homely, old-fashioned *Spray*. We swapped computer games, ate cookies, and told our parents that we were going to another boat to watch television. Instead, we played hide and seek in the dark.

With Ben as the seeker, Jessie and I ran the length of the main walkway before hiding in the shadows of a fly-bridge cruiser tied up at one of the floating docks. Breathless, hearts pounding from running, we waited for Ben to find us. On the other side of the dock, a powerboat rocked when someone moved about in the cabin. It was long, low, and fast. Empty beer bottles filled the drink holders and an unlikely yellow ball lay on one of the cockpit seats. The uncertain murmur of voices from inside and a faint haze of light escaped the curtained portholes.

Ben had ten minutes to find us. He saw Robin and Mark even before he clattered down the ramp. They were from Fort Lauderdale, on their grandparents' motor cruiser for spring vacation. I pushed Jessie behind some boat steps next to the powerboat and crouched beside her. Ben would see us if he as much as glanced in our direction. His shoes squeaked on the planks when he passed. He continued down the main walkway to search the far end of the dock. Jessie started to speak, but stopped when I held my finger to my lips.

I pointed at her, then to the stepped box. I lifted the side. "Get under here," I whispered.

She giggled before clamping her hand over her mouth, gleefully nodding. It wouldn't be for very long and there were large vent-holes in the sides. She wriggled under, squirmed around to get comfortable, and then curled up so the stairs would fit over her. Keeping in the shadows, I crept down the main walkway to find a spot for myself.

At the end of the dock, Ben was searching *Frivolous*, Tyler's family's big racing yacht. Tyler Cassidy III was mega-rich. Ben busted Tyler in the bow pulpit and yelled, 'three down, two to go.' I ducked behind a sport-fishing boat. There was just enough room between the boat and a concrete pile for me to fit, precariously balanced on a steel pipe. Technically, I was still on the dock. He soon found me, shrieked 'one left,' and hurried off to find our sister. I lagged behind, casting a furtive glance toward Jessie's hiding place. A man was standing on the stairs, about to get off the powerboat, one foot planted on the top stair, the other poised indecisively on the side deck. He turned to talk to someone out of sight. I strained to hear what he said; however, I was too far away.

Ben ran back to me. "Where's Jessie?"

I couldn't help smiling. At the time, he was looking right at the steps. "You won't see her even when you're on top of her."

With no sign of Jessie, and eager to finish the game before his time ran out, Ben raced back to where he'd found me. The man on the boat steps suddenly glanced at his watch and shook his head.

Tyler ran up and gave me a friendly nudge. "Where is she?"

Before I could answer, the man strode down the middle of the walkway. I jerked Tyler out of his way. The man glared at us, went a few paces, and turned around.

"Kids aren't allowed on the docks," he said coldly, no hint of a smile.

"There's no sign," Tyler said, completely unflustered.

"No boat, no dock," the man continued in the same cold tone.

Tyler boldly returned the man's stare. I envied his confidence, his sureness that he belonged. "Boat," Tyler said, pointing to *Frivolous*, which dwarfed every yacht in the marina, 76 feet long and 19 feet wide. "Which boat is yours?" he asked sweetly.

"None of your business. Someone ought to take a belt to your ass." He turned on his heel and left, nearly knocking into Ben, on his way back to where we were standing.

When the man was far enough away that he wouldn't turn around, I hurried to the boat stairs, tilted them up, took Jessie's hand and pulled her after me.

"That makes five! I won," Ben shouted when he saw Jessie.

Jessie started to whine. At 8:55 pm, I wasn't going to argue about it. Yelling assent to meet Tyler the next day, we hurried back to the *Spray.*

Jessie's whine became a near yelp. "Josh!" She stopped.

"What's up with you?" I demanded, pulling at her to get her moving again.

She toyed with the end of her braided pigtail. "He's going to murder someone, Josh."

"What are you talking about?"

"I heard him under the steps."

"Heard who?"

"Some man on the boat. He said a bad word." She looked around nervously and leaned up to my ear to whisper a word I heard every morning before my butt hit the bus seat.

"What else did he say?"

"'I'll kill him if he doesn't pay.' He was really mad."

"It doesn't mean he's going to kill someone, Jess. People say things they don't mean when they're angry."

Jessie looked unconvinced. "I'm still telling Daddy."

"You can't. We were supposed to be watching TV on Tyler's boat, remember?"

"If he finds out you were playing on the dock without your life-jacket, you'll be grounded for a month," Ben added, forgetting to mention that it was his idea to play hide and seek in the dark.

Jessie chewed on her bottom lip. I walked faster, dragging Jessie after me. When we reached our boat, our mother was rinsing out wine glasses.

Our father interrupted his CD to point out, "You're an hour late."

"Daylight saving, Dad," Ben said before he disappeared into our cabin.

I hoped he hadn't forgotten the piling as he frowned at me. "We've a full day of sightseeing tomorrow. Brush your teeth and hit the sack."

I saluted his last command of the day, trying hard not to smile.

Chapter 10

"Cast off in ten minutes," my father announced the next morning. He'd returned from his jog in such a hurry that he hadn't taken changed from gym shoes to boat shoes, one of the lesser rules on his never-ending list.

He looked around the table. In the puzzled silence that followed, I kept my head down. Beside me, my brother and sister went on eating breakfast.

"I thought we were staying until Friday for the mail to catch up," I finally asked, skipping the part about 'sight-seeing' all day.

"It's not worth $80 a day to tie the *Spray* to a couple of piles, Victor."

No one argued. I knew it wasn't about money. He was leaving because there were too many people. He'd always been that way; however, he was getting worse. We hurried off to say good-bye to our hide-and-seek friends before he started the engine.

I envied Robin and Mark for their normal lives. They had a real house and relatives. Other than my grandmother, I had no relatives, or if I did, I'd never met them. Yet I had always wondered about the photographs on the nightstand next to my grandmother's bed. Only one photo was of my family, taken in summer at Virginia Beach. She said the others were families of people she worked with. In one photograph, a man and a woman each held a baby; in the other, a mother knelt by two children, a toddler and a boy about Jessie's age. The women looked like my mother.

+ + +

Day after day, we motored from dawn to dusk, through a maze of islands, lagoons, canals, and creeks of the Canaveral National

71

Seashore. Dense thickets of red mangrove trees rose on roots that lifted the trunks out of the water. They appeared to be walking while carrying so many birds and nests that the branches brushed the water. Wading birds rose into the air when we came close to shore, and hordes of crabs scurried up to the water's edge, only to dart away again. Vast fields of grass waved gracefully below the surface, home to schools of tiny minnows and striped mullet, and lumbering manatees—there were warning signs everywhere.

We sailed 120 miles down the Indian River, and motored through narrow sounds and busy canals, until we arrived at Lake Worth on the outskirts of Palm Beach, a popular resort. It was also the closest departure point to the northern Bahamas.

A fleet of boats awaited us, some with sailors who welcomed us with cheerful waves; however, my father anchored near the shore, as close as he could get to the small inlet that served as the dinghy landing. We shuttled back and forth in the dinghy, lugging groceries from the local shopping plaza to the dinghy, and ferrying them out to the *Spray*—everything from toilet paper to animal crackers. We filled the lockers, the refrigerator under the counter, and the freezer, like an old-fashioned icebox with its lid on top. We posted letters to friends and washed clothes. Except for a trip to a marine store to buy spare parts, my father remained onboard, finishing last minute projects to prepare his boat for departure.

He was in the cockpit when I lifted up the last bag of groceries. I climbed the ladder, ready to watch TV until dinner. His binoculars lay on the seat beside him. He seemed more agitated than usual. I followed his gaze to where a flotilla of dinghies waited for their owners. A man dressed in black from head to toe seemed to stare back at us.

"We'll talk later," he said curtly, turning to me.

My father came down the stairs later that evening as my mother was preparing dinner and Ben was setting the table.

"We'll leave at 6:00 am tomorrow," he announced when he sat down at the table.

"The wind won't be too strong, will it?" my mother asked from the galley. The wind was as good a way as any to voice the worry we all felt about what lay ahead.

"A cold front's on the way."

"What does that mean?" I inquired, although silence made more sense.

"Fifteen knots from the south west, gusting to 20. It couldn't be better."

My mother stopped slicing tomatoes. "As fast as that?"

"Fifteen knots and moderate seas are ideal."

"What are moderate seas, Daddy?" Jessie asked, looking up from her toy cat.

"Moderate seas means the waves are average."

"How big are average waves?" I'd studied statistical averages—means, modes and medians, but I wanted numbers, not generalities.

"About five feet," he said. "Nothing to worry about."

I glared at him. 'Well I'm worried,' I wanted to say. Reading dozens of books and sailing down the Intracoastal Waterway was one thing; casting off for foreign parts was another.

When no one spoke, he continued, "Tomorrow's forecast is ideal. As the front moves through, the wind will strengthen and shift northwest with waves ten feet high."

"Grandma said she was thinking about flying down to see us," Ben said quietly.

Jessie nodded, no doubt full of hope. I knew better. His mind was made up when he sounded like that.

"We leave in the morning," he said flatly.

I kept my head down while my mother banged pots and pans in the galley.

"It's 56 miles across, the same distance we sailed down the Indian River on Wednesday," he added. Not even a hint that he cared about his family, or that the rest of us wanted to stay. "This time tomorrow we'll be eating dinner in the Bahamas."

"If we're lucky," I whispered to Ben.

My father glanced at the Captain, who gazed down at us from his gilded frame on the bulkhead. "I don't know about anyone else, but I'm ready for dinner."

Chapter 11

I'd hoped for storms; however, the weather report was accurate—a blue sky with patches of puffy clouds. Despite a thunderstorm during the night, it was perfect weather for sailing. My father started the engine as soon as the sun rose. Alone, he hoisted the dinghy and raised the anchor. We were underway before we had breakfast. We hadn't gone more than a handful of miles before he stopped at a marina to refuel. The store overflowed with sailors taking advantage of the weather to make the trip to the Bahamas. They rushed back and forth with last minute purchases, everything from chewing gum to magazines. We bought a dozen donuts for breakfast, while my mother searched for postcards and brochures for her scrapbook, and my father paid for 103 gallons of diesel fuel at the marina office. With our water tanks topped off and eight jerry cans strapped to the rails, we were officially leaving the U.S.

Cheered by a 20-cents-per-gallon discount for bulk fuel purchases, my father steered past marinas, cruise ships, and container ship terminals cluttering the harbor entrance. He turned east, towards the Atlantic Ocean. Beyond the breakwater, the beaches and high-rise hotels of Palm Beach stretched to the horizon on either side. Even though there was no wind, the waves began to grow, pitching the *Spray* up and down and rolling it from side to side, banging the halyards against the mast. The ocean appeared unspeakably large.

The smell of the sea replaced the swamp's rotting reeds and mud. It was fresh, salty, and blue-green, not the gloomy brown of the last 40 days. Astern, the buildings along the shore were bland, rectangular boxes facing the morning sun—their windows like mirrors, their balconies already indistinct.

"If you're going to phone your mom, you should do it before we're out of range," he said to my mother after we'd motored for half an hour.

She'd tried four times the night before; however, there was no answer. This time, my grandmother answered on the first ring.

"We're leaving for the Bahamas," my mother explained. A few moments later, she added, "I would've liked a few more days, but he's just being careful." She didn't mention the weather. Instead, she looked at me for a few moments, then Ben, then Jessie. "They're sitting next to me, Mom. They miss you as well."

My mother talked for a few minutes before she handed the cell phone to Jessie. When she finished, Ben took over. Finally, it was my turn. My father looked up from his chart plotter, impatient. He checked his watch.

"We're paying by the minute. Keep it short."

My grandmother's voice was barely a whisper. I could tell she'd been crying. "Thank you for emailing the photos, Josh," she said, her voice tight. "I have the one of you and Ben catching crabs in my purse."

"I don't know when I'll be able to send more."

"There'll be a lot of places where you can send email," my father said loudly, drowning out most of what she said next.

I stood up. "It's too noisy up here, Gran. I'm going downstairs."

In the cabin, I forced the cell phone against my ear to block out the conversation in the cockpit, the muffled reverberation of the motor, the slosh of waves against the hull. The pitching and rolling was worse down below.

"Are you keeping out of trouble?"

I assumed she meant 'with my father;' that seemed to be my biggest trouble spot.

"I'm trying. It's not always my fault."

"What happened?"

"Nothing. I still don't know what I did wrong. I carried stuff down to the dinghy while Mom took Ben and Jessie to the supermarket for another load. A man offered to help me, that's all. I think he confused me with some other kid because he called me 'Alex' a couple of times. He seemed surprised when I didn't answer."

"Did you tell him?" she asked abruptly.

"He saw everything he wanted to see through his binoculars. I told him I didn't ask the man for help, but he wasn't interested. He was mad at me for no reason at all."

"Josh," she began.

"Victor, say goodbye to your grandmother. I need you up here," my father shouted from the cockpit. I said a hurried good-bye.

When I stepped into the cockpit, he handed over the wheel to my mother. We raised the sails and he turned off the motor. The *Spray* wallowed with the waves, sails sagging, creeping across the sea at a rate that would take three days to reach the Bahamas, if we got there at all. He soon started the motor again to do what he called 'motor sailing.' At 8:30 am, we were still within sight of land. The promised breeze was on the way; you could smell it. All of a sudden, the billowing sails filled and became stiff as the sheets tightened on the winches. We scudded along, heading southeast. The waves grew larger, and were farther apart, some with whitecaps. The *Spray* rushed along the troughs, rose up the face of a wave, and plunged down the other side, sending sheets of water high into the air.

We listened to golden oldies on a Palm Beach radio station until it became a fuzzy crackle. About the same time, we hit the north-rushing Gulf Stream. Seaweed gathered in clumps sloshed by waves that came from every direction. The ocean's dull green became a sapphire's dark blue, almost half a mile deep. My father changed course to due east and called for his CD of Serge Prokofiev's piano sonatas. Prokofiev was not a shared favorite. As much as the surging, sideways five-foot waves, it seemed to cause an exit below—my mother, Ben, and Jessie, dogged by bouts of nausea. My cast-iron stomach seemed to have something in common with my father. Still, I wished I hadn't eaten those three powdered donuts at the marina.

The life-jacket rule had now expanded to include a safety harness, its strap connected to a steel ring bolted to the cockpit floor, or attached to sturdy nylon webbing if one dared leave the cockpit. I didn't. The harness was uncomfortable, yet far preferable to being flung overboard with no land in sight. My job was lookout for other vessels. By mid-morning, 17 boats stretched across the horizon. Only a few boats were smaller than the *Spray*. Most were chartered fishing boats, charging headlong through the waves, or trolling slowly. With so much going on, I forgot about the *Spray* sinking on its own and began to worry about colliding with one of the mountainous container ships or oil tankers traveling the Straits of Florida.

Apparently unaffected by such a possibility, my father suggested lunch. I put chunks of canned tuna in pita bread with a squirt of mustard, the mere smell leaving my mother and siblings even greener. My father smiled approvingly and engaged his self-steering system—levers and ropes connecting a wind-vane and rudder.

He stretched out on the seat, sandwich in hand, wagging his finger to Prokofiev. "Your grandfather loved to play this."

I was about to ask about why when the compass needle wavered erratically. He noticed it too.

"The boat needs to be balanced," he muttered after he altered course for the fifth time.

"Is Ben's *Britannica* weighing down the bow?" I asked hopefully.

"It isn't helping, but balance on a sailboat is more complicated than shifting the weight."

My wisecrack earned me yet another lecture on the physics of sailing, balancing forces on the sails, the hull, and the keel. It made more sense when it was actually happening.

"You learned that from books?"

My father studied the sails. "You can't learn everything from books. Take the wheel for a while."

"Now?" My stomach tightened as each gust of wind shoved his boat in a different direction.

"You need to learn how to handle waves," he said, releasing the steering wheel and stepping back to make room for me to stand in front of him. Even small waves shoved the *Spray* off the course he'd painstakingly calculated to correct for the current. The first large wave took all of my strength to force the wheel back. "Let the wind do the work," he said impatiently, pushing on a wheel spoke to bring his boat back to the heading he wanted. "Pay attention. It's not that hard, especially with the motor running."

'For you maybe,' I wanted to say, but didn't.

He steered away from the wind to pick up speed, which he called 'bearing off,' turned back to rise up the face of the next wave, and then veered off again after the wave passed the stern. He moved away and I gripped the wheel ready for the next wave, which promptly crashed against the bow.

"Bear off next time," he shouted in my ear.

I cursed under my breath and tried again. After 30 minutes, his critical barks had slowed to an occasional 'watch for the wave.' When he acknowledged my progress with a gruff 'much better,' I felt my muscles relax and noticed I'd loosened my death grip on the wheel.

"Not as good as an autopilot, but you'll do."

I wasn't sure if it was a joke or a compliment. While I steered, he played Prokofiev's *Opus 33, Love of Three Oranges*. It was less painful than the piano sonatas, though the story was stupid. A prince with incurable hypochondria searched for three oranges containing princesses, while a bumbling witch, a wizard protector, and an unreliable sidekick got in the way. He turned up the volume when the whoosh of water passing by drowned out all but the loudest parts. Finally, even he couldn't stand the noise and turned it off. That was okay by me.

At 3.15 pm, Grand Bahama Island was a low gray haze on the horizon, the wind already dying as the front stalled across Florida. After an hour, we could make out the West End water tank and the shapes of buildings. It looked like any small town on the east coast of Florida.

For the first time, we hoisted the yellow, 'quarantine' flag, required of vessels upon entering foreign ports. As we approached the Old Bahama Bay Marina, the sails came down. I dragged the fenders and dock lines out from underneath the cockpit seat. Beyond a sand spit dotted with palm trees was a bay surrounded by pastel-colored cottages and two-story condominiums. At ten minutes to five, we tied up at the dock among dozens of pristine motor cruisers and sport fishing boats. At least we were getting better at the docking part.

Bahamian law allowed only the captain to go ashore to complete the formalities of arrival. My father rushed off. He soon returned, our stamped passports and a cruising permit in hand, and $350 poorer. He wasn't about to pay to stay at the marina for the night. With the sun low in the sky, he motored from the marina towards Settlement Point and the vast expanse of Little Bahama Bank. As far as the eye could see, the water was the color of my grandmother's brooch; a blue so distinctive that only 'turquoise' described it. There were patches of stilted mangroves, beaches, and fields of marsh grass between groups of metal-roofed huts. We dropped anchor in crystal-clear water, near a rickety post, far away from other yachts. To the west, where the day expired in a fiery sunset, were home, family, and friends—a day, or three years away. We got out the portable barbecue and grilled hamburgers for a late dinner. When Ben said he wished we had some apple pie and ice cream, I knew exactly how he felt.

+ + +

Other than a few local fishermen in motorboats chugging across the bay, no one was awake when I came on deck. The morning sun cast long shadows over the mirror-like water. Below, finger-sized fish weaved through clumps of sea grass dodging the larger fish. I enjoyed the solitude until my brother emerged from the cabin. Within moments of dropping his line in the water, he caught a small silver fish that fought like a much larger fish.

My father appeared in the companionway, blinking in the sunshine. Ben proudly poked at the tiny fish dangling from the end of his rod.

"You could use it for bait to catch a bigger fish. I know someone who caught a lot of big fish that way," he reminisced.

I nudged Ben and shook my head, 'don't ask,' while he looked around, taking in the sweeping curve of the shore, the shimmering water surrounding the *Spray*, a lone pelican sentry on the nearby post, two more perched on the end of a distant wharf.

"It's just how I imagined it would be." He knelt on the cockpit seat beside me and looked over the side. "The water is so clear it looks shallow."

"'Shallow sea' is 'baja mar' in Spanish," Ben piped up. "That's how they got 'Bahama.'"

I remembered how much I enjoyed Spanish lessons with Señorita Gaitán. "It's Ba-ha, not Bar-jar." Ben responded with a shrug and a rude gesture.

Our father ignored us and surveyed the yachts east of Sandy Cay. Within half a mile, there were a six boats anchored in blue-green water. His gaze went from boat to boat as if searching for someone or something. With a hint of a smile, he took off his T-shirt and cannon-balled into the sea. He emerged, shaking water from his head like a dog after a bath.

"I've always dreamed of doing that," he called out. "Come for a swim, but don't dive in. It's too shallow." He kicked and sculled away leisurely, floating on his back.

Ben and I jumped in, disturbing an iridescent school of minnows, emerald-green parrotfish darting among them. Time after time, I came to the surface, breathless, not believing what I'd seen—huge brown starfish, delicate sponges, a stingray, and exotic marine species that I couldn't begin to identify. I spotted a giant barracuda next to our anchor. It sat on the sand, surrounded by unoccupied conch shells. The barracuda circled the anchor before it speared through the water and disappeared.

Chapter 12

The next day, we ferried our bicycles to shore by dinghy to explore the western side of Grand Bahama. Thirty minutes after we arrived at Deadman's Reef, the wind began to strengthen. With flying sand stinging our skin, we headed back. The wind blew so hard that we walked our bikes the last two miles to the rutted, sandy track leading to the fishing village where we left our dinghy. It was a welcome sight, and worth every cent of the three dollars my father gave to a man to guard our dinghy.

We should've made two trips to the *Spray*; however, no one was willing to wait on the beach with the blustering wind. We piled the bikes in the middle of the dinghy; my mother and I huddled in the bow, and Jessie, Ben, and my father crowded into the stern. Halfway to the *Spray*, the outboard engine coughed and stopped. After a dozen pulls on the starter rope, my father unscrewed the cap on the top of the outboard motor. He looked into the gas tank, then at me. Apparently, running out of gas was my fault because I was the last person to refill the tank; however, he didn't say a word. He dragged the oars out from under the bicycles and rowed as hard as he could. It wasn't enough. After a dozen strokes, he jumped out of the dinghy into chest-deep water to stop the dinghy from blowing away.

"We'll end up on the sand bar," he shouted over the wind.

"Not if we get a line from the *Spray*," I suggested. Gusts buffeted the dinghy, making it rock violently. It was all he could do to hold on.

Ben's voiced his solution. "We ought to row *Squirt* to shore and wait till the wind dies."

The dinghy didn't have a real name, just a string of letters and numbers on either side of the bow. Jessie named it '*Squirt.*'

My father considered Ben's suggestion, not mine. "Even rowing flat out, we'll end up miles down the beach, probably in the mangroves."

My mother gave my idea a boost. "Getting a line to the *Spray* is the only way, John."

"I'm thinking about it," he said.

"It's not that far. I could swim it easily," I offered. At least he'd been listening.

He glared at the useless motor, then at me. "It's 200 yards. I don't have a line that long on the *Spray*."

"There are ropes under the seat in the cockpit. I could tie them together."

A wave broke over his back, soaking him. Water streamed from his goatee. He looked like Captain Slocum, struggling to get his *Spray* off a sandbar at Castillo Chicos, Uruguay.

"It'll be easier coming back. I won't be going into the wind," I added.

After another howling gust, he nodded. "Okay, get in the water."

I clambered over the side of the dinghy. The water came to my shoulders; however, the buoyancy from my life-jacket made wading impossible.

"Take your time. It's not a race," he shouted after me.

Waves slapped my face. Without goggles, my eyes stung. Within the length of a swimming pool, I'd swallowed a lot of water. The gusts pushed me back despite the effort I put into swimming. Before I was halfway, I seriously doubted being able to reach the *Spray*, yet turning back was unthinkable. I kicked as hard as I could. Suddenly, the *Spray* loomed over me. Exhausted, I struggled up the stern ladder, aware of water rushing past me. The wind pushed the *Spray* back. It could only mean that the anchor had come loose. The rickety post was already a long way away, the distance between the *Spray* and the shoals shrinking rapidly.

The nearest boat, only recently arrived, resembled a trawler with high bows and a dubious wooden mast. A man in a pink shirt was in the cockpit, black binoculars draped around his neck. He stared at me after I waved and shouted that the *Spray* was drifting. He cupped a hand to his ear, gave an exaggerated shrug, and disappeared into the cabin. It infuriated me because sailors always helped each other in an emergency.

My father could see that his boat had started to drift. He bellowed something. It was blowing so hard that whatever he said was lost. I had a dreadful image of running aground and him holding me responsible, even if it wasn't my fault.

Once, during a thunderstorm, he'd used the engine to keep the *Spray* from running into the marshes until he could reset the anchor. For five weeks, I'd watched him start the engine and raise and lower the anchor with the electric windlass; however, I didn't have the key to open the cabin and turn on the battery power. I cursed the windlass, the anchor, the wind, my father, his boat, and his lectures, which always began with 'In an emergency, think first, then act.' I closed my eyes and tried to think.

There was a spare anchor in the storage compartment in the bow. He used it to pull the boat free after running aground. I hurried forward, opened the hatch, and struggled to lift it out. I hauled the anchor to the side, dragging chain and coils of thick rope behind me. Worrying about damaging his precious woodwork, I heaved anchor and chain into the water. A lot of the rope raced over the side before I realized I had to stop it. Yards of rough, nylon rope tore through my hands until I let go. Stunned, I watched another 100 feet snake over the gunwale.

My hands burned as if they had held molten metal. Somehow, I wrapped the rope around the anchor post. The line snapped taut, embedding the anchor, creaking as the wind pummeled the boat. I leaned over the railing and the contents of my stomach gushed out. I was shaking with cold when I stumbled back to the cockpit. My hands were red raw. I hollered if I touched anything.

The lockers under the cockpit seats held fenders, dock lines, a hose, and spare kines. I dug down, clenching my teeth against the pain, shoving things to the side or throwing them into the cockpit until I found the two ropes, still in the packaging. They were the floating kind, same as swimming pool lane lines. With one end secured to a winch, a knot in the middle, and the other end tied around my waist, I jumped over the side. My feet hit the sand, jarring my spine.

For a few seconds, the water took away the heat in my hands. They stung when I started to swim. Despite the rope I dragged behind me, the return journey was much shorter. The waves boosted me forward. My father heaved me over the side of the dinghy and I collapsed on the floor. Hands hurriedly untied the rope from around my waist. He took up the slack and fastened the rope to the towing ring at the bow of the dinghy. No one spoke when they saw my hands. My mother simply shook her head and hugged me.

My father went hand-over-hand along the rope, to the *Spray*. He used the winch to haul the dinghy back. There was no other way when the wind was blowing that strong. While he went about starting the engine and getting the anchors up, I went below with my mother. Life-jackets, tossed down the stairs, cluttered the floor. Charts, navigation guides, and two of Ben's encyclopedias covered the table. Jessie's stuffed toys occupied the seat. I shoved them aside, while my mother looked for bandages and ointments in the first aid locker.

She sat down, took my right hand in hers, and straightened my fingers. Angry red streaks covered my palm and fingers. "You're lucky."

I returned a feeble smile. "Me, lucky?"

She looked up from spreading ointment over my hand. "You've always been blessed," she mused. I winced when her finger touched the biggest welt. "It could be a lot worse. Somehow, no matter what happens to you, you're always okay at the end."

Her finger traveled slowly up my forearm, barely touching my scars.

"Was I lucky when I fell on the heater?"

She glanced up. "You were very lucky."

+ + +

When I went upstairs three hours later, my father greeted me with a curt nod. He concentrated on steering, watching the depth sounder, the chart plotter, and the shallow water ahead.

"Where are we going?" I asked.

He pointed to a low, shrub-covered finger of land extending out from Grand Bahama Island. "Mangrove Cay. If this wind keeps up, we'll be better off in its lee."

I waited until he looked up from the chart plotter to check his bearings. "When I filled the tank, I put the gas cap back on properly. I made sure it was tight."

"I don't want to talk about it." He took a deep breath. "After today, we've all got to pay more attention to what we're doing."

"We should've checked the anchor while we were swimming yesterday." At the time, I'd been more interested in the barracuda than the anchor.

He grunted. "How do your hands feel?" he asked after a while.

87

"They only hurt if I use them."

I examined my hands. Antiseptic ointment and bandages completely covered them. My father glanced at me before turning away. I expected a lecture about 'thinking before acting.'

"If the *Spray* ran aground, it's likely the wind would have pushed her onto her side. We might have lost her," he said, biding his time.

"There wasn't a lot of time to decide what to do," I hedged.

"You did the right thing by putting out a second anchor. Same as using those floating ropes; that was clever." He had more to say. "If we hadn't run out of gas, none of this would've happened."

"I tightened the cap," I protested.

"When the outboard is tilted back, the fuel drains out if the cap isn't on tightly. When I unscrewed the cap, it was already loose. It didn't come loose by itself. You have to be careful when others depend on you," he said.

He looked at nothing in particular. When he was like that, it was best to let him be.

Chapter 13

The gale raged for two days. It battered the shallow sea of Little Bahama Bank until white-capped waves stretched across the horizon. It rained for hours at a time, running in rivulets across the cabin roof, pouring from the scuppers. Twice, we listened to crackling calls on the VHF radio from boats seeking assistance; however, tiny scrub-covered Mangrove Cay sheltered us from the worst of the storm. The *Spray* bucked, strained, and swung from side to side, yet the anchor held fast. Schoolwork helped to pass the time, although holding books wasn't easy. I struggled to use the tips of my bandaged fingers to poke at the keyboard of my computer.

My rope burns also forced me to watch Ben shuffle the cards when we played poker, a process more painful than the burns. He tediously reinserted each card in the deck, as if getting one out of place would invalidate the laws of probability, or expose him to allegations of cheating. We listened to the rain, the wind shrieking through the rigging, our cabin bouncing up and down with every wave that walloped against the bow.

"Why is Dad always mad at you?" Ben didn't care. He was just curious.

"You tell me. You're the rocket scientist."

He thought about it while he straightened the deck. "He almost never gets angry with me or Jessie. Sometimes it's like he's angry at himself."

"I'm older so I have to set an example." It sounded like something my father would say.

"Mom says it's because of what happened to you."

I answered with a shrug. I didn't see what my arms had to do with it. No longer interested, Ben put the cards away, pushed aside a pile of clothes, and flopped onto his bed.

"Let's play 20 Questions," he suggested. Twenty Questions was his favorite game.

"Let's not and say we did," I grumped.

As though I'd said 'great, let's', Ben began. Five minutes later, when I learned that he had denied that Harry Truman was a musician, albeit a bad one, I threw a shoe at his head.

"Be quiet in there, Victor!" my father shouted over his music.

+ + +

In the time it took to eat breakfast, the leaden skies vanished, leaving behind ripples and blue skies all the way to the horizon. While the rest of my family swam and snorkeled, I sat in the cockpit and waited for my hands to heal. I was glad to be free of the stale, damp cabin; even if the sun blazed down like summer in a Norfolk trailer park. I sought shade beneath an ugly plastic sheet draped over the boom, and read.

Sunrise and sunset were the bookends of every day. We traveled at a leisurely pace, putting up the sails whenever possible to conserve diesel fuel. In the morning, the wind was barely enough to move the *Spray;* yet a breeze always arrived by noon. Unlike other cruising boats that visited the string of tiny islands on the eastern side, my father preferred solitude. He negotiated a twisting channel among sandbars, running aground three times, so we could visit the palm-tree-covered beaches and mangrove-lined inlets of Great Abaco Island. We stopped at out-of-the-way places, each more beautiful than the last, all inhabited by exotic birds and rare fish species that would make an aquarium a conversation piece. When we weren't swimming, sightseeing, doing schoolwork, or cleaning up, Ben and I fished. Every night we ate fish, fried, barbecued, sautéed, or baked in the oven. When my brother suggested we try fish sushi, my mother responded that perhaps chef training was a prerequisite.

For several days, we stayed at Mores Island, on the western side of Little Bahama Bank. It supported two small villages, The Bight and Hard Bargain, a landing strip, and a handful of fishing boats. We had the southern half to ourselves except for a three-masted schooner at the other end of the beach—a charter boat full of 'noisy nudists' according to my father. If they were, I didn't see them.

Diving on the coral reef along the unprotected ocean side was more exciting than snorkeling across shallow sand and grass banks. There were vast numbers of colorful fish: butterfly fish, parrotfish, blue and yellow angelfish; and sharks. On the second day, I saw three, each as big as a person. I struck out for shore. When I could stand up, I tore off my snorkel, pointed to where I'd seen them, and screamed 'Sharks!' No one showed the slightest interest. My mother and father lay on their beach towels, while Jessie decorated a sandcastle with shells and bits of palm fronds. Ben looked up from exploring a rock ledge and waded towards me, his mask pushed up on his forehead.

"They came by here a few minutes ago. They're Caribbean Reef Sharks. *Carcharhinus perezi*." He tortured the scientific name. "They won't attack unless they're provoked," he added.

"Why don't you go provoke them?" I retorted.

Ben scanned the reef, looking for the sharks while my heart thumped in my chest. "You can tell from its dark fin tips and a small dorsal fin," he went on. "Its nose is pointed compared to most sharks. They're harmless," he insisted.

So was sitting on the beach, I decided. I didn't go back in the water for the rest of the afternoon. When I ventured into the water the following morning, I kept close to shore. Streamlined shadows went back and forth over the reef, showing no interest in me. I still kept an eye on them.

+ + +

From Mores Island, we sailed to Cross Harbor, the jumping off point to cross the Northern Providence Channel. The Channel wasn't wide, about 50 miles; however, we had to wait for the right conditions to cross during daylight. Two days later, we raised the sails before the sun rose. We exchanged turquoise water for emerald green, then sapphire blue. The channel was more than two miles deep. By noon, the winds had become light and we drifted for hours, our sails sagging from the mast, our destination in tantalizing sight. It was 5:00 pm when my father finally decided it was time to motor the rest of the way. We anchored off Eleuthera Island after sunset. Ben felt compelled to inform us that 'Eleuthera' was 'freedom' in Greek, named by English Puritans fleeing religious persecution.

Sunrise revealed a new and improved island paradise. We ate breakfast in the cockpit, balancing bowls of cereal in our laps since my father had disassembled the dining table to give the wood another coat of varnish. Glistening pieces covered his chart table and workbench. No one minded. It was too hot below anyway— without a breath of wind, the heat building up, and the sun so bright that without sunglasses, it hurt to look at the water.

"We could visit Spanish Wells," Ben said, after telling us how Spanish sailors had come ashore there to fill their water casks before setting off for Spain.

"Why don't you do that and we'll go to the beach?" I suggested.

My father ended the debate. "Your mother and I want to see Dunmore Town."

That, of course, meant that we all wanted to see Dunmore Town. Ben's unexpected silence brightened my day considerably. Apparently, the Britannica didn't have much to say about Dunmore Town.

We rode our bikes across the island to take a water-taxi to Harbour Island. Wood-framed, pink houses lined the streets of Dunmore Town, most with shady porches behind white picket fences, surrounded by gardens of tropical flowers with hibiscus sprouting over walls made of chunks of bleached coral. For three dollars, I bought a shell necklace from an old woman who made them using tiny crimson and white shells she picked up from the beach.

On the way back, we stopped for an early dinner at a roadside stand decorated with conch shells and driftwood. Willie, the proprietor and cook, made spicy conch fritters while you waited. Willie was dark as night with teeth as white as sand. His eyes were yellow, his eyebrows white and gray knots, and there were flecks of gray in his dreadlocks. He moved slowly even by island standards. If you're already in paradise, why rush?

When Willie lowered the fritters into boiling oil, my father got out his wallet. "What's de big hurry, Mon? You on de two-day vacation?" he asked with a broad grin.

"We're sailing around the world," my father replied, fumbling among Bahamian dollars mixed up with US money. They were worth the same; however, the Bahamian buck had a picture of Queen Elizabeth on it.

"Around de world and you taking de chiles, Mon?"

"If it works out, that's the plan," my father replied as if some doubt remained. "They'll learn a lot more than going to school."

With a flick of his wrist, Willie rotated the wire basket of fritters in the bubbling oil. "I'm wid you, Mon. A chile needs learnin' he cain't get in school."

"That's true, but they still need school," my father hastened to add.

A truck roared down the road, swerving erratically while a dark arm waved vigorously from the window. Willie waved back. "De boys here, dey don't finish school, but dey makes plenny cash on de boats."

"Catching conch?" I said 'konk' like Willie, and added, "Mon."

Willie laughed as if I were hilarious. He lifted the basket from the oil, shook it, and sent oil droplets flaring across the grill. "I pay a dollar for dese, Mon. Is lobster dat pay big money." He watched Jessie play with a sleek, black cat. "My nephew, Jomo, he sixteen. He got lots of money, Mon," he added. He placed the basket on a paper towel and pointed at a red motorcycle parked next to his pink and turquoise bungalow. "He got hisself dat motor bike."

My father eyed the prices on Willie's chalked menu. "Looks like lobster's the way to go."

Willie chuckled. He squeezed lime juice over the fritters. "Ain't all lobster, Mon. Lobster season end April Fool Day. When de money run out, Jomo work de cigarette boats."

"Doing what?" my father asked.

Willie answered with a careless shrug. "Jomo carry, he cook, he do what need doing. Dey camps out near dat cay call Norman's." He put our conch fritters on paper plates and added a splash of sauce with a ladle. "Willie make de best conch fritters in de Bahamas, Mon," he declared.

Chapter 14

No one needed a watch in the Bahamas. We ate when we were hungry and we slept when we were tired. The island pace even affected my father. He put his projects aside and lounged in the cockpit. I'd never seen him so relaxed. Nevertheless, on Sunday morning, after chatting to some sailors on the radio, he decided to leave Eleuthera Island, though not the usual way.

On the chart, much of Middle Ground Shoal was marked with 'VPR' for 'Visual Piloting Rules,' and 'Numerous shallow coral heads.' We motored slowly through exquisite shades of light blue and green—beautiful but dangerous with its sand bars and reefs. A glancing blow from a rock could tear the side out of the *Spray*. I stood in the bow for three hours, signaling where the water was deeper.

"Go that way," I called to my father, urgently waving right because shadowy, swirling water was dead ahead. The bow veered away from the rippled water. Another patch immediately appeared. "Stop!" I shouted, waving both arms, which was the signal we'd agreed on. He stopped the *Spray* and hurried forward. "I couldn't see it," I explained.

I took off my sunglasses and blinked at the sea—the sun's glare made it difficult to see below the surface until I was directly above it. Shadowy water churned, forming eddies in the swell. There was no way to navigate through the reef. We'd have to turn back.

"That was good practice," he said.

I searched his face and saw no hint of sarcasm. I also saw no hint of turning back. He simply shifted into forward gear and motored on. The color of the water suddenly changed to dark, deep blue. I slumped against the railing and pushed my cap back to wipe the sweat from my brow. If he did it again, hopefully it wouldn't be on my watch. Shortly, Ben and I unfurled the sails and he switched off the engine. The *Spray* sprinted south as if released from captivity.

A 90-mile string of tiny islands defined the western edge of Exuma Sound, an island for every day of the year, they say. Most were uninhabited, lacking fresh water except when it rained, and none had the lush vegetation I expected to see in the tropics. We watched the islands go by, looking for the perfect place to stay, avoiding islands like Highbourne Cay with multi-million dollar homes. At Norman's Cay, our captain charged headlong into a narrow pass, seeming smug despite an undersea cliff rushing up to greet him. After avoiding several rocky outcrops, he entered an inviting lagoon with dozens of boats.

"That's a drug runner's plane," he said, pointing out the partially submerged remains of an airplane. "Norman's Cay was Carlos Lehder's base."

"He was the leader of the Medellin cartel," Ben piped in. His 'Medellin' sounded like 'medallion.'

"Is there anything he doesn't know?" I asked under my breath.

"They were the worst of the lot. They made the Mafia look like altar boys. In the 1980s, people disappeared if they ventured near here," my father said, sounding disturbingly like Ben.

I pressed for anchoring and exploring, but true to form, he decided otherwise. He motored out Wax Cay Cut, turned to starboard, and cautiously negotiated rocky bars and coral heads into a narrow gap between two islands.

Bush Hill was uninhabited, tiny, and so difficult to reach that few yachts would bother to visit. Surrounded by shallow sand bars, he dropped the stern anchor and both bow anchors close to the shore. He used the engine to pull the anchors into the sand by going back and forth; however, even with three anchors to keep the *Spray* in place, he wasn't happy.

"If you boys want to do something useful, see if the anchors are dug in properly."

Ben and I jumped in with fins, snorkels, and masks to follow the anchor chain down to the main anchor, embedded in sand and broken-up coral. The second anchor was buried under a clump of sea grass. Then, we checked the stern anchor. Beside it was a large Queen conch, like those on the walls of Willie's roadside stall. It had the same spiral shell, mottled cream and brown on the rough upper surface to resemble the sand around it. The outer lip on the bottom of the shell was glossy yellow and white, changing to pink on the inside, like the houses of Dunmore Town. I carried it back to the *Spray*, ready to make conch fritters until my father pointed out that we were just inside the northern boundary of the Exuma Cays Land and Sea Park; no fishing allowed.

+ + +

The next morning, ominous clouds on the horizon confirmed another cold front heading our way. With schoolwork postponed until the afternoon, Ben, my father, and I swam ashore. An iguana scuttled down the beach within feet of us, curious yet cautious. Before long, a second iguana appeared from the low brush, and then another. Soon, there were eight of them running around, some a yard long, all with bumpy, gray-brown backs and what looked like sunburned lumps on the loose skin around their necks. Ben tried to coax an iguana to come close enough to touch.

"It's a *Cyclura cychlura figginsi*." His knowledge of biology exceeded his Latin.

"It's a friggin' lizard!"

He gave me a sour look as the iguana darted off. "The Exuma iguana is one of the world's most endangered reptiles."

97

"And for good reason. It's too friendly." My father stood up, impatient to go.

We left the iguanas frolicking on the shore and followed a track through clumps of sparse brush, past trees scorched by the sun and beaten into submission by the constant breeze. When we stopped to rest, a bird with a long, pointed tail and an orange beak burst from a nest hidden in a limestone ledge. It was the first white-tailed tropicbird we'd seen, one of the most beautiful and unusual birds in the Caribbean. While my father and brother waited for it to return, I explored by myself. I hadn't gone very far when I came upon a clearing, surrounded on three sides by stunted trees. On the open side, a path led down to the sea. Papers, crushed beer cans, and empty liquor bottles littered the sand.

"Hey Mon, dere's been a big party here," I called out. My father came over, his expression silently critical. "Do you think some sailors left it?" I asked.

"I'd like to think otherwise, but who else would come here?" He kicked a bottle so that the label was visible. "You might be right about the sailors. I doubt many locals drink Scotch." He stalked across the clearing and stopped abruptly. "This looks familiar," he said to himself.

I hadn't noticed the drum, like the plastic pails I used to hide behind in the barn. "It looks like the one that got tangled on the propeller."

"They probably carried their drinks in it." He looked around the clearing, pulling at his goatee. "From the look of the sand, they were here since it last rained."

I hadn't noticed the sand until he mentioned it, crusted under a few cans strewn among the bushes where animals and people hadn't disturbed it. "It rained when we visited the pineapple plantation," I said, thinking back to four, or was it five days ago.

My father squatted to pick something up from the sand. After a moment, he began scraping with the side of his hand. He was an assistant store manager. He knew the price of prune juice and where to find romaine lettuce. Instead of looking like he was cleaning up a spill in aisle six, he reminded me of a TV detective at a crime scene.

"That's interesting."

"What is, Mon?" I walked over.

He held out a hollow cylinder that glistened like gold. A second, shiny cylinder was under his thumb. "They're .357 shells," he said, scraping away thin layers of sand with his other hand. A sliver of gold appeared. He didn't pick it up.

"You think they shot somebody?"

He glanced up. "Don't jump to conclusions. These shells mean someone either reloaded a handgun or used a semi-automatic, that's all."

"I'm impressed!"

"Don't be. They probably drank too much and started shooting at iguanas. It's the sort of thing you'd expect from people who'd leave a mess like this." He stood up, surveying the dark clouds spanning the sound. "Where's Ben?"

"Dat nature boy, 'e go to de beach, Mon."

My brother stood knee-deep in the sea, peering under a rock ledge. I waded out to get him, although we had a long time before the storm arrived. We stopped at every rock ledge for Ben to identify fish, shells, and seaweed. Suddenly, the breeze vanished and it became very quiet, as if the approaching storm had sucked up the air. The deep water of Exuma Sound turned violet under towering clouds, boiling black underneath. Long wisps swirled down to the sea before an advancing gray wall of rain. We walked faster.

A jagged flash ruptured the clouds. I counted to ten before the thunder boomed. With lightning just two miles away, we jogged along the shore, the water beside us glowing like luminous sea slime. The wind returned in a rush, whipping the sand around us until we plunged into the sea to swim to the *Spray*. The rain began when we climbed the ladder. With a jet-engine roar, the wind grew stronger. We hurried down to the cabin, water dripping from our shorts, holding on tightly as the *Spray* bucked up and down and tugged against the anchors. Instead of lecturing us on the effect of water on varnished wood, my father rushed to disconnect the electronics as a precaution against lightning strikes. Just as he finished drying his head, there was a dazzling flash and a simultaneous boom. Everyone jumped. Jessie howled.

"That was close," our captain said matter-of-factly.

Uncharacteristically, he spared us the lecture about what would happen if lightning struck the *Spray*. It was supposed to travel down the masts, which connected to the keel, thereby passing into the water without causing damage. It wasn't a theory I wanted to test. If it didn't work, the results included possible electrocution, fire, and sinking.

A few seconds later, another flash lit up the cabin with a bang that hurt my ears. I barely heard him shout, "Nobody touch anything metal."

My mother clutched Jessie. Ben and I cowered beside them. Across the cabin, Captain Slocum stared from his frame. He'd survived terrible storms. The halyards banged against the masts and the boat creaked. With a deafening crash, the lightning struck again, lighting up the cabin like a thousand camera flashes going off at once. It was over before anyone screamed. My father looked around for signs of damage in the eerily dark cabin.

"I think it hit us," Ben murmured.

My father peered through a porthole. "It's blowing 50 or 60 knots out there. I hope the anchors are bedded in." He glanced at me. If the anchors pulled free, it was clear whose fault it would be.

The storm battered the *Spray*, shoving it back against the bow anchors, all the while rolling from side to side. The wind tossed our boat about like a giant with a toy, tearing at the rigging with a high-pitched wail. Lightning flashed through the hatches and portholes, and thunder followed, like bombs exploding.

The torrential rain ended with the thunder and lightning; however, the wind continued in relentless gusts. With the noise and the *Spray* rocking wildly, it was impossible to do schoolwork. Ben took to his berth with his encyclopedia to study iguanas, Jessie read *Charlotte's Web*, my mother worked on her scrapbooks, and my father made spare dock lines with precise splices. After looking through his book on rope work, I made a wristband using cotton cord and a braid knot like Jessie's three-stranded pigtail. With success on my wrist, I made a bracelet for Ben, a small one for Jessie, and another for my mother. Her bracelet was uncomfortable so it went on my other wrist, both bands sliding up and down and getting in the way. Little did I know that after being in saltwater, the cotton would shrink so much that the only way to remove a bracelet was to cut it off with a knife.

We resumed routine the following day, with two extra hours of schoolwork to make up for what we missed because of the storm. I did my work rocking in a hammock hung under the boom, wafted by an ocean breeze, smelling salt air, and watching clouds pass overhead. My father came upstairs and busied himself tidying up and checking for damage after the storm. When I looked up, I found him studying me.

"You need a haircut, Victor," he said, as if noticing the length of my hair for the first time.

I put on my tattered, stained Yankees' cap, the peak facing backwards. "Is cool, Mon."

"The transformation is almost complete." He sounded almost sad.

"What transformation?" I inquired innocently, though I knew what he meant. With my suntan, bracelets, and shell necklace, I'd turned into an island kid. My accent, a poor imitation of Willie's, only added to the perception.

"You look like him," he said unexpectedly.

"Who?" He didn't answer. "Who do I look like?" I pressed.

"My brother," he said. I gaped at him. It was the first time he'd mentioned having a brother. "He left when you were three." For a moment, he seemed about to say more. "I'd appreciate it if you didn't mention it again," he ended, turning away.

It seemed pointless to point out that I hadn't mentioned the subject in the first place. He went to the bow and stayed there until my mother called us for lunch. We stayed at Bush Hill for two more days, making our departure when another boat arrived.

Chapter 15

We'd been motoring past shallow sand bars for a hour when we passed dozens of sharks milling in a tight circle. Dark-tipped dorsal fins sliced through the water, tails swirling, churning the surface to a whirlpool. They were small, only a few feet long, but as a gang, they were menacing. They fought to the center before other sharks shoved them away.

"I wouldn't like to be in the middle of that," my father said, steering closer.

Personally, I thought that was the understatement of the year. I hated sharks. They were indifferent to my opinion—like my father seemed indifferent to my shark anxiety. To hide it, I joked.

"Is dere lunch time, Mon. When de shark 'ungry, 'e got no manners." My 'Willie' accent had improved with practice; however, he still didn't smile.

"Caribbean reef sharks are harmless. If you don't bother them, they won't bother you," Ben repeated his mantra, leaning over the side to look.

As usual, Ben's rational science failed to comfort. Didn't shark communities hide the odd sociopath?

"I wouldn't jump in," my father said. On that, we agreed.

On a day without equal, schoolwork still waited. I stalled. When my father noticed I was still on deck, he pointed to his chart book. The gesture was enough—if I sat in the sunshine, it would be for a navigation lesson using his charts, compass, and ruler to figure our position. He called it dead reckoning, which struck me as self-explanatory.

I sat on the cockpit seat, his chart book before me. He rattled off approximate distances and compass readings so I had to adjust for magnetic variation. He'd changed course a half-dozen times since our last known position.

"We're a mile from Shroud Cay," he barked after I'd gotten our position wrong. Navigation was a religion to my father. "Do you have any idea how accurate the Captain's navigation was?"

"Better than mine?" I asked brightly.

Anyone else would have laughed. "He could calculate his position over thousands of miles of ocean, and be a mile off."

As usual, I tuned out. 'A hundred yards separates sailing and running onto a reef...' I'd heard it so often that I could repeat the entire sermon word for word. This time, I'd placed the *Spray* only two miles off course, just outside the Exuma Cays Land and Sea Park. I was half as accurate as Captain Slocum with two months of experience. I thought it better not to mention it.

The Park, a haven for marine wildlife, required tying up to a mooring ball to protect the coral. At Shroud Cay, the only available space was next to *Orel*, a motor cruiser built like a trawler. A stubby, bald-headed man stared at us as we drew abreast. He resembled a tropical garden gnome with a floral shirt and shorts so long that they covered his knees.

"We'll stay here tonight because we don't have a choice," my father said seeming irritable there was no other spot. "Victor, I'll need you in the bow to pick up the buoy."

I yearned to toss back, 'Sure thing, Hubert,' but thought better of it.

"Moor your *Spray* of top of me, why don 't you?" the gnome rasped and disappeared into his cabin. Joy all around, I thought to myself.

"That's odd. Our name's on the stern." My father's voice was wary.

"You built it to look like the Captain's *Spray*," my mother reminded him.

"Orel's Russian for 'eagle,'" was my father's only response.

"You know that from playing Russian music?" I asked. Though genetics seemed to have skipped me, only DNA could explain my brother's computer-like absorption of data. I got no answer.

"I'm sure I saw him when we refueled at Palm Beach," he went on, glancing again at *Orel*.

"Maybe he's motoring around the world," Ben suggested.

I'd seen *Orel* too, near West End, where the *Spray*'s anchor had dragged; but I didn't say so.

+ + +

Warderick Wells Cay was a popular destination in the Exuma Cays Land and Sea Park, with a skeleton of a sperm whale washed up on the beach, sinkholes and caves buried in the limestone, and the ruins of a Loyalist plantation. A fixed mooring cost $15 per night, free if the crew worked for a day in the park. My father volunteered the five of us to work the following day, saying it was time we did something useful. It was really about the 15 bucks. The park warden assigned us trash collection, the job no one else wanted. There was plenty of it: plastic bags, lunch wrappers, drink cans, cigarette butts, even clothing.

At noon, a park ranger lugged a battered garbage can up the trail. She pushed back her hair, opened her backpack, and handed out bottles of chilled water. Flattered by her praise on the amount of garbage we'd collected in three hours, I told her about the trash we discovered a week earlier.

"Drug smugglers probably left it," I concluded just as my father came over.

"I'm afraid Victor has a rather vivid imagination," he interrupted.

"You're from England, Mr. Walker?" She had a strong British accent.

"Boston," he said curtly.

"Ah, yes, right; well Victor here might be spot on. Drug runners sometimes camp on the islands, and worse," she continued.

"Like what?" I asked.

"A body turned up two days ago."

My father's face darkened. "Where?"

"Near Shroud Cay. The sharks made rather a mess of it." She might've been talking about the nesting habits of loggerhead turtles.

My mother, who'd taken a break from garbage detail, raised her hand to her mouth. "We saw a lot of sharks near Shroud Cay. They were circling something, but we couldn't see what it was."

"With sharks, one never knows. Don't forget your free showers. Cheerio." And with a wave as cheery as her initial greeting, she was gone.

+ + +

We sailed along the chain of islands to George Town on Great Exuma Island. Behind Stocking Island, a hundred yachts spread out across a nine-mile-long anchorage once frequented by pirate ships. Without explanation, my father docked at the busy marina. After a minute in the office, he returned, fuming.

"The blighters want two dollars a foot for a marina in the middle of nowhere!"

"We could anchor and use the dinghy," Ben suggested.

"I need to fix the self-steering system. I need the dock."

"We've got to go shopping anyway," my mother soothed. We were out of lots of things, from hot dogs to toilet paper.

"I could do with a shower. It's been a while." He scratched peeling skin from his arms.

"Only ten days," I said, wrinkling my nose, although there wasn't a smell; daily dips in the sea took care of that.

"We'll stay for a night," he decided.

We left him dismantling his self-steering system, and went to find the supermarket. It was near the inlet to Lake Victoria, a metal shed painted orange; inside, a clutter of cardboard boxes sliced open to show off their contents. The prices were high, the selection limited, less than a small, 24-hour convenience store. My mother splurged on a taxi to get back to the marina after we filled its trunk with groceries.

"It cost $35 to fill the water tanks," he complained when we staggered aboard loaded with shopping bags. "That's 30 cents a gallon. Don't waste it!"

"Everything's expensive here,' my mother said evenly. "Toilet paper cost a dollar-fifty."

"It was two bucks for the soft kind," I added.

"Mom bought the cheap stuff." Ben opened his bag to show him.

Jessie's excitement overwhelmed good judgment. "We bought ice-cream too."

With our self-sacrificing virtue exposed as fraudulent, my father drew a breath, the usual prelude to criticism.

"Double dips with sprinkles. Imagine having waffle cones here." My mother's voice was an unflustered challenge. It went unmet.

+ + +

The next morning, while my father pondered the pulleys and gears of his self-steering system, we went sightseeing. The houses in George Town reminded me of Dunmore Town—pink or dazzling white, trimmed with yellow or blue in as many shades as the sea. Chickens strutted across the roads, ready to fight anything that ruffled their glossy red and black feathers. We found a market where Bahamian women made and sold straw baskets under a huge ficus tree that had shaded pirates trading their booty. A woman sold fresh-baked bread from the back of a van, while she sat under a green umbrella, her bare feet resting on a wooden crate.

My mother had picked out two loaves when Jessie pulled on her arm. "That man's staring at us," she whispered.

My mother glanced over her shoulder at the man shopping for souvenir baskets. He glanced away, using his walking stick to move baskets aside. My mother searched her purse for change and handed over eight Bahamian dollars and a handful of coins.

"Let's go see who's won, your father or the steering system." She grasped Jessie's hand and, despite our protests, herded us back to the *Spray*.

+ + +

"Back so soon?" my father inquired. His apparent victory over the steering system had apparently cheered him.

"A man was staring at us," Jessie announced.

"Well, we're a fine looking crew, why wouldn't he?" My mother's voice was cheerful; however, her look at my father wasn't.

His good mood dissipated. He started the motor. "Victor, prepare to cast off. We have to leave by noon or pay for an extra day." It was 10.56 am. "We'll find somewhere less crowded."

"It's not crowded over there." I pointed to Monument Beach, a perfect spot to anchor—lots of space between boats, a few minutes to the dinghy dock, and overlooking the white sand beaches of Stocking Island.

"No."

"Why can't we stay here for a couple of days?" I asked, realizing that he meant to leave George Town.

"We could rent a car and see the plantations," Ben added hopefully. He rattled off names from the colonial past: Steventon, Mount Thompson, and Ramsey.

My father ignored us. Soon, our only connection to George town was chatter on the VHF radio, with reminders to other families of a dinghy race off Hamburger Beach and a treasure hunt at Kidd Cove. Our family motored on.

Most yachts going to the Caribbean followed the reef to Cape Santa Maria, east to Rum Cay, and then south to the Turks and Caicos Islands, island hopping and taking advantage of the trade winds all the way to Puerto Rico. We had just lost sight of land when my father turned to starboard. We passed through a gap in the reef.

"Too many tourists," he explained in response to the unasked question.

I always wondered why he designated other travelers as 'tourists,' as though we were indigenous people who, for some reason, chose to dress like tourists from Norfolk, Virginia. I started downstairs.

"The water's shallow ahead. I need a lookout," he called from behind me.

+ + +

Long Island bristled with the beauty of cacti-covered cliffs and stark, uninhabited beaches. We arrived late in the afternoon. Donning fins and masks, Ben and I snorkeled circles around the *Spray*. Within minutes we'd hauled up two conchs, used a hammer to smash through the shells, inserted a knife to cut the muscle, and pulled out the slimy parts—the intestine and claw. Only a handful of white meat remained, enough to make conch salad: raw conch sprinkled with salt, green peppers, onions, tomatoes, and lime juice. We ate dinner in the cockpit and talked about exploring the island. The sun set as a great orange ball, mocking our pitiful attempts to make conch shells into horns.

We left at sunrise, and never set foot on land. My father said it was ideal weather to cross Crooked Island Passage, though more likely was waking to find a boat anchored a mile north of us. An hour later, with Long Island far behind us, the wind increased, the *Spray* surging down the waves and slamming into the troughs. Despite my father's modifications to the self-steering system, his boat still wandered off course, just not as much.

"Take the wheel," he ordered, already on his way aft.

I left my math book on the seat. It was the first time he wasn't beside me. I gripped the wheel too tightly and over-corrected against the waves, which seemed bigger than ever.

"Head up five degrees and let the wheel go!" he shouted from the stern. 'Head up' meant steer closer to the wind.

I wanted to ask 'is it fixed?' when the *Spray* barged straight ahead into the waves.

"You can steer for a while. I need to have a look at the handbook," he announced on his way downstairs.

With no angry shouts from the stern, I became more confident. When he returned, he looked green.

"Jessie puked again, and Ben's not far behind her." He was in a bad mood, likely due to the yellow spots on his shirt.

A few minutes later, he called out for me to let the wheel go again. The self-steering system worked perfectly. I settled into the lee corner of the cockpit with my math book, an uninspiring introduction to probability dueling with Mikhail Glinka's opera, *Russlan and Ludmilla*. He based it on one of Pushkin's fairy tales— a Grand Duke's daughter kidnapped by a dwarf wizard, a wicked fairy who imprisoned her, a magic ring, and a handsome hero who saved her. My father delighted in its rushing scales and turned the volume up to compete with the roar of water going past.

"His complex melodies set the style for a century of Russian music," he claimed.

"It's too complex for me," I replied crossly.

He looked at the math book and turned down the volume.

Chapter 16

A string of puffy cumulus clouds stretched along the horizon, mirrored in a vast, shallow lagoon. We anchored near the southernmost tip of Acklins Island. Except for a huge white motor yacht, anchored in deeper water about half a mile away, we were by ourselves.

"We'll stay a day or two." My father's face was red from sun and wind. When no one spoke, he added, "Next stop is Great Inagua. It's only 85 miles, but we need a rest."

"Even if we leave at dawn, we'll have to sail at night," I pointed out.

"Only for a couple of hours, Victor. We'll be there by 10:00 pm."

"Can I use the dinghy to look for conch?" I asked before his sniping became shouting.

"Where?"

I pointed towards Salina Point, a low headland where Acklins Island ended and tiny Castle Island began, its lighthouse towering over the trees. It was an ideal place to find conch.

"It's nearly four o'clock. Be back by six," he said, looking at his watch. "Don't go past the reef. If you land, stay on the beach. Don't race the outboard, and take Ben with you."

We lowered the dinghy and headed off to a small beach littered with limestone rocks, overlooking turquoise water and dark patches of sea grass. We swam out together, into a strong current that pushed us towards the reef.

On the first dive, we found more conchs than we could carry and still swim back to the beach. When we surfaced, we weren't alone. Ben saw it too—the olive-gray dorsal fin of a shark following a zigzag path in its search for food. Suddenly, it was between the shore and us. We stopped swimming, treading water with our flippers while the current swept us towards the shallow flats. The shark reversed direction. Instead of returning to the reef where it belonged, it resumed its meandering patrol along the beach.

Ben pulled his snorkel away. "It's a hammerhead," he asserted, seeming undaunted. Then, more timidly, "A big one."

According to Ben, there were 375 species of sharks in the world. Sixty-eight of them lived in the Caribbean. He was studying them one at a time, memorizing Latin names, habitats, and distinguishing features. The shark's steeply raked dorsal fin was taller than any I'd seen, curving at the top, and ending with a pointed tip; but not even Ben could determine shark species from that.

"Don't move," I ordered. If the shark didn't realize we were there, it would eventually move away. "We'll go around it," I decided. There was no choice but to leave the conchs where we found them and let the current carry us away.

Suddenly, the huge tail swirled and the shark disappeared. Scared to the pit of my stomach, I scanned the water. When the dorsal fin reappeared, it was close to the reef. An escape route was open to the beach, now even farther away, and we would have to swim against the current.

"Swim slowly and don't splash," I whispered.

We began to swim, making as little movement as possible in the water. We'd gone only a few yards before the shark turned again, its fin cutting through the water. It headed away from the beach, towards us. I'd prepared for a situation like this by memorizing page 124 of *A Practical Guide to Lifeboat Survival*. It advised facing an oncoming shark, shouting in a high-pitched voice, or hitting it on the snout to make it go away; above all, not fleeing since that attracted even more attention. The stark reality of razor-sharp teeth separated theory from practice.

"It's a hammerhead. I'm certain of it," Ben said matter-of-factly.

"Be quiet!" I snarled, looking around.

An inflatable runabout approached Salina Point from the ocean side, its outboard engine howling, leaping into the air when it bounced over the waves. Two men were in the boat; however, it was so far away that they probably couldn't see me waving, or the shark, which had veered away again, zigzagging back to the reef.

"Go! Swim!" I gave Ben a push.

I kept watch on the shark, waiting until Ben was well on his way to shore before I started to swim. In his hurry, Ben's flipper smacked the surface. It wasn't loud, yet the shark instantly whirled around. I made noise of my own, flailing against the current. The shark charged towards me, its tail making eddies in the water, its dorsal fin pushing up a wave. When it was only a few yards away, it turned onto its side, exposing a white underbody, a huge pectoral fin, and eyes like black beads on its flattened head. The runabout slewed in a dramatic turn, and threw out an immense sheet of water. I couldn't see Ben, or the shark.

I screamed, "Get my brother," and struck out towards the runabout, thrashing at waves and foam.

One man leaned out over the bow. With a heave, he jerked Ben up and dumped him into the boat. I swam as fast as I could, terrified that the shark was somewhere underneath me. I swam straight into the end of a boat hook. I grabbed it with both hands and held on, still kicking. When I reached the side of the boat, the other man seized me under the arms and swept me out of the water. He pulled off my mask and snorkel and I collapsed to the floor amid fishing rods and tackle boxes. I couldn't stop shaking even after he wrapped a towel around me.

"Talk about cutting it close," he said. "That was a big one."

"It was a Great Hammerhead," Ben proclaimed, as if it was a species of sea horse instead of a man-eating shark. "*Sphyrna mokarran* are supposed to be shy," he added doubtfully.

"They are shy, only not when they're hungry. You're lucky we came along when we did. A few seconds later and it'd be chow time. You okay, kid?"

I looked up into an old man's face. He rubbed my shoulder and smiled reassuringly as he helped me unfasten my swim fins. He had white hair cut short and curly white eyebrows. His skin was like wrinkled brown leather. He looked like someone's grandfather.

"That shark nearly had you for dinner," he said, glancing over the side as if expecting to find the shark waiting, mouth open. "He was this close to your flippers when we scared him off." He held his hands apart. I gulped, which made him smile. "What are you doing way out here?"

I shivered. "D-d-diving for c-c-conch."

"Did you find any? There ought to be lots. Nobody ever comes down here."

"We only j-just started l-look-looking, but there were l-lots."

I trembled, suddenly cold. I tried to breathe deeply. It hurt inside my chest.

Ben watched me from the other side of the runabout. "What's wrong with him, Sir?"

"He's okay, but I don't know who 'Sir' is. I'm Sal. "

"He needs to get his breath back. Most people would have filled their pants if a shark got that close to them," the other man said. He was half-a-lifetime younger, with close-cropped, dark hair, and the same Florida tan. His eyes looked like the shark's.

"A drink will settle him down," the old man said. His accent was deep and throaty, an elderly New Yorker. However, it was more than that; he sounded Italian. "See what you can find, Tony."

The young man opened a cooler and pulled out two cans, knocking off ice chunks before he opened them. "Thanks to his wife, all we've got is diet lemonade."

"She won't let me drink anything with caffeine. It's bad for my heart. No sugar because I'll get fat. I wouldn't care except the stuff's disgusting with rum."

I gulped a mouthful. The drink was so cold that it hurt going down. The sun seared my face. I closed my eyes, blocking out the glare from the water, seeing red behind my eyelids. All I wanted to do was sleep, even if it meant lying in the bottom of the boat.

"I reckon we'd best get you boys home," Sal said after a while. "I take it you're not from Acklins?"

"No Sir. We're from the *Spray*." Ben pointed towards the masts, visible above a low hill of windswept trees.

"You be pirates, says I, come to bury your treasure on me island."

"No sir. We're sailors. Our dad's sailing around the world," Ben explained, ever serious.

"Sailors, ye say? Then I won't throw ye back." Sal grinned and I gave a halfhearted smile. It was impossible not to like him. "Hey Tony, jump in and get their dinghy, will you?"

"I'll take a rain-check this time, Sal."

"How about you, Shorty?" Sal nudged Ben playfully. "Want to go for a swim?"

Ben's eyes went wide. He shook his head. "No sir!"

"I'm Sal, remember? You reckon he's still down there?"

Ben looked over the side. "My encyclopedia might be wrong about them being shy," he said, less certain of his facts.

"He probably thought you were tuna. Sharks don't really care. Tuna, boy, both of 'em taste like chicken of the sea. You're just crunchier."

Sal ran the runabout onto the sand so that Tony could attach a towline to our dinghy. With a final joke about hand-feeding sharks, he backed away from the shore. We rocketed around the point, smacking down waves that dared to get in the way. *Squirt* bounced along behind. Too soon, we stopped beside the *Spray*. My father appeared in the companionway.

"These boys tell me they live here," Sal said, waving at Ben and me.

"I'm afraid so." My father stepped into the cockpit, leaned over, and glared down at me, his grim expression exactly what I expected. "What happened this time, Victor?"

"A hammerhead got between us and the beach," Ben answered for me.

"With the flats being as big as they are, a lot of fish go by Salina Point," Sal added. "There are always a few sharks hanging about."

My father nodded as if he knew that already. "I've warned them to be careful when they go swimming. So far, sharks haven't been a problem."

"Normally, they aren't. Until today, all I've seen there are reef sharks."

"It was probably taking a shortcut around Castle Island," Tony added. "The big sharks usually stay on the other side of the reef."

117

"You should have seen it, Dad. It was enormous." Ben hopped up to the *Spray*'s deck, catching fins, masks, and snorkels as Tony tossed them up.

"Are you getting off, Victor?" my father asked when I didn't follow.

I tried to get up. My legs felt numb.

"I reckon he's still in shock." Sal had a sympathetic smile for me. "It's not every day a boy comes close to being mauled by a shark."

"Thanks for bringing him back in one piece," my father said with a marked lack of enthusiasm.

"The name's Sal. Sal to everyone, including my priest, although Shorty there insists on calling me 'sir.'" Sal winked at my brother and absently scratched his weathered brown arms.

After a moment, my father said, "I'm John."

He leaned over the rail and shook hands with Sal and Tony while I clambered to my feet. I grabbed hold of the *Spray*'s safety rail and looked back. I needed to thank Sal for saving my life. I couldn't find the words.

Instead, I said, "Thanks for the ride, Sal." He said everyone called him Sal.

"No problem." Sal turned to my father. "Staying long?"

"A couple of days, no more." He made it sound as if he couldn't leave fast enough.

Sal smiled at me. "You can do me a favor for a couple of days. Don't go looking for conch near Salina Point." His tone was more amused than scolding. "You might want to try between here and my boat," he added, pointing towards the motor yacht, which was obviously his home. "There ought to be lots of conchs. If you find more than you need, bring them over. I pay two bucks a pound, shelled and cleaned."

I placed my foot on the top of the runabout, ready to climb up. I took a deep breath. "Thanks Sal."

"Get the dinghy, Victor," my father said crossly.

"Tony will do it," Sal countered swiftly. "He needs to take it easy for a while."

I hauled myself onto the *Spray*, climbed over the safety rail, and slumped onto the cockpit seat. My father tied the dinghy to the rail. He didn't say a word. I scrutinized the sweeping shoreline, the solitary house on Salina Point, water so blue that it appeared artificial. I looked everywhere except at my father. I barely noticed the runabout backing away, Sal waving to Ben and me, saying something about us coming over to visit him whenever we wanted. The outboard roared and the runabout rose from the water, accelerating rapidly. It bothered me to see them go.

When I couldn't stand the silence, I said, "It wasn't my fault."

My father gave an exasperated sigh. "When are you going to be responsible?"

"I checked for sharks before we went in the water. It came out of nowhere."

"It did, Dad," Ben added. "It wasn't Josh's fault."

"You always have excuses, don't you Victor?"

"Why are you blaming me? I didn't know the shark was there."

"You and Ben could've been killed!"

"You think I don't know that! I'm sorry, okay?"

119

The runabout was a hundred yards away, when it turned around. It slowed down as it returned to the *Spray*. Sal stood up, leaning against the seat back as the runabout puttered past.

"I forgot to tell you. When the shark closed in, he stayed so his brother could swim to shore," he called out.

"The kid's got guts."

It was the last thing I expected my father to say.

Sal looked at me and nodded slightly, as though we had something in common. "He swims like a tuna too." With a deft turn of the wheel, he pointed the runabout in the opposite direction. "You're invited to dinner tonight. Nothing fancy. About seven o'clock. We'll have drinks on the bridge and watch the sunset."

Ben's pleading, "Can we go?" interrupted my father's stillborn excuse.

"Thanks, that's kind of you. See you then."

Ben and I exchanged a high-five.

Chapter 17

My father steadied the dinghy and waited for his crew to climb down, his gaze fixed on Sal's motor yacht. While he lacked party spirit, he'd dressed with care, and insisted we do the same. My long trousers still had creases and my button-down-collar shirt scraped at my neck, both prickly in the tropical heat. He'd apparently missed Sal's 'nothing fancy.'

I shoved up my shirtsleeves as soon as I took my place in the bow of the dinghy. "I look like a dork."

"You look like a guest," he snapped.

With five people crowded into *Squirt*, it was impossible to go faster than a crawl and not get wet. Ten minutes after setting off, the ultra-modern motor yacht loomed over us like a small ocean liner, a brilliant white ocean-going ship with three levels. The sun bridge bristled with radio antennae. The middle level had enormous windows, dark and shiny as obsidian. On the lower level, the portholes were oval-shaped and big enough to need curtains. My father called it 'Queen Mary.'

"Jealous, John?" my mother teased with a hint of warning.

We passed the yacht's stern, its name, '*Marionette,*' and home port of Bridgetown, Barbados, painted in gold and black. Sal waited by the boarding stairs. Bleached cotton trousers and a colorful-as-sunset silk shirt replaced the stained shorts and T-shirt he wore when fishing.

"Yo, Sharkbait, ya didna see no shark frens coming over, didja?" Sal called out when we came alongside, a conspiratorial smile fully acknowledging his Brooklyn origin.

I beamed back. I'd never had a nickname other than Noah Junior. He extended a hand to my mother, assisting her from our scruffy dinghy onto his gleaming steel stairs.

"Welcome aboard. It's not often that I have two beautiful woman aboard," Sal declared, his voice like a rasp grinding away wood.

"I'm flattered." My mother smiled and brushed out the pleats in her dress. My sister giggled from beside her. "Thank you for inviting us."

"You're a lucky man, John," he said over her shoulder, still holding her hand.

"Sal, thank you so much. We're very glad you came by when you did," my mother said.

"It was a fluke. I usually fish the flats. I thought I'd try outside the reef for a change. We wasted three hours before we got tired of the waves." He looked at me, as much as saying if they'd arrived a few seconds later, I'd be dead, or missing a leg.

Sal radiated happiness the same way my father did gloom and doom. Oblivious to my father's silence, Sal guided us into the main cabin, apologizing for the mess, which was imaginary by our standards.

"My granddaughter, Daniela, always spends the summer with us, so I'm meeting my wife in Puerto Plata at the end of the month. If the *Marionette* isn't spotless when she arrives, she'll turn around and head off again," he joked.

The main cabin was bigger than the trailer we'd left in Norfolk, with no expense spared. My father took in the rich mahogany paneling, the oil paintings of sailing ships, the intricate models of the *Cutty Sark* and the *USS Constitution,* and didn't say a word.

"Where's your wife now?" My mother wanted someone else to talk to as much as I did.

"Martinique. Marion prefers the southern islands. I'd rather fish here, but she gets bored sitting around while I'm fishing. We're both happier this way," he added with a grin. "I love her dearly, which is one of the reasons why I called my boat '*Marionette*.'"

I looked up. "A marionette's a dancing puppet, isn't it?"

Sal looked at me approvingly. "I also dance to Marion's tune. She gets what she wants, and I get to pay for it. Of course, when a woman is as pretty as Marion and your momma it doesn't matter."

My mother smiled; my father didn't.

A circular staircase led up to the bridge-deck. Creamy canvas stretched overhead shaded the still -fiery sun, and cloth-covered seats surrounded a teakwood table with a platter of food already set out. Beside it were crystal glasses, delicate plates with an angelfish pattern, and little silver forks. My stomach growled. Lunch was a midday memory of crackers and cheese without snacks to refresh it. I picked out a few nuts from a big bowl. Immediately, my father gave me a disapproving look

"The macadamia nuts are there to eat," Sal said with a casual gesture.

My father shook his head when Sal asked him what he wanted to drink. He didn't touch the tray of food. Apparently, good manners stopped with dressing up. I retreated to the railing, out of his way, anxious that he not offend Sal, angry that he seemed dedicated to squeezing the happiness out of our lives.

The Bight of Acklins stretched as far as the eye could see, mere wisps of cloud floating over Long Cay and Crooked Island. I could hear Tony in the cabin below on a shortwave radio.

"Sal wants you here no earlier than Tuesday. Five days! Not before! Over."

123

The reply came in crackling Spanish. I understood a few words, enough to know he wasn't pleased. Tony gave a string of numbers for latitude and longitude, and repeated them. I moved farther away when Sal addressed my father directly.

"Ben said you were sailing around the world. Marion and I have always wanted to do that. Unfortunately, we've never found the time. How long will it take you?"

My father glanced up at Sal's question.

"Sal asked you a question, John," my mother said. My anger increased on her behalf. Her good manners made the battle uneven. It always did.

"Three years, give or take." He didn't deliver his usual lecture about Captain Slocum's voyage around the world.

"We moved aboard two days before Christmas." Not surprisingly, my mother added, "It seems a lot longer."

Five months on a boat that was a fraction of the size of our previous home! We were always in each other's way. No privacy. Stale air if the weather was bad. Queuing to use the head, climb the stairs to the cockpit, or go through a doorway. No wonder she sounded peeved.

"I can't imagine doing a trip like that with kids. It must be very stressful," Sal said. He rubbed his brow, driving bony, brown fingers through his bristly hair.

My father perked up. "It'd be a lot easier if they followed the rules." He looked at me.

Sal turned in my direction too, inclining his head. "You don't like rules?"

I shrugged in response, my face flushed, hating my father.

"That's why we have incidents like today."

"Or maybe because sharks are sharks," my mother said, clearly at risk of testing her manners.

"He sounds like me at that age," Sal chuckled, apparently untroubled by my parents' bickering. "I was always getting into trouble." He nodded at me, like a nervous tic. It wasn't. "It was a brave thing you did today, Sharkbait. You don't mind if I call him that, do you?"

My father shrugged and helped himself to shrimp from the platter and a glass of wine. As always, his mood improved once he'd ruined everyone else's. "Victor doesn't like the name we gave him," he said coolly.

Sal seemed amused when he glanced at me. "Can't say I blame him. What did you do before you decided to sail around the world, John?"

"This and that. It seems like I've spent most of the last ten years building the *Spray*."

"Dad built it all by himself, just like Joshua Slocum," Ben added.

"I'm impressed," Sal remarked. "Most people wouldn't know where to start, or wouldn't make the effort."

"What do you do, Sal?" I asked, curious as to how he came to be rich.

"I buy and sell diamonds. There's a good market for them when it's duty free. Unfortunately, the trade attracts some undesirables."

Although my father said nothing, 'I bet it does' hung in the air.

Chapter 18

Sal taught me how to fly-fish. From noon until sunset, we drifted across the immense lagoon of the Bight of Acklins, or stood knee-deep in the shallows. I learned how to cast, how to make a 'fly' that looked like a tiny shrimp, or an intricate insect, and techniques to catch bonefish, permit, and tarpon.

On Tuesday, our fifth afternoon of fishing at Acklins Island, a big powerboat was alongside the *Marionette* when we returned. It was as long as the *Spray* and half as wide, with a swept-back windscreen. A colorful bird rising out of flames, and the name, '*Firebird,*' emblazoned the side. Sal pulled up next to the powerboat, switched off the outboard motor, and thumped hard on its hull. A man stepped into the cockpit, his shirt open to his waist, displaying a thick, gold chain and a gorilla's chest.

"Hola! Is good place, Sal. Es privado," the man declared.

"You're early!" Sal's sharp-as-a-knife tone took me by surprise.

The man's eyes narrowed. He stepped away from the gunwale, folded his arms across his bare chest, and regarded us. "El muchacho. Quién es él?"

He wanted to know who I was.

"None of your business, Javiero."

Javiero pointed at the *Spray*, his eyebrows a question mark. Sal glanced at me. I was sure he was warning me to keep my mouth shut. Javiero polished his tobacco-stained teeth with his tongue, back and forth, until it was clear that Sal wasn't going to elaborate.

Tony suddenly appeared at the railing of the *Marionette*. He stared down at Javiero.

"Tony will take over for me today," Sal said, his irritation clear. "All of it better be there."

"You count. Tony count. It make no difference. It all there."

"Count it twice to make sure, Tony," Sal instructed. "I'll be gone for a while."

"Sure Sal. I'll take care of it," Tony said.

Sal turned to Javiero. "I want you in Lupe' on the 19th. Next Wednesday. Be there!"

He pushed the runabout away from the powerboat and started the outboard motor. Behind us, Javiero strained to lift a red cooler high enough for Tony to take hold of the handles.

"Who's he?" I asked.

"No one worth knowing. He brings supplies from Nassau for me. It's the only way to get things here besides flying them in, which costs an arm and a leg. Things we're short of, that's all."

"You don't trust him, do you?"

Sal seemed to think that was funny. "You got that right. Colombians are all crooks."

"Like all Italians are in the Mafia?" I asked, grinning.

"Notta all Italiano are Cosa Nostra, Sharka-bait. Justa the men with pretty women," he joked in his New York-Italian accent. It always made me laugh. "With men like Javiero, you always count. Last time, I told him to bring a dozen bottles of champagne. He brought me ten and said two were smashed on the way. A hundred bucks a bottle that cost me."

"Why do you do business with him if you don't trust him?" I asked.

"I ask myself that every time I see him. Javiero's an ass, but his boat is useful. That cooler is full of ice cream. We're out, you know." He looked at me over his sunglasses before breaking into a good-natured grin.

In five days, Ben, Jessie, and I finished all the ice cream on the *Marionette*. Sal seemed delighted by the achievement. I would miss him a lot. And the ice cream. He pointed the runabout at the *Spray* and opened the throttle.

"Javiero's only got one line out," I observed, still looking behind. "His boat will hit the *Marionette* for sure."

Sal glanced back. The bow of the powerboat drifted out, bringing its stern close to the *Marionette*. "Babbo!" He slowly shook his head. "In the old days, he wouldn't last long. I'll radio Tony. He'll take care of it." He picked up the microphone.

"Tony's your bodyguard, isn't he?" I asked when he'd finished talking.

"He's busted a few knees." Sal laughed. I couldn't tell if he was joking or not.

When we said good-bye, he said we'd meet again when I least expected it, because that was what happened in the Caribbean. I hoped he was right.

+ + +

My father started the engine at 4:00 am. It woke me up. I lay in my berth, listening to the whir of the electric windlass and the clank of the chain when he raised the anchor. I stumbled on deck before he came down to get me. We motored cautiously into the night, my father watching the depth sounder while I peered ahead. As we crept past the *Marionette*, a flashlight flared in the darkness. It blinked several times from the sun bridge. We were too far away to shout, so I switched on the cockpit lights, stood up, and waved vigorously.

"Sit down before you fall overboard," my father ordered.

"I'm wearing a life jacket." I waved again.

"Do what you're told and don't answer back!" He leaned over and flipped off the light switch. I started downstairs.

"He's rich. He's happy. Of course you hate him," I said under my breath.

"Being rich has nothing to do with it, but there is something I don't like about him."

I stopped in the companionway. "What?"

"People aren't always what they appear." It was his usual answer when he didn't trust someone.

I liked Sal. He taught me to fish and told funny stories about growing up in Little Sicily, New York City— he was very allergic to cats, and his mother kept two of them.

"Or what you want them to be," I whispered.

"Now you're up, you can lend a hand," my father said. He'd heard me.

I steered and he raised the sails. The wind barely filled them. The dim outline of Salina Point drifted by.

From the lighthouse on Castle Island, the course to Matthew Town on Great Inagua Island was 162 degrees, a straight-line distance of 81 nautical miles. My father stood behind me while I steered, looking over my shoulder, nudging me when the compass needle varied from the heading.

"Focus," came the anticipated staccato.

"I can't see the sails in the dark," I countered, bad feelings still in control.

When I heard the sails fluttering like bats in the night, I tried to adjust by bearing away slightly before slowly returning to the

129

heading he wanted. It was always too much or too little. He pushed down on my hand to turn the wheel.

"Listen closely. You should be able to sail with your eyes closed."

I always thought it odd that although he loved beautiful music, his voice was harsh. You wanted it to stop, or maybe it was just me. I stared at the compass and the indistinct shapes of sails until they became blurred. He cranked the winch and pulled in a few inches of mainsheet. The fluttering stopped.

"Head up a few degrees," he ordered.

As soon as there was enough light to see what I was doing, he sent me back to bed. When my mother sent me to deliver his breakfast, his mood hadn't improved. I was glad I had four hours of schoolwork.

By noon, the wind had increased. With 70 miles left to Great Inagua Island, we slogged though the waves, the wind growing, the sky darkening. Over the next hour, we skirted gray walls of rain. Lightning flashed into the sea. The *Spray* barged into the waves, braking at each crest before surfing wildly down the other side. My father took down the mizzen sail, furled the outer jib, and put a reef in the mainsail. Even with reduced sail area, the *Spray* continued its relentless heaving cycle, burying its lee rail in the waves, rising up sharply as though gasping for air before its next downward plunge. Water swirled around the cockpit floor, ankle deep, before it disappeared down the drains.

I stayed on deck with my father. Huddling in the corner of the cockpit, breathing deeply, and staring at the horizon seemed to help. Tchaikovsky's *Marche Slave, Opus 31,* blasted from six waterproof speakers.

"He composed it in five days," my father suddenly shouted over the fury of the wind. He steered with one hand, and conducted his orchestra of waves with the other. The madness of Captain Ahab was in his eyes. Only the white sperm whale, Moby Dick, was missing.

"This is the sixth time you've played it."

He didn't care. "We're going about. Take the wheel. I'll do the jib."

Going about moved the sails from one side of the boat to the other. It was always a rush to stop the sails from flapping, which could damage them. Suddenly, the outer jib unraveled from the forestay.

"The flaming furling system is busted," he shouted. The jib flailed, each crack as loud as a gunshot and shaking the boat violently "Are you taking the wheel?" he demanded.

He shoved my legs to get past, as though I was a sack of sails in the way. I got to my feet and silently took his place. I gripped the wheel with both hands. Salt stung my eyes and fear soured my mouth; however, I didn't throw up. He tried to roll up the jib by cranking the furling line onto a winch. After two turns, he stopped and cursed under his breath.

"It's tangled. I'll have to go forward to fix it. Watch out for the waves."

He climbed out of the cockpit and waited until the *Spray* plunged into a trough before he dashed forward, always keeping one hand on the rail. When he reached the bow, he wedged himself into the pulpit, and began to untangle the furling line. Immediately, the wind blew harder than ever, pushing his boat onto its side for long minutes at a time.

After a long gust flogged the sail, my father roared, "Bear off. You'll rip it to shreds."

Quickly, I steered away from the wind. The *Spray* heeled and a wave crashed over the bow. Sheets of spray hid my father from sight. When he crawled back to the cockpit, he was drenched to the skin, even under his jacket. Water streamed from his straggly beard.

"I can't fix it," he gasped. "I'll have to drop the jib." He found a length of rope beneath the cockpit seat and rushed back to the bow in a lull between waves.

"I don't want to do that again in a hurry." He clambered back into the cockpit. For a moment, I thought he might actually smile. He didn't. He slumped onto the seat, wiped his face with his hand. "You did a good job steering."

The *Spray* crashed and bucked through the gale: punching into the waves, rising up, careening down the other side, slewing into the churning troughs. At the peaks, I gaped at endless lines of white caps, wave upon wave, some breaking like surf. In the troughs, unnatural hills of deep, dark blue surrounded us. Up and down, with no rhythm except it repeated relentlessly. My stomach was queasy, the taste in my mouth, revolting. I spit it out and consoled myself with the thought that at least I wasn't throwing up like my brother and sister. My mother looked ghastly. Her face was white, her lips compressed. She didn't even offer to make dinner.

With the onset of night, the wind decreased and the waves became smaller. We hauled up the jib, took the reef out of the main, and raised the mizzen sail. The clouds and the sea sopped up the moonlight, leaving only the foamy crests of waves passing by.

Waves breaking on a reef woke me up. My father and I had dozed off. Without a word, we leaped to tack away with a frenzied hauling of the jib sheets. The chart plotter's reading condemned us. We had come within a stone's throw of the reef. I fought to stay awake, staring into the dismal night, listening to the disconcerting sound of nearby surf. Finally, my father tapped my shoulder, pointed to dots of light from houses just a few miles away, and started the motor. At 2:10 am., after 22 hours, we anchored off Matthew Town, Great Inagua Island.

+++

When I awoke, the cabin was hot. The sun blazed through the hatch and onto my face. My head ached and my scalp itched from crusted salt. My berth moved beneath me, lifting up and plunging down, just as it did when we were underway. Ben's berth was vacant, an amazing recovery from a virtual coma of seasickness. I struggled into dry clothes, not having the foggiest idea of how I got undressed and into bed. The main cabin was tidy, the hatches and portholes wide open. There was no sign of yesterday's chaos, or my family.

Yawning, I climbed the companionway steps. They'd dragged the dinghy up the beach, away from the waves that rolled ashore, and left me to fend for myself. On either side of the *Spray*, yachts formed a jagged line along the parched, windswept shore.

Matthew Town revealed no redeeming features. Rusty-roofed buildings, ragged palm trees, electric poles, water towers, and radio antennae baked in the sun. In the distance, a concrete pier extended into deep water. What appeared to be snow-covered hills were vast piles of salt, a million tons of it. On the other side of the town, a long, curving peninsula ended in a moonscape of gray grass, skeletal shrubs, and a lonely lighthouse. A line of clouds on the southwest horizon situated Cuba, 60 miles away.

When I went below to scavenge for food, I found a note on the galley counter:

'Gone to find doctor for Jessie. Back soon. Love Mom.'

Beneath, Ben had printed, 'Dad said no school today.'

Only one apple was left of the dozens of apples we'd bought in Florida. It was mealy with a brown mark on the side. I gnawed around it, feeling like Jim Hawkins on the *Hispaniola*. I went upstairs again, gave the beach a cursory glance, and stretched out on the cockpit seat. I soon fell asleep in the sun.

Something bumped against the side of the *Spray*. Thinking it was my family returning, I blocked out the sun with the crook of my arm, and settled into a more comfortable position, my back aching from lying on the hard seat.

"Yo, Sharkbait," brought me back to life.

I sat up, blinking. Sal's head protruded over the side of the cockpit.

"Look who's finally awake," he said.

I squinted in the sun, disbelieving despite Sal looking at me with a friendly smile and the *Marionette* docked at the end of the pier. "What are you doing here?"

"Refueling. Would your mom and dad like to go to lunch?"

"They took Jessie to the doctor." Then, I told Sal about our rough voyage.

"I don't know why your dad didn't wait. I told him the front would move through in a day."

"Once his mind is made up, it's impossible to change it."

After an awkward silence, Sal asked, "Do you think your parents would mind if I took you to lunch?"

My father would mind; however, lunch with Sal trumped the stale bread and peanut butter I'd eat on the *Spray*. I hadn't eaten anything except an apple and a chocolate bar in 24 hours. With my stomach settled down, I was ravenous.

"I could leave them a note," I suggested hopefully.

"Tell them we won't be gone more than an hour or so."

I hurried down the stairs, missed a step when the *Spray* heaved up and down, and barely avoided falling. Beneath Ben's neat printing, I scrawled:

'Josh went to lunch with Sal. Back soon.'

I grabbed a pair of sandals on the way out of the cabin, climbed over the rail, and waited for a trough in the waves. Below, Sal's runabout bounced like a cork in a stream.

"Now!" he shouted, and I jumped.

He opened the throttle and headed to the beach, driving the runabout onto the shore so we could get off without getting our shoes wet. The *Spray's* dinghy was a little farther up the beach, away from the waves.

The restaurant was a converted house built of stone and painted lime green. A crowd of local people gathered at the bar, mostly men, gossiping and drinking mugs of beer. Every table was in use. Luckily, Sal knew Rosemary, the owner. Soon, we were seated and looking at the menu: American hamburgers and hotdogs, and fish, chicken, and conch. The cook fried everything, including the hotdogs. I ate until my belly bulged. Then, we talked.

Chapter 19

Three-foot-high waves stretched from the Matthew Town pier to the lighthouse, pitching and rolling the *Spray*, yet my father worked on the jib furling system, squeezed between the railings over the bowsprit. He glanced up one time after Sal's runabout left the beach. He got to his feet only after I'd climbed aboard and Sal's runabout was pulling away from the stern.

"I took him to lunch. I hope you don't mind," Sal called out.

"Thanks," my father responded. The waves shoved Sal's runabout farther away from the *Spray*.

"How's Jessie?"

"She's fine. When she woke up this morning, she hurt near her kidneys. According to Virginia, it's a symptom of dehydration so we took her to the doctor. Three hours we waited, then he saw us for all of three minutes."

"That's island time for you. The things that happen quickly, you never expect. The rest take forever," Sal chuckled. "Bonefish run on island time, don't they Sharkbait?"

I grinned back. Some days we fished for hours without a bite. We interrupted the monotony by saying 'anytime now,' hoping it would invoke a strike. Bonefish always hit the lure hard and fast, ripping half of the line from the reel with no warning at all.

Sal gave me a sociable nod and motored away.

My father staggered back from the bow, gripping the rail, his anger obvious. "You were told to stay here until we got back."

Behind him, Ben's head poked cautiously above the companionway hatch. He quickly ducked down, keeping out of sight. Not standing on the stairs was included in rule number six;

'companionway procedures' on the list my father taped above the refrigerator.

"Mom's note didn't say that."

He exploded. "You need permission to leave the *Spray*! That's the rule."

I considered saying it wasn't on his list. "You weren't here so I couldn't get permission."

Like augers, his eyes bored holes into me. "Do you know why we left Acklins when we did?"

I shrugged, not particularly interested in his self-serving reasons. Sal's runabout was halfway to the *Marionette*, skimming across Victoria Bay.

"I wanted to get you away from him. That man's a bad influence."

I almost laughed. "How?"

"That fly-rod must be worth hundreds of dollars."

I felt years of anger seething. "Yep, generosity is so wrong." After Sal taught me how to fly-fish, he gave me a rod and reel and a box of equipment. The rod was handmade. "He's got dozens of fishing rods. He didn't need it."

"Maybe you can explain why Santa Claus is here, in this God forsaken hole?"

"They're refueling. He's on his way to Puerto Plata to meet his wife and granddaughter."

My father took a deep breath. "Something's not right."

"Like what?"

He just shook his head.

"You don't like anyone! You never have. You go out of your way to avoid people. When we stop, it's because no one is there, and if there are other boats, we're so far away that we can't see anyone."

He looked away. I hoped I'd hurt him. He turned back. "I don't trust him."

"Him and the rest of the human race," I retorted, past caring. "He's the only person I've talked to since St. Augustine."

My mother came on deck. "Josh has a point. He could use some time with kids his age," she said in a quiet voice.

"Should we have stayed at George Town?" He waited for her to disagree. She didn't. Instead, she turned to me.

"Josh," she began. "You spent five days with Sal; we don't know anything about him. We don't even know his last name."

I looked up. "Sal likes having me around because I remind him of Dante. His son liked to fish as much as I do." He scowled at me. She waited for me to continue. "He died eleven years ago, when Sal lived in New York. They were out shopping for birthday presents for Sal's granddaughter when someone shot at them from a car."

"Maybe..." My father shook his head. "It doesn't change a thing. I don't want you near him."

"Why? Because you don't like him?"

"Why isn't important!" he snarled.

"He doesn't need you shouting at him."

He turned to my mother, his anger barely restrained. "I don't like it. It's too much of a coincidence."

"What is?" I asked.

He spun around. "That's none of your business, Victor!"

"I know you're worried, but there's no need to take it out on him," she said, giving him a cold look.

Instead of arguing, he looked at his watch. "I'm tired of being tossed around. If we leave now we can reach Lantern Head Harbour before dark."

Lantern Head Harbour was the last stop before setting out for Luperón, on the north coast of the Dominican Republic.

"After what we went through yesterday, we need a break," she said firmly. She stared him down. "We'll stay another day so Jessie gets a proper rest, otherwise you leave by yourself."

"Until we know more about him, we need to be careful. I know I've seen him before, and that bothers me," he said, always having the last word.

He went to the stern, down the ladder to our dinghy. Watching him, alone, his back hunched over as he started the outboard motor, I wished we'd never left our trailer in Norfolk.

+ + +

My mother said she wasn't worried when my father missed dinner; however, I worried, certain that he'd gone to the *Marionette* to tell Sal to keep away from me. I lay awake for hours, waiting for the sound of our outboard motor, listening to Ben's sonorous breathing and the halyards banging against the masts as the *Spray* rolled with the waves. At midnight, when his old-fashioned ship's clock chimed the end of the first watch and the beginning of the middle watch, I decided to find him.

Scattered lights were still on in the town. Bright dots of light spaced along the distant pier pointed out to sea. I padded barefoot to the stern, climbed down the ladder, and eased into the water to swim to shore. I tried not to think about sharks. Even the sociable sand shark that frequented the beach looking for handouts was dangerous at night.

I dried off with an old towel I took from our dinghy, still where he'd left it on the beach, thinking I should've left a note; however, it was too late to go back. A faint noise came from behind me. I turned and stared at the sea, shivering in wet, clinging clothes. The *Spray* was a silhouette against the sky, rocking in the swell. My imagination didn't consider the physics of sound. Despite how faint it was, I decided my father had shouted from the end of the pier.

I ran down the beach, sharp pieces of broken pansy shell stabbing my feet, passing the mountainous salt dunes that loomed out of the night. Finally, I scrambled up to the road and ran down the pier until I reached the *Marionette's* stern. I rested behind a stack of pallets, breathless, watching two men in the salon, like ghosts behind glass.

For a minute, Sal talked so quietly that I missed what he said. Suddenly, his voice became louder, impatient with anger.

"I'm tired of your screw-ups, Morello."

"Is not my fault, Sal. The supercharger not work right."

It was obvious my father wasn't on the *Marionette,* yet I curious about Sal's middle-of-the-night visitor. I'd heard his voice before, though I couldn't remember when or where.

"Get it fixed. While you're at it, get rid of the name!"

"I get it done, Sal."

Sal stepped into the doorway. For a moment, a rectangle of light framed him, his hair white as salt. "I want you in Lupe' on Wednesday morning," he said over his shoulder. "That's six days from now!"

"Plenty of time. I need four more for Miami. You get Tony take care of it," Morello said.

"You screw up again, Morello, and I'll have Tony take care of you." If Sal had glanced up, he would have seen me leaning over the rail. Instead, he turned and stared into the darkness where a freighter's navigation lights glowed.

I quietly crossed the pier to the other side, safely out of sight behind a stack of wood-slat crates draped with curls of dried seaweed. The stench of rotting fish was overwhelming. Maybe my father was right about Sal.

Farther down the pier, I stopped to look over the railing. A powerboat bumped against the truck tires serving as fenders against the piles. It looked like Javiero's boat. It wasn't. Instead of a bird on fire, they'd painted flames and a name that I couldn't read because of the angle.

I hurried down the beach, eager to be back in my berth before anyone noticed. However, my father stood beside the dinghy, his hands on his hips. He kicked at *Squirt*. His foot bounced off the inflated rubber tube and nearly unbalanced him. He cursed and kicked again before he tried to drag the dinghy to the water's edge. I was next to him before he realized. He glared at me.

"What are you doing, sneaking around in middle of the night?"

"Looking for you."

"How'd you get here?" he slurred. It was the first time that I'd seen him drunk. I didn't like it.

"I swam."

His hand brushed my chest. "You must've. You're still wet."

I fetched the anchor that he'd tried to pull through the sand. Neither of us spoke while we dragged *Squirt* down the beach and climbed in. Waves tried to flip the dinghy over.

"Make yourself useful and row." He flopped down next to the outboard motor. "Quietly! Don't want to wake everyone up."

Chapter 20

It was late the next morning when my father stomped down the stairs and over to his chart table, a glossy mahogany and maple counter cluttered with rolls of charts and navigation equipment. He inspected the rows of CDs that filled the shelves above, selected one, and inserted it into the player. Igor Stravinsky's *Le Sacre du Primtemps* blared in the cockpit until he adjusted the volume. It was Stravinsky's most famous work, 'a landmark in music, filled with tension and anger,' my father said. No wonder it was a favorite, I thought. Europe was at the brink of war and plagued by widespread depression when Stravinsky composed it. It caused a riot at its premiere in Paris.

No one looked up from the schoolbooks and papers that covered the table. The sound of his feet on the floor was warning enough. He stopped by the bulkhead next to me and stared at the Captain's photograph. He cleared his throat.

"We're leaving for Lantern Head Harbour."

My mother took a deep breath.

"We've a long trip ahead of us. I want to get as close as we can to the Dominican Republic before we leave Great Inagua." On the way out of the cabin, he tapped my shoulder. "I need you on deck."

I left my work on the table and followed, anticipating a lecture. I didn't say a word while he got his boat ready to leave. I tidied up the cockpit. My father waited until I finished coiling the halyards and sheets. He looked at the end of the pier. The *Marionette* was gone. One of the tramp freighters that plied the Caribbean islands had replaced it. It was a football field long, its superstructure dented, its hull streaked with rust. Cranes swung back and forth, placing cargo on waiting trucks.

142

"I doubt we'll see him again. If we do, I don't want you to go near him," he said.

At that moment, I hated my father. It wasn't about Sal. He always worried about being near other people. He'd been like that for as long as I could remember.

+ + +

Around four pm, we arrived in Lantern Head Harbour. My father steered a course close to only boat there, instead of motoring around the harbor to find a more secluded place. It was a lot smaller than the *Spray*. Gas bottles, fuel cans, and plastic storage containers cluttered the deck. A potted tomato plant hung from the boom, its leaves dangling over a wooden steering wheel so old that it might have belonged on the Captain's *Spray*. Attached to the aft railing were an odd-looking self-steering mechanism, a barbecue grill, a couple of worn-out fishing rods, and a life ring bearing two stick-on letters, remnants of the vessel's name, which was hand-painted on the transom. A rubber dinghy covered with mismatched patches drifted off the stern.

"Ahoy there, *Down Under*." My father followed the traditional greeting of sailors with, "Anyone home?"

A tousled head poked through a hatch. White lather covered the lower half of the man's bristly face. "Blimey, you're the last person I expected to see here," he called out cheerfully.

My father pointed the bow at a rocky headland that guarded a lagoon and a sandy beach.

After a few moments, the man called out, "Sorry, mate. You look like someone I knew back home. You staying long?"

The *Spray* kept turning. "For a night or two."

The man waved his arm around while shaving with the other hand. "Pick a spot. Nowhere's bad 'less it's blowing a gale. Then, everywhere stinks till you get to Lupe."

143

"How long have you been here?" my father called out.

"Since the money ran out. I might have to get a job soon. I'm getting tired of drinking rainwater and eating what I catch." He dabbed his face with a towel before casting an appreciative eye over the *Spray*. "Good looking boat you got there. Based on Slocum's Spray, ain't she?"

My father beamed. No lecture needed. "As close as I could get. She's a foot longer."

The man watched us pass. "You interested in a potluck dinner?" he shouted. "I hooked a grouper this morning. I'll bring it if you bring the beer and sides. On the beach in an hour?"

My father agreed with a wave, not bothering to ask where on the beach we would gather. We dropped the sails and anchored nearby. Except for marinas, it was the closest the *Spray* had been to another yacht.

Bruce McKenzie's passion to sail around the world matched my father's. It disturbed me that he'd been away for two years and he was only halfway. He talked with my father late into the night, about cruising routes, places to visit and places to avoid, and how to make the money last longer. The following day all they did was sit in the cockpit, talk about sailing, and drink beer. I couldn't remember a time when my father's mood had been better, or an entire day without Russian music.

+ + +

Saturday evening, May 15, my father listened to the weather report and made notes on a pad. He came over to the table, pushed aside dinner plates, and opened his chart.

"It should take about 35 hours to get to Luperón," he began.

"A day and a half at sea?" My mother sounded resigned. She rubbed Jessie's shoulder.

"It'll take longer if the weather doesn't cooperate," he said.

I sat across the table from him. Even with the chart upside down, I could see what worried him. The trade winds usually blew from the east in that part of the Caribbean, 175 miles into the wind with nowhere to stop on the way.

"Will it cooperate for 35 hours?" Ben asked as though my father could somehow arrange it.

My father looked up as if he expected the question. "Just tomorrow, but we'll take advantage of it. We'll motor when the wind is too far to the east." He paused, looked around the table, and began his lecture. "The passage isn't heavily trafficked, but we'll need to look out for other vessels. There'll be two watches. Four hours on duty, and then four hours for sleep. We'll leave at 4:00 am. I'll take the first two watches. Ben, you'll be with me, starting at 8:00 am."

Jessie clutched her stuffed cat. My mother hugged her. "Don't worry. You'll be asleep most of the time."

Jessie shook her head determinedly. "Why can't we stay here?"

My father didn't answer, fixing his gaze on my mother. "You'll need to adjust the sails and keep track of course changes. He knows what to do," he added, nodding at me.

My first watch started at noon, when with eight bells from the ship's clock, the forenoon watch ended. With the self-steering operating properly, there was nothing to do except occasionally survey the horizon and glance at the compass. Jessie played in the cockpit and ate candied ginger, which Bruce had provided as his remedy for seasickness. It seemed to be working, provided she didn't eat the whole jar, which seemed to be her current plan.

At four o'clock in the afternoon, I woke my father and Ben for their watch. We'd gone 61 miles, slightly ahead of schedule. The only problem was the wind, steady at 12 knots. What started from the northeast slowly shifted east. We winched the sails in until they were drum-tight. The heading was still farther south than he wanted. My father started the motor when I went down the stairs, ready to climb into my berth and sleep for four hours.

At 8:00 pm., Ben woke me up. The sunset was spectacular, dinner wasn't—tuna fish and salsa smeared over stale bread. I played my guitar and my mother watched the compass. At midnight, I fell into bed and was sound asleep in seconds.

My father's prolonged shaking did nothing for my mood when he woke me at four in the morning. I staggered into the cockpit with a handful of cookies, bleary-eyed and wishing watches lasted eight hours instead of four. He recorded the end-of-watch position in his logbook. I didn't ask how far remained. The wind had faded during the night. He'd used the motor throughout his watch, yet even then, landfall was at least a day away.

"Do you think you'll be okay by yourself, Josh?" he asked while I tightened my safety harness and clipped the tether to the floor ring.

My mouth dropped open, surprised both by his question and him calling me 'Josh.' I glanced down the companionway. "Where's Mom?"

"With Jessie. She's sick again."

My stomach tensed.

"She's not as sick as last time," he added. "I'd stay with you, but I need to sleep for a while. I could sleep in the cockpit," he offered; however, he didn't mean it.

I gazed into the night. Waves whacked the bow as the *Spray* sailed slowly onward. The sea sucked up the moonlight until it was difficult to see the sails. They fluttered until the self-steering adjusted the course.

"All you have to do is watch out for other boats. Don't leave the cockpit except to go downstairs." Instead of a lecture about responsibility, he said, "If you need help, give me a call. Remember, the important thing is to..." He waited for me to finish.

"Write down the position, heading and distance every hour, and whenever it changes," I said tiredly. "And watch out for lights."

Boats sank when they ran into things: reefs, other boats, whales, floating debris, and worst of all, the huge steel containers that fell off freighters during storms. Only boats had warning lights. The rest lurked in the darkness and waited for unsuspecting sailors.

"Keep her properly trimmed..." He yawned. "The hardest part is staying awake. Do you want anything before I go to bed? A drink maybe?" I shook my head. "Thump on the hatch if you need me. There's only two hours until dawn," he added before he went below.

He'd never left me alone on deck for longer than a few minutes, never for four hours at four in the morning. Sunrise was at 5:54 am. I had to stay awake until then. After that, I wouldn't have to worry about falling asleep. As soon as he was gone, I wanted something to drink. It was too late to call him back.

The first hour dragged. When I started to fall asleep, I fetched my guitar and played *Yesterday*, again, and again, and again. Bored with that, I invented variations to McCartney's composition until the sky lightened in the east. Sunrise began as a faint yellow glow on the horizon, expanding until an orange disk suddenly rose from the sea. The leaden-gray ocean became dark blue and the eastern sky burst into radiant fire. Warmth touched my cheek and the chill of night fled like a vampire at dawn. Even as the *Spray* came alive again, I struggled to keep my eyes from closing.

My father reappeared at 8:00 am with cookies and a glass of milk. He checked my scribbled notes of time, position, direction, and distance. I waited, not eating.

"Why every half hour when the wind shifted one time?" he inquired, glancing up.

Two hours earlier, the wind increased and shifted back to the northeast. I'd eased the sheets and picked up two knots and five degrees. He should've been pleased.

"I thought... if I wrote it down every half hour, when the bell rang, instead of on the hour. It helped keep me awake.... If something went wrong you'd only have 30 minutes from the last position."

"It's a good idea. We'll do that from now on."

My next watch started at noon. I dozed on the cockpit seat while my mother kept watch and cut up travel brochures for her scrapbook despite Jessie's sweaty head in her lap. Ben buried his head in his encyclopedia. My father stretched out on the other side of the cockpit, content to listen to funky Caribbean music on a local radio station. Our destination was a cloud-covered smudge on the horizon.

Chapter 21

The scent of the rain forest arrived on the breeze, not like the salty Bahamas. The island ahead, its mountain peaks disappearing into clouds, was reputed to be the most beautiful island in the Caribbean. Columbus thought so in 1492; however, that was before his *Santa Maria* ran aground farther up the coast. He called it 'La Isla Española.' Hispaniola was 'The Spanish Island.'

The remaining miles rushed by with the same trade wind that had carried Columbus. Soon, steep, forested hills rose up from the sea, meeting a lush paradise of jungles tumbling down from the mountains. Plantations were patches of bright green velvet scattered over the foothills.

Hispaniola rolled off the tongue along with tales of square-rigged ships, swarthy pirates, and gold escudos spilling from treasure chests. I imagined Luperón surrounded by walls with cannon. Instead, the luxurious buildings of a new tourist resort lined the shore. Palm trees, sunbathers, umbrellas, thatched-roof beach huts, a strip of sand, breaking surf—it ended at a rocky outcrop. A forest covered the headland on the other side of the harbor entrance. My father steered for the gap.

Suddenly, he spun the wheel, turning back to the safety of deeper water. He bellowed, 'Victor, get the chart!' like it was my fault.

I scrambled down the stairs while he cursed under his breath. His chart showed one reef extending halfway across the harbor entrance and another reef to the east. We'd seen the waves breaking over them. Between the reefs were dark areas; they could be deeper water, rocks, or big clumps of seaweed.

"Where are the buoys?" he demanded, looking up. White ointment covered his nose, the rest of his face tanned from spending every day in the sun.

The chart showed buoys to mark the channel. If they existed, they hid among pieces of Styrofoam and plastic bottles tied to fish traps. He started the engine and lowered the sails. Cautiously, he motored into the harbor entrance, constantly glancing from paper chart, to chart plotter, to depth sounder, to the churning water ahead. The channel narrowed, the ocean swell lessened, and the water became cloudy. We passed two buoys, one green, one red. A little farther and yacht masts sprouted above mangroves. Luperón was a popular 'hurricane hole'—100 boats spread across a bay protected from the ocean and wind by surrounding hills. As we approached the outlying yachts, the VHF radio crackled to life.

"'De say-boot arrive een Luperón, stop dere eet eese," a disgruntled voice demanded.

The 'say-boot' was the *Spray*. Between outbursts of Spanish and garbled English, he told us it was too late for the customs and immigration officers to visit. He ordered us to drop the anchor and have no contact with other yachts until the officials boarded and inspected the *Spray* the following morning. He went on and on. My father was so tired that he was happy to oblige.

+ + +

The customs officials and their military escort arrived in an old wooden launch with smoke wheezing from a noisy outboard motor. A metal awning kept the sun and rain off the officials, while seven men dressed in camouflage fatigues and armed with automatic rifles stood in the stern. When the launch was an arm's length away, the marines swarmed over the rail.

"Armas?" one man demanded of my father. "You have firearm on boat?"

After a moment, my father glanced at my mother and shook his head. Two men stood guard and the others searched the *Spray* for contraband. The search soon moved down to the cabin. They inspected every locker before the customs officers climbed aboard. One man carefully handed a black briefcase to another before he crossed from the launch. A third man remained in the launch under the awning, his feet propped up on the seat, his arms folded on his chest until he swatted at the gnats that hovered over his head.

"El Commandante," a soldier explained. He smirked. "Last night he drink too much."

It was impossible to tell whether El Commandante commanded the navy, the army, or the police. A Panama hat covered his face, shielding his hangover from the morning glare.

The customs officers wore starched white shirts and shorts, gold-braided caps, and polished belts with leather holsters for their pistols. The older man proceeded through a formal introduction of names, titles, and immigration laws of the Dominican Republic. His assistant, unshaven and acne-scarred, waited with the briefcase. He watched us suspiciously, his eyes darting back and forth as if a middle-aged man, his wife, and three children posed a threat.

"Your passports have stamps for arrival in Bahamas, but not for departure. Why?" the official asked after he inspected our passports.

My father's mouth opened. For once, he said nothing.

"We're sorry, sir. I guess we didn't realize," my mother said.

The official turned to her and raised an eyebrow. "And you also didn't realize you needed a clearance certificate?"

"Clearance certificate?" she repeated.

"I can handle it," my father interrupted.

The official's mood suddenly soured. "Captain, all vessels arriving from the Bahamas must have a clearance certificate; and your passports must be stamped on departure. Surely you know this?"

When he stopped talking, I noticed Ben and Jessie waving vigorously from the bow. It was as far away as they could get and still be on deck.

I was about to join them when Ben shouted over his shoulder, "Josh, the *Marionette* is here."

There was no mistaking the *Marionette*. As it approached, the horn tooted. I grinned and waved.

"Sal is friend?" the official inquired politely.

"Yes, he's a very good friend," my mother said quickly. "Sort of a godfather to Josh, our son."

My father started to say something, but stopped. The official's attitude had changed.

"Welcome to Luperón," the man said, his smile suddenly bright. "I will tell El Commandante that Sal is your friend, Señor Walker. We hope you have a good visit."

He opened the briefcase. With unexpected efficiency, he canceled the $50 fine imposed for not having a clearance certificate, collected the entry fee of $75, stamped our passports, and completed our visitors' cards. They left in a hurry. Their next vessel, the *Marionette*, awaited them at the wharf at the far end of the harbor.

"What's Sal doing here?" my father demanded of me.

I shook my head and wondered when we'd leave, by nightfall most likely. However, after my father raised the anchor, he motored around Puerto Blanco to find a good place to anchor. He avoided the government wharf and the yacht club, finally venturing into an out-of-the-way inlet that reminded me of the dirty water, mud, and mosquitoes of the Carolina swamps. Vast numbers of birds filled the mangrove trees, and snowy egrets pecked on the mud shoals. There were several yachts already anchored where my father decided to stop. On a big catamaran, a wiry, dark-skinned girl lay in a hammock slung under the boom. She was reading, one leg dangling down, her foot pushing at a winch on the cabin roof to make the hammock sway. She waved to me and I waved back. Pointing to her book, she held up two fingers, two hours to finish her schoolwork. She pointed to the shore. I nodded eagerly.

+ + +

She rowed a red, inflatable dinghy over to the *Spray* while we sat in the cockpit eating lunch, planning a family trip ashore for the rest of the day.

"Hola!" she called out. "Welcome to Puerto Blanco."

Expecting to fend off a collision, my father stood up and watched while she brought the nearest oar to the side and worked the other oar back and forth to bring the dinghy closer to the *Spray*. When it was clear that she knew what she was doing, he sat down again.

"Hello, and who might you be?" my mother asked.

The girl beamed up at her with a mouth full of perfect white teeth. "I'm Imani Keats." She pointed to the catamaran. "I've lived on *Nauti-kat* since I was five."

She was friendly and funny. 'Imani' was Swahili for 'Faith.' She gave us her life story with a practiced flourish. Her mother was a dentist who operated her practice from the catamaran, her father a retired ice hockey player from Toronto, Canada. During seven years, their travels had taken them throughout the Caribbean. After spending their third winter in Luperón, they'd sailed to Miami. They were heading back to the Virgin Islands to stay until the hurricane season ended. Imani knew what was worth seeing, what to do, and what not to do.

"Always chain your outboard to your dinghy," she advised, "but even that won't work if they've got bolt cutters. Luperón's not like the Bahamas. The worst thing they do there is siphon your gas tank. It happened three times before my dad realized it wasn't my doing."

My mother directed her gaze at my father. "That's interesting. We ran out of gas in the Bahamas." He shrugged in response. "Is there anything else we should know?" she asked.

"Whatever you do, don't drink the water," Imani said, shaking her head. She made a wry face and added, "I won't go into the details, but if I did, you'll wish I hadn't. Not at all nice."

When we stopped laughing, Imani asked if she could take Ben and me to explore the town. I was astonished when my father agreed, so long as we took Imani's dinghy.

We rowed to the wharf on the other side of Puerto Blanco, weaving an erratic course among the anchored yachts and fishing boats. Like *Squirt*, Imani's dinghy was difficult to row. A week earlier, it had an outboard motor securely chained to a stainless steel ring. In the middle of the night, thieves had stolen it. They swam to the catamaran, untied the line, towed the dinghy to the shore, and cut the chain with a hacksaw to remove it.

The *Marionette* took up one side of the government wharf. I stopped rowing to look. Five, bare-to-the-waist workers washed the windows and buffed the shine.

"A patrol boat usually docks there. It always leaves before the *Marionette* arrives," Imani said when she noticed my interest. "It's the same every other month. Sal always stays in Luperón for three days. Never longer."

"How do you know Sal?"

"Everyone in the Caribbean knows Sal," Imani laughed

She pulled with her oar to turn the dinghy towards a pier packed with dinghies, three deep. It was conveniently located where the road ended and the wharf began—across from the Bar Luperón, a metal shed with tables and seats lined up outside.

+ + +

The road into town was like the worst back road in the hills of West Virginia—sometimes thinly covered with asphalt, full of potholes, and lined with pigpens and ramshackle houses. Closer to town, jumbled signs advertised laundry, automobile repair, and welding done while you waited. Clothes hung from lines strung between brightly painted houses, jammed together and deformed as if the ground heaved up under them, their tin roofs battered from above. They painted everything, including the electric poles, as high as a person could reach on a ladder.

Luperón had only 8,000 people, not nearly enough to explain the bicycles, cars, motorbikes, trucks, and buses racing along narrow streets with a deafening roar. Chickens scrambled to avoid mangy dogs, and stubborn mules carried crates of farm produce. Naked toddlers came out to stare at us before they ran off to hide. Grizzly fishermen gossiped and cleaned their fish beside sidewalk merchants selling food and designer-label clothes. Young women wearing the latest fashion flirted with teenage boys who recklessly swerved their motorcycles around grandmothers lugging straw baskets across the street.

Luperón was an endless conga from one end of the town to the other —a thousand boom boxes played 'merengue,' a salsa-like concoction of saxophones, drums, scrapers, and electronic instruments; fast, metallic, and loud. We wandered past men sitting on boxes around a yard enclosed in chicken wire. They drank beer and compared their plumed, fighting cocks, placing bets, and watching them squabble and prance in the prelude to sparring. At the market, we met two other kids who lived on yachts in the harbor. There were 20 more like them in Luperón, kids who traveled the world instead of living in houses in suburbia.

When we returned to the *Spray*, dinner awaited us: fried chicken, plantain chips, spicy rice, and beans, from Louisa's Chicken Shack. My father took great delight in observing that the entire meal cost less than five dollars.

Chapter 22

Wednesday, May 19, arrived with a humid drizzle that turned into in a tropical deluge. As suddenly as it started, the rain ceased and the wind returned. Soon, only a few straggling clouds remained. After listening to a discussion on the VHF radio about the best type of anchor for the harbor's muddy bottom, my father turned the volume down and came over to the table.

He consulted his watch. "Eight-thirty. It's time to get going."

"To go where?" my mother asked. The night before he'd talked about staying for a week.

"Santiago, and then the mountains. It'll be a change from the sea."

"What about La Isabela?" Ben interrupted. He'd spent the previous evening reviewing Hispaniola's history in his encyclopedia. "It's the first European settlement in the New World and it's only ten miles away," he added hopefully.

"We'll see it, but not today." My father turned to my mother. "They can do school work on the bus to Santiago."

Ben looked to me for support. I chose a trip to the mountains over ruins.

+ + +

A bus went from Luperón to Santiago every two hours, the next one at 9:00 am. Apparently, no one noticed the sign, or relied on it. For 20 minutes, we stood in the street, dodging cars and trucks and waiting for the promised bus. Dozens of guaguas stopped to offer us rides. A guagua was a private mini-van built to carry between 6 and 12. Instead, they carried double the number. Guaguas honked their horns and pulled up beside you if the driver thought you wanted a ride. If they were traveling too fast, they

157

merely slowed down and the fare collector, the cobrador, leaned out and shouted the destination. If it was going where you wanted, you waved and ran after it.

My father became increasingly agitated. When the next guagua arrived, he negotiated a family fare of 100 pesos ($2.90) and we piled onboard. It wasn't so crowded that we couldn't do schoolwork; however, it rattled and bounced so much that it was hard to concentrate. The guagua lacked glass in most of its windows, and the seats had holes; which was typical, along with no air-conditioning, no timetable, and no route map. It stopped at Imbert. Three passengers headed off to the waterfalls. The rest changed to other guaguas, going to the resort towns on the coast, or south to Santiago.

Santiago was an old, sprawling city, choking in car exhaust, as loud as it was dirty. New, four-story buildings packed the center of the city, painted white or tropical pastel, with signs attached to every surface. People rushed from store to store, across busy streets oblivious to the traffic. There were lots of elaborate stone buildings and a huge monument, all worth visiting. However, we weren't in Santiago any longer than it took to my father to decide that at $20 each, the bus tours to the mountains were overpriced. Instead, we used a succession of guaguas: one to Concepcion de La Vega, then another to the village of Jarabacoa.

The 'Jarabacoa Express' had been a family minivan until wooden benches replaced upholstered seats. The outside was red and blue and decorated with pieces of broken mirror. Duct tape held loose panels together, and the front bumper dragged close to the road. A roll of baling wire rested on the dashboard so the driver could make repairs on the way. We squeezed inside, along with six other people and three smelly farm dogs, and shared the last bench with a tired-looking woman who had two noisy children climbing over her. The seat was wide enough for three people; however, eight people squeezed onto it. Ben sat on my father's knees, Jessie perched on my mother's lap, and I squeezed between them.

The driver, or chofer, drove with one hand and used his other hand to wave to children who ran out of tiny, tin houses when the van rattled past. He drummed to blaring music, chatted with the passengers, and avoided livestock and the remains of mudslides with aggressive swerving, all the while maintaining a speed that made the van shudder. Jarabacoa was in the foothills of the tallest mountains in the Caribbean; however, the guagua was so packed and the windows were so dirty that we could only guess at the hillside coffee plantations, jungles of pine trees mixed up with palm trees, and cascading ribbons of waterfalls.

While we waited for the last guagua to arrive to take us to La Ciénaga, we snacked on crunchy chips made from plantains,wandering through streets strung with power lines and overhead signs, our heads craned back to stare at steep mountains that disappeared into the clouds. All of a sudden, my father turned around and crossed the street. My mother shrugged and led the way into a store displaying trays of dulce de leche, a Caribbean sweet treat—soft, gooey fudge made from milk flavored with coconut. We crossed the road to find him waiting for us in front of a sign that read, 'Yaque del Norte Rafting,' '4 hours US $10 each,' 'English spoken.'

My mother licked fudge from her fingers. "Rafting, John?"

He shrugged, yet I could tell he was excited. "We don't have time to go to La Ciénaga and do more than wait for the next guagua back here," he said. La Ciénaga was the end of the road. From there, hikers made the long trek to Pico Duarte, over 10,000 feet high. "It's only $35. The kids are half-price," he explained. He pulled out his wallet and began to search through a wad of notes: US dollars, Bahamian dollars, and Dominican Republic pesos.

We climbed into the back of the Yaque Del Norte pickup truck and sat on wooden box seats. Above us, pipe scaffolding held up a rubber raft that bulged over the sides of the truck. The engine struggled to start. The driver gradually coaxed it from a death rattle to a roar and the truck careened onto the street, rocking erratically on worn out shock absorbers.

"Rafting?" my mother shouted. She was also amused.

He grinned back at us. "It won't be as bumpy as this."

The truck's transmission whined an earsplitting protest as it labored up a twisting road along the side of a gorge. Far below, a river cascaded over rocks that had crashed down, leaving ugly scars in the hillside and recent rubble strewn over the narrow road. The steep incline kept our speed to a crawl; however, even a crawl was too fast when there was no safety rail. The farther we went, the worse the road conditions became. Huge rocks rose up from the road, battering the truck so badly that the engine struggled to keep running. We passed through a village of tumbledown houses, a general store, and a busy local bar. The driver slowed down and waved at men lounging on the front porch. A mile later, after skidding around a hairpin curve, the truck turned off the road to La Ciénaga and began a slow descent into the gorge. The stench of burning brakes worried me all the way down.

The road was no more than a path when it stopped before a waterfall veiled in mist. A rain forest surrounded us, tangled vines, ferns, and orchids like my grandmother grew in her overheated sunroom. The driver and guide manhandled the raft off the rack and dragged it to the rambling Rio Yaque del Norte. Our guide, a lanky, constantly grinning college student handed out an assortment of tattered life-jackets, scratched helmets, paddles with broken ends, and a legal form releasing all claims.

We clambered into the raft, my father in the front. We gaped in delight at inquisitive parrots as our raft glided along in the leisurely current. Six minutes later, the first rocks appeared and the guide told us to hold on. The raft picked up speed as the gorge closed in, a roaring, white, wet funnel through which we were shot over a ledge, drenching us thoroughly. After that, it got worse, except my father's mood got better. He loved the 'Mike Tyson,' a vertical drop of 12 feet that jarred our spines and nearly tossed Ben out of the raft; and he wanted to repeat 'The Cemetery,' full of tombstone-shaped rocks. We survived to drift on a meandering river, oohing over waterfalls tumbling into deep pools, precarious rope bridges, noisy parrots, and exotic tangled vines. All too soon, the ride was over. The pick-up truck waited at a bend in the river to take us back to Jarabacoa.

We returned to Luperón through Santo Tomas de Jánico, once famous for its gold. Farmers had stripped the hills of trees, replacing them with coffee bushes in strict rows. Our guagua made good progress until the hard-clay road deteriorated to a rutted cow track. After an hour and a half of bumping, the little town of Jánico was a welcome sight. Another guagua took us to El Rubio, where we drank lukewarm sodas and waited for a ride to Mao.

From El Rubio, the road followed a river, crossing back and forth on wonky, wooden bridges. The bridges creaked and we held our breath, yet the guagua kept going. It stopped at farming communities according to the whim of the driver. I was half-asleep in the late afternoon sun when an elderly man in a threadbare suit struggled on with a cardboard box full of hand-printed T-shirts instead of the usual basket of fruit or vegetables. The van staggered off before he sat down. He stumbled, emitting a loud, flatulent boom that sounded like a trombone. The box toppled from his arms to the floor, scattering T-shirts in the dirt and trash.

"Venganza de las habas!" someone snickered. Revenge of the beans.

The driver stomped on the brakes and fiddled with the radio while the old man picked up the T-shirts, dusted them off, and carefully refolded them, all the while grumbling.

"Josh, isn't that Sal?"

I barely heard my mother over the din of commercials and music as the driver switched from one radio station to another. I glanced uneasily at my father. His head rested on the back of the seat, sound asleep. She peered through a film of dust, grubby fingerprints, and spots of food on the inside, and dead insects on the outside. Ahead, the road widened to provide waiting space for a single-lane bridge. Three vehicles were queued up, though not waiting to cross. One of them, a farmer's truck, had a canvas tarpaulin draped over its wooden-slat sides. Rust riddled the truck, which carried a sign that said 'Azúcar de Tavares SA, Barahona.' It had come a long way—Santa Cruz de Barahona was a port on the southern coast of the Dominican Republic.

"That is him, isn't it? Next to the truck?" she asked again.

Between the farmer's truck and a red pick-up truck, were two men. Neither was Sal. However, I recognized Javiero, leaning against the pick-up truck, and Morello, who walked from behind the farmer's truck, smoking a plump cigar.

Suddenly, the guagua lurched forward. As it rumbled towards the bridge, Javiero looked up, shielding his eyes from the dust, while I stared down at him from behind the grimy side window. A white plastic drum without a lid sat on the pick-up's open tailgate. It was full of pale, round nuts. Dozens of drums filled the pick-up, stacked in rows as high as the cabin roof.

"Where did you see him?" Just in case, I kept an eye on my father.

"He went behind the truck. Probably buying more of those macadamia nuts he likes."

I skewed around in my seat to look through the rear window as the guagua rattled onto the bridge. On the other side of the truck, two men talked. One man might have been Sal. His hair was snow-white. The other man stepped deeper into the shade as our guagua passed. He belonged in an office with his white shirt, gray trousers, and creamy Panama hat. He seemed bored with his arms folded across his chest. The blue sedan at the front of the row, the cleanest car I'd seen all day, was probably his. It certainly wasn't a rental car, not with its long radio antenna.

The guagua turned left off the bridge, rapidly picking up speed.

+ + +

The next guagua stopped in every village and farming settlement from Mao to Luperón. Finally, the sea came into view, a sweeping beach, long lines of breakers, palm trees silhouetted against the sunset's red-orange. I awoke stiff, sore, and hungry when the guagua arrived in Luperón. Again, our $5 dinner came from Louisa's Chicken Shack, a huge platter of greasy plantain chips and a family-sized bowl of spicy chicken stew, which my sister said burned her mouth.

Tired and full, we resisted the trek to the government wharf. My father waved and a motoconcho immediately swerved to the curb. Another motoconcho going in the opposite direction turned around and stopped next to the first one, both roaring their motors. My father shouted our destination and handed over two dollars before putting Jessie and Ben on the back of one of the motorcycles and getting on behind them. I climbed onto the other one, my mother behind me, and held on for dear life, screaming with delight as our motoconchos hurtled down the main street, none of us with helmets.

The motoconcho drivers missed the dinghy dock, taking us to the end of the wharf, squeezing past a red pick-up truck parked next to the *Marionette*. On the way back, I glanced into the rear of the pick-up truck at a pile of bricks with chalky mortar on the faces.

The lights were on in the *Marionette*'s main cabin. Sal stood at the open doorway, surveying the darkened wharf, eating nuts and tossing the shells over the side. I looked away quickly; however, it was too late. My father saw him wave.

He lectured me during the ten-minute ride back to the *Spray*, raising his voice over the noise of the outboard motor and the wind. We were both damp from the spray that blew across the dinghy, yet he kept me in the cockpit while the others went below to get ready for bed.

Finally, I demanded, "Why can't I see Sal again?"

"Because I said so!"

"That sucks."

To my surprise, he stayed calm. "I've told you there's something about him that bothers me. I've seen him before. I can't put my finger on where or when, but he worries me. That's all you need to know. I don't want you anywhere near him. He's not what he seems."

Too tired to argue, I left him there, the halyards banging against the masts, the wind strong enough for the *Spray* to tug hard at the anchor.

Chapter 23

The squawking and chirping in the mangrove trees started at sunrise, and was much louder than usual. Unable to sleep and curious about what had the birds so agitated, I went on deck. Egrets pecked on the mud flats a dozen yards away—the anchor had dragged during the night. A bold parrot, a noisy Hispaniolan Amazon, perched on the teak handrail. It tilted its head and inspected me with disdain, as if it sat on the shoulder of Long John Silver.

When my father came up the stairs, the parrot fled for the safety of the mangroves, a flash of green with splashes of red and blue on its wings. He looked at the shore, strode to the bow, yanked on the anchor chain, and came back to the cockpit.

"We need a bigger anchor," he grumbled.

"Or one that works."

He snorted and tried to start the engine. The starter clicked in the engine room below, the batteries too weak to crank the engine.

"We used the engine two days ago. There should be plenty of power left." He stared at me, as much as saying that his flat batteries were my fault.

"Maybe we left a light on while we were away yesterday," I suggested, scratching a mosquito bite near my elbow.

"I turned them off." He turned away, heading down the stairs. "Enjoy the sunrise. I've got work to do."

Months earlier, he'd installed three solar panels and a wind generator; however, they were useless until he finished the wiring. He started work immediately, drilling holes, poking wires, and banging locker doors. We took our schoolbooks upstairs and kept out of his way. He was still pulling wires when Ben rushed to the toilet. He had diarrhea, probably from drinking the water. Already grumpy, my father postponed the afternoon trip we'd planned to La Isabela.

I asked my father if I could go ashore to meet some of the kids who lived on the yachts in the harbor. He looked up from the electrical panel he'd been working on since lunch, annoyed at the interruption.

"Not by yourself!"

He connected the last wire to a brass terminal and turned the main switch. A gauge on the panel registered electrical current flowing from his solar panels. His chart table light flickered weakly and the radio crackled. He switched them off at the panel.

"We left in a hurry," he said without looking up. "You can go if you stay away from Sal, and you take Jessie to the market."

Every morning, local farmers sold their produce from the backs of their trucks, shouting prices for stacks of bananas as tall as a man, boxes of eggs, and tubs of exotic tropical fruits and vegetables. The farmers departed at lunchtime, leaving a dozen wood and canvas stalls to reopen in the afternoon. They sold everything you'd find at a mall, from clothes to electronics. One stall cornered the market on secondhand toys and games, its wobbly tables attracting kids like bees to ripe melons.

"Put the portable radio in your backpack. I'll listen on Channel 68 when there's enough power. Keep a close watch on Jessie."

"Yes sir." I snapped a salute.

"You look like a hobo! Change your shirt and put on some shoes!" he added. My feet were grimy after three days without a swim.

+ + +

Across the harbor, Morello and Javiero had tied their powerboats alongside the *Marionette*. I steered the dinghy close enough to see a man painting red and yellow flames and curls of smoke to cover up the name of one boat. Only four letters remained. 'O', 'L', 'I' and 'C', and those would soon be gone. When it was finished, it would look like the water was on fire.

After I finished securing the dinghy at the dock, I glanced across the wharf at the *Marionette*, my father's warning burning in my ears. Jessie watched silently.

"What's up with you?" I asked. We hadn't spoken since leaving the *Spray*.

She shuffled her feet. "I know why you didn't want me to come."

I shrugged and squatted down to check that I'd chained the outboard motor to the dinghy. Every yacht owner had stories to tell about things disappearing. Only that morning, Imani and her parents had rented a car to drive to Santo Domingo to buy a new outboard motor and a much thicker chain.

"You want to see Sal, don't you?" she asked.

I didn't look up. "No!"

"I promise I won't tell."

I stood up and put on my backpack. It wasn't heavy with only a bottle of water and the portable radio, just inconvenient to carry. I started walking, glad we were only going to the market. After wearing flip-flops or going barefoot for two months, my shoes were uncomfortable.

"I like Sal too," Jessie said, hurrying to keep up.

With the *Spray* anchored in another branch of the harbor, my father couldn't see the wharf. I stopped and took a deep breath. "I guess we could visit for a few minutes. Maybe he has some ice cream left."

I followed Jessie back to the *Marionette's* gangplank. No one was on the wharf to see us, only a man and a woman sitting at a table in the shade of a tree next to the bar and they were looking the other way. I'd been on the *Marionette* so often that Sal said I'd earned the right to make myself comfortable, so with Jessie trailing behind, I strolled up the gangplank and into the lounge. No one was there. However, I could hear a husky mutter from behind a wall of cabinets. I resisted the urge to call out, thinking I'd surprise Sal the same way he'd surprised me the last time we met. I peered around the corner into the galley. He sat at a polished stainless steel table, his back to me.

"Hi," I said, stepping out from behind the cabinets.

Sal spun around so quickly that he kicked a cooler under the table, knocking it against two large suitcases. "What are you doing here?"

"I didn't get to say goodbye at Matthew Town."

He pushed himself up from the chair, a smile slowly replacing his scowl. "I was wondering when you'd visit."

"Jessie's here too." I moved so that Sal could see her behind me.

"Where's Ben?"

"He's home, as sick as a dog, and feeling sorry for himself," I said, wondering if I'd come at a bad time.

Sal regarded me oddly. "I didn't know you'd lived in New York."

I glanced down at the 'I love NY" logo on my chest and shrugged. "It's my dad's. I've never been there." I took my backpack off, lowered it to the floor, and pushed it against the wall so it was out of the way.

"I thought you might remember..." He stopped and leaned back against the table. "Why don't you watch TV in the salon? I'll bring in some ice cream when I'm done. Coconut and strawberry, right?"

Jessie's eyes lit up at 'strawberry.'

"What are you doing?" I asked, stepping closer.

Sal sidestepped to block my view, but not fast enough. My mouth dropped open.

"Look at all the money," Jessie murmured from behind me.

Pictures of Ben Franklin's face and Independence Hall, Philadelphia, covered the table. Close to the wall, the money was new, the bills neatly stacked into precise, rectangular blocks.

"We'll come back later, when you're not busy," I muttered.

Sal stared at me like Captain Slocum without a goatee. I backed away until I pushed into Jessie.

"Josh," he began. He glanced behind him. $100 bills were stacked five, six inches deep, and twice that height next to the wall.

"You rob a bank or something?"

Sal laughed. "No need to rob a bank. I own one in the Caymans.

"Where did it come from?" Jessie asked.

"Business has been good lately," he said quietly.

"It looks like it's been very good," I said just as quietly.

"It's really quite simple. Most people in the diamond business use cash. That way the government doesn't know how much money they've got." He glanced again at the stacks of bills behind him, pulling at a shaggy eyebrow. "Most people would think it's fun to count money, but the bills stick together. It's worse if they're new. I'm lucky this time. Most are older than you."

"A lot are new." The bills stacked next to the wall were crisp and clean, touched a few times at most.

"That's mine."

I was about to ask who owned the rest when several loud bangs came from the lower deck. We turned at the same instant.

"Carpenters," Sal explained before I could ask. "Marion wants more storage space. I'm having it done before she arrives. It's okay for you to be here, right?"

"Daddy doesn't know," Jessie peeped.

Sal watched me. "He doesn't trust me."

"He's like that with everyone. He thinks he's seen you before."

"Perhaps he has."

Javiero came up the stairs. "Hey Sal, more bricks and we ready to go." He stopped when he saw Jessie and me. "What they 'ere for?" he demanded.

He lugged a plastic drum. The lid and a roll of duct tape were in his other hand. Instead of macadamia nuts, chubby white bags filled the drum.

"I came to see Sal." I mustered a defiant stare. Javiero glared back at me.

"I'll be down soon. Take that with you," Sal said to Javiero, nodding at the drum.

"What's in it?" I took a step closer.

"Esnortiar." Javiero smirked. He pinched the tip of his nose. "You know what is esnortiar, muchacho?"

"That's enough!" Sal barked. Suddenly, he wheeled about. "Go watch TV. I won't be long."

I winced at his tone. "What's wrong, Sal?"

Javiero dropped the drum on the floor with a heavy thud. He kicked it across the shiny teak floor. It stopped next to me. I glanced down at fist-sized bags packed in tight layers, like fine sugar or flour in plastic sandwich bags. When I looked up, he smirked again.

"Is ten kilo, muchacho," he boasted. "Is 300 grand."

"Stop kidding him," Sal growled.

"Muchacho, he see too much," Javiero sneered, drawing his finger across his throat.

"Shut up!" Sal snarled. He shoved back his chair. It banged against the wall and toppled over.

"Hey, Morello," Javiero called. "Come here. Is little problem." He had a way of baring his teeth that made me think of a rabid dog. "Is big problem for you I think, muchacho."

He came closer. I smelled aftershave mingled with sweat. Bristles shadowed his face, and his chest hair, like twisted black wire, extended up to his neck. Without warning, Sal shoved him out of the way.

"I'll take care of this," he said quietly.

Javiero rocked on the balls of his feet, flexing his hands, ready to grab me. "If you let him go, he go to police."

"Sal?"

Sal flinched. "Be quiet, Sharkbait." He turned to Javiero. "He'll keep his mouth shut. You have my word on it."

"This muchacho you call Sharka-bait, he not your son."

171

Sal exhaled. "He'll do what I tell him." He glanced at me, and then Jessie.

Morello came up the stairs. He stopped behind Javiero, his arms folded on his chest.

"Is the kids from Acklins," Javiero explained. "Muchacho, he know too much."

"He wouldn't know anything if you kept your mouth shut," Sal cut in.

Javiero waved his hand at the money on the table. "I tell him nothing he don't know." He pointed to the drum beside me. "Muchacho, he see us yesterday. At the bridge, he see us unloading."

Sal flinched. "What are you talking about?"

"On guagua, he was. He see me. He see you. He see truck. He see everything. Maybe he tell police. Maybe now you think muchacho is problem, eh?"

"If he went to the cops, they'd be here, or I'd have heard something."

"No witnesses, Sal. Not unless you want trouble with Cartagena," Morello said.

"I'll deal with them after you've gone. Until then, they can go in the guest cabin."

Sal grabbed my arm and spun me around, his fingers like talons. His other hand gripped Jessie's wrist. The more I tried to twist away, the harder he squeezed.

"Let me go!" Jessie shrieked.

"What are you doing? Stop hurting her!" I shouted.

When he didn't let go of us, I kicked at his shins. Javiero and Morello laughed as Sal pushed me down the stairs ahead of him.

I'd never been on the lower deck before. The first cabin was luxurious, its mahogany walls lacquered like a grand piano, a painting of a sailing ship in a gold frame opposite the door. The closet doors were open, colorful dresses strewed over the bed. Two sheets of plywood from the back of the closet leaned against the wall. Behind the closet was a large compartment with white drums stacked floor to ceiling. At the head of the bed, dozens of round, six-inch buoys took the place of pillows—all yellow, all with the letter 'R' clearly marked on the side, all with a length of orange rope attached.

I stumbled when Sal thrust me forward. Before I could regain my balance, I struck the door frame and fell to the floor.

"Do exactly what I say and everything will be okay," Sal whispered when he pulled me to my feet.

"Is his leg broke?" Javiero laughed from the stairs, holding up the duct tape.

With another push, Sal propelled me into the next cabin. A final shove sent me sprawling across the room, like a toy tossed away in a tantrum. He didn't look at me when I got up from the floor again. My face flushed red as if he'd slapped me.

"Get on the bed."

I tugged on Jessie's arm and pulled her after me. There were a dozen little pillows on the bed and a satin bedspread with embroidered shells.

"Hold out your hands. Now!"

Javiero handed Sal the roll of tape. He peeled off the end, dragged off several inches, and stopped. "Take those things off your wrists."

"They don't come off." I held out my hands so he could see. The cotton string had shrunk so much that the only way of removing my bracelets was to cut them off.

With a shake of his head, Sal began to wrap the tape around my wrists. Most of the tape stuck to the wristbands; however, the edges grabbed onto my bare skin.

Javiero came closer. Amused, he pointed at the scars on my forearms. "Is dangerous play with fire."

I thought Sal hesitated before he pulled the tape even tighter, ripping it from the roll with a sound like tearing cloth. I winced, but he didn't care. He taped my ankles the same way. He finished by heaving me back onto the bed so that I bounced up and down. I glared at him and he smiled back. He pulled a long strip of tape from the roll. For a moment, I thought he was going to tape my mouth. Instead, he jerked his finger at Jessie. Obediently, she came to her knees, crawled closer, and held out her hands. Jessie's bracelet was loose. He pushed it up her arm before taping her wrists together.

"That'll keep you busy for a while," Sal chuckled.

Javiero smacked his lips, blowing a kiss before he left. The door closed behind them. Their footsteps went down the corridor and into the first cabin.

Jessie trembled against me. "Why's Sal being so mean?"

"Don't worry. He told me everything will be okay," I shushed. "It's just for show, so they'll leave us alone." I wasn't sure about anything.

"My hands hurt." She held them up for me to see.

The tape was so tight on my wrists that my hands were slowly turning darker. I tried to force my hands apart. The tape tore at my skin. When I couldn't feel my fingers, I chewed on the tape. Before I could spit it out, I swallowed a piece of tape. Duct tape tasted awful. I gnawed at it anyway, mostly where the tape bulged over my wristbands, listening to Sal in the adjoining cabin.

"Don't threaten me with Cartagena, not after what happened in the Exumas."

"Not my fault, Sal," Morello protested. "I tell you, the patrol boat come from nowhere."

"I'm not talking about running into the cops. Icing that local kid wasn't smart."

"Still not my fault," Morello argued. "The chase scare him bad. Jomo want to quit, but I say no. Fool run to the beach, only he don't swim so good with bullets in him."

I tore at the tape, shredding it with my teeth and spitting out bits of plastic and rubbery adhesive until a small hole exposed the bleached string of my wristband.

"Why don't you take out an ad, Morello?" Sal said.

"On bill-board," Javiero laughed. "Your face is too ugly for TV."

"When you're finished, tighten the straps. I don't want the drums shifting. And be careful replacing the panels in the closet. Don't force them in. I want the clothes back in the same order you took them out."

"Sure Sal. Is something to eat before we go?" Morello said.

"Make yourself a sandwich. Check on the kids when you're done."

"What you do with them?" Javiero's voice hastened my chewing.

"I haven't decided. He'll keep his mouth shut. I'm not sure about his sister. Don't worry. They'll disappear."

"Take them offshore. Sharks chew on their legs." Javiero laughed.

While Morello and Javiero banged and hammered in the next cabin, I gnawed at tape strands until a horrible gummy taste filled my mouth. I locked my fingers together and forced my elbows apart. Still, the tape wouldn't break. I kept chewing, ripping and tearing, twisting my wrists apart until the tape stretched into thin, wet cords. They broke with a loud snap. I nudged Jessie to show her my hands were free, holding a finger to my lips.

All of a sudden, footsteps came down the corridor. I lay down next to my sister, curled up, and hid my hands under my chest just before the door was flung open.

"When sharks finish with you, muchacho, your momma won't know you," Javiero sneered.

I mouthed a vulgarity from a high school locker room. He jerked the door shut and locked it from the outside. After his footsteps faded, I pulled at the tape around Jessie's hands. She whimpered and her face scrunched up when the adhesive stuck to her skin. As soon as her hands were free, I started on the tape around my ankles.

There were two portholes in the cabin, one over the bed, the other over a marble-topped table. They looked large enough to squeeze through. I climbed onto the table, unlatched the porthole, and opened it. Nearby, Javiero's powerboat bumped against the *Marionette*, and the man who had been painting Morello's boat had finished and left. The inner flange made the opening much smaller, jamming my shoulders when I poked out my head to see if I could fit. Disheartened, I sat back, rubbing my wrists, itchy from strips of soggy tape stuck to my skin. Ben could have wriggled through the porthole with no trouble at all.

"Come here, Jess."

"It's too small," she protested, vigorously shaking her head.

"No it's not." I hopped to the floor and started towards the bed, ready to drag her to the porthole and force her to climb out if she didn't cooperate.

Jessie got up, still shaking her head. She took a reluctant step and stopped. "Why don't we shout for someone to help us?"

"Because the flaming wharf is on the other side." I sounded just like my father. I took a deep breath. "No one would hear us. Jessie, please get on the table. They could come back any second."

When she didn't move, I lifted her onto the table and pushed her down into position. Grudgingly, she put her head through the porthole. She jerked back. "It's too far!"

"It's like jumping off the *Spray*." It wasn't.

I tried to turn her around so she could slide through the porthole feet first. She thrust me away. "You have to, Jessie. It's our only chance."

"You said Sal will let us go."

I shook my head, cutting her off. "It's not Sal I'm worried about. You heard what Morello said. He's got nothing to lose by killing us."

My sister frowned at me. "I can't swim to the *Spray*! It's too far."

"You don't have to. You know the rocks where the road ends? That's as far as you have to swim." Jessie tried to scramble off the table. I grabbed her arm and stopped her. She shook her head with seven-year-old determination while I nodded. "Once you get to the rocks, go to the bar. There are two sailors sitting outside..."

"Mr. and Mrs. Henderson, they live on *Valare*. Mommy and I met them...."

"Ask them to take you to the *Spray*. Mom and Dad will know what to do."

With no help from Jessie, I got her legs through the porthole. She squirmed back, complaining that the edge of the porthole scraped her thighs. I pushed at her hips. After a few more inches, her bottom squashed against the stainless steel frame. She was half in, half out, clinging to the edge of the table. I hoisted her shoulders off the table and rammed her through the porthole. She squealed, flailing her arms at me. When I let go, she made a loud splash. She spluttered to the surface and pushed away a palm frond, her hair floating around her. She gave me a mean look and dog-paddled away, bravely ignoring a rotting mullet. I waited until she passed the *Marionette*'s bow and disappeared from sight. With nothing else to do, I lay on the bed and picked flecks of duct tape from my wrists.

Chapter 24

Ten minutes passed on the digital clock beside the bed while I waited for something to happen. When I heard footsteps coming down the corridor, I curled up on the bed, my hands under a pillow.

"Hey, Sharka-bait, you swim with sharks soon. Then, you really be shark bait. What you think about that, muchacho?" Javiero shouted through the door. The key turned in the lock and he threw the door back. A moment passed before he realized. "Where is she?"

I nudged the hump beside me. Six small pillows under the bedspread made a formless lump, not a girl asleep. Javiero didn't say a word. He drew a knife from his pocket, snapped the blade into place, and sauntered over, his thumb rubbing along the honed edge.

Behind him, Morello puffed on a cigar. "You 'ave cojones, muchacho, but is better you tell him before he cut off your tongue."

Javiero was looming over me when he saw the open porthole. He cursed, using Spanish words that weren't in my language course. His knife snapped shut and went back in his pocket. He dragged me from the bed and held me at arm's length, powerful sinews stretched tight beneath his dark skin, a sinister black tattoo of a snake from his wrist to his elbow. His breath was disgusting. I turned away.

Morello sucked on his cigar. "Where she go?" He made a point of blowing smoke in my face.

I mustered my courage. "Vaya al diablo!" Mexican kids in my class said it when we played basketball.

Javiero smirked. His arm pulled back slowly as if flexing his shoulder. His fist struck hard into my side, just below my ribs. I crashed onto the bed. They roared with laughter while I struggled to inhale. I'd never had the wind knocked out of me. It was a dreadful feeling of my lungs no longer working.

Even as the air rushed back, Javiero tore at my arm again, dragging me up. I tottered before him, my stomach heaving, trying to keep down my lunch, every movement a stab of pain. He thrust me out of the cabin. I stumbled along the corridor, up the stairs, and into the galley. The money was gone. In its place were the scraps of a meal: salsa, grated cheese, and beer cans. Javiero dragged me into the main cabin; and Morello went to get Sal from the bow, where he leaned against the railing, talking with Tony. Jessie must have gone right past them on her way to the wharf.

"Muchacha is gone," Javiero growled when Sal entered.

Sal stared him down. Finally, he asked, "How?"

Javiero jerked my wrist up to show him the strands of tape hanging from my wristband.

"She get out window, Sal," Morello added.

"The porthole?" Sal looked at him in disbelief, and then glanced in my direction.

I stared back at him, afraid he'd seen me looking at the bar at the end of the dock, even though there was no sign of Jessie.

"She must have gone by the stern. We'd have seen her otherwise."

He stalked across the cabin to the windows overlooking the aft deck. For two minutes, he surveyed Puerto Blanco with binoculars, from one end to the other, searching every yacht. Even the closest boat was a long swim for a seven-year-old girl.

He came back, shaking his head at me. "How long ago?"

"She's probably talking to the cops by now."

"The police are the least of my worries. The question is what to do now?" He tapped his lips thoughtfully, as if considering which fly to cast.

"That's easy, Sal. We kill him."

"Shut up, Morello. And lose that cigar." Sal's irritation matched mine—the fumes were disgusting. "Javiero, fetch Tony in here." He turned, looked at me, and slowly shook his head again. "Why couldn't you just do what I told you?"

I glared at him while we waited for Tony. My side throbbed from Javiero's punch. If I moved or breathed too deeply, pain stabbed through my chest. I wondered if my ribs were broken, or if I had what my mother called 'internal hemorrhaging.' She'd seen people die from it in the emergency room at Norfolk General.

"We'll leave immediately," Sal said after informing Tony of Jessie's escape.

"Ten minutes, Sal," Tony said. "What about Mateo? He's on the payroll and he's never done more than look the other way every two months."

"Let him know what's happened." Sal paused, his eyes flitting back and forth from me to Javiero and Morello. "By the time his parents report it, we'll be out of here. Tell him to act concerned, but stall. Say the kid may have done something bad and his sister's covering it up. Have his men drag the harbor."

"That ought to buy us a couple of weeks," Tony joked, already on his way to the door.

"Javiero, take your boat around the harbor and look for the girl. Maybe we'll get lucky. Call me on the radio if you find her. I want her in one piece!" Sal turned to Morello. "Find their yacht and keep an eye on it. It's the only gaff rig in the harbor. You can't miss it."

Morello looked at him blankly. "What is gaff?"

181

"Look for a white ketch with a blue stripe.'"

"What is ketch?"

"It's got two masts, you idiot." Sal sighed wearily. "Just find the '*Spray*' and keep an eye on it. Anything unusual, let me know. Both of you listen to the radio in case I need you back here."

Morello and Javiero left as the *Marionette*'s huge diesel engines rumbled to life, sending vibrations through the ship.

Sal regarded me. I looked everywhere except at him. "All you had to do was trust me for a couple of hours."

"Is that why you tied us up?" I sneered, spitting contempt.

"I would've let you go after they left."

"I heard you tell them how you were going to take care of us." My face burned with shame. "'They'll disappear.'"

Sal looked at me as if I'd kicked him. "I meant disappear so they can't find you. If it was up to them, you and Jessie would be dead by now."

"What's in the closet?" It was hard to get the words out.

"It's not what you think."

I shuddered, anger substituting for being let down. "I think you're a drug dealer."

"I handle the money for them, that's all."

"Drug money!"

He squared his shoulders. "About half of it's from drugs. The rest is mine. Like I told you, I trade diamonds. I'm good at it."

"Why trade drugs if you're so flaming good?" I shook with rage.

He gazed out the windows at the hills surrounding Luperón, green splashed with brown where farmers had hacked into the rainforest.

"You might find it hard to believe, but I give it away," he said quietly.

Javiero and Morello cast off, roaring engines, spewing smoke, churning the water, leaping to fend off each other's powerboat.

"A couple of first rate sailors, those two," he said with a disparaging shake of his head. He looked back at me, suddenly old. "When Dante died, I tried to get out of the business."

"I'm sorry about Dante, but you got what you deserved."

"You don't know the whole story." Javiero and Morello raced each other across the harbor before he went on. "Back then, the cops were ratcheting up the pressure. A couple of families decided they could make more money working with the Colombians. I had the know-how to handle the money so they made me the banker. I never asked for the job."

I stared back. I hated him.

"By the end of the year, the Russians moved in and started duking it out with Colombians. They killed my son to get at me."

"You said it was an accident, a stray bullet."

Sal's shoulders hunched. "They wanted to send me a message."

He walked slowly around the cabin, pausing to look at a game-fishing rod and a photograph of Dante standing beside a Bluefin tuna taller than he was. He stopped before a painting of a large ketch heeled under sail, a forest green spinnaker billowing in front, fingering the gold frame.

"It wasn't long before my wife and I got a divorce. She couldn't stand to look at me." He turned. I stared at the floor. "I

183

wanted to get out, but there's an old saying in Sicily, 'once in, you're in till you're dead.'"

"I hope they catch you and you spend the rest of your life in jail."

"I'm no choirboy, but there are far worse things in the world than what I do."

"Like murdering Willie's nephew, Jomo?"

"I had no part in that. Morello screwed up." He paused. From the tremor, the *Marionette* was pulling away from the wharf.

"What are you going to do with me?"

"Maybe they're right about feeding you to the sharks," he said with a poker face. "Maybe I'll drop you off somewhere up the coast. I haven't decided."

He smiled at me. I didn't smile back. He crossed to the pilot station and yanked the microphone from the radio. "You're an enterprising young man. John ought to be proud of you instead of pointing out your faults."

"Dante wouldn't be proud of you if he knew what you did."

Behind me, Sal said, "Don't try calling for help." He locked the doors, pocketing the key before he started up the spiral stairway. "I don't want to send Tony to shut you up."

The *Marionette* weaved through the anchorage, so close to the shore that I could've escaped before anyone realized. From behind thick, dark tinted windows, I watched a dinghy zoom out of the cove where the *Spray*'s masts protruded above the mangroves. My father knelt on the floor, balancing the dinghy as it raced over rippling waves. I hoped he was going to get Jessie, but more than likely he had to go to the hardware store for electrical wiring. It was always the same when he did a project.

I waved frantically to get his attention. He went out of his way to avoid looking at the *Marionette*. I stopped waving just before Rick, another of Sal's crew came into the cabin. Rick was Tony's younger brother. He worked in the engine room and shared steering duties with Tony. He sat down at the computer station and switched on the monitor. I slumped into a plush, leather seat, utterly dismayed. My rescue depended on my little sister. She could barely swim; she chewed on her pigtails; and she talked with a stuffed cat.

Chapter 25

The *Marionette* cleaved the ocean swell surging into the harbor, making what appeared to be a normal departure until the headlands and beach were behind us. It slowed to a crawl when Javiero's powerboat came alongside. After a minute or two, Javiero's boat veered off and headed northwest, towards the Bahamas, traveling so fast that it was soon gone from sight.

I remembered the portable radio in my backpack when the *Marionette* was so far from shore the tourist resort was barely visible. Given the sun, Sal's boat was heading more or less north; however, without an accurate position, the radio was useless. As calmly as I could, I ambled over to the computer. The screen showed a digital version of the ship's bridge.

Rick looked up from monitoring the *Marionette's* engines. "What do you want?"

I looked over the line of icons along the top of the screen. "We don't have radar on our boat. I've never seen one working before, that's all." It was a lie. I was so nervous that it was all I could do to speak clearly.

Rick clicked on the radar icon. "That's the coastline," he said, pointing to a bright edge on the monitor.

I leaned closer. My hand shook when I pointed to a fast moving dot on the radar screen. It headed away from the Dominican Republic. "Is that Javiero's boat?"

"His boat's nearly invisible on radar. It's the 2:00 pm flight from Puerto Plata to Miami."

For some reason, you didn't see airplanes on our radar. I peered over his shoulder, pretending to be interested while I tried to make out the numbers on the bottom. The *Marionette's* position was Latitude, 20° 0' 20 North; Longitude, 70° 57' 4 West. The latitude would be hard to forget.

"I'm hungry. Can I get something to eat?" I asked, backing away.

"Sure. Just don't make a mess. Sal's mad already because of you."

Before I reached the galley, I'd repeated '70, 57, 4' eight times in my head. My backpack lay on the floor where I'd left it. When I bent to pick it up, the *Marionette* slowed down and changed course, headed closer to the coast, towards Haiti. Now, the sun shone though the port windows, so diluted by the dark glass that it barely made shadows.

I looked inside the refrigerator, pushing aside slabs of cheese, assorted salami, and bottles of olives. As if looking for crackers, I opened and closed cabinet doors, repeating '70, 54, 7.'

"I've got to use the bathroom, if that's okay?" I shouted.

Rick didn't reply, not about to waste his time talking to me now that I wasn't a friend.

I hurried down the stairs and along the corridor. The first cabin was pristine, not even a wrinkle in the bedspread, the pillows perfectly aligned. The cabin at the end of the corridor was Sal's stateroom. Exquisite African woods paneled the walls, with nooks for the things he wanted to see every day. At the center was a silver-framed pencil sketch of pretty, dark-haired girl, who I assumed was his granddaughter. I went into the bathroom and latched the door. It was as far away as I could get. The bathroom seemed as big as the *Spray*'s main cabin, with a Jacuzzi-bath, an immaculate white marble vanity, gold-plated taps, and mirrored walls all around.

My father's lecture on radio etiquette for emergencies drummed in my ears—'be precise' and speak slowly and clearly,' using the appropriate level—'Sécurité' (warning), 'Pan-Pan' (urgency), or 'May-day' (distress), then 'all vessels', 'the name of the vessel followed by its position,' and finally the problem. Most of it had to be said three times. He also said the signal from a portable radio wasn't very strong. It worked best when there were no obstructions, so I opened the porthole and poked out the antenna.

I switched on the radio, checked that it was Channel 16, the international hailing and distress channel, and pushed the transmit key. "May-day. May-day. May-day."

Maybe I should've said 'Pan-Pan' instead. My situation deserved more than 'Sécurité', while 'Mayday' was too extreme. It was for things like boats sinking. At the time, his radio etiquette lecture didn't seem like a lot to remember.

"This is Josh Walker from the *Spray*. I've been kidnapped. I need to get a message to my mom and dad," streamed from my mouth. "My position is 20, 20 North. No, it's 20, zero, 20."

Someone sprinted down the corridor, shouting and slamming doors in the cabins along the way. Sal's crew probably monitored the radio—most vessels did when underway

"The longitude is… 70-something. It's 70 degrees, 74 minutes." However, it couldn't be that, not with 60 minutes in a degree.

A sideways shove caused a stack of towels on the vanity to slide off. Before the ship straightened, I heard Sal and Javiero talking outside the bathroom. The doorknob turned and stopped.

"I'm busy in here," I shouted. "I'll be finished in a minute."

The knob twisted several times, increasingly urgent. I jumped back from the porthole. Before I could put the radio in my backpack, the door exploded inward, leaving a splintered frame where the lock had been. Javiero filled the opening until Sal thrust

188

him out of the way. He stormed in and jerked the radio from my hand. Without my finger on the transmit key, the radio switched to receive status, buzzing with static from another more-powerful radio.

"Where did this come from?" I stared back at Sal until he noticed my backpack on the vanity counter. He clapped his hands together, not at all what I expected. "What am I going to do with you?"

"Tie bricks on him," Javiero sneered.

Sal spun around. For a moment, I thought he might throw the radio at Javiero. "I thought you were smarter than Morello. No one heard him. These toy radios won't transmit more than a mile." He gave me a long-suffering look. "Why did you have to visit today?"

I looked him in the eye and said, "I thought we were friends. I wanted to say goodbye."

"If you keep your mouth shut, I'll let you go."

Javiero glared at me from behind Sal. "No! Get rid of him!"

Sal turned on him. "I told you I'll handle it. He'll do what I tell him."

Javiero stepped past the shattered frame. The door sagged from a single hinge. He smashed it against the wall. He stopped, face to face with Sal. They looked like a pair of fighting cocks in a dusty pen in Luperón.

"Muchacho is nothing to me. I do it for you."

Muscles bulged obscenely under Javiero's shirt, yet Sal pushed him away with the heel of his hand. I bolted for the opening behind Sal before he could stop me. I ducked under his arm. Javiero sidestepped with the agility of a mountain lion, barring my escape. Instead of merely blocking the gap, his fist smashed into my face. My head snapped back and my knees buckled under me. I toppled

189

back onto the toilet. When I tried to get up, I slumped to the floor. My face was on fire. Blood covered my hands and ran into my mouth until I couldn't breathe without spitting it out. Distantly, I heard Sal and Javiero arguing.

"There's no need to hurt him."

"'You want him escape?" Javiero rocked on the balls of his feet, his fists clenched.

"He can't go anywhere!"

Blood poured from my nose and dripped on the floor. Sal offered me a towel. I shook my head, splattering spots on white marble. He dropped it beside me.

"He cry like muchacha." Javiero's snicker made me try to get up. It was all I could do to prop myself against the bath.

"Get out!" Sal bellowed, his face flushing crimson.

Javiero pretended to kick me before prodding Sal's shoulder. He poked him again, much harder. Sal stepped back. He trembled with rage, his face becoming darker and darker. Suddenly, he began to gasp. He shuddered, staggered a few steps, and grabbed the towel rail to steady himself.

"Is heart attack, Sal? Maybe you die." Javiero glared at me. "You come with me, muchacho. Bring that." He pointed at my backpack.

I shook my head, blood dripping from my chin. Javiero pushed Sal aside, took a step closer, and raised his fist in my face. I struggled to my feet and stumbled after him, clutching my backpack to my chest, along the corridor, up the stairs, past the galley, into the main cabin. Through the windows, distant palm trees clumped along an unspoiled beach. We slowly passed curls of smoke coiling above the roofs of a village, steep hills rising behind it. He stopped in front of the doors leading to the aft deck. He tried the handle. When it didn't open, he hammered on the glass. Rick got up and ambled over to unlock the door. He stiffened at my bloodied face, yet said not a word.

Javiero dragged me outside. I clung to the stair railing, determined not to let go. He jabbed at me as if he was punching a bag. He kicked at my legs. I kicked back, holding my backpack in front of my face. Without warning, he grabbed my arm, jerked me away from the stairs, and shoved me over to the safety rail. He leered down at me, his breath suffocating.

"Let him go," Sal ordered from behind us. He gripped the door frame with white knuckles, weak and red-faced, my radio still clasped in his hand.

Javiero pulled on my arm and hauled me closer to the stern where the railing dipped lower. The ocean roiled with waves and foam on either side of the transom. Though the *Marionette* had slowed to a crawl, a curving white swathe stretched behind.

"Propellers chop you to mincemeat." Javiero yanked hard on my arm.

The *Marionette's* powerful diesel engines were barely audible over the sound of waves smacking the hull. I swung my backpack at his head. I missed. It sailed across the aft deck.

"Hey, Javiero!" Tony stood beside the inflatable runabout, secured on the upper deck. "Sal told you to let him go. I'd do that, if I were you."

His arm slowly came up from his side, until his gun, a big, black, automatic pistol, pointed at Javiero.

"Sal is old man with bad heart." Javiero smirked. "I tell Cartagena you take over."

"You want me to whack him, Sal?" Tony sighted down the barrel.

Javiero froze. "Muchacho know enough to put us away, Tony."

Sal staggered a few steps. He leaned against a lounge chair. Even that was an effort for him. "I'm not worried... He'll keep his mouth shut..."

"He will if he's dead." Javiero shoved me against the rail.

"He's smart, Javiero. He knows what's good for him, unlike you." Tony was implacable.

"You are stupid as dog!"

"Can I whack him, Sal?" Tony had both arms straight.

"We call Cartagena. They decide, okay?"

Sal shook his head. "Not this time."

Tony's gun was unwavering. "You want me to find a spot to drop him off?"

"Ought to take him to Haiti... Make him walk back..." Sal managed a hoarse chuckle. He turned to me. "That beach is La Isabela... You think you can swim there?"

"You might as well feed me to the sharks," I sniveled through my clogged nose. Blood covered the front of my shirt. Sal shook his head almost fondly.

"Is too late, old man," Javiero growled.

Sal looked at him uncertainly. "What's too late?"

Javiero jerked his head at a small, gray, inflatable dinghy racing towards the *Marionette*, hurdling waves, my father clinging to the sides. Usually, he puttered along, leaving little more than a ripple behind, conserving fuel and preserving the engine.

"Sal, he's got a knife!" Tony shouted.

I heard the knife blade snap into place. Before I could jump back, Javiero grabbed my shoulder with his free hand. He spun me around so that I was between him and Tony. The razor-sharp blade pressed into my neck. When I tried to jerk away, Javiero lifted the knife under my jaw, forcing my head up.

Sal let go of the chair and stepped back, breathing heavily and holding up his hands. "Okay, Javiero. We'll do it your way."

"Tell Tony to put it away."

"Sal?" Tony pressed.

Sal glanced at *Squirt* like a bothersome mosquito. "I need you back at the helm, Tony." In an odd, calm voice, he added, "Island time. No need to panic."

'Anytime now' was always the punch line for his 'island time' jokes. Almost nothing happened quickly in the Caribbean. When something did happen quickly, it was always unexpected.

Sal stepped forward as Javiero dragged me closer to the stern railing, his knife forcing me to the tips of my toes. Suddenly, my father was alongside the *Marionette*, plunging up and down over the waves. He was a few yards away when he turned the dinghy towards the landing platform. It was moving too fast to stop. He swerved away, barely missing the *Marionette* and nearly tipping the dinghy over.

"Let my son go!" he roared.

Squirt raced in a wild circle, its wailing engine belching a cloud of blue smoke.

Sal nodded as if nothing had changed between us. "Bonefish," he said.

I figured it out a moment before the massive diesels beneath our feet unleashed 4,000 horsepower all at once. It was enough to make the *Marionette* leap through the water like a bonefish after taking a lure. It made a sharp turn, tilting like the *Spray* in a strong gust. Thrown off balance, Javiero stumbled backwards, taking me with him. Simultaneously, Sal punched, his right fist driving into Javiero's chest. I heard something crack. Sal's other hand grabbed my wrist, trying to wrench me away from Javiero before we crashed against the stern railing. Javiero finally let go of me when we toppled over the side.

Behind the *Marionette* was a washing machine of foam and churning water, dragging me down. I kicked and clawed at swirls white with bubbles, back to the surface. I gulped a breath before I went down again, long enough to see Tony leaning from the bridge deck. His pistol pointed directly at me, both arms stretched out in front of him. Javiero floundered towards me, his head covered in foam, his arms flailing as if he couldn't swim. When I came to the surface again, I couldn't see him.

A wave broke over my head and I choked on salt water and blood running from my nose. Again, the water pulled me down into a mist of pink bubbles. I looked into Javiero's face one last time before I resurfaced. I kicked off my shoes and began treading water.

My father hauled me over the side of the dinghy and held me while I coughed up water. I slumped to the floor, my head between my knees. When I recovered enough to look up, my father simply said 'you're okay,' and hugged me.

"Jessie?"

"She's okay too."

When I tried to explain, the words came out in a gasping, garbled rush.

"Now isn't the time, son." He looked over my shoulder.

The *Marionette* had turned around and was on the way back, slicing through waves and throwing out spray as high as the bow. It headed straight for us. My father and I exchanged a glance before he leaped across the dinghy. He jerked rapidly on the rope to start the outboard motor. It spluttered, hiccuped smoke, ran for a few seconds, and then stopped with a metallic rattle. After three attempts to start it, he gave up.

"It's frigging ruined!" Only he didn't say 'frigging.'

The *Marionette* veered away. High above us, Sal leaned over the bow. Beside him, Tony gave directions to Rick, who steered from the bridge deck.

"Is he okay, John?" Sal called out.

My father looked at the blood still dripping from my nose. "He'll live."

"It didn't go quite as I planned."

"What's the plan now?" my father inquired, his calm demeanor surprising.

Sal studied his fingernails, roughened and split from spending his days fishing on the shallow flats of the Bahamas. He looked from his hands to me, and smiled curiously. "You might like to know that I'm taking your advice."

"What advice?" I wished he would leave me alone.

"About getting out. I'm going to sail around the world." He paused, his gaze shifting to my father. "Your *Spray* got me thinking, so I did some research on Joshua Slocum. You have the same surname as his first wife. I wasn't sure until then."

My father didn't say a word. Crow's feet pulled at his eyes.

Sal walked beside us as the *Marionette* passed by. "If you'll unfasten your outboard and drop it over the stern, I'll be on my way. I figure it'll take an hour to row to shore, another hour to get to the cops, a couple of hours of interrogation. That's four hours before they start searching. I'll be in Cuba by then."

He removed the batteries from the radio, zipped it inside my backpack, and tossed it into the dinghy. My father opened the combination lock, unfastened the chain, and unscrewed the clamps that held the outboard motor on the transom. He lifted it up and let go. It crackled and sizzled, leaving steam and a trail of bubbles before it disappeared into the water.

"We'll meet again," Sal said. I returned a cold-hearted stare. He turned to my father. "We have too much in common not to." He nodded to me, barely moving his head. He signaled to Rick and the *Marionette* bolted for the open sea.

Chapter 26

We rowed without stopping for an hour and ten minutes, my father on one side of the dinghy, while I hunched over the other side, on the brink of throwing up. I did my best to keep up with him until my hands stung, raw with blisters. He constantly corrected our course, making extra, harder strokes. We didn't speak. I tried once, to ask how he found me. With a jerk of his head, he ordered, 'row!'

Waves grew out of the ocean swell as we neared the shore. In an exhilarating rush, a wave picked up *Squirt* and flung it towards the beach. The surf broke around us in a flume of foam, carrying the dinghy into the small cove below Cabo Isabela, the same bay where Columbus and the settlers disembarked in 1493. We hauled *Squirt* onto the beach, tired, sunburned, and angry. My father removed the caps and opened the valves to let out the air before he collapsed beside me on a patch of sand littered with broken rocks. He soon got to his feet and began pushing down on the dinghy to hasten deflation. After a while, he stopped and looked at me, his brow furrowed.

"I told you to keep away from Sal. You disobeyed a direct order. You endangered yourself and Jessie."

His tone, his posture, everything about him was harsh. He made too many rules and enforced them without regard for extenuating circumstances. This time, he was right, yet I stared at the sand, silently grateful for the shade of a stunted tree.

"We've a lot to talk about. Right now, we need to get to the police. It'll be suspicious if we don't report it," he added, speaking almost to himself.

He stomped on the side tube. The valve wheezed out air. I scanned the horizon behind him. Patches of cumulus clouds rose like the white domes of distant, gray cities.

"I'm sorry."

"You're lucky to be alive." His voice wavered. "If I hadn't needed extra bolts for the solar panels, you might not be here."

"I'm sorry about the outboard."

"I can always buy another one. I can't replace you." He stood over me, blocking out the sun. "Or Jessie," he added pointedly, his way of letting me know that I'd let him down.

"She told you what happened?"

"Not a lot. She was scared stiff when I found her. She said there were drugs onboard." He waited.

"Javiero called it esnortiar." He looked at me as if he hadn't heard properly. I pinched my nostrils and snorted, imitating Javiero. "They store it in plastic drums like you used to build the *Spray*."

"You remember that far back?"

"Before I started school, I played in the barn while you worked on the *Spray*. You yelled at me if I disturbed you, so I hid behind them."

He seemed about to smile. Instead, he pushed down on the bow to hasten its collapse.

"Javiero and Morello deliver it using their powerboats," I continued. "Remember the boat that nearly ran us down outside Oriental? That's Morello's boat."

"No way! We've seen dozens of boats like it."

"I saw the name. The '*Aquaholic*,' or it was until a few hours ago. They changed the name."

"Even if it is the same boat, it doesn't prove anything except it was on the waterway at the same time we were."

"It's not a coincidence!" Then, I told him what I thought he needed to know.

"It's possible I suppose." He knelt on the bow. "Maybe you'll become a detective. You've got the mind for it." It sounded like a compliment until he added, "You're lucky you're still alive. Tony tried to shoot you."

I shook my head. "Sal would never do that! He was furious when Javiero punched me. He tried to catch me before I fell overboard."

"He's still a drug dealer. They're all the same. They kill anyone who gets in their way." He tramped back and forth over the dinghy, pushing out the last of the air. All of a sudden, he stopped. "Tony might have been aiming at Javiero, I suppose."

We rolled up *Squirt*. Carrying 90 pounds between us, we scrambled up a limestone bluff, past a sign pointing to La Isabela Sitio Arqueológico, the 'well-situated rock' that Columbus chose for a colony. No one spoke more than a few halting words of English in the tiny fishing village of Cabo Isabela. Outside the general store, we found a guagua going to Luperón. We hoisted the dinghy onto the roof racks and squeezed inside, a ten-mile ride, which he used for a lecture on what I should and should not say to the police.

+ + +

In the middle of Luperón's main street, with trucks and motor cycles swerving around us, a policeman directed us to the Commandancia. The Commandante handled anything that happened at sea.

"Up dere, up dere," he said, waving his hand about as he directed peak hour traffic.

"Dónde?" I asked 'where?'

"Usted habla Español? Excelente! La oficina del comandante está en la colina. Van tres calles y dan vuelta a la derecha. Vaya al extremo," he jabbered, gesticulating wildly before he stepped out of the way of an onrushing guagua.

I was overwhelmed. Señorita Gaitán had not prepared me for this. "I think he means we go that way," I said, struggling to hold my share of *Squirt* while pointing ahead.

My father regarded me in grim silence before he started down the street in the general direction of a nearby hill. I followed, lugging half a dinghy to a low building of concrete block, tin roof, and narrow windows with thick bars. Parked outside, and surrounded by chickens, cows, and mules, were two dusty Jeeps equipped with sirens, search lights, and bristling antennae. A solitary tree shaded a spotlessly clean sedan. We left *Squirt* beside it.

The spring-loaded door squeaked when it closed behind us. Inside, a tired-looking man read a book, occasionally tilting his head to listen to radio transmissions. He glanced up, dropped his book on the counter, and picked up an official-looking form.

"What is name?" he inquired of my father.

"John Walker."

"Muchacho is son?" He stabbed his finger in my direction.

"Yes. Victor's my son."

The officer regarded him, his form, and me, in that order. Momentarily confused, he studied the form again, scowling. "Is not... Josh?" It sounded like 'hoss.'

"His name is Victor Joshua Walker," my father said very slowly.

"Is address S-p-r-a-y?"

"Yes."

"I think Commandante Gomez will see you," he said, nodding sluggishly.

We waited five minutes until Commandante Gomez finished his phone call and came out to meet us. For a government bureaucrat, he looked flustered. His white shirt had sweat stains under the arms and his tie was loose around his neck. He told me to wait and escorted my father into his office. The door closed behind them, blocking out the hum of a fan. I lingered next to a notice board cluttered with posters of criminals wanted for crimes like stealing motorcycles and cattle rustling. By the time I finished translating a warning about an increase in theft of outboard motors from tourists' boats, it was my turn to go into the office.

The Commandante asked questions and wrote down what I said on a note pad. It was obvious that he wasn't impressed with what I had to say. He repeated the questions and checked off my answers, all the while glancing from me to my father. Finally, he folded his arms and focused on me as if I'd done something wrong.

"You are certain you can identify the men who were at the bridge?" he finally asked.

It struck me that something I'd said upset him. "Yes sir. I got a good look at them."

He frowned. "Where was this, Señor?" he asked my father.

"I've no idea. I was asleep. We were coming back from Jarabacoa."

The Commandante shoved his chair back and stalked across the room to a wall painted in three shades of green and decorated with maps of the region, newspaper cuttings, and 'wanted' posters. He stopped before a map of the Dominican Republic, surrounded by notes and dotted with colored pins. He stabbed his finger near the center of the island, and then traced a line back to Luperón via Santiago.

"We went that way. We came back through Mao," my father clarified.

"Mao?" The Commandante shook his head. "There are no drug routes near there."

"What routes do they normally use?"

The Commandante cleared his throat. "It comes by ship from Colombia." His finger touched the southern shore of the Dominican Republic at the capital, Santo Domingo. "From here, it goes by truck to Puerto Plata. There's no reason for drug smugglers to go to Mao," he added.

"What if they went the other way, over the mountains? Through Jarabacoa," my father suggested, his elbows planted on the Commandante's desk while he studied the map.

"It makes no sense to go that way. It is backtracking."

"Are there no other places along the coast to land drugs besides Santo Domingo?"

"There are a few," the Commandante allowed cautiously.

"Going through Mao might make sense if the drugs arrived elsewhere," my father suggested. Having made his point, he sat back and stroked his goatee.

"The truck had a sign on its door." I stared at the map, searching for a name. "It might've been Barahona, sir."

"Impossible! Only crocodiles live there! The province of Barahona has mountains with coffee plantations. A few farmers. Nothing more!"

"How would it get from Barahona to here?" my father asked.

The Commandante answered with a dismissive shrug. When my father leaned closer to examine the map, he pointed to a road winding across the Cordillera Central mountain range. "The road from San Juan de La Maguana to El Rubio is very bad. It is slow and dangerous. It makes no sense!"

"We were going from El Rubio to Mao," I said.

The Commandante stepped to the side, blocking my view of the map. "Tell me again what happened at the bridge."

Back in his seat, he made himself comfortable, leaning back and putting his feet up on the corner of his desk, his arms folded, his fingers keeping a silent beat. I repeated what I'd told him three times already.

"You saw these men, Señor Walker?" he prompted.

"I told you I was asleep at the time. My son saw them."

"You would recognize these men if you saw them again?" the Commandante asked me.

"Javiero and Morello, I would for sure." I took a deep breath. "One man might have been Sal. There was a farmer too, but I only got a glimpse of his face."

"You said there were five men. What of the last man?"

"I didn't see him very well. He was behind the truck, in the shade." The Commandante appeared to relax, yet his eyes roved constantly. I had a strange thought. "Maybe he didn't want anyone to see him."

"You're very observant, muchacho, and you are smart too; however, you should be careful what you say. These are dangerous men."

"Why would they transfer the drums to a pickup truck so close to here, sir?"

"It's safer if each person knows only a small part of the operation. Which is why it's so important to catch the people at the top," my father said impatiently. "What happens now?"

"I will personally conduct the investigation and make the official report," the Commandante replied. "We take drug smuggling very seriously in my country."

"When will you arrest them?" My face ached, my side throbbed, and my feet were sore. I wanted revenge.

"First we must find evidence that a crime was committed before anyone is arrested." With one eye closed, the Commandante examined his tobacco-stained fingers. He turned to my father. "It seems your wife was right to be worried, Señor."

"Pardon?"

"She reported your son was missing. I immediately ordered a search of the harbor in case he drowned, unnecessarily, as it turned out." He fixed his gaze on me, picked up his pen, and began tapping against his note pad. "You may go, unless there is something you haven't told me."

My skin prickled. I needed a long, hot shower. I'd settle for a sponge and lukewarm water. "You know what I know," I chafed, tired of answering questions, and frustrated after telling parts of my story numerous times.

"Señor Walker, you may return to your boat. However, you must remain in Luperón."

"I'd like to leave here as soon as possible," my father objected.

"Of course," the Commandante sneered. It was like talking to a fox. "If what you have told me is true, you are much safer here."

The telephone buzzed. He raised a finger to show he would be quick, and leaned to pick it up. His eyes held mine until I looked away. Wolf, not fox, I decided.

"Commandante Mateo Gomez," he intoned. "Cuál es él?" (What is it?)

Mateo was a common name in that part of the world, yet a chill ran through me. I nudged my father's foot to draw his attention from the maps on the wall.

"What is it?"

"Can we go?" I whispered. The Commandante looked up, lifting the telephone away from his ear to hear. "I'm really tired," I added, imitating a yawn and not covering my mouth.

My father gave me a disapproving look. "Commandante, if you're finished, I'd like to take my son home."

With a wave, the Commandante dismissed us. Just as we were about to leave, he cupped his hand over the receiver. "Do not leave town, Señor Walker." He looked at me again, and nodded, the corners of his mouth twitching as if trying not to smirk.

Outside, my father hoisted the dinghy onto his shoulder, and at a brisk pace, led the way towards the harbor. I followed him across the parking lot before I stopped to look back. The color of the car at the bridge was blue, like the car parked under the tree. The antenna was a dead giveaway. I hurried after my father, trying to avoid rocks and pieces of glass.

"What was that all about?" he demanded when I caught up.

"I forgot to tell you. Sal told Tony to talk to someone called Mateo. That's the Commandante's name." I expected him to say it was another coincidence.

A police Jeep with flashing lights and screaming siren sped down the road leading into the town. It swerved to miss a mule carrying a stack of bamboo and sent chickens and piglets scrambling for safety.

"Mateo's a common name," my father said after the noise faded.

"He works for Sal. He was supposed to handle it as if I'd drowned. That's why he started a search of the harbor," I said stubbornly.

My father hurried along, leaving the impression that he hadn't heard a word I'd said. What was the point of telling him I'd seen the car at the bridge, or that the man talking to Sal wore a creamy Panama hat like the one on the Commandante's desk? I jogged to keep up, skirting patches of blacktop baked by the sun.

The marina provided a pontoon boat for people to use to go back and forth to the wharf when they didn't want to use their dinghies. The pontoon boat was a familiar sight in the harbor—scraped and dented, with a constant metallic rattle. When we arrived, it was just coming in with the evening crowd, every seat filled like an overloaded guagua. We were the only passengers on the return trip.

Chapter 27

A gull perched on the end of the *Spray*'s bowsprit as if it belonged on our crowded little yacht, now safely anchored away from the shore. A welcoming committee greeted us after we hefted up *Squirt* and climbed aboard—Imani's mother and father back from buying an outboard, a lone sailor from Miami, and a couple from South Africa had come to offer assistance to my mother. Ben sat on the cabin roof, pale and exhausted, while above him, Imani and Jessie rode the boom like a mule, their legs dangling down for balance. Again, I recounted what happened on the *Marionette*. Everyone said I was lucky to be alive.

"I'd be surprised if the police do anything. This part of the world runs on corruption," Imani's father said when I finished. Mr. Keats was several inches taller than my father, with broad shoulders and bulging arms; however, beneath the surface lurked a nomad, his only worry being where next to anchor.

"It's possible that Sal's bribed El Commandante," my father said.

"What did he say about the drugs?" Mr. Keats asked.

"Not much. I don't think he believed us. Of course, other than Victor's claim that he saw some bags of white stuff on the *Marionette*, there's really no proof," he replied.

"What about the drums in the closet and what I saw at the bridge?" I persisted, deciding that with 'Victor,' little had changed between us.

"They'll say it's coincidence," Mr. Keats said. "The same thing happened when our outboard was stolen. Imani saw it in the back of a truck."

"I got the number plate, but the police didn't care," Imani piped in from her perch on the boom. "'Una coincidencia,' only they couldn't explain why it had scratches in the same places."

"If the Commandante's working for Sal, nothing will happen," my mother said.

"Not necessarily," my father said. "We need to talk to the U.S. Coast Guard. If they catch him red-handed…"

"You could contact them on your SSB radio," Mr. Keats suggested.

"Sal's smart enough to monitor the Coast Guard frequencies." My father smiled. "If we can find someone to pass on a message, they might surprise him."

He turned to me. The decision wasn't mine; however, I knew what he wanted me to say. "He'll go to jail, won't he?" I asked, breaking the awkward silence.

"If they find him with the drugs, otherwise it's your word against his."

I wasn't sure I could go to court and give evidence against Sal. I felt empty and tired, the hate gone. I sat in the cockpit and listened to Mr. Keats and my father down in the cabin. There were hundreds of channels on our SSB radio, beeping and squawking as they went from one to the next, sometimes snippets of garbled conversation in other languages. An American drawl boomed out of the speaker, broadcasting from a ranch outside San Antonio, Texas, 1,600 miles away. There was a brief exchange of information before they set up a telephone link to the Coast Guard Station at Corpus Christi in the Gulf of Mexico.

+ + +

That night, I fell asleep when my head hit the pillow. Usually, I read and listened to the waves lapping at the bow. After five months on the *Spray*, I could distinguish an outgoing tide from the wind picking up and making larger waves. There were other sounds too—the rattle of an anchor chain, sometimes the friendly squeaks of a dolphin pod. Mostly the sounds came from engines, mechanical vibrations traveling through the water. The sound of engines woke me up, not the throaty chug-chug of a yacht's diesel engine, or the sputter of a small outboard. It was a ragged growl, like a lumping, multi-headed beast stalking its prey.

Suddenly, I was wide-awake. Ben continued to snore lightly as he always did when he lay on his back. I eased out of my berth and groped for my shorts while peering into the main cabin. A shadow lurked near the chart table. The hollow clunk of wood hitting wood followed a scrape like chalk on a blackboard. It made my skin break out in goose bumps. I tiptoed to Jessie's berth before I recognized my father's goatee. He pulled out the drawers from under the chart table and placed them one on top of the other, a scrape followed by a clunk.

"What are you doing?" I whispered.

He spun around. "Go back to bed, Victor."

"What are you doing?"

He answered with a grunt, picked up a screwdriver, and squatted down. He skewed his head to look under the table.

"I never thought I'd need to get this out," he said to himself.

"You want the flashlight?"

"No!" He banged his head on the frame. "Blast these screws!" He looked towards the companionway. "Get up there and keep an eye on the boat. Don't let them see you," he whispered.

I climbed up the stairs until my head was just above the sliding hatch. I moved my head from side to side, straining to see in the faint light.

"It's passing Imani's boat, near the shore. What are you looking for?"

He didn't answer. I stared into the gloom until the moon came from behind a cloud. The swept-back profile of a long powerboat glided across the water. Flames and curls of smoke painted its side in shades of silver and gray.

"It's Morello's boat," I whispered.

Something clattered loudly. My father scrambled around on the floor. "Damn! I've lost the flaming screwdriver! Get down here!"

I scrambled down the stairs and began to feel around for the screwdriver, crawling towards the galley. I found it under a ledge. My father grabbed it and knelt down in front of his chart table. Again, he peered up. He shoved frantically, cursing when the screwdriver slipped from his hand. I handed it back.

"What are you doing?" I whispered.

"There's a piece of plywood under the table. Supposed to slide back, but it's stuck."

"Why's it stuck?"

"I wanted it tight so it didn't open accidentally. I need you to reach up under the table. I'll push up on the plywood. Stick this in the gap and force it back," he said in a low, tense voice. He put the screwdriver in my hand and closed my fingers around it. "Don't drop it."

I squatted next to him, weaving my hand through the framework, scratching my wrist against the point of a screw before I found a flat panel secured by two wooden rails. When he pushed up, I jammed the end of the screwdriver into the gap and levered it until something cracked. The panel slid back and dropped into my father's hands. He withdrew it from the framework. Carved into gray sponge were five rectangular, plastic-wrapped packages, a box of bullets, and the gleaming outline of a handgun. It looked like one of the snub-nosed revolvers cops used on TV.

Before I could ask, the powerboat was next to the *Spray*, its huge engines vibrating through the hull. All of a sudden, the rumble ceased. Ripples replaced it, lapping the side of the *Spray*. It swayed as the weight balance changed, just enough movement for the halyards to slap against the masts.

My father nudged me and brought his finger to his lips. "Two of them," he whispered.

He pulled the revolver from its hole and pushed the cylinder to the side, quietly closing it again before he raised a finger, pointing up. There was no mistaking the sound of careful footsteps creeping over the cabin roof. He pushed me past his chart table, and into the shadows behind the engine room. A moment later, a man peered down the stairs, blocking the moonlight.

"Eh, Morello," he called out. "Is dark down there."

"Get out of my way, fool." Morello stepped onto the cockpit seat. "Muchacho is mine."

A foot appeared in the dark companionway, seeking the first step. The stairs were steep and narrow. We ascended and descended always facing back, never forward into the cabin, critical details pertaining to my father's companionway rule. It was easy to miss one's footing the other way. With one foot planted on the top stair, Morello's other foot searched for the next step. My father leaned closer, reaching behind the stairs. Before Morello found the second step, he shoved at the foot on the top step. Morello pitched forward, flailing for the handrails beside the hatch to stop from falling. He plunged through the companionway and slammed onto the galley counter. It was plastic that looked and felt like stone.

I thought Morello was dead. I stepped from my hiding place to gawk from beside my father. Suddenly, Morello struggled to his knees and pointed his pistol at me. My father shoved me aside and kicked him twice in the side of the head. Morello crashed to the floor again.

"Hey, Morello? Miss dat step, eh?" the other man called out.

My father darted back, thrusting me towards his chart table until we were out of sight. "My leeg eese broke, I theenk," he groaned, feigning a very convincing accent.

He lifted his revolver, holding it with two hands, sighting down the barrel, his feet apart–the same stance that Tony had used. The other man jumped into the cockpit and stuck his head through the companionway. He looked into the barrel of my father's gun and backed away.

"Okay, Mon. Is cool, okay? Is cool, Mon," he jabbered.

Without warning, he brought up his pistol. My father sidestepped at the same instant and fired his revolver with a deafening bang. He leaped over Morello's inert body and scrambled up the stairs, shouting for the other man to stop. I followed him, pausing to add a kick of my own.

The powerboat's engines bellowed to life. It took off, heaving the *Spray* aside, and roared into the night, leaving a trail of foam to the shore. It stopped with a loud crash. A man jumped off the boat and sank knee deep in mud. The boat exploded before he reached the mangroves, lighting up the cove like a lightning strike. The shock wave punched the side of the *Spray*.

My father turned to me, the fire blazing behind him, casting a red glow over his boat. "'A man will defend himself and his family to the last,'" he said softly.

I remembered what Captain Slocum said next. "'For life is sweet after all.'"

He smiled. We watched flames shoot into the night, like a trailer on fire.

Almost an hour after the blaze petered to glowing coals, the Commandante arrived, delivered by the smoke-belching Customs launch. Two marines both with automatic rifles at the ready, hopped onto the *Spray* before he stepped across. He plopped onto the cockpit seat and loosened his tie, no doubt considering what to do about Morello. He was strung up on the foredeck, his hands secured with duct tape, raised over his head by a jib halyard.

"I warned you these are dangerous men," he began, glaring at me. He glanced behind him at a red-haired man dressed in a creamy coarse-linen suit. "From your embassy, Señor Walker. Someone made a radio call to your Coastguard."

My father met his eyes. "There are dozens of boats in Luperón. Could be any of them."

The man waited until the boats bumped before he grabbed the rail and clambered aboard.

"Roland McNair," was all he said. He shook my father's hand, wiped the cockpit seat with a paper towel he took from his pocket, and sat down.

"This is the boy who thinks he saw drugs," the Commandante began.

"Muchacho lies," Morello shouted.

"Speak again, and my men will silence you!" The Commandante looked steadily at me. "Tell him."

I told my story for what I hoped would be the last time, and my father gave his version of what happened during the night. He left out the compartment hidden under the chart table and his Smith and Wesson handgun. Instead, he'd pointed our flare gun at the intruder.

"There was a gunshot," the Commandante said.

My father shook his head. "It must have been the powerboat backfiring." He lied without batting an eye.

The Commandante turned to Morello. "You work for Sal?"

"I want a lawyer," Morello said.

"Lawyer?" The Commandante chuckled. "Contact your embassy."

Still, he looked at me suspiciously. With a gesture to the marines, Morello was unleashed and manhandled to the cockpit.

The Commandante leaned back, his arms crossed on his chest. "Now, you tell me what happened."

Morello bared his teeth at me. "All lies. They try to kill me."

"Mr. Walker is a dangerous man, no?" the Commandante jeered.

Morello held out his hands, twisting his wrists. He nodded at the smoldering remains on the mud. "Si, Commandante. He destroy boat!"

"He says you kidnapped his son; is that a lie too?" The Commandante inspected his manicured nails.

"Everything they say is lie." Morello glared at me. "Muchacho lie like dog."

All I wanted was to go back to sleep; however, sleep had to wait. The interrogation continued until the sun rose on Morello's blackened boat. Egrets scavenging the exposed mud flats for worms scattered when the launch approached. Four marines searched the charred remains. Soon, they shouted back 'cocaína, cocaína'. They found 10 drums in the cabin.

When the launch chugged back to the *Spray*, the Commandante got to his feet. He jerked his head at Morello, a marine on either side of him. Shiny handcuffs had replaced duct tape.

"You need lawyer, I think."

Morello struggled until he came face to face with me. "Sal make big mistake with you."

"He made a bigger mistake with you," I replied, emboldened by daylight and my father standing beside me.

Morello glared at me. "Caribbean is dangerous place for you, muchacho."

My father's hand was firm on my shoulder. "Get this scum off my boat."

One of the marines shoved Morello so hard that he had to jump onto the launch or fall into the water. "I have friends. They will find you," he boasted.

"I look forward to meeting them." My father sounded remarkably calm.

The marines forced Morello to sit on a wooden bench. He twisted around and screamed, "Muchacho, all of you, muerto!"

'Muerto' was 'dead.' I gave him the finger when my father looked away.

The Commandante saw it. He raised an eyebrow, and with a sly smile, asked, "You know what is 'el gato,' muchacho?"

"The cat," I replied. One of Señorita Gaitán's jokes had begun with 'a dog, a cat, and a mouse went to the market.'

"A cat has nine lives. You have one," he said in a voice so low that only I heard.

I knew what he meant. Before I could reply, he stepped across to the launch and sat under the shed.

Roland McNair remained on the *Spray*. "We appreciate your getting involved," he said to my father.

He smiled ambiguously, keeping an eye on the launch. Again, the Commandante had folded his arms across his chest. He stared at me as if daring me to say that he was the man I'd seen at the bridge.

"If we keep an eye on them, it helps to move things along," he went on.

"I'm certain the Commandante is part of it," my father said quietly

"I've heard rumors in Puerto Plata that he might be. He knows what he's doing, unlike some of these clowns," he said, nodding at Morello. "There'll be a reward for him. Javiero Orejuela too, if his body turns up. As for the rest, we'll see what happens. When the press picks up the story, I assume you'll want to remain anonymous?"

"I'd rather not have the publicity."

He gave me an awkward 'high-five' and shook hands with my father before he jumped awkwardly onto the launch, joining the Commandante under the shed.

Chapter 28

El Commandante's written order arrived by launch within an hour of him leaving. For our 'safety', he confined us to the *Spray* until further notice, anchored in the main harbor, directly opposite the government wharf. He enforced his order with a guard, who watched us through binoculars from a Jeep parked at the end of the wharf. The same morning, my father sent a request for reconsideration, also in writing, with a copy mailed to Roland McNair at the US Embassy in Santo Domingo.

After four boring days, there was no response. Nothing happened quickly in the Dominican Republic, where the local people moved at a sea snail pace. Only tourists scuttled about during the heat of the day, like crabs on the mud flats. We watched them from our jail, shaded by a temporary awning strung over the boom.

Between schoolwork and visits from Imani, I strummed Johnny Cash jail songs on my guitar and waited for news. There was nothing on the local radio stations about Sal, or Javiero, or Morello, just a few sentences about a powerboat blowing up in Luperón. Every evening we listened to news broadcasts from America on the SSB radio. There was nothing new, like the weather report that my father tuned to after the news—muggy and hot until the trade wind returned.

Late on Monday afternoon, the launch arrived with another letter from El Commandante. We gathered in the cockpit and waited for my father to open it.

"He's lifted the order for us to stay on the *Spray*," my father said after he'd read a page of poorly translated Spanish. "We can make day trips if we inform the Commandancia before we leave Luperón. The *Spray* stays here until he decides otherwise."

"Can we go to La Isabela tomorrow?" Ben had fully recovered.

"By bike. We need the exercise," my father said. "Something's happened to change his mind."

+ + +

I expected the worst, yet the third item of the eight pm BBC World Service News shocked me.

"Early this morning, in a joint operation with the Royal Bahamas Defense Force, the U.S. Coast Guard boarded a motor yacht off San Salvador Island, in the eastern Bahamas," a crisp, public-television voice announced. "They recovered a suitcase with $20 million in cash, and cocaine with a street value of $48 million. A U.S. Coast Guard spokesperson said the evidence pointed to a gun battle with a rival drug cartel. The owner of the yacht, mafia boss, Salvadore Saccoccia, and his crew are missing, presumed dead.

"For many years, Saccoccia was a pillar of New York society. He founded the Dante Fund, providing millions of dollars a year for research into childhood diseases, and he was an avid supporter of the New York Philharmonic."

My father's head jerked up with an 'I told you so' look. The corners of his mouth twitched, a conceited smile in the offing. "No wonder he looked familiar."

The rest of my family looked at me as if I was responsible.

+ + +

Not much remained of the first European colony in the New World, just a few rocks piled under metal-roof shelters. Unable to stomach Ben's enthusiasm, I meandered across the plaza, overlooking the bay where I'd seen Sal for the last time.

My mother came up behind me. "Sal's cunning." She rested her hand on my shoulder.

"Like a fox," I agreed. "He's out there somewhere."

Wispy clouds lined the horizon. To the west, a container ship headed to Cuba; northeast, a yacht was so far out to sea that its sails were dots, two white, one green like a spinnaker. On the other side of the plaza, my father, Ben, and Jessie explored the foundation walls of Columbus' house.

"He loves you a lot, Josh. More than you realize," she said quietly.

I shook off her hand and wondered how she knew what I was thinking.

+ + +

Nine days after our trip to the mountains, we boarded the same crowded guagua going from Luperón to Imbert. However, instead of going south to Santiago and the mountains, or visiting the waterfalls at Imbert, we changed to a guagua going to Puerto Plata, 25 miles down the coast. After two days of rowing *Squirt* across the harbor, or waiting for the pontoon boat to ferry us to and from the government wharf, my father decided it was time to buy another outboard motor. Puerto Plata had a marine store.

The guagua stopped for workers to get on and off at five fancy resorts before it let us off near the Puerto Plata train station. We wandered through the old part of town, past the white towers of the Church of San Felipe, along noisy streets lined with Victorian-era buildings, a rainbow of pastels assigned with meticulous care to elaborate details: cornices, columns, and architraves. There were restaurants and outdoor cafes intermingled with shops that sold trendy Caribbean clothing, sunglasses, suntan oil, postcards, cigars, amber jewelry, and vast quantities of plastic souvenirs. Puerto Plata seemed an unlikely location for a marine store until we saw the bustling waterfront. Two wharves extended out into a harbor sheltered by Mt. Isabel de Torres. A cruise ship prepared to depart from one wharf; at the other, two freighters were unloading and loading. Between the wharves was a long line of super-sized sport-fishing boats, luxurious motor yachts, and dozens of sailing boats.

"I wouldn't mind staying here for a while," I said.

"Even with the smell, I'd rather be in anchored in Luperón." My father headed into Puerto Plata Centro Marina store.

He walked the line of outboard motors stretched along the back wall, from massive engines of 260 horsepower for offshore fishing boats to tiny trolling motors. Finally, he squatted down and inspected one of them.

"This one might do. It's got half the power of the old one so it won't last very long." He examined the handwritten price tag. "Outrageous!"

My mother came over. "How much is it?"

"You don't want to know." He inspected the tag again and shook his head in disgust. "It's got three lousy horsepower, and the price is ten times what our old one cost."

"It was secondhand," she reminded him.

"It was professionally reconditioned! I could have bought the same piece of junk in Luperón and saved the bus fare."

"It's not as if we have a choice. We need another outboard. The Keats went to Santo Domingo to buy theirs."

"We'll go there tomorrow," he decided. "I need something to write on."

She opened her handbag to look. At the front of the store, the door buzzer sounded the arrival of another customer.

"Assuming El Commandante lets us go." She'd taken to calling him 'El Commandante' too. The trick was saying it the right way.

"He'll have trouble stopping me." He glared at me, his stony expression unrelenting. "We'll be lucky if this one lasts six months before it falls apart. Finding parts will be impossible, assuming they even make parts..." He went on and on.

My mother stayed because she had no choice. I moved away. Not all of the outboards were inferior. Two outboards were the same brand as our previous one. One of them was the engine my father should have bought in the first place—more than double the power of his old engine. It was both electric and rope-pull start. I gulped at the price—$6,000, and didn't draw attention to it.

"The other possibility is to wait until we get to Puerto Rico and buy it there," my father said without much enthusiasm.

"Maybe we could find a motor at the flea market?" Ben suggested.

"We might get lucky and buy the Keats' old outboard." My father directed his sarcasm at me; as much as saying we'd have to give it back, which would also be my fault.

My mother diverted him. "The sign says to ask about reconditioned motors at the front desk."

"There's no harm in asking."

On the way to the front of the store, he diverted to the paint section. Ben and I went over to the fishing section to look at trolling lures. Five minutes later, my father carried a tin of varnish to the front of the store. He waited until the sales clerk finished writing in his order book.

"Señor, a sign at the back of the store says you have reconditioned outboards. I might be interested in buying one, if the price was right." He expected everyone to bargain with him.

"Si, Señor. We have five motors in the workshop."

"I want one with about six horsepower."

"Won't the new one do? It is an excellent motor, Señor, ideal for a small inflatable."

"What are you talking about?"

Even from the fishing section, I could hear his frustration. Without thinking, I headed towards the front door.

"The outboard, Señor. You can take it with you, or we can deliver it. Tomorrow morning, if you wish." He had an annoying blink.

My father stared at him. "I don't know what you're talking about."

"You're not ready to take the outboard, Señor?"

"I'm interested in buying a reconditioned outboard, if the price is right," he repeated as if for my benefit.

The sales clerk threw up his hands. "But you have a new outboard." He turned the order book around so that it faced towards my father. "You are John Walker, owner of the *Spray*, currently at Luperón?"

Instead of answering, my father read the last entry. "Fifteen-horsepower, four-stroke, electric-start outboard." He stared at the bottom of the page. "It says 'paid $5,500 cash.'"

"The three-year warranty is expensive, Señor."

"I don't understand," my father said simply.

My mother stepped forward. "May I ask who paid for it?"

"Your friend, the man who just left. He paid me in American dollars." He opened a drawer, reached inside, and pulled out a sheaf of notes, each with Ben Franklin's face.

"Was he an old man with white hair?" I asked, not really believing what I was thinking. There was no other explanation.

My father spun around. I thought he was going to shout at me. "Sal's hundreds of miles away," he said calmly.

"Who else could it be?" My mother was clearly amused. "I'm sure he's giving it to us to make up for the other one."

I grinned back at her, realizing the deception. Salvadore Saccoccia disappeared at San Salvador Island, 350 miles away. Two days later he was back in the Dominican Republic, where he was least expected.

"We can't accept it," my father said with a determined shake of his head, his moral compass never off course.

"He paid for it, Señor. I took off $500 because he paid in cash."

The bundle of notes were crisp, touched only a few times. Sal took what was his and left the rest behind for the Coast Guard to find. I bolted for the front door, not caring that my father called out for me to stop. I ran across the street, dodging guaguas, cars, trucks, and motorcycles to reach the harbor. I jumped onto a bench and scanned the busy docks. A few boats looked like Javiero's—long and low, with fiery colors on the side. Sal could be on any of them, or none of them.

The cruise ship began to pull away from the wharf, sounding its horn to warn a small trawler passing too close, its pint-sized, vividly attired captain unaware as he prepared his dock lines. A white ketch, vastly larger than our *Spray*, backed away from the dock directly in front of me. A woman and two men prepared to raise the sails while a girl looked on. She reminded me of Señorita Gaitán, beautiful, with long dark hair. Another man stood by the steering wheel, watching astern. White hair peeked under his captain's hat. I waved and shouted. I was certain he saw me. He didn't wave back. I felt like *Squirt* with the air let out, wilting in the afternoon heat, painfully aware that I'd made a spectacle of myself by waving at strangers.

The man spun the wheel and the yacht turned towards San Felipe, the fortress that once guarded the harbor against pirates. He looked over his shoulder. I waved again, just to make sure. He nodded, just once, like a nervous twitch. The stern slowly came into view, revealing the boat's name, '*Maid Marion,*' executed in the same black and gold script as the *Marionette*. My heart raced and sank at the same time.

From behind me, my father said, "Despite what you think, he's not Robin Hood."

I jumped from the seat and moved away from him. "Since when do you care what I think?"

"I care!" He looked past me, watching the trawler. "With luck we won't see him again."

"We're leaving?" I choked at the thought of saying goodbye to Imani.

"The sooner the better. We'll buy an outboard in Puerto Rico."

"Sal tried to do the right thing," my mother said in a voice that did not tolerate objection. "We'll keep the outboard."

At midnight, we quietly motored out of Luperón harbor. For six months, we followed the long chain of Caribbean islands from Puerto Rico to Trinidad, then along the seemingly endless South American coast to Brazil. Other boats went west to Panama, avoiding the current and taking advantage of the trade winds, but not us. When Slocum sailed around the world, there was no canal through Central America.

Chapter 29

Endless oily gray waves rolled westward, slowing the *Spray* as if it dragged a sea anchor, yet offering a boost when it passed over the crest. For a few moments, each wave restored life to a yacht almost becalmed in the stifling air. Six hundred miles south of the Equator, the heat was intolerable—the deck too hot for bare feet, the glare from the sails agonizing without dark sunglasses, clothing clinging with sweat. I dozed, stretched out on the cockpit seat, my New York Yankees cap pulled down to block out the blistering sun, waiting for a breeze to arrive.

He came on deck ten minutes before noon to check on his crew. He looked around, prepared to find fault, the sails not set properly, navigation incomplete, the cockpit untidy. "It's still there," he observed after a while.

A boat had been on the horizon since we'd left São Luis two weeks ago. Only fishing trawlers and yachts traveled that slowly, and almost none of the latter. People who wanted to go south from the Caribbean first headed east to the Canary Islands near Africa to avoid the current racing up the South American coast. Only my father, or a fool would sail the course we were on.

He brought out his binoculars and focused on the tiny speck off the stern, almost lost among undulating waves. It was too far away to determine more than it didn't have sails. Then, he checked the compass heading and made a note in his log before he nudged my leg.

"I'll take the rest of your watch," he said. "I made tuna fish sandwiches."

The tuna was fresh, caught from the stern with a trailing line and a silver lure, 60 pounds of iridescent green fish as tall as my sister. All of a sudden, I was hungry.

"Put on Tchaikovsky," he called after me.

I stopped in the companionway. "I'm tired of Tchaikovsky."

"Then pick one you like. I haven't heard Stravinsky's *Firebird* in a while."

"Anything as long as it's by a Commie composer."

"How many times do I have to tell you to stop muttering? Anyway, it's pre-revolution Russian."

I inspected his long rows of CDs, avoiding Stravinsky and works by Tchaikovsky that I'd heard so often I could hum with the orchestra, finally selecting one of my father's homemade recordings. He'd labeled it 'A B, New York 1995.'

"Your watch doesn't end for another ten minutes." Ben didn't look up from his encyclopedia. Despite leaving the vast mouth of the Amazon River astern three weeks ago, he still read about its plant, animal and fish species, from waking up until falling asleep.

He looked like a bad-tempered smurf, his hair greasy and disheveled, still tinted purple from when we crossed the Equator. At the time, we were stuck in the Intertropical Convergence Zone, hot and no wind, yet tradition demanded we celebrate with bizarre rituals. I counted myself lucky—there was no one to see my blond hair was dyed blue.

I yawned and gnawed on a sandwich, stale homemade bread with a slab of tuna, not paying attention to him going over the mating habits of piranha, or my sister's chatter in the aft cabin. As far as I was concerned, the southern hemisphere differed only by latitude and opposite seasons, and my choice from my father's music library. Although I hadn't heard the CD before, it was familiar, a piano and violin, a melody like an old friend who appeared out of nowhere.

Suddenly, my father stomped down the companionway. "I didn't tell you to put that on." He stabbed his finger on the eject button. Flamboyant, African-inspired music blared from the radio.

"You told me to pick one. It sounds like Tchaikovsky." It reminded me of his *First Piano Concerto*—a little awkward, yet ingenious.

My father stared past me, at Slocum's photograph on the bulkhead over my head. He was a shadow from a century ago, with a lot in common with my father, not the least being single-mindedness and a need to control. Their physical similarity ended with their goatees. Captain Slocum was very nearly bald, while my father's hair was like mine—sun-bleached disobedience, only much darker.

"There's no harm in listening to it, John," my mother said from behind him.

"It's not something I want to discuss." He'd been in a bad mood since we entered the North Brazil Current. It pushed us backwards whenever the wind eased.

"At least tell him why."

"I don't have the time. Please don't play it again." He started back up the companionway. "Get some sleep, Victor. There's a storm on the way. A bad one," he added over his shoulder.

I wanted to ask 'how bad.' Instead, I glared at his back.

"We'll head out to sea," he added.

Staying close to the coast offered less current and safe harbors, the nearest 60 miles behind us; however, no one dared question our captain's decision.

What little wind there was, soon disappeared. The *Spray* wallowed, the engine pushing us towards the oncoming storm, halyards wearily slapping the mast. The sea, like the sky, was the color of lead in every direction. It made me uneasy until I fell asleep. When I woke up, the wind was back, blustery gusts that turned the sea even darker.

My father kept a list of things that we needed to do in case of a storm. Down below, we put things away, prepared food, and tied down anything that could come loose; while he strapped the dinghy to the deck and tied down the sails. He came down to lock the hatches and portholes. Satisfied that we'd secured everything, he took me aside.

"I'll need you on deck. Everyone else will be throwing up."

While he dragged the storm sails from the bow locker, I pulled on my plastic trousers and jacket. Bright yellow was supposedly safer in foul weather. My boots came to my knees. I tightened my life-jacket and safety harness and followed him up the stairs. The sky was dark with billowing smoky trails under the clouds.

"The wind's swinging around. It won't be long now," he said as we raised the storm sails. They were tiny but tough, built to withstand winds that could rip other sails to shreds. When he was back in the cockpit, he turned to me. "Do you remember anything from when you were three?"

"I remember you building the *Spray*."

"You were four when I laid the keel. How about before we moved to Arcadia Park?" I shrugged a response. "Do you remember hearing that music before?"

"Should I?"

"When you were three, you stayed with my parents for the summer."

"Wasn't that when they died?"

"Maybe it's better this way. Some things are best forgotten."

"Like how I got these?" I asked, looking at the burn scars on my forearms. My father looked too, only for a moment before he turned away. "What were they like?"

He cocked his head. "You don't remember them at all, do you?"

I shook my head. Suddenly, my skin crawled. It hurt to breath. My ears felt like they were going to explode. He opened his mouth to say something. No sound came out. The *Spray's* masts and rigging hummed. When, I looked up, a vast, dark funnel blocked out the clouds.

"Microburst! Hold on!" my father screamed.

It plunged down, radiating out rather than swirling up like a tornado, getting louder until my head throbbed. With a roar, the wind heaved the *Spray* onto her side. The bow dipped deeply, the deck canting at a gravity-defying angle. I plummeted down, flung from the cockpit towards the sea. Only the lifelines saved me. My father hauled me back. I clung to him, my gut churning. The *Spray* spun around and lurched over a huge wave before slewing into the trough, the storm sails cracking like a 21 gun salute. It ended as abruptly as it began. Miraculously, nothing broke.

My heart thundered. I was certain we wouldn't survive. As far as I could see, the sea boiled, whipped white, sweeping towards us. The roar grew louder, like an out-of-control locomotive bearing down, until blinding sheets of water crashed onto the *Spray*. I thought we'd roll over for sure. My father fought back, gripping the wheel with white knuckles and staring blindly ahead. I'd never been terrified, or as uncomfortable—the front of my jacket slapped my neck red. Sheets of spray cascaded over me, finding openings in the sleeves and under my hood, brine sloshing through my clothes, chafing cold, clammy skin. For hours, I rubbed salt from my eyes, making them itch even more.

The waves were more frightening in the dark, invisible until a wall of water loomed up before us, a battering ram that shoved the *Spray* out of the way. A sideways surge preceded each wave; the stronger the rolling motion, the bigger the wave. There was no way to avoid the waves—even the smallest were bigger than any wave I'd ever seen. The *Spray* rose up to greet them, as if stubbornness could make the waves get out of her way. As the bow lifted, hundreds of gallons of seawater gushed over the gunwales with a deafening thump, swamping the deck and flooding the cockpit ankle-deep. My father clung to the wheel, his safety harness bracing him against the torrents of water, conducting Tchaikovsky's *1812 Overture*, which played over and over again

The waves grew even larger into the night, white crests easily half the height of the mast, sometimes breaking like surf. Fearing his boat would capsize, my father hove to, his tiny storm trysail sheeted tightly and the rudder locked in the opposite position. We waited out the storm with the bow pointing towards the wind, the *Spray* rolling and bucking incessantly.

After one wave lifted the *Spray* so high it seemed we'd never get over it, he laughed maniacally. "I wish Sarah was here to see this," he shouted after the crest passed. The *Spray* charged wildly down the other side.

I cowered in the corner of the cockpit, fighting seasickness and a persistent fear that the masts would break, that the next wave would shatter a hatch and we'd sink. "This is crazy. We should head for shore," I shouted back.

"We're safer at sea than entering a strange port in a storm, especially at night."

"At least they'll find our bodies washed up on the beach."

"These waves are nothing to worry about. I built her to sail through a hurricane."

Another gigantic wave slammed into the bow, shaking the *Spray* violently. Water streamed down his front. Like Joshua Slocum, my father was unyielding.

+ + +

In the middle of the night, the wind slowly lessened. We took turns keeping watch, drifting in and out of restless sleep. The storm blew itself out the next day, leaving a long, rolling swell and a steady breeze that pushed us towards Rio de Janeiro.

Chapter 30

Rio de Janeiro was so hot in late November that even with every hatch and porthole open, and a cloth chute suspended over the bow hatch to scoop up the wind, only a breath of sultry air wafted through the *Spray's* cabins at night. In the morning, the chute seemed to pull in the sounds of the city waking up—the hum of traffic on Avenue Infante Dom Henrique, noisy seagulls squabbling over scraps in the marina's smelly garbage cans, ten feet away on the quay. It was enough to wake me up.

"You sure it's his boat, Faro?" a man demanded.

"The stern, it says '*Spray.*'" He sounded foreign.

"There's only one way to find out," a third man said, adding a handful of words. He sounded like the announcer on my father's Prokofiev CD—the *Sixth Symphony*, recorded in Kiev.

I stood on my berth and peeked through the hatch. Three men walked down the quay, the early morning sun casting long shadows ahead of them. They made their way among dark-skinned vendors preparing pushcarts for another day of peddling trinkets in the Parque do Flamengo. One man looked like a badly dressed tourist in tartan shorts, a Panama hat, a ridiculous checkerboard shirt, and socks nearly up to his knees. He barely reached the shoulders of the man on his right. That man might have been a government official, his gray business suit not out of place in bustling Rio de Janeiro. He reminded me of my old science teacher, Mr. Metwager, a demanding, wiry man with sunken cheeks, who was often the brunt of 'Gestapo' jokes. The man carried a walking stick with an oversized handle, which he used with flair, not as if he needed it. The other man was tall, with the broad shoulders and closely trimmed hair of an Olympic athlete. Dressed entirely in black, he looked as if he belonged in New York. I ducked behind the wind chute when he turned to look back.

They walked on after the short man climbed aboard a trawler-style motor yacht. Its bow pointed to shore, like the *Spray*, unlike the other yachts docked at the Marina da Glória, which had their bows pointing out. I'd seen him before. This time, he stared at our boat with a malevolent scowl. The other two men disappeared among boats stored on stands. I pulled on a T-shirt and went aft to tell my parents.

My father's side of the bed was empty—he'd gone for an early morning jog. I woke my mother and told her. "What do they want with us?" I asked when I finished.

She stifled a yawn. "They're most likely from the marina. You father mentioned something about a problem with the electrical supply."

"I'm sure I've seen them before."

She sat up. "Where?"

"One of them, the dumpy dude, I saw in the Bahamas. His boat looks like a trawler. I think the buff guy was at Palm Beach when we were getting ready to leave. And the third man; remember at the market in George Town? It might have been him."

She mulled it over. "You're not certain?" I shrugged. She rubbed sleep from her eyes. "It's probably nothing at all." She leaned over and found her watch on the shelf next to the bed. "It's seven thirty. He won't get back for another half-hour." She looked up abruptly. "I want you to point them out to me."

From the cockpit, I scanned the quay, the waterfront park, the marina pavilion, back and forth through the parking lot. She handed me binoculars and I searched in every parked car before I spotted one of the men standing close to a palm tree. 'Buff guy' had taken off his jacket. The other man sat alone in a nearby car. My mother focused the binoculars on each man as I pointed them out.

233

Suddenly, she sat down and pulled me onto the cockpit seat beside her.

"We need to let him know."

"He usually runs along the beach." I didn't know where he went after that.

"He'll go right past them on his way back. Josh, I want you to take *Squirt* along the shore and look for him," she said in a low voice.

After telling me to be careful, she stood up and ambled to the stern. She might have been enjoying the early morning sunshine as she untied the dinghy. Casually, she draped the painter into the dinghy. On the way back, she unclipped clothes from the rail where she'd hung them to dry. When she shook out a beach towel, distracting the men's view of the cockpit, I scrambled into the dinghy. Hidden behind the *Spray*, I started the outboard motor and pushed off. After dodging the yachts moored in the marina, I raced past the breakwater into Guanabara Bay, a breathtaking expanse of blue water. Pão de Açúcar and Corcovado towered behind the high-rise buildings of the city, the gigantic statue of Christ the Redeemer a brilliant beacon in the early morning sun.

I'd almost reached the end of Flamengo Beach before I spotted my father among the trees. I headed towards him, waving and shouting until he saw me. He jogged down to the shore.

"What is it, Victor?" He stopped running on the spot when I told him.

"Who are they?"

"This isn't the time." He kicked off his running shoes, waded out to the dinghy, tossed his shoes in, and clambered over the side. I moved to take my usual seat in the bow. "You steer!"

I turned towards the marina, opening the throttle just enough that the dinghy planed, no faster because my father insisted it wasted gas and wore out the engine.

"Go as fast as you can." I didn't expect him to say that.

Squirt skimmed across the water, making its own breeze. I slowed only when I passed the breakwater. The two men were still in the parking lot. With dozens of yachts between them and us, and their attention focused on the *Spray*, they didn't notice us. He ordered me to turn into a gap between two yachts tied up at the quay. The *Spray* was only five yachts away, on the opposite side of the pier. He scrutinized the two men again.

"Who are they?" I asked. He didn't answer. "Are we leaving?"

We planned to stay in Rio de Janeiro through Christmas, four weeks away.

"First things first. I need a diversion; a couple of minutes ought to do it."

I pointed out the trawler on the far side of the marina. It seemed to pop up everywhere we went.

He scratched the nape of his neck. "That's the second problem."

"Why don't we call the police?"

"And tell them some men looked at our boat?" He made it sound foolish.

Undaunted, I suggested, "How about the fire brigade?"

He beamed. "That ought to get their attention."

"I could call from the public telephone." It was on the side of the main pavilion, near the laundry.

"You'd avoid them if you went behind the building." He told me what he wanted me to do. He made it sound easy.

My father heaved himself onto the pier and I puttered away, heading to the other pier. He ambled down to the main quay like a sailor taking a morning stroll before it got too hot. He turned right and stopped at a pushcart to buy a newspaper. He opened it up and buried his head among the pages as he approached the *Spray*, stealing quick peeks all around. At the last moment, he hurriedly clambered onto the bowsprit and disappeared down the front hatch.

He said to wait a few minutes, but on a whim, I tied *Squirt* to the pier using the anchor rope, leaned over the bow, and unfastened the painter. With a hard shove on the pier, *Squirt* drifted past a small yacht. A gentle push on its bow brought *Squirt* to the trawler's stern. With my heart going twice its normal rate, I tied one end of the painter to the trawler's stern platform, and dropped the rest in the water. A few pulls on the anchor rope and *Squirt* bumped against the pier.

After sneaking a look around, I climbed onto the dock and sauntered along the quay, pausing to pet a mangy mutt searching for food scraps. He said 'look normal, don't rush.' As soon as I was out of sight of the parking lot, I ran, dodging pushcarts, hawkers selling their trinkets, and people walking their dogs. I slowed down behind the marina's main pavilion, trying to stop gasping, my heart hammering. When I peeked around the corner, only a delivery van separated me from the two men. The driver shoved boxes into the rear and slammed the door, muttering in Portuguese as he climbed into the cabin. The van left, leaving no way to get to the telephone without them seeing me.

Their interest converged on the *Spray* when my mother emerged from the cabin. She walked to the bow pulpit and leaned out to flip the electricity switch several times before examining the cable plug. She retraced her steps, coiling the cable. Ben appeared within seconds. He climbed off, staying close to the *Spray*, idly looking about for someone to play with.

I hurried back the way I'd come, searching for another telephone.

"Buy candy cheap?" A boy blocked my way. He held out a grubby green packet. "Mentos?"

He was a street kid, skinny with sunken, sad eyes, ragged clothes covered with paint spots, sores around his mouth. Ugly welts covered his arms and legs. Most of the street kids were beggars; a few lucky ones had pushcarts or carried their wares in cardboard boxes. They sold candy, magazines, drinks, and cigarettes, anything a tourist might want. I shook my head.

"Telephone?" I held my hand to my ear.

"Vaque Tona?" My sister liked Vaque Tona—gooey chocolate and caramel frosting in a bell with a ring pull on one end and a plunger on the other.

"Telephono?" I demanded, wondering what it really was in Portuguese.

He pointed at the pavilion. He followed me, a few paces behind, persistently offering cheap candy. I skirted the ramp and hurried through the boat storage area, crowded with yachts on stands, some stripped of paint, others with fresh coats. Not far away, the man under the tree watched my brother practice tying knots in the *Spray*'s dock lines before carelessly draping them around the bollard. All the while, the stray dog sniffed at his feet.

The street kid nudged me, his hand out, wanting a tip for directing me to 'telephono'. It was the same public telephone, in plain sight of the car. I backed away. A dockworker carrying a bucket full of paint-covered rags to the dumpster stopped to let me go past. However, he shoved the street kid aside and tossed the rags into the dumpster. The boy scrambled up, cursing him out in Portuguese. With a shrug, the man resumed slapping paint on a yacht. The smell from the dumpster made me stop. I turned around and beckoned. The boy came over, back to pushing Vaque Tona.

"Cigarette lighter?" I asked, holding out a five-reais note.

He grinned. "Si cigarro? Gringo want Camel, eh?" 'Gringo' sounded like 'green-go.'

"No, cigarette lighter." I motioned, flicking my thumb up and down.

He stuck his hand in his pocket, pulling out a cheap plastic lighter. I gave him the money and he followed me to the dumpster. My hand shook as I flicked the lighter and reached over the side of the dumpster, not at all sure I could do it. The rags, full of solvent, burst into flame. I jerked my hand away, shuddering. My scars prickled. Sweat covered my face.

"If anyone asks, it was him," I said, pointing to the man in the car. "He likes to burn things." I don't know why I said that.

Fire exploded from the dumpster. I turned and ran. The boy laughed behind me. Someone shouted. I kept running. When I finally looked back, half a dozen people had gathered to watch the blaze and billowing black smoke, including the man who'd been under the tree. I couldn't see the man in the car.

My father suddenly stood up in the *Spray's* cockpit, shouting for me to hurry as he reversed away from the quay. In the bow, my mother hoisted Ben aboard, the stray dog yapping at his sudden departure. I jumped into *Squirt*, untied the anchor line, and pushed off. For the first time in six months, the outboard motor wouldn't start. Again and again, I turned the start key. I tried adjusting the controls, every possible combination of choke and throttle until the battery died. When I pulled the starter rope, it sputtered smoke.

"It sounds like it's flooded. Give it full throttle," my father bellowed.

I opened the throttle and yanked hard on the starter rope. More smoke and a wheeze. After five more pulls, the motor coughed, almost starting.

"Try the choke!" was his next advice.

"You won't be as lucky next time, Alex."

I glanced up at the voice and a name that wasn't mine. The man in black leered down at me from the stern of the mock-trawler. I barely glimpsed '*Orel*' before its motor roared to life. For a moment, water churned from its stern before it stopped abruptly with a very loud bang.

On the next pull, the outboard started and *Squirt* leaped away, throwing me off balance. Before I regained control, the dinghy had bounced off the bow of the small yacht. I careened past yachts docked along the quay, towards the breakwater and the *Spray*.

$+++$

"Good job on the trawler. They'll be stuck there for hours, cutting their prop free," my father said after I tied off *Squirt* and climbed aboard. He glanced at the column of smoke over the marina. "Not quite what I had in mind, but all told, it worked out nicely." The rumble of a jet taking off from the airport masked the sirens of the fire trucks.

"Who are they?" I demanded.

He didn't answer. Instead, he stared at Corcovado, the gigantic concrete statue of Christ the Redeemer a tiny spike reaching from the granite summit. We'd planned to visit that afternoon to watch the sunset.

"You ever going to tell me the truth?" I was angry.

"They have me confused with someone else."

The bay sparkled in the early morning sun, deserted except for the *Spray*. The plane climbed in slow motion, banking steeply as it turned into an endless blue sky. He steered a collision course to the beckoning bald knob of Pão de Açúcar, the diesel engine straining at maximum power. I slowly calmed down.

We were dangerously close to running aground when he spun the wheel, not towards the harbor entrance, the other way, into the mountain's shadow.

"A long time ago I learned that the best place to hide something is where it won't be noticed and where it's least expected," he said, smugness lurking in a hint of a smile.

Ahead, hundreds of yachts lined Botafogo beach, most clustered around the Royal Yacht Club. We stayed there until the day after Christmas.

Chapter 31

At noon, January 13, I exchanged watches with my father, both of us bleary-eyed as we recorded the *Spray's* position—512 miles south of Montevideo. We still had 750 miles of dangerous ocean to reach Tierra del Fuego. With every mile south, the waves grew larger, the wind, colder and stronger.

With my schoolwork finished, I crawled into my berth, looking forward to four hours of sleep.

"I need to take down the sails. Everyone else is asleep," my father said, shaking me.

"I wasn't?"

"You can sleep in tomorrow. The weather forecast said a pampero is on the way."

Pamperos formed in the pampas grasslands. Usually, they stayed there. However, they could leave land with almost no warning, and with great force—the initial gusts could attain hurricane strength. The majestic cumulus clouds that had towered over Argentina now scraped across the horizon, headed our way. For an hour, the clouds raced towards us, blocking out the land, a vast, flattened mushroom cloud looming behind, the sea gray and threatening.

"We'll miss the worst of it," he declared, motoring at full speed to avoid the storm front.

When the wind arrived, it was so strong that it hurled the *Spray* about with gut-wrenching force, heaving it through the waves as if they didn't exist. We'd prepared for the worst. 'Running under bare poles,' my father called it, not even a storm sail aloft.

"The Strait of Magellan by Friday, if this wind keeps up," he bellowed at the height of the tempest, his smug prediction of outrunning the storm long since forgotten.

"What about a straight jacket?" I shouted back.

He glared at me, seawater streaming over him, his hair in wild disarray, somehow retaining control as the howling wind tried to bully his boat into submission. Huge waves crashed over the stern. The *Spray* slewed from side to side, dragging 600 feet of anchor rope behind. That rope may have saved our lives when breaking waves and screeching gusts tried to turn her over.

When the wind weakened to manageable levels, he hauled the rope aboard, intending to raise the mainsail to steady the *Spray*. He gave orders and I carried them out, my stomach knotted as I winched the sail higher. It flailed in the gusts, the boom swinging wildly, the gaff squeaking in unrelenting protest even after it reached the top. The instant he steered away from the wind, something cracked overhead, like two cars colliding without the squeal of tires. The line securing the top of the gaff had broken away from the mast.

"Get it down!" he yelled.

He turned the boat around, facing into the wind. I released the halyard and scrambled onto the cabin roof to get the sail down before it ripped, clinging to the mast with one arm and using the other to grab fistfuls of cloth. I was exhausted long before we'd furled the sail and strapped down the gaff.

"Next time, clip yourself on. You're lucky you weren't swept overboard, Victor."

I bristled. My head throbbed from lack of sleep. I wasn't in the mood for a reprimand I didn't deserve. "Next time your frigging sail can rip itself to shreds."

"Get below!"

Twelve hours later, we anchored in the Golfo San Jose to make repairs.

+ + +

When I came on deck the next morning, my father sat in the cockpit, contemplating the masthead through binoculars. He was so quiet that I hadn't realized he was there.

"I've got a job for you, assuming you've got the guts for it," he said gruffly. I felt him watching me, waiting for a response.

"I'm the kid with guts, right?" I don't think he remembered saying it.

"How would you feel about going up the mast?"

"You want me to climb up there?" I asked testily.

It was a long way from the deck to the top of the mast. It wasn't like climbing a tree—no branches to hold on to and no bark for a foothold.

"You can if you want. I'd recommend using the bosun's seat," he said, still looking up.

The bosun's seat had a plywood bottom, sail cloth sides with pockets for tools, and a harness. He fitted it to me and tightened the straps. He said I could turn upside down and not fall out—I wasn't about to test it out. He issued me an adjustable wrench along with new bolts. All I had to do was replace the bolts that had come loose in the storm and reattach the lines. He used the mainsail halyard, one end fastened to the bosun's seat, the other end wrapped around the biggest winch. He cranked the handle until my toes swung free of the deck.

"Watch out for the shrouds," he cautioned.

His shrouds came closer as I went higher. I pushed away from them, swinging back and forth until I grabbed hold of the mast. I felt queasy and I was only one third of the way up. I worried about the halyard breaking and the harness coming undone. He kept turning the winch.

"If I have to do this again, I'm putting you on a diet," he called out.

"Something other than tuna fish sandwiches?" I yelled back.

He stopped to take up the slack in the backup halyard before he cranked the winch the rest of the way. From the top of the mast, Golfo San Jose was an inhospitable place with no sign of human habitation. However, the view was breathtaking—tall cliffs with tiny windswept trees, like burrs in an olive-green carpet of tussock grass, gulls and cormorants wherever I looked. An albatross soared past the cliffs before swooping along a promontory extending into the bay. I'd seen albatrosses every day since leaving Rio de Janeiro, never as close as it passed by the *Spray*. I watched it wheeling about, suddenly realizing that out of sight from the *Spray's* deck, huge wind-sculpted boulders sheltered a colony of sea lions. The males on the outskirts flapped their flippers and thrust their heads together, disputing control of the 'harem.' I heard only the faintest squeals, the wind blowing their din onto the cliffs.

"Tighten those bolts as hard as you can," my father shouted after he'd secured the halyard.

I wanted to shout, 'why don't you tighten them?' He didn't have to contend with a bone-chilling breeze. With my legs clamped around the cold metal mast, I used one hand to hold the gaff fitting over the holes and the other to insert a bolt, all the while worrying about dropping his precious wrench overboard. It was like clinging to the top of a power pole that bucked violently as the Spray rolled and pitched. The bolts went in easily just as he said they would; however, three bolts didn't stop turning when I applied force to the wrench—only the last one was snug against the fitting. After attaching the ropes, I watched the sea lions while I waited for him to lower me.

I wasn't alone. Perched on a boulder like a leprechaun, a man in a grass-green shirt scanned the bay with binoculars. He slowly turned around until he stopped abruptly, as if he knew someone was watching him. I descended in jerks, a few inches at a time. A minute later, I stood on the deck while my father unfastened the bosun's chair from around me.

"You did a good job," he remarked.

"Next time, I'm sending you a bill," I said, choosing humor over the shrug I wanted to give.

"I know I'm always on your case about being responsible, Victor."

"The wind was going to tear the sail if I didn't get it down," I disputed, tired of 'Victor,' his lectures, his erratic moods.

"It wasn't worth the risk. You need to think things through, especially if there's a chance of being injured." He paused, looking past me. "Only when something or someone is very important to you do you take that kind of risk. Those are the hardest decisions of all. Sometimes you do what you think is best, and you're still wrong."

He clapped me on the shoulder, imitating a hug. It was better than nothing.

We watched the albatross glide to the cliffs, its wings eight feet across, the edges outlined in black. Suddenly, it veered away, its wings barely moving.

"The man from *Orel* is over there," I said, waving at piles of boulders on the shore. He frowned. "He's following us, isn't he?"

"That seems to be the case."

"Who is he?"

"He has me confused with someone else!" After a few moments, he added, "Maybe it's better you know." He took a deep breath. "The man who's following us is the insurance investigator for the fire at Arcadia Park. He thinks Mrs. Mason's new husband started it."

"That doesn't explain why he's following you."

"Walker took out a million-dollar policy on each of the kids and his wife a week before the fire, and then he disappeared. We have the same last name. We left at the same time. It's coincidence, but it's suspicious." He regarded me, daring me to dispute his explanation. "With luck we'll lose him by the Strait of Magellan."

Chapter 32

I woke up when someone shoved me. I burrowed deeper into my pillow, ignoring the voice in my ear. My pillow smelled moldy, my blankets were damp, and so was the thin layer of foam rubber I slept on. All of my clothes were wet. My father shook me again and dragged the blankets away. Reluctantly, I lifted my head and blinked into the glare of my reading lamp.

"I need you on deck in five minutes," he boomed.

I clamped my arm over my ear, trying to drown out his order. He was louder than the waves whacking the bow. He squatted beside my berth, his wet weather gear dripping puddles of water on the floor, his hair sodden, his beard straggly, his face red from the wind and spray. He looked tired, older than his 45 years. It was the middle of summer; however, that far south was like winter. We kept the portholes and hatches closed and breathed stale air to keep the cabin warm. Day after day, the wind blew from bottom of the world, driving icy waves across the ocean. Being outside for four hours at a time was miserable—always cold and wet from intermittent rain squalls and blinding sheets of spray, hurled into the cockpit by passing waves. It was worse at night.

"Time already?"

"It's 3:30."

"I've got 30 minutes," I complained. My watch started at 4:00 am.

He shook his head. "The barometer's dropped steadily for an hour. I want another reef in the sails before the wind gets too strong." He got to his feet. "Don't waste time getting dressed."

Storms cells swept up from the vast ice shelves of Antarctica, arriving with no more warning than a rapid drop in barometric pressure. I could tell from the noise and the *Spray*'s bucking motion that the weather had worsened since my last watch ended. Then, the wind blew steadily with waves averaging eight feet high and far apart. While I slept, the wind had grown stronger and the waves had become much bigger. They lifted the bow so high that I slid back in my berth. At the crest, the *Spray* paused like a roller coaster car at the top of the ride, just before it dropped into the trough with a frightening rush. The biggest waves lifted the self-steering rudder out of the water and the *Spray* slewed sideways until the self-steering regained control.

Wearily, I unclipped the side of the lee cloth and sat up to put on my wet-weather jacket. "What's the forecast?"

He answered with a shrug. In that part of the world, weather forecasts and actual conditions seldom corresponded for very long, and they took forever to down load using the SSB radio. I listened to him clomp through the main cabin on his way back to the cockpit. When I tried to put on my pants, a sudden, sharp pain struck deep inside my belly, as if someone stuck a spear in me and twisted it. Hesitantly, I poked my finger into my side. As quickly as the pain came, it went. My stomach had been tender since we left Punta Arenas, the only town in the Strait of Magellan. That was a week ago. The island of Diego de Almagro was the last land we'd seen. It was three days and 400 miles behind us.

When I stood up, I felt nauseous. "Mom?" I called. There was no answer. "Anyone?"

"She's upstairs already. Dad wants you on deck, now!" Ben shouted from the galley.

He swaggered back and braced himself against the bulkhead. I wedged myself against the locker, taking shallow, quick breaths while he gnawed at his daily ration of Chilean candy.

"It's the middle of the night and you're eating Princess' Arm?" Just the thought of almond nougat, plum jam, and chocolate in a marzipan wrapper turned my stomach.

"It's not me who's about to throw up," he observed with an experienced eye.

The spear stabbed again and I clutched my side. "Get Mom!"

The pain became a nagging ache that roamed over my front, never stopping long, always returning to the same place. I slumped onto my berth, squeezed my eyes shut, sore from salt and lack of sleep, and waited.

"What's wrong?" my mother asked from the doorway. She sat on Ben's berth and placed her hand on my forehead. "You look terrible. Are you seasick?"

"Hurts inside." I waved over the right side of my abdomen.

"Where exactly?" she asked.

I put my finger midway between my belly button and right hip. She replaced my finger with two of hers, and gently pressed in. It was tender below her fingertips, yet it didn't hurt as much as it did when I pushed with my finger. When she took her hand away, I almost cried out.

My father loomed in the doorway. "What's taking so long?"

"He's sick. I think it's appendicitis. He's tender over his McBurney's Point. It's a bad sign."

He rubbed his forehead, muttering 'damn' under his breath, "Maybe it's something he ate?"

"If I'm right…" She glanced at me. "He should be on his way to hospital."

"Could it be something else?" He fixed his gaze on me.

"John, it's enough that it might be appendicitis. Out of three kids who get an appendectomy, one doesn't need it. We can't take the chance."

"Aren't there tests?"

"Of course, there are tests. I need a lab to do them." My father was about to say something when she turned to me and asked, "Josh, how long has your stomach been sore?"

"A few days."

"Have you been since then?" She meant to the bathroom. When I shook my head, she glanced up at my father. "How far are we from a port?"

"Patagonia is 80 miles east."

Patagonia was a clutter of islands and a vast area of glacial wilderness in southern Chile. Even if my father could navigate through the islands without running onto a reef, there were no roads and no towns for hundreds of miles in any direction.

He turned to my brother, concerned yet still chewing Princess' Arm. "Go to bed, Ben!" He pulled on his goatee, suddenly uneasy. "Three days maybe."

"We don't have three days. It could burst any moment."

"How long?"

"It usually ruptures within 12 to 24 hours of the pain becoming worse. I'll start him on antibiotics right away." She brushed my hair back from my forehead. "At least he hasn't vomited."

"After dinner," I murmured so he wouldn't hear me.

My mother rubbed my forehead. "I wish you'd told me." She turned to my father. "It may have ruptured already. Short term, I can treat the infection. He needs an operation as soon as possible."

I swallowed, thinking I might vomit again. My face grew hotter. Ben climbed onto his berth, licking sticky nougat from his fingers before he opened his Britannica. Suddenly, a wave heaved the *Spray* onto its side. My father lunged through the doorway, flailing for something to hold on to until he regained his balance.

"Weather's getting worse. As soon as I've put in another reef, I'll radio the navy base at Punta Arenas. If we're in range, maybe they can send a helicopter."

As he turned to go, she stopped him, pulled him close, and whispered, "We need to get him to a doctor."

He stared down at me, his face grim. "Everything will be okay. She worries too much." He hurried though the main cabin and scrambled up the stairs. The companionway hatch slammed shut behind him.

Between waves, my mother searched through the first-aid kit, bandages, ointments, dozens of dark glass bottles in lift-out trays, medical instruments, and vacuum-sealed surgical packs. She sat on the end of my brother's berth and prepared two syringes.

"Ben, go brush your teeth." She gave him a gentle push to get started.

With reassuring competence, she pushed the sleeve of my T-shirt up to my shoulder and dabbed a swab at my arm, spreading yellow antiseptic in a widening circle. I winced when she jabbed in the first needle.

"This is a broad spectrum antibiotic. It'll stop the infection." Her thumb slowly depressed the plunger. She pulled out the needle and pressed the cotton pad tightly against my arm to dull the pain.

"All I need is a shot?" I asked, hope springing eternal.

"You're the lucky one in this family, Josh, but you're not that lucky. Your appendix has to be removed. Unfortunately, there isn't a hospital nearby."

I didn't blame my father, although we traveled the world because of him. I eyed the second syringe. "What's in that one?"

"Morphine sulphate. It'll stop the pain. Morphine is named after Morpheus." She jabbed the needle into my arm.

After she pulled it out, I forced a feeble smile. "The god of dreams."

"My mom would be happy that you still remember her stories." Her voice wavered.

My berth surged under me the same way it did when a big wave approached. She felt it too and momentarily clutched the wood rail. When the wave didn't hit, we breathed out in mutual relief.

"Once this takes effect, you'll sleep till it's over."

"Am I going to die?"

She patted my shoulder. "Kids usually spend a few days in hospital, sometimes as long as a week if there are complications. No one dies from it."

Without a roar, a massive wave rolled the *Spray* onto its side, flinging me from my berth onto my mother. Ben screamed from the main cabin. My stomach cramped, disgorging whatever remained in it. A second wave crashed against the hull. My mother clutched me while I coughed and gasped. A few seconds later, after a loud bang, a third wave walloped the *Spray* from astern, shaking everything it its path. She clambered to her feet, shouting at Ben to be quiet. I staggered after her, expecting to find the hull stove in, icy seawater gushing through a gaping hole in the side. In the galley, pots, plates, and boxes of food had spilled from the lockers. My sister was bawling. There was blood on her forehead. I slumped onto the seat and held onto the dining table, my side throbbing mercilessly.

My mother hammered on the companionway hatch until he shoved it back. Outside, the sails cracked like rifle shots in the shrieking wind. He scrambled down the stairs, shaking off water.

"What the hell happened this time?" My mother was at her best in an emergency.

"Friggin' gybe! The gaff fitting broke again. Ripped the mainsail."

Oblivious to chaos, he stomped over to his navigation table and switched on the radio. It crackled with static as he rotated the dial, switching from one frequency to another. There were no squeaks and squawks, none of the familiar jargon of Ham radio operators.

"I was afraid of that."

My mother let a long sigh escape. "Now, what's wrong?"

"Antenna's busted. I'll need to go up the mast to fix it." He dragged a chart from its slot, unrolled it, and gave it a cursory look before getting to his feet again.

Another rogue wave crashed into the *Spray*. The Captain's portrait tumbled from the bulkhead wall and clattered onto the table. Jessie screamed until the *Spray* began to right herself, rolling wildly from side to side. My mother clung to the galley counter.

"Slocum said 'even the worst sea is not so terrible to a well-appointed ship.'" My father seemed almost happy. "Golfo de Penas has lots of protected coves. I'll fix the radio and call from there."

He hurried back up the stairs. She called after him to be careful. Ben followed him, stopping when his head cleared the companionway. A moment later, he ducked down as the hatch slid shut.

"His mainsail's in pieces."

"Ben, clean up the galley. Jessie, Josh is going to sleep in your berth. You can help by moving your toys to the bow." I held up the Captain's picture for her to see the cracked glass. "Your job is not to throw up on his precious captain," she said, wry humor drawing a smile from both of us.

My father looked exhausted when he scrambled down the stairs. Taking down the mainsail reduced the *Spray's* rolling, though it still pitched violently when waves thundered by. He tossed his wet weather gear into the locker behind the stairs and dried his face with a towel before he came over and looked down at me.

"How's he doing?" He sounded a long way away.

"He's starting to doze off. I should've noticed something was wrong with him."

"Not your fault," he said.

It was difficult to keep my eyes open. Was he smiling at me? I couldn't be sure with his goatee.

+ + +

My body burned in my dream—red, orange, and yellow flames licked the walls around me, unbearably hot. The flames grew bigger, hotter, the screaming louder. I couldn't stop it no matter how hard I tried.

"He's got a fever of 105. We don't have a choice." My mother's palm was a cold fish on my forehead.

"Ben, take Jessie to our cabin." My father sounded worried too.

She leaned over me. "He's waking up. I'm not sure I can do this. Ten years is too long."

"You haven't forgotten," he said, seeming in no doubt.

254

She pulled out trays from the first aid locker, dumping the contents of one of them on the galley counter. "I'll need you to assist. You can start by getting more light in here."

She ripped the plastic from a surgical package, spreading out a sterile cloth, medical instruments in plastic sachets, tweezers, forceps, and scalpels. I dozed off, waking again when my father scooped me up from Jessie's berth and carried me to the dining table. He'd draped a sheet over it, another over the spare berth and the bulkhead. I looked up at five reading lights stuck to the cabin roof with long strips of gray duct tape.

"What do you want me to do now?" he asked.

She looked up from *Emergency Medical Procedures*. "Take off his clothes. You might need to shave him. Then, wash his front with antiseptic."

I cringed, unable to speak. When he finished, he covered me with a sheet. She came over with a syringe, swabbed my shoulder again, and stabbed it. I felt nothing, not even a pinprick.

"Go back to sleep, Josh. You're going to be fine."

She loomed over me with another syringe. Latex gloves covered her hands. A white cloth masked her nose and mouth. A scarf covered her hair. It was hard to keep my eyes open. The Spray rocked back and forth, not rolling, or pitching up and down as it did among steep waves. It swayed gently as if sinking into the water. I sank with it.

+ + +

When I opened my eyes, I looked into Jessie's face. "Mommy, he's awake," she called out.

My mother hurried downstairs, my father close on her heels. Suddenly, my family lined the side of Jessie's berth, all speaking at once. I closed my eyes again. The berth moved beneath me, calm like the Sargasso Sea. The debris of the oceans gathered there with great fields of seaweed, never to leave. It was hot and briny, without wind or current. It was a sailor's Hell.

When I woke up, they were gone. Everything back to normal; remnants of schoolwork covered the dining table; the Captain looked down from his place on the bulkhead, no longer behind glass; Tchaikovsky played in the cockpit. I looked up. Behind my head, taped to a locker, was an upturned bottle. A clear plastic tube led down to my arm and a needle. Outside the cabin, my brother chattered about glaciers and fjords. He came down first, lugging one of his encyclopedias back to the bow cabin.

He left it on the table and greeted me with a happy, "Hi." It was an effort to smile back. "Mom operated on you just in time. There was pus everywhere."

"Thanks for sharing that."

Ben grinned. "She sucked it out with a bilge pump."

"After she sucked out your brains!"

He knelt on the seat. "What's it feel like to have your appendix removed?"

My mouth was parched. It hurt to swallow. The pain in my side was gone. "I don't recommend it."

"It sounds like you're feeling better," my mother observed.

I hadn't heard her come down the stairs. She lifted back the blanket and leaned over me. I raised my head and looked down at my belly. Yellow skin covered my front. On my right side, purple and brown skin disappeared under my boxers. Evenly spaced knots of what looked like fishing line closed an ugly gash three inches long.

When she glanced up, she touched my arm. "All things considered, you're still the luckiest person I know. It could've been much worse." She didn't elaborate, and I didn't ask.

"Did you really use a bilge pump inside me?"

She scowled at my gleeful brother. "I flushed your insides with saline solution. We used a sterile plastic tube and a spare bilge pump to suction it out."

I glared at Ben's back as he carried his encyclopedia back to our cabin. "I hope you catch it," I croaked after him.

"Appendicitis isn't something you catch." She pulled out the drip-feed needle and replaced it with a gauze pad before she checked my temperature. "How do you feel?"

"Tired."

"You slept for three days. Are you hungry?"

Sitting up took an enormous effort. She spoon-fed me lukewarm chicken broth and raspberry-flavored gelatin. When I finished, I tottered to the head and back to my berth. She helped me climb in, straightened the blankets over me, and wiped my face as if I was still a child.

"You need to sleep," she said when I asked for my guitar.

'I'm not sure I want to. I had a horrible dream, over and over."

"Tell me."

"There was a man who looked like Dad, only he was older and he played the piano." She nodded for me to continue. "There was fire all around us. He tried to drag me away from it."

My mother brushed back my hair. "They should have called Morpheus the god of nightmares, not dreams."

"The man in black was there too."

"Morphine does that," she said, almost to herself. "Is that all you remember?"

"I remember being in a hospital." I stopped. For a moment, it seemed real. "I was there for weeks..."

Her eyes darted to the scars on my forearms. "You were on morphine then as well."

"From when I fell on the heater?"

"You nearly died, Josh," she said so quietly that I wasn't sure I heard her.

Chapter 33

Tired of my family constantly talking about the Andes Mountains, I struggled up the stairs to see for myself. The *Spray* sheltered in a tiny, saw-toothed cove behind an island in Golfo San Esteban, surrounded by pristine, snow-capped peaks. A glacier crept from the flank of Cerro San Valentin, the highest mountain in Patagonia. Its journey ended with a boom whenever a chunk of ice as big as a house plummeted into the sea. The water, like polished green jade, was so deep that my father couldn't anchor. Instead, he'd tied lines to boulders on the shore.

I hunched down in the cockpit to escape the breeze, wrapped in a blanket cocoon, the frosty air restoring my lungs while the sun warmed my face. There were no buildings, fences, or fields, and no boats. I'd never seen a more beautiful, or inhospitable place.

"We won't have to worry about that insurance investigator finding us here," I said.

"What investigator?" My mother put her scrapbook aside.

"I told Victor why that boat was following us," my father replied. She seemed baffled. He stood up, impatient as ever. "I need to do repairs. We'll head to Más a Tierra as soon as he's ready to travel."

Back to following Joshua Slocum's route, our next port of call was one of the islands in the Islas Juan Fernández. Más a Tierra was the home of Alexander Selkirk, marooned for 52 months before a ship rescued him. His story inspired Daniel Defoe to write *Robinson Crusoe*. It was ten days north, if the wind stayed in the west.

"I've looked at your maps," my mother began.

"Charts," he interrupted, as if he already knew what she was going to say.

"Do what you need to do to fix your boat, but we're following the coast. Josh needs to see a doctor to make sure he's okay."

He nodded back at her.

"Mom, how did you know what to do?" I asked after he left to fetch his tools.

"I assisted at dozens of appendectomies at Norfolk General. I must have learned a few things over the years," she said, watching him. "I couldn't have done it without him."

+ + +

For two weeks, we pursued the coast of Chile—deserted, craggy islands and empty, endless stretches of beach that bore the brunt of the Pacific Ocean. We stopped at shabby fishing villages and trading ports full of small rusting ships and rundown warehouses. Every day, I grew stronger. At Concepción, when I finally did see a doctor, even my cautious mother agreed that I'd fully recovered. The doctor congratulated her on a minimal scar, which I thought boded poorly for local kids.

While a boatyard made repairs to the mast and sail, and repainted the *Spray*'s bottom, we trekked through the Andes Mountains. By the time we returned, my belly looked almost normal.

In the middle of April, we loaded the *Spray* with supplies, filled the fuel and water tanks, and set a course for Easter Island, which my father hoped to reach in 20 days. We'd never been at sea without sight of land for 2,000 miles. The breeze lasted for 300 miles until we entered the horse latitudes. Feeble puffs filled the sails barely enough to move the *Spray*, often disappearing for hours at a time. On a good day, we traveled 85 miles, often less than 50 miles, never running the engine because my father conserved fuel like a miser. Boredom set in, made worse by the muggy air and sloppy waves. My mother finished one scrapbook and started another to record our journey from Rio de Janeiro.

Few yachts sailed to Easter Island. It was out of the way with hazardous anchorages, the main harbor barely big enough for three yachts to huddle behind a breakwater. On the other side, the ocean surged relentlessly, threatening to drive the *Spray* onto an unforgiving shore of black pitted lava, spilled from the cliffs. Beyond the straggling town, Easter Island resembled a golf course without trees—a drab carpet of grass draped over three modest volcanoes and dozens of small conical pustules. We stayed for three days, long enough to walk to every one of the gigantic statues that guarded the island's perimeter.

Trade winds accompanied our departure, stronger than usual for that time of year. Day after day, we punched through steep waves. We lived with noise, endless banging and squeaking, the *Spray* heaving up and down, nothing horizontal except for the horizon. Even the simplest chores became difficult when everything sloped, always holding on with one hand, whether pouring a drink, eating, or using the head. Spills splattered the galley and dining area, the bathrooms stank, and tempers frayed as we stumbled back and forth. Waves tossed the *Spray* in such a random way that I bumped into things so often that dark bruises covered me. I washed my hair once in a week! Even sleeping was difficult, tossed against the lee cloths that kept us from falling out of our berths. After a few days, I was exhausted, yet unable to do more than nap for a few minutes at a time. Every night, I stared into the darkness with bloodshot eyes, constantly worrying about something breaking during my watch.

Before my watch ended at dawn, my mother took over and I went below. My father sat at his chart table, listening to the weather forecast on his SSB radio, a crackling, garbled inventory of zones and likely weather conditions. I gave him our position.

"We've still got a day before we get to the halfway point." He was grumpy as I'd ever seen him. "The good news is we're missing the worst of it. It's blowing 40 knots 500 miles north."

He leaned back in his chair after changing the radio frequency to the Pacific Net, which sailors used to keep in touch. When no one spoke for a while, he lay on the floor and began his daily regimen of 50 sit-ups. Ben was asleep on the settee, Volume 9 of the Britannica cushioning his head. I shoved him to make room.

"I saw another albatross, a really big one," I said in his ear.

Nature boy jerked up, blinked, rubbed his eyes, and went back to sleep. I snacked on raisins and sipped lukewarm water, envying people who had refrigerators with a constant supply of ice.

"...foxtrot-zero... CQ Kilo ... six-delta... bravo. Over." 'CQ' meant 'seek you.' Radio operators used it to establish contact. "CQ Kilo...six... Vessel Sierra...Romeo Alpha...."

The metallic voice, distorted by static, passed almost unnoticed, yet my father and I glanced at each other. He rushed to the chart table and adjusted dials on the radio, enunciating our call sign like a BBC announcer. "You're not coming through clearly. Over."

"Kilo... delta... bravo ... message for you," the radio operator said.

The radio hissed and crackled loudly. "John ...I was coming back from... two nights ago and I saw..."

My father frowned at me. I nodded nervously. "Sarah is that you? Over."

My grandmother didn't answer right away. "... safe... worried about you..."

"Sarah, I can't hear you? Over."

The loudspeaker erupted with might have been an unruly New Year's Eve party—whistling, squeaking, and squealing, drowning out whatever she said. He clenched the microphone.

"Bad copy. Too much interference. Can you repeat? Over."

The radio fizzled and popped until another man said. "I'd be interested in any news about them." His voice was familiar. Before I could be certain, the buzzing grew louder.

"...had to leave... Be careful," my grandmother said.

"I hear you loud and clear in Honolulu, Hawaii. I can relay to your party. Over."

I was certain it was Sal. Before my father noticed, our radio erupted in static. It was so loud that he turned off the radio.

"John?" my mother inquired, peering from the companionway.

My father stared at the microphone. "Your mom just called. Too much static to hear her. You know how she worries about the kids."

"She sounded upset," I said as my mother hurried down the stairs.

"What did she say?" When he shrugged, she lost it. "Damn! I knew something bad would happen."

"We don't know that anything happened."

"She saw something that scared her," I said.

He glared at me. "Sheer speculation, Mister."

I didn't care if I made him mad. "She said she saw something, and that she was safe."

"What she said was 'safe', not that she was safe. And she worried about us. That's all. Maybe she saw a weather report for the southeast Pacific."

My mother launched a counterattack. "We should have telephoned her from Easter Island."

"There's no need to worry. She said she was okay."

"You just got through telling Josh all she said was 'safe.'"

For a moment, my father seemed to ready to dispute. He conceded with a shrug.

"She wouldn't call us unless there's a problem," my mother said. "We'll go back to Easter Island."

"That's not possible."

"It's possible and sensible." She sounded just like my grandmother.

"Something bad has happened," I said. "She's never used the radio to contact us."

I felt his eyes bore into me. "You're on watch, Victor."

"I'm eating lunch," I snarled. I grabbed another handful of raisins from the box.

"It's not worth the risk, John. We have to go back."

"Mom's right!"

He looked right through me. "Easter Island is a thousand miles straight into the wind. It'll take two weeks if we're lucky. The Marquesas Islands are nine days away if the wind keeps up. We'll try the radio again when the reception is better. If anyone can take care of themselves, she can."

Chapter 34

With the first light of dawn, cumulus clouds mushroomed into a sky streaked with mare's tails. The clouds gathered over the Marquesas Islands, draping the peaks of extinct volcanoes. Including the brief stop at Easter Island, we'd spent seven weeks at sea. Those clouds were a very welcome sight.

Soon, we were close enough to see land where the sun penetrated the clouds—shadowed, sinuous ridges and deep gorges that plunged over vertical cliffs into the sea. Here and there, dark spires like the statues of Easter Island, thrust through countless green hues. Coconut palms grew everywhere, poking from the volcanic boulders along the shore and sprinkling the hills until they became too steep. Waves pushed by the wind, grew even higher as Hiva Oa rose up from the ocean. They swept across Traitor's Bay, and thundered onto rocky cliffs sending up huge plumes of spray, salty mist shrouding a plantation house with a wide, white veranda, flanked by jungle plants.

"This is paradise." My father beamed at the bright morning sun. "The perfect place to relax for a while." He struggled to maintain his balance as the Spray rolled from side to side.

Captain Slocum, having sighted a nearby island, sailed on to Samoa; however, I didn't say that, not when my father had talked of sailing to the Marquesas for as long as I could remember.

"That would be nice," my mother said.

"We'll call your mom as soon as we find a telephone. I'm sure there's nothing to worry about."

He'd tried to contact our grandmother, using a ham radio operator to find out that she'd transmitted her message from Omaha, Nebraska, which made no sense at all. There was no reason why my grandmother would go there. Another radio operator telephoned her house in Richmond, Virginia; however, there was no answer.

With the sails furled, he motored into a small inlet behind a breakwater. It was so crowded that it was difficult to find a place to anchor. There wasn't a marina and the main quay was no more than a stone wall. The dinghy dock was a square of concrete with tractor-tire bumpers for protection. A lanky redheaded teenager watched us as a wave threatened to heave *Squirt* onto the twisted steel stanchions.

"Better not fall in," he called, clearly amused. "The water's so murky you can't see the sharks. They're thick around here. One mauled a poodle last week."

We jumped to the dock between waves, grappling for something to hold on to, slipping on greasy, green slime, seawater soaking our clothes. We hauled the dinghy out of the water and carried it to safety as the morning drizzle began. We hurried away from the stench of rotting fish, hordes of flies, filthy oil drums, building materials, and piles of crushed stone. Fish scales and cigarette butts covered the laundry—a broken concrete slab equipped with rotting washboards, rails to hang clothes, and a faucet dripping rusty water.

Undaunted, we went into the general store, hoping to find fresh milk, croissants just out of the oven, and a telephone. A sweaty man covered with black tattoos tried to sell us dented cans of food and freezer-burned meat. We exited quickly. On the verandah, an enormous rat scuttled away from the remains of a loaf of French bread. Across the road, hand-carved letters under a crude roof welcomed visitors with 'Bienvenue A Hiva Oa.' Below, scraps of electrical wiring tacked to the post indicated where a telephone had been.

"If this is paradise, what's purgatory like?" I said under my breath.

My mother fumed too. She glared at my father, not saying a word. The heat and humidity made it unpleasant to breath.

"First things first. We'll look a telephone after I take care of the paperwork."

The immigration office was the local police station, a long hike up a muddy road. No one wanted to walk. My legs felt like rubber, the ground rising and falling like waves, and my feet throbbed in tight sneakers. The police station was a modest bungalow surrounded by an overgrown garden with dozens of chickens. Compared to other countries we'd visited, there were no lengthy forms to fill in for French Polynesia. Instead, a man in a pretentious, pressed uniform demanded $5,000. It was a deposit to ensure our prompt departure when our visas expired.

"There's no charge if you get a visa before you arrive," he admonished.

Having learned it was better not to complain, my father asked if he could pay the following day.

My mother interrupted him. "Can we use a credit card?"

"We'll pay in cash," my father insisted. "American dollars are okay?"

"French Polynesian francs only, Monsieur. It is returned when you leave." The policeman smirked at my mother as if she was the first woman he'd seen in a month.

We emerged into sun. The tropics surrounded us—the peaks of Mt Temetiu and Mt Feani glistening wetly after the clouds peeled away, a vast green amphitheater cradled between them, colonial style houses scattered over the hills, trees weighed down with exotic fruits, red splashes of hibiscus flowers hiding among leaves so glossy that they seemed artificial.

"This must be the most beautiful place on earth," my father said. He took one look at my mother's face and added, "I'm sure we'll find a telephone in the village."

Nearly the same number of people lived in Atuona as in the trailer park where I grew up; however, the Marquesan Islanders were much friendlier. Little pickup trucks stopped beside us to see if we wanted a lift. Each time, my father said no. We needed to walk after being 'cooped up for so long.' A horde of dark-skinned kids with shiny black hair burst from a school. Jessie stared at a group of giggling girls. I knew how she felt. One of the girls directed us to the post office in the center of town.

After buying a phone card, we crowded around the public telephone. My father laboriously dialed the international code, the country code, the area code, and my grandmother's phone number.

"She should be home by now," he said smugly. He held the receiver away from his ear so we could say 'hello' together. It clicked several times.

"The number you have dialed is no longer in service. Please check the number and dial again."

He glared at the telephone as if it was broken. He checked the numbers he'd written on a scrap of paper and dialed again to make sure.

"Let me try?" My mother dialed rapidly, and then waited for a connection.

"It doesn't make sense." Now, he was worried. "Maybe she forgot to pay the bill."

It took ten minutes and another phone card before my mother talked to a real person at the telephone company.

"I'm trying to find out why her number isn't in service," she explained for the fifth time.

"It was disconnected, Mam."

"She'd never have her phone disconnected without letting us know in advance," I said. My grandmother had moved across town a week before Christmas. The following day, she sent us three letters, each with her new address and phone number.

"Ask if she has a new number," my father said.

My mother jabbed him with the telephone and stalked away as if she already knew that there wasn't a new number. She sat down on a cheap plastic chair before the only computer on the island with public Internet access. We gathered around her. Our email account had 213 messages, mostly junk. My grandmother sent two emails, the last one two days before the radio call.

"I have settled into the new place. Everything is okay. Jag is still sick. I have another appointment with the vet in 15 minutes. More tomorrow," my mother read aloud.

"Probably an allergy. Nothing out of the ordinary otherwise." His conclusion was hard to fault.

"One of us will have to go home."

She stood up, knocking over the chair. It clattered on the floor. At the counter, a post office official muttered something in French. I picked up the chair, placed it before the computer table, and waved back.

"Mommy can't go. She has to stay with us!" Jessie was adamant.

My father rubbed his chin. "I'll go. It won't take more than a week. You'll be safe here."

My mother glanced at me. "You've said that before, John."

He followed her gaze. "This has nothing to do with what happened then. Maybe she finally got a cell phone and decided she didn't need a regular phone."

I didn't point out that a cellphone couldn't explain why she'd tried to contact us by radio, or why she hadn't told us about it in an email.

+ + +

We spent the afternoon getting money changed for the departure deposit and our passports stamped, stocking up on supplies, ferrying drums of diesel fuel to the *Spray*, buying fresh fruit and vegetables from local farmers, and finally, eating a chow mien dinner at *Snack Make Make,* the cheapest restaurant in Atuona.

"We need to talk," my father said to me after we climbed aboard.

My mother bustled Ben and Jessie below. I sat on the cabin roof, guessing I was due for a lecture on my attitude, or lack of responsibility, or any of a hundred other things.

"I can't imagine how Slocum sailed around the world by himself." He stopped to watch a dinghy speckled with patches putter towards us. "I'm counting on you while I'm away."

At times, the dinghy disappeared behind waves, its undersized motor barely able to push it over the crests.

"Bit of a surprise, what?" my father remarked when the dinghy was close enough to recognize the man in the stern.

Bruce tossed a line and my father hauled his dinghy to our boarding ladder. A passing wave sent it crashing into the *Spray's* stern. Before the next wave arrived, Bruce flung himself across the gap and onto the boarding ladder. He grinned broadly. He'd changed little in the year since we'd last seen him. Stubble sprouted from his cheeks and chin. His forehead was like wrinkled brown leather with peeling pink spots at his temples.

"G'day, mate." Bruce and my father shook hands like old drinking buddies. "How's your trip been?"

"We've had a few problems." He didn't elaborate.

"Me too, mate. I got whacked by a hurricane last year," Bruce chuckled. "I ended up on a beach in Cuba. After I fixed her up, I had just enough money left to pay for the Panama Canal, so I figured it was time to head home. You go 'round the Horn like you planned?"

"We went through the Straits of Magellan. We were lucky with the weather. It wasn't too bad."

"Bit of a coincidence, you turning up today. You just missed your mate from New York."

"I don't know anyone from New York." My father turned on me. "Victor, help Ben and Jessie tidy up down below."

Bruce went on regardless. "I went to pick up my new mainsail at the airport this morning and there he was, waiting for the flight to Tahiti."

"Hold on, Bruce," my father interrupted. "Victor, what did I just say?"

I ignored him. I'd done my share, day after day, night after night, standing watch on his boat. When I went below it would be to sleep, not to tidy up.

Bruce breezed through mutiny. "He wouldn't give his name. Weird, huh? He knew all about you, though he didn't know you're following Slocum's route. I told him you'd blow past here. He's on his way to Samoa by now."

My father jerked his head, leaving no doubt that he wanted me gone. I took my time leaving. Behind me, Bruce continued.

"Sounds European, Poland or Hungary, or wherever."

"Buff guy in black clothes, right?" I asked from the stairs.

271

"Like diesel soot, mate." Bruce grinned. "Gotta wonder why you know him, but your old man doesn't? I reckon that's why he said you were sharp as a tack."

My father snapped his fingers and pointed below. I ducked below the hatch, lingering on the stairs, full of unanswered questions.

"He showed your photo to everyone," Bruce went on. "I recognized you right away. You sure you don't have relatives in Australia, mate?"

"None that I know. It sounds like he expected us to be here?"

"He knew you left Concepción in April. It's a good bet you'd turn up here. Not much of a friend, if you ask me, but he's keen to find you, or he's got more money than sense. Before he left he gave me a hundred bucks and said there'd be a lot more if I called him when I saw you again."

My father's laugh sounded more like a grunt. "If he's who I think he is, don't waste your time."

"My feeling exactly, mate. I ran into someone else who knew you on my way through the Panama Canal. I tied up alongside him and we got to talking. Said he met you at Acklins' Island after your eldest out-swam a shark."

"Sal," my father said.

"That'd be him. Nice old guy. He could make a living telling stories," Bruce enthused.

My father loomed over the companionway. "Yeah, he's a nice old guy alright."

He was pissed at me again.

Chapter 35

Just before daybreak, my father switched on the light over my berth. I didn't recognize him at first. He'd shaved off his beard and dyed his hair dark.

"Get up." He dragged back my sheet. He only did that when he was in a hurry, or angry. "I need you to take me to shore."

Still groggy, I pulled on yesterday's clothes and clambered from my berth. It made no sense. The plane to Tahiti didn't take off until midday. From there, he'd fly to Los Angeles, and on to Virginia.

My mother was already dressed. She greeted me with a nod and a wink, a sure sign she wasn't angry with me.

"I've made tuna fish sandwiches. They're on top of your overnight bag," she said to him.

She went back to gluing postcards from French Polynesia in her scrapbook, slapping them down. He busied himself checking his wallet. I watched them sulk, the silence excruciating. Their spats never lasted longer than a few minutes.

"Why did you shave?" I asked.

"I don't have time to explain," was his curt reply.

"There's no need to be rude to him." My mother peeled away a misplaced card.

He stiffened. "I shaved if off because I felt like a change." He unrolled a chart on the dining table—Polynesia, its islands scattered across the Pacific like confetti outside a church. "Leave as soon as Victor returns. I've plotted the course."

"John, if you don't think it's safe for us to be here while you're gone, then you ought to stay."

"This is a precaution!" He pointed to Ua Huka, one of the 15 islands that made up the Marquesas Islands. "If everything goes okay, I'll look for you here in a week. Nothing longer than a day's sail. Shouldn't be difficult," he added when no one spoke.

"Why don't we stay here until you get back?" I asked.

"The bay's too dangerous when the wind picks up."

Winds from the south swept into Atuona Bay. It made more sense to move to the protected side of Hiva Oa. "How will you get to Ua Huka?"

He looked at my mother. "If there's a problem…"

"I know what to do." She leaned to kiss him. It lasted longer than normal. "Be careful."

"You too. I'll see you in a week, otherwise Plan B like we talked about. Listen to the Pacific Net every day, eight am and eight pm." He picked up his overnight bag, stuffed the sandwiches inside, and started up the stairs, making more noise than he needed to. "I don't have all day, Victor," he called impatiently.

+ + +

An amber sky inflamed Hiva Oa's twin volcanoes. The air was sultry, still lacking the sticky humidity that followed the morning deluge. Along the shore, rangy sea birds cawed, flapping and pecking at each other. We climbed into *Squirt* without saying a word. My mother stayed in the cabin.

"Far end of the bay." He pushed away from the *Spray*.

"The dinghy dock is closer," I said. "The waves aren't as bad as yesterday so it'll be easier to land." Mosquitoes thrived where he wanted to go.

"Just for once, will you do what you're told?"

I kept my head down and motored slowly past the Aranui, a small freighter-cruise ship that went back and forth from Tahiti to the Marquesas. It had arrived during the night. We were nearly at the end of the bay before he spoke.

"I'm sorry." He stroked his bare chin. "Do I look different without it?"

"You don't look like Slocum anymore." It took some getting used to.

"It feels strange not having it. I started growing it when you were four."

"I always thought you grew it so you'd look like him while you were building the *Spray*."

"I wish it was that simple."

"Bruce said you look like someone he knew in Australia."

"I've never been there. Get in as close as you can." He pointed to an opening in the trees. Sharp, black basalt rocks lined the shore.

Before the outboard scraped bottom, I stopped the dinghy with the bow pointed into the sloppy waves.

"I left a book on the table for you," he said. "Stevenson's *In the South Seas*. Early on, he says the first experience of a South Sea island is like your first love. It should be a special memory."

"Like the rat we saw yesterday?"

He returned a dry smile. "Like the book, it's a bit gruesome in parts." He hopped over the side, holding up his bag and shoes. "Don't tell anyone where you're going."

"What about Bruce?"

"I'm not sure I trust him. He borrowed to buy his new sail." He looked back, Bruce's yacht barely visible in the huddle of boats.

"When someone is that short of money, there's no telling what he'll do."

"What are you and Mom fighting about?"

"I'm depending on you. I hope she listens to you more than she does to me."

"What are you fighting about?"

"She's worried about the man in black. She thinks I should stay. She's seldom wrong. She is this time," he added. "Last night when I went for a run, I checked at the airport. He's on his way to Samoa." He waded towards the shore, carefully placing his feet as muddy water surged around him.

"Be careful."

"I will," he said over his shoulder. After a moment, he turned around. He looked as gloomy as ever. "Tell everyone I said goodbye."

I waited until he reached the rocks. We exchanged waves. Dozens of squawking parrots flapped among the trees as he headed towards the road. He hoped to hitch a ride to the airport.

+ + +

At 7:30 am, my mother and I quietly hauled up the anchors. No other sailors were about as we crept out of the harbor, keeping as far away as possible from other yachts.

"Do you want to steer or put up the sails, Josh?" my mother inquired—my father never asked; he thought 'captain' was the nautical version of 'despot.'

While Ben cranked the winches, I scrambled over the cabin roof, removing sail covers and releasing lines, returning to the cockpit to help him tighten the halyards, just the last couple of inches—not bad for an eleven-year-old boy whose main exercise was carrying his encyclopedia back and forth.

With the mainsail, jibs, and mizzen sail aloft, the *Spray* bounced over the waves. Soon, the waves grew bigger, the wind stronger. Sheets of water flew over the bow, rushing down the scuppers before it went over the side. We changed course according to my father's instructions and adjusted the sails to add another half knot. With the self-steering system doing the work, we settled back.

"I hope it's like this all the way to Ua Huka." My mother was trying to be cheerful.

"I don't like sailing without Daddy." Jessie blinked away tears. "What if something bad happens?"

"Nothing bad will happen."

"What if something breaks and you can't fix it?" Ben asked.

"Nothing will break, Ben." She sounded exasperated.

"What if Daddy doesn't come back?" Jesse was ready to bawl.

"He'll be back as soon as he makes sure that Grandma's okay." My mother glanced over her shoulder. Behind us, Hiva Oa rose steeply from the sea, bulbous clouds already gathering around its volcanoes. Against the dark cliffs, a sail was a brilliant white speck. "Nothing bad will happen."

We sailed 15 miles before the wind began to die down. Three hours later, we were halfway, sweltering under the sun, the sails sagging, the *Spray* wandering over the sea, leaving little more than a ripple behind.

"We won't make it by dark." My mother looked aft. Other than a tiny sail on the horizon, there were no boats.

"Use the motor," I suggested.

"Dad wouldn't. Diesel fuel costs too much. It pollutes the atmosphere too." Ben was studying environmental science.

"He isn't here."

My mother smiled sincerely for the first time since the argument. "We'll motor slowly."

We lowered the sails and started the engine. For five hours, we chugged towards a smudge that gradually took on the shape of an island, a jagged profile against the sunset-streaked sky. The closer we came to Ua-Huka, the more rugged it became. Volcanic pillars, like fat fingers, became increasingly difficult to see as the light faded. With the navigation lights switched on, we headed along the southern side of the island, where according to my father's instructions; we would find a suitable place to moor. All I could see were barren, scarred cliffs. There was a constant roar as waves thundered onto a shore littered with intimidating rocks and broken coconut trees.

My mother clenched the wheel as waves shoved the *Spray* close to a towering dark wall. While she cursed under her breath, her three children strained to see in the night. The cliff ended, opening to a small bay, the valley beyond dotted with lights. Other lights swayed as incoming waves rocked the boats in the anchorage. She steered the *Spray* into the center of them before lining up the bow with the waves.

"We might want to use two anchors." I was ready to go forward, life-jacket on, straps tightened.

My mother held me back. "We're not staying here."

"The waves aren't that bad," Ben said.

"I'm not worried about the waves, Ben." She pointed to a lonely light, a single star a few miles offshore. "It's that yacht we saw earlier. It followed us from Hiva Oa."

"You're as neurotic as he is."

"Being careful isn't neurotic, Josh." She switched off the navigation lights before turning towards the headland we'd just passed.

"So what if someone followed us? I don't understand why he doesn't tell the insurance company he had nothing to do with the Masons' trailer catching on fire." I almost added, 'assuming it's true.'

"It's more complicated than that."

"Did he have something to do with the fire?" Ben had heard the same explanation.

"He did in a way. It's not what you think." The *Spray* lurched when a big wave swept under us, rushing towards the cliffs. She waited until it crashed onto the shore. "He'll explain when he gets back."

After a while, she looked over her shoulder. The light was still there, no more than three miles away; however, without navigation lights the *Spray* was invisible. I stared at the light until it disappeared behind the headland.

"Where are we going?" I rubbed my eyes, knowing a long night was ahead.

"Nuku Hiva," she said. "You'd better get some sleep. I'll wake you at midnight."

I slept on the cockpit seat.

+ + +

When I woke up, I felt as if I hadn't slept longer than a few minutes. My mother sat opposite me, her thighs providing pillows for Jessie and Ben. The sea gleamed under the moon, a light breeze fresh on my face.

"We're way off course." I pointed at the compass; we were headed southwest.

"'Head for Ua Pou. Twenty miles out, bear northwest for Nuku Hiva,'" she read from a scrap of paper.

"That's dumb."

"It isn't if he wants us out of the range of radar before we change course."

"He knew someone would follow us?"

"'Hope for the best and plan for the worst.'" She sounded exactly like him.

There was no sign of the yacht, or any other boat, when we raised the sails and set the self-steering on the new course to Nuku Hiva. My mother napped on the cockpit seat between my brother and sister.

With dawn, dark ridges emerged from the sea, fingers spreading out to separate bays, each leading to a broad valley that rose up to towering volcanic peaks. We turned north with the coast a few miles away, the sails full of wind and boosted by the tireless swell from astern. In the lee of Cape Matauaoa, we motored to Anaho Bay. It was a semicircular cove enclosed by mile-long headlands. A fringe of coconut trees lined the beach, giving way to a dense forest of trees ripped by patches of rock. It stopped when the hills became too steep, turning into misty black pinnacles that diverted the trade winds.

My mother motored around the bay, closely watching the depth sounder. I was in the bow, looking out for dark spots, coral heads under crystal-clear turquoise water. My father was on a jet thousands of miles away, yet nothing changed; she chose a spot to anchor far away from the three other boats already there. Much closer was a long, narrow, white sand beach ending in a rocky promontory. We saw water spout from a blowhole moments before the morning downpour began.

Chapter 36

Anaho Bay was all but deserted—a few fishermen's shacks, a restaurant indefinitely closed for repairs, and a tiny Catholic church with a thatched roof, sand floor, and stools made of coconut trees There was no dock, shops, telephones, or roads. Without a boat, the only way out was a hiking trail, one way leading to the ocean, the other to Hatiheu, a village in the next bay.

Two days later, after we'd caught up on schoolwork and cleaned the *Spray* from bow to stern; we hiked to Hatiheu so that Ben could see an archeological site. By then, we'd learned firsthand about no-nos—hordes of tiny sand flies that swarmed down from the hills, with a bite that swelled up and itched. No-nos were plentiful among the trees, bearable on the beach, and only a few ventured over the water as far as the *Spray*. We covered ourselves in mosquito repellent, even under our clothes. Secure from attack, we headed up the hill, sliding in ankle-deep mud and climbing over boulders covered in slippery moss. Mud covered my legs, splattering on my face and arms. In the still humid air, beads of sweat trickled down my forehead and dripped from my nose. A gang of no-nos buzzed my head, not stopping long enough for me to swat them.

"A bunch of old stones is worth this?" I snarled at my brother, shoving aside tree branches and tangled vines.

"They dated some artifacts to 95 BC. That isn't old; it's ancient! It made historians rethink how Polynesia was settled."

"Now you're a frigging archeologist?" My mother and Jessie were a long way behind.

"They were cannibals." My gruesome brother seemed to think people eating each other made ruins worth visiting.

From the ridge, I looked out over craggy hills and saw-toothed bays. A spine of vertical slices of rock, like enormous vertebrae, protruded out of the next hill. Clouds swirled past the highest peaks with long wisps trailing behind. Towering coconut trees, brilliantly plumed birds, and a profusion of flowers made an exotic Garden of Eden, yet evil still lurked in the reek of rotting undergrowth. Cannibalism wasn't that far away.

"You can smell the frangipani." My mother had finally caught up. She wiped her brow and turned to look back the way we'd come, the wind on her face. "John thought Hiva Oa was paradise. I wish he was here to see this."

"He'd be overjoyed. Almost no other people."

She gave me a reproachful look until I conceded. Except for no-nos, frequent bouts of rain, and having no one to talk to except my family, it was paradise.

On the other side of the hill, the village of Hatiheu straggled beside the bay. No more than a few hundred people lived there, though it had a red-roofed church, a one-room school, and an infirmary spread along a single road. My spirited brother led the way down, oblivious to a wall of mist with rain not far behind. We took shelter under a banyan tree, a fig tree that surrounded an existing tree with thick aerial roots like gaunt ribs. Soon, a man and a woman slithered down the hill, snatching at vines and bushes to stop from sliding in the mud, their clothes already soaked, their legs daubed black.

"May we share your tree?" the woman shouted over the rain beating down.

My mother waved and they hurried over to join us, crowding close to get out of the rain. They had the same 'can-do' manner typical of people who sailed around the world.

"The daily deluge, right on schedule." Water dripped from the man's chin. "We're the Carletons. Our boat's the *Rigmarole*. I'm Roger."

"I'm Megan," the woman said on cue. "We're from Southampton."

"We're the Walkers." My sister did a fair imitation. "Our boat's the…"

My mother interrupted her. "I'm Virginia. The kids are Josh, Ben, and Jessie in order of size."

"You're from the *Spray,* aren't you?" Megan wiped her face with a sweaty handkerchief.

Jessie didn't hesitate. "That would be us."

"When I saw you drop anchor, I said that's it, didn't I dear?" Roger said.

"Exactly how he described it." Megan continued dabbing her cheeks.

My mother stiffened. "Who?"

"The little man with the toy trawler," Roger said with a snicker. "God only knows how he made it this far."

"I don't think we've met anyone like that."

My mother's guarded response matched my own fears. Who else could it be but 'dumpy dude?'

"You'd remember him." Megan was insistent. "He has awful taste; green shorts and a shocking yellow and purple striped shirt."

My mother and I exchanged a quick glance. As unlikely as it was for a small motor boat to cross the Pacific Ocean, it could if it carried enough fuel.

"He went to every boat to ask if we'd seen you. He's gone now. He left on Tuesday, headed to Taiohae," he continued.

"I'm sure you can contact him on the Pacific Net. He has a SSB radio." Megan said.

They had the same gray hair cut short and sun-weathered faces, matching khaki shorts, white golf shirts, and leather sandals. Like my parents, it seemed as if they knew what the other was thinking.

"We've run into him before. I'd prefer that he doesn't know we're here." My mother rested her hand on Jessie's shoulder, hinting she had reason to be careful.

"He is rather odd, I must say," Megan agreed.

Eventually, the rain slowed to drizzle. Through the mist, men unloaded trucks, stacking bags of dried coconut on the black sand beach far below.

"The Aranui arrives tomorrow," Roger explained.

+ + +

It was a few minutes before 7:00 pm when we boarded the *Spray*. Exhausted, we rinsed off mud and repellent. My mother turned on the SSB radio a half-hour ahead of schedule, hoping he had something to report and could get to a radio. Instead, there was a discussion about repairing a diesel motor in French Polynesia. It went on and on, a hundred cruising sailors giving their opinions on anything mechanical, from finding parts to deficiencies of certain engine models.

When it ended, a woman said, "Calling the *Spray*. Calling the *Spray*"

There was no mistaking my grandmother's voice. She was nervous, yet like a college professor giving instructions to sophomores, she precisely said each word.

"It's Grandma!" Ben's shout reached from my parents' cabin. He was teaching my sister to play chess.

I put my guitar aside and bolted from my cabin, reaching the radio at the same time as my brother and sister. He snatched the microphone to respond.

My mother grabbed his wrist with a floury hand—she'd been making fish cakes for dinner. "Put it down!"

"She sounds like she's close."

It wasn't often that I had a chance to correct Ben. "There's no way of telling. SSB radio waves bounce off the ionosphere."

My mother lifted her eyes. "Only you and John would know that."

"Calling the *Spray*. Hello." My grandmother was confident, full of life as usual.

In the background, a man quietly coached, "Say 'over.'"

"Calling the *Spray*, over," my grandmother repeated.

"I want to talk to Grandma!" Jessie pushed past Ben.

"Be quiet so we can hear," I said, sounding just like my father.

All of a sudden, my mother snapped off the power switch.

"Why did you turn it off?" I demanded.

She exhaled like *Squirt* did when we deflated it. "Hope for the best, expect the worst. He expected another radio call. We won't answer until he says it's okay."

"You're as crazy as he is." I pulled away when she tried to touch me.

"Josh, you don't understand."

"Then, explain it to me!"

"We don't know what happened. Until we know, it's best not to…"

"We could find out by talking to her," Ben interrupted, as frustrated as I was.

I didn't need to hear any more. "None of this makes a damned bit of sense. We can't talk to Grandma! Creeps are following us where ever we go, and he cares more about following Slocum!"

"He cares enough to fly back to Richmond," she said.

With her hand on my shoulder, she steered me to the table, Ben and Jessie trailing behind. I looked up at Slocum, staring down from his frame, still lacking glass. My father had the same eyes. They searched the horizon day after day, or looked right through me.

"You think something bad happened to her, don't you?" I demanded.

"That man speaking in the background worries me."

"I don't understand why Dad doesn't tell the insurance company what happened," Ben said.

"Because it isn't that simple, Ben."

"The insurance thing is bullshit! He did something bad, didn't he?" I remembered his face on the night of the fire in Norfolk.

"I told you it involves him, but not like you think."

"Yeah; he'll explain when he gets back. I got it, Mom!"

She switched on the radio again. My grandmother had finished. Twenty minutes later, after several sailors finished complaining about their slow voyage from the Galapagos Islands, my father came on. It was 8:45 pm.

"I have a message for *Squirt*."

"That's us," Jessie squeaked, jumping up. "Can I talk to Daddy first?"

"The situation is as before," he said. "Mr. Black was at Richmond. He hasn't left town as I thought. Take appropriate steps. I'm on it, going a new way. Out."

After an ominous pause, my mother turned off the radio.

"What's he mean, 'as before?'" I asked.

My mother abruptly shook her head, wiped her hand over her eyes, and slowly stood up.

"He didn't use proper procedure," Ben pointed out. "He never said the call signs, not even where he was calling from."

"Daddy sounded so close." Jessie started to sniffle.

"He's probably at one of the marinas in Norfolk or Portsmouth. That was the plan." My mother leaned on his navigation table, confronting long rows of CDs.

"We should've told him Grandma called us on the radio tonight," I said.

"He'd have heard her if he was listening earlier." Ben was trying to be helpful, but SSB radio transmissions were unpredictable.

"Who's Mr. Black?" Jessie asked.

"He means the man in black, Honey."

"The good news is he's on it," I said.

My mother flinched at my sarcasm. "He was sending us a message, Josh. When he said 'I'm on it,' he emphasized 'on.' The first time Grandma called us from Omaha, Nebraska. He's probably going there next; it's the only thing that makes any sense. I've no idea what he meant with 'going a new way.'"

"What does 'take appropriate steps' mean?"

"He means we should be alert, that's all. There's nothing to worry about. We'll do what we always do." She looked at each of us in turn.

Ben and I exchanged a quick glance. He didn't believe her either.

Chapter 37

We spent the following afternoon exploring the only coral reef in the Marquesas chain. Big sharks frequented the outside of the reef, along with manta and leopard rays, so we swam in waist-deep water on the beach side. It swarmed with schools of tropical fish: goatfish with yellow stripes on blue, crimson cardinal fish, blue and gold striped angelfish, fusiliers, and parrotfish. Exotically shaped and colored shells and black spiky sea urchins littered the sand. Rock lobsters darted from one crevice to the next. They were large, each big enough to feed several people. I went back to the *Spray* to fetch my father's homemade spear gun. He'd fashioned it from a length of aluminum tube and a piece of elastic cord, and it fired a spear made from steel rod. It worked when the lobster hid in a crevice and I could get close enough to shoot before it escaped. After Ben and I caught two lobsters, we waded back to the beach.

"Dad wouldn't be happy." Ben directed my attention to the yachts moored at the far end of the lagoon.

Now, there was another yacht anchored close to our *Spray*, a white ketch with a green stripe, the largest boat in the bay. I was sure I had seen it before.

We filled our arms with shells, lobsters, fins, masks, spear gun, and towels and began the trek to our dinghy. Suddenly, Jessie dropped her shells and stared, her hand shielding her eyes. A moment later, she screeched like one of the gray-backed terns that constantly wheeled overhead, and ran along the beach, whooping and waving her arms.

Ben slapped at no-nos buzzing his face. "What's got into her?"

"Someone's sitting in our cockpit," I said, hurrying towards *Squirt*.

My first thought, that someone was stealing our home, was unlikely—not in Anaho bay, with a population of five plus a dozen or so sailors. However, what replaced panic was just as unlikely. I didn't believe my eyes. Neither did my mother and Ben.

"It's not possible!" My mother did the unthinkable; she stood up in the dinghy to get a better look, breaking several rules including no life-jacket. She sat down when it almost flipped over.

"It's Grandma! It's Grandma!" Jessie bounced up and down.

As we approached the *Spray*, all doubt disappeared. There was no mistaking my grandmother from behind, her hair pulled into an orderly bun, her clothes tidily pressed. Suddenly, she glanced over her shoulder and grinned.

She welcomed us warmly, hugging her grandchildren one after the other, all chattering at once while my mother kept back, barely talking except for a soft-spoken, 'I'm glad you're okay, Mom.'

"You're all so brown," my grandmother gushed. "And you, Josh, you're so tall. I can't believe how much you've grown in a year."

Ben grinned. "He started puberty... finally."

"How did you get here?" I asked, glaring at him.

"With a great deal of difficulty." My grandmother sat down so that Jessie could climb onto her lap. "Where's John?"

"He's gone to find you." My mother was worried, yet I could tell she was as happy as I was. "We tried to call you, but your phone was disconnected."

My grandmother stroked Jessie's hair, tangled with sand and wind knots. "My house burned down." We stared at her, needing more details than that. Finally, she said, "That's why I'm here."

My mother looked miserable. "That's what John meant. 'It's the same as before.'"

My grandmother suddenly reached for her handbag, a bulging leather satchel on the cockpit seat. She dragged it closer and opened it far enough to peek inside. She patted the side. "Luckily, he's a very good traveler."

The bag moved as if something was inside it. Jessie's eyes grew wide. She leaned over and pulled the bag wide open.

"It's Jag!" she shrieked.

"I couldn't leave him behind, not after all we've been through."

Jag poked his head through the opening and looked around, bewildered, not at all like a cat that viewed the world with scorn unless he wanted attention. Jessie lifted him out of the bag, crooning while she stroked him, her face smothered in Jag's fur, spotted like camouflage.

"The day of the fire, I took him to the vet. He might've been eating my orchids and I couldn't take the risk. I heard the sirens while I was there, but I didn't think anything of it." She patted Jessie's shoulder. "When I got home the fire was out. There was nothing worth saving."

I could tell my grandmother was holding something back from the way she looked at us.

"There was some nonsense about a gas leak from my stove, only it wasn't an accident. I knew I couldn't stay in Richmond, so I drove all night and most of the next day."

"You drove all the way to Omaha?" Ben made it sound like she'd driven halfway cross the US.

"I picked the most unlikely place I could think of. How did you know I went there?"

"We figured it out from the call sign, and talking with other radio operators."

"I could've sent email, only I didn't know when you'd get it. I had to let you know I was okay. I found Phil on the Internet. He used to work for a radio station so he had a lot of equipment. When I told him what happened, he wanted to help."

"How did you get here, Mom?" My mother was as suspicious as he was.

"I was lucky. A friend of yours came on the radio when I tried to call you from Omaha. He was the only lead I had, so Jag and I flew from Denver to Honolulu to meet him. He's very allergic to cats so Jag had to stay in my cabin." She smiled at me. "He refers to you as 'Sharkbait.'"

"That would be Sal," I said. The big ketch was Sal's *Maid Marion;* no wonder it looked familiar.

"I couldn't have found you without him, although I still don't know why he helped me."

"I don't see how Sal knew we were here?" Ben said.

"Someone told him you were at Easter Island, so the Marquesas made sense. We didn't know where in the Marquesas until we called on the radio last night. A nice English couple said you were here," my grandmother replied.

"That would be Megan and Roger." I could tell my mother wasn't happy about it.

My grandmother stood to stretch her legs. "Apart from losing my house, I'm glad I'm here. I can see why John always wanted to visit Polynesia. Look, there's even a dolphin to welcome me!"

A few yards from the *Spray*, the dorsal fin of a big, white-tip shark sliced through the water.

+ + +

Shortly, an inflatable dinghy headed in our direction. Sal was just as I remembered him, white hair, curling eyebrows, leathery skin scorched brown, and scrappy fisherman's clothes. He waved when he saw me, and I promptly waved back, relieved that my father wasn't with us. His wife, who might have been a model when she was younger, sat in the middle of the dinghy. A girl about my age sat in the bow. She looked Italian, her skin dark against a white blouse, her hair pulled back into a long, curling ponytail. As the dinghy drew nearer, I realized I'd seen her before.

"Yo Sharkbait!" Sal shouted over his motor. "You still swimmin' wid dose shark frens?"

"When I'm not fly fishing." I waved my arm the way he'd taught me.

The dinghy swerved abruptly and the motor died. As it came alongside the *Spray,* I caught the line he tossed and tied it to the rail.

He grinned at me. "Island time still works. The things that happen quickly, you never expect."

I grinned back. "The rest take forever."

He climbed aboard, followed by Marion, his wife, and his granddaughter, Dani, which was short for Daniela. She barely mumbled 'hello.' Whenever I looked at her, she looked away.

Suddenly, Sal noticed my father was missing. He frowned. "Where's John?"

"Daddy went to find Grandma," Jessie had her arms full of contented cat, staying as far from Sal as possible.

"How did you join the *Maid Marion's* crew, Dani?" It was obvious my mother didn't want to talk about our captain.

"I'm always with Nonno for the summer." Dani was the only person I'd met who didn't call him 'Sal.'

293

She peeked at me. Her eyes were brown like Sal's. She smiled like him too. I wanted to impress her, to say something funny. My tongue felt too big for my mouth.

"Unfortunately, she goes back to school at the end of August." Sal's constantly dripping nose made him sniffle. "We want her to stay longer, but her mom wants her back." He turned to me. "I hear you've had some adventures since Luperón."

"He can tell you over dinner. You're eating with us," my mother insisted. "We'll put Jag in the bow cabin so he doesn't bother you. I'll need fruit, and two more lobsters, Josh," she added, as if all I needed to do was dive down and pick up a couple.

+ + +

Bananas, papayas, mangoes, and breadfruit grew wild, although birds scavenged most of the fruit. The trees had been part of someone's garden, the house having disintegrated long ago. The jungle had consumed everything except a few rotting planks, foundation stumps, and stones along the sides of a path.

"It looks like a big grapefruit." Dani pointed to a pamplemousse, a yellow-green fruit eight inches in diameter.

"It's sweeter." I pulled off one, worked my thumbs through the thick skin, and forced it apart. Inside was white and dripping with juice. I handed her half. She regarded me warily until I ate some. She peeled off skin and sucked on a giant segment, making a wry face in the process.

"It grows on you," I laughed.

At the risk of agreeing with my brother, in the jungle everything grew on something else, or fed on it. Nature boy never tired of pointing out symbiosis. There was moss wherever I looked, ferns, lichen and clinging vines. Orchids were splashes of color destined for Ben's rapidly growing specimen collection.

"Like Polynesia?" Dani could tease like her grandfather.

I'd told her when we first arrived, I hated it. "I've never been happier, even though the no-nos are a pain and it rains every day."

She smiled. Like me, she reeked of repellent and her hair was damp from the last afternoon shower. Still undecided, she ate another piece of pamplemousse—French for pomelo from Asia, Ben's *Citrus maxima.*

We rambled along the path until it joined the trail to Hatiheu, stopping at the creek to cool off. A thin ribbon of water cascaded from a cleft in an imposing black wall into a pool before tumbling over volcanic rocks. We followed the creek through the jungle, wading or hopping from rock to rock, all the way to the beach, emerging opposite the *Maid Marion.*

Ben and Jessie waited for us by the dinghy with tomatoes and avocadoes they'd purchased from one of the houses at the far end of the beach. On the way back, we stopped at the reef. It took ten dives to catch a lobster. Another lobster got away when the elastic inside the spear gun broke.

+ + +

We sat in the cockpit, eating lobster salad, coconut rice, and cornbread that my grandmother had baked, talking and listening to snippets of news and well-intentioned advice on the Pacific Net until the sky grew dark and the Southern Cross appeared.

"I hope you didn't have to out-swim a shark this time," Sal said to me, after enthusing about the lobsters I'd caught.

"You really beat a shark?" Dani asked.

"I was lucky. The shark had already eaten." Finally, I got her to laugh until it hurt.

"Mommy always says he's the lucky one in the family." That night, Jessie talked more than I'd ever seen, always to Dani, constant girl-chatter as words stored up inside her rushed out.

"Sarah tells me you've had some adventures since I last saw you," Sal said to my mother. "Josh almost died from appendicitis?"

"It ruptured so Mom had to operate on him," Ben said, sounding like a doctor.

"You're lucky to have a mom who's a doctor," Dani said.

"She's a nurse." Nature boy was into facts, not feelings.

Dani looked at him strangely. "But Nonno said…"

"I'm a nurse," my mother interrupted. "He's still lucky though. I might've been an accountant."

Sal chuckled. "Doctor, nurse, it doesn't matter. He was in very capable hands."

"There's another boat arriving." I pointed it out, a light at the entrance to Anaho Bay. Too close to the horizon to be a star, it had to be a fishing boat or another yacht coming into the bay.

"It's getting crowded. If Dad was here we'd leave in the morning," Ben joked.

"Speaking of leaving, I'm nearly ready to call it a night. Do you want to fix your spear gun before we go?" Sal said, turning to me.

I started downstairs to get some elastic cord from the locker where my father kept his spare parts.

"Turn the radio off and put on some music while you're below," my mother said. It was too late for my father to contact us.

"Which Russian composer would you like to hear? We have all of them," I said.

Sal chuckled. "Let's see if you do. How about… Borodin's Third Symphony?"

"We have it, only Dad doesn't like to play it."

"I still remember hearing Borodin's great grandson conduct the New York Philharmonic. A dozen years ago it was, *Pre-Revolution Russian Concertos,* one of his best performances."

"Sal!" My mother's tone said 'enough'.

"After all that's happened, isn't it time?" My grandmother sounded tired.

"I'd rather it not be now."

Dani and I exchanged glances when Sal abruptly got up. "I hadn't realized it was so late."

Marion stood too. "Thank you for a delightful dinner. It's been a long day."

I watched them climb into the dinghy. Dani gave me a questioning look. I said a polite goodbye. Inside, I fumed.

I waited until they'd gone. "What was all that about?" Somehow, it was my father's fault.

"Later. We still need to organize below." My mother owed me an explanation, not another ploy. "Ben, you'll be in the spare berth. Josh, you take Jessie's berth. Mom, I'm putting you in the bow cabin. Jessie, you can sleep with me until your father gets back."

"There's no need for the boys to move. The spare bed, berth, or whatever it's called will do just fine."

"You can't climb over the dining table, Mom."

"Why can't Jag and I share with Grandma?" Jessie was ready to bawl.

"Of course, you can, Sweetie. I'll sleep in the spare bed and the boys won't have to move."

"Mom, can we do this my way? It's difficult enough as it is."

"I'm sure he's okay." My grandmother gave Jessie a hug. "We'll share the front room, okay."

My mother conceded with a tired smile. We went below and carried blankets, pillows, books, toys, and clothes back and forth. Only Ben's encyclopedia remained where it was. There was no place for it in the main cabin. He carried one volume to his berth and climbed in. Like my new berth, it was like lying in a coffin tucked under the deck. A canvas flap stretched across the open side, providing token privacy and too much enclosure.

I went on deck to get the spear gun. The air was humid, slightly cooler than it was during the day. Saw-toothed peaks loomed over the bay, shadows against the star-filled sky. A faint breeze wafted down, bringing the smells of the tropics: fruits and flowers, and rotting coco-palm leaves. The *Maid Marion* was the closest yacht, so far away that I couldn't see more than its masthead light and a few pinpricks of light coming from the portholes.

Back in my berth, I dismantled the spear gun, removing the end caps, withdrawing the slide from inside the tube, and extracting the broken elastic cord. Reassembly took longer—it really needed two pairs of hands to insert the slide and ensure that the lengths of elastic were the same size. When I drew back on the cord to make sure the slide moved freely, it needed adjustment—the elastic was too tight to reach the latch. It could wait until morning. Ben said goodnight and turned off his reading light. There was a faint murmur from the bow as my grandmother once again told the story of Actaeon and Diana.

+ + +

I jerked awake, smelling fumes. It wasn't the stench of diesel from the engine room. It was the same smell the outboard had when it leaked. My sheet was wet and it stuck to me when I sat up. I yanked it away. Gasoline was everywhere. It even dripped from the ceiling. My mouth opened to scream when I saw a shadow in the cabin I used to share with Ben. Not twelve feet away, a man leaned over my sister. I got a better look at him when he turned to the berth where my grandmother slept. He had square shoulders like my old swim coach. He doused her with gas before he moved silently through the main cabin, splashing from a gas tank as he went. When he disappeared behind the engine room, I slid out of bed.

There wasn't time to retrieve my father's handgun, even if I could open the sliding panel and figure out how to use it without killing myself. Instead, I grabbed the spear gun, fitted the spear, and dragged back the elastic. I ducked behind the galley counter as he came out of my parent's cabin. 'Buff-guy' knelt on the seat and leaned across the table to pour the last of the gasoline on my brother.

When he turned, he saw my berth was empty. Then, he saw me. Unhurriedly, he placed the gas tank on the table while I struggled to hold back the elastic. I couldn't stretch it more than seven or eight inches before it slipped through my hand, not even halfway. I pointed it at him. He stared at me like a snake charmer's cobra, moving inch by inch across the seat. His eyes were as dark as his clothes.

He smiled as if a smile made a difference. "You were lucky before. This time your father's not here to save you." His accent was Russian.

"I'm still lucky, asshole."

He charged out of the seat and I let go of the cord, releasing the spear. For an instant, I thought it hit him because he lurched back. Slowly, he looked over his shoulder. The spear skewered my father's photo of Joshua Slocum. He turned back, smirking.

"You're not as lucky as you think you are, Alex," he sneered.

"My name's not Alex."

"Oh, but it is. They named you after your great, great grandfather. Are you as musically talented as he was?" He edged closer.

"You don't know what you're talking about."

"You don't remember the first time you saw me, do you?"

"It was in Florida." I gripped the spear gun tube. He was still too far away to hit, the galley counter between us.

"Before that, when you were three? Do you remember what happened after the fire? You should; you were in hospital for a month."

The gasoline smell made me dizzy. I needed fresh air. I glared back at him, ready to thrust when he came within reach. "It's news to me."

"I would've finished the job, except a nurse came in. After that, your family vanished. We wasted years looking for you in Australia. Not a sign of any of you until we saw your grandmother's photo in the newspaper. It should have ended at Arcadia Park."

I lunged. He deflected the tube, grabbed my arm, and twisted it back, all in a second. It felt like he ripped my arm out of the socket before the tube clattered on the floor. Both hands locked on my neck, his thumbs forced in.

"Pressing here stops the blood from flowing to your brain," he leered in my face.

He could have snapped my neck if he wanted. Instead, he applied just enough pressure. I flailed wildly, my head about to explode. He followed me down to the floor when my legs gave way, straddling me with his thumbs jammed into my neck. Ben came from behind him, his arms reaching over his head. He slammed down the *Britannica*, stunning the man.

"Mom!' Ben screamed from beside me. He tried to drag the man off me. A lightweight eleven-year-old, he would need a block and tackle to budge him.

"What's going on?" My grandmother had a wet sheet wrapped around her.

My mother emerged from the aft cabin, her nightgown soaked. "There must be a fuel leak, Mom. There's no need to panic. Diesel fuel won't explode."

"MOM!"

When she turned to ask what Ben wanted, she finally saw me sprawled behind the galley counter, pinned under the man. It took their combined effort to get me out from under him. I staggered to my feet, coughing until I collapsed. She hauled me up again.

"What on earth?"

"Gasoline," I wheezed in a voice that wasn't my own.

"Oh my god! Mom, get Jessie!" She shoved Ben towards the stairs, ignoring his protests. "Now Mom, not tomorrow!" she screamed when my grandmother didn't follow.

"I'm getting some clothes. Jessie, what on earth are you doing?"

Jessie wailed. "I'm not leaving without Jag."

"Jessie, come on." My grandmother dragged Jessie by one arm, snatching one of my T-shirts from a pile on the settee as they passed.

My mother pushed me to the stairs and made me climb, one step at a time. "Josh, get in the dinghy! I'll look for Jag."

I stumbled to the stern. There were two dinghies, *Squirt,* and a tiny, two-person inflatable with paddles.

"Jag's up here," Ben shouted. "I've got him."

I climbed down with a death grip on *Squirt's* line. Ben was next, holding our squirming cat by the scruff of the neck. The floor of the dinghy was awash with gasoline, the fuel line ripped from the outboard.

With my family aboard, my mother pushed away from the Spray and got out the oars. When we were a safe distance away, she carefully felt my neck.

"Your luck nearly ran out," was all I heard.

I didn't need to hear that. I was about to say so when a flashlight searched the water. It came from the mock trawler, between the *Spray* and Sal's *Maid Marion*. It settled on us, like deer in the headlights.

"We'll head for the beach." My mother did her best not to splash as she jerked at the oars.

Chapter 38

We were a strange looking sight had anyone been walking on the beach at five o'clock in the morning—my grandmother wearing my 'I love New York' tee shirt, my mother in a flimsy nightgown she bought in Rio de Janeiro, her children dressed for a hot tropical night in their underwear. Everyone watched the *Spray*, expecting a fireball to light up the sky at any moment.

"Why on earth would he try to kill us?" Ben voiced my thoughts as well.

"Who is he?" my grandmother asked.

"One of them." My mother looked around, shaking her head. "I really don't know."

"Buff Guy's no insurance investigator, that's for sure." When I breathed, my head throbbed. My neck hurt so much I had to sit down. My father was gone when we most needed him. I was tired of lies and excuses that made no sense.

"Josh, he was wrong to lie to you, but now isn't the time." She sat down between my sister and me. "He was following us, Mom. We haven't seen him since Rio. John said he was at Richmond."

"He didn't follow me here." My grandmother looked around uneasily. "I was careful about that."

"Even if he did, it doesn't matter, Mom. They would've found us eventually."

"Who are they?" I figured I had a right to know who was trying to kill me.

"Josh, I promised. He thinks you're safer not knowing."

"Mommy, I think I see him." Jessie clasped Jag tightly.

Ben walked to the water's edge and peered into the gloom, tilting his head from side to side. The *Spray* was a dim shadow against the sky, her masthead light almost lost in the stars.

"He's getting into his dinghy."

"We can't stay here." My mother got to her feet. "Stick close together. I don't want anyone getting lost."

She took Jessie's hand, bundled Jag against her chest, and led the way. Soft, silent sand gave way to dead palm fronds that crunched under our feet. Jessie hobbled along, her feet curled up to avoid splinters. After a dozen yards, the jungle took over; slimy mud and decaying leaves squelched under our feet. The thick undergrowth was impenetrable except for a few narrow tracks that were difficult to find even in daylight. Thorny branches scratched our skin or snagged the few clothes we wore. One branch ripped my mother's nightgown. We stopped to untangle it.

I thought I could hear someone coming closer. I wasn't the only one. My mother hugged Jessie tightly. Ben and my grandmother held hands, all of us blindly looking about for the source of the sound. The jungle thrived around us, foraging rats, mating insects, a wild pig rooting among leaves. I concentrated so hard that my ears hummed.

"And I used to think your trailer park was scary."

At another time, my grandmother's whispered comment would've been funny, not with a man in black stalking us, his clothes like an invisibility cloak. I was certain that he was in two different places when something snapped, not a branch, a mechanical click. Three clunks followed in quick succession. Other than movies, I'd never heard a gunshot muffled by a silencer. I knew what it was, my mother too. She held her finger to her lips.

"He's coming towards us," Ben whispered.

My mother shoved him down when a flashlight flared to our right. It shifted back and forth, pausing erratically. It stopped directly over our heads, so close that even the slightest movement would draw his attention. Eventually, he moved away.

"Grandma, you're bleeding," my sister murmured.

My grandmother's face was very pale. Blood seeped from a deep gash near her ankle. "It's nothing, sweetie. Just a scratch." Her hand shook as she wiped it away. She turned to my mother. "It might confuse him if I head back to the beach."

"We stick together." My mother was barely able to hold on to our squirming cat.

"That's what he expects us to do."

Instead of arguing, my mother nodded. My grandmother hobbled away. I had an appalling thought that I'd never see her again.

We forced our way through tangled vines and exotic ferns. I was sure we were heading back to the beach until I stumbled over a stump. It was a palm tree trunk driven into the ground, part of the foundation of a house, a few rotting wood planks scattered about, and an abandoned garden edged with stones. I recognized the pamplemousse tree, the path to Hatiheu not far away.

"I can't hear him," Ben whispered. "Maybe he's given up."

Suddenly, Jag leaped from my mother's arms and disappeared into the night.

"Jag!" Jessie cried, too loudly.

An oversized grapefruit exploded, splattering juice and bits of rind over my face. We fled, slipping and sliding on the muddy trail. We ran all the way to the creek before we paused to catch our breath. Right away, another bullet thumped into a tree a few feet away from my brother. My mother jumped into the creek, dragging

305

Ben behind her. I shoved Jessie after them, keeping low and scrambling over slippery boulders as the man crashed through the undergrowth. To my right, a wild pig hurtled past. It squealed when it slammed into a tree.

"You're next, Alex!" the man shouted.

Somewhere in the darkness, someone called, "This way!"

Jessie stopped too. She gripped my hand. "Daddy?"

"Ya soskucheelsya," our pursuer jeered.

"I can't say I've missed you," my father shouted back.

"You came on the Aranui, Comrade?"

"What would you do?" My father was closer.

"Take the bait, same as you, though I expected you on today's flight."

"I thought you might have someone waiting."

He answered my father with a round of muffled gunshots. Birds burst from their roosts among the trees, flapping and screeching in the darkness. Jessie shrieked and flung up her arms to protect her face when they came too close. She slipped and fell in the water, floundering until I pulled her out. From the noise behind us, the man in black was closing rapidly. I pulled her after me, paying no heed to her cries as I tried to catch up to my mother and brother, clambering over rocks, wading through knee-deep water, ducking low hanging branches. When I stopped, the beach was close enough to hear waves lapping the shore.

A tree ripped from the ground thrust tangled moss-covered limbs over the creek. It was the last obstacle to overcome. Just ahead, the eastern horizon glowed, silhouetting the *Maid Marion's* masts. I could see lights shining from portholes, another light on deck.

Something brushed my arm. My father whispered, "Keep moving. Don't stop again, no matter what." He gave Jessie a hug before he crept away.

I pushed my sister under the tree trunk into a labyrinth of roots and vines. Spiders' webs stuck to my face. I clawed them away and shoved at her, urging her on. The creek widened on the other side of the tree, trickling over stones embedded in the beach. My mother and brother waited for us beside an inflatable dinghy only a hundred paces away. Instead, of running with me, Jessie tottered a few steps and crumpled onto the sand. She tugged at my hand. Her ankle was the size of a tennis ball.

"It appears your luck has run out, Alex," came from behind me. 'Buff guy' smirked despite blood smears on his face, his shirt ripped to shreds, his left shoe lost in the jungle.

"Why are you doing this?" I pulled Jessie to her feet. pushing her towards the beach.

"Payback for what happened in New York," he said.

"I've never been there."

Jessie hobbled a few feet before she fell down again.

"You were born there." "You got those scars on Long Island."

"I fell on a heater in our trailer."

He said to keep moving. I backed away from Jessie, away from the beach.

"You got them when your grandparents' house burned down."

"You were there." I was never so certain about anything.

"You do remember." He dabbed a black handkerchief against his forehead.

My father lurked among the palm trees. Crouching low, he crept closer.

"Did you use gasoline then too?" I had to keep him talking. Now, there were four people next to the dinghy, and my father was only a few yards away.

"It was during Zagarovsky's trial so it had to look like an accident." His eyes darted between Jessie and me. "I turned on the gas. Unfortunately, there wasn't enough to explode properly."

"You tried to kill my other grandmother the same way." I could barely get the words out.

"I scared her so she'd lead us to you. Unfortunately, we lost her after Omaha. No loss because you turned up at Hiva Oa." He pointed his gun at my head.

My father leaped across the intervening sand and tackled him at mid-thigh. It knocked him off balance and stopped him from shooting me. He stepped back and slammed his pistol into my father's face. My father staggered, yet he still dragged him down. They fought for the gun, a jumble of knees, elbows, fists, and butting heads. 'Buff-guy' was bigger and stronger. It was only a few seconds before he dislodged my father long enough to point his pistol at me. He fired as I lunged away, like leaving the diving blocks in a 50-yard race. I plowed into the sand. The bullet missed me, yet I could've been dead. I was so scared nothing worked. I heard a loud grunt and my name before I raised my head. My father was too distracted to stop the fingers squeezing into his neck. His face was already darker.

I crawled across the sand. As soon as I reached his side, a powerful blow sent me sprawling onto my back. I was trying to get to my knees when I heard a hammer claw smash into a conch shell. The man toppled onto the sand. Tony stepped over his legs, his pistol aiming at the man's bloody forehead.

Sal hurried across the beach with my mother and brother. He gave me a passing glance before he shone his flashlight next to my father. "Recognize him, Tony?"

"Dmitri Barkov, ex-KGB. The Bratva's top man."

"Russian mafia; they give Sicilians a bad name." He turned to my mother. "How is he?"

She knelt by my father. I couldn't see his face. Ben could. He backed away.

"I treated worse at Norfolk General every Friday and Saturday night." Her disciplined calm always amazed me.

"Sarah..." my father gasped.

"She's safe on the *Maid Marion.*" Sal smiled at me. "You must've learned shark baiting from her. She swam the whole way, bleeding from her leg, and at night too."

"He's coming around, Sal." Tony planted his foot on Barkov's chest. "You want me to off him?"

"No..." My father tried to get up. "Call the police." Blood covered his face.

Sal snorted. "Are you crazy? Zagarovsky's out of prison. You need to vanish right now."

"Who's Zagarovsky?" Ben asked.

"A Russian drug dealer. Barkov's boss. I'm surprised he's not here. He usually has others do the legwork, and then he turns up to finish the job. Probably the same reason why Faro's not here." Tony stopped when Sal coughed.

"Is he short and wears ugly shirts?" I said.

"That would be Mogilvich. He's harmless unless he's got the upper hand," Tony chuckled. "You wouldn't want your daughter marrying him."

"That's his boat," I pointed out the trawler, a shadow without anchor lights. "He followed us all the way from Florida."

"I'll take care of him." Tony sounded as if he relished the opportunity.

Sal tapped his lips. "He couldn't have gotten here without an automatic pilot. Set it for north so it looks like they're heading to Hawaii. Once you're out of the harbor, open a seacock part way. It ought to take a couple of hours before it sinks. It'll be out of radar range well before then."

Again, my father tried to intervene. My mother hushed him.

Chapter 39

The sun dropped under the afternoon clouds, shooting golden rays across Anaho Bay. The mountains glowed with the concentrated colors of sunset, the jungle a myriad shades of darkening green. The shadows grew longer, stretching the *Spray's* masts across the lagoon, her bow pointed to sea as if eager to go. Within minutes, the sun disappeared again, hidden behind rocky pinnacles, turning them into guards like the gigantic statues on Easter Island.

I picked notes and chords on my guitar and strung them into soulful lines. One line was the clouds drifting over the jagged peaks, another palm trees whispering, yet another, the waves washing onto the shore and yachts swinging at anchor, everything that I wanted to remember about the South Seas islands. The cedar face of my guitar was hazy with age, yet each note was as clear as the day Ignacio Fleta made it in Barcelona.

My father watched me, one finger keeping time. He was more relaxed than he'd been for months. When I finished, I thought I saw the start of a smile. He still looked strange without his beard.

"That was truly beautiful." Sal seemed distracted. Crows' feet pulled at his eyes.

When Sal had suggested a traditional Polynesian pig roast on the beach, my father was indifferent, yet they'd spent most of the day hiking to Hatiheu to buy the pig. The rest of us dug the pit, made the fire, and wrapped pieces of pig and tropical vegetables in banana leaves before burying them among glowing hot coals. We sat on the sand for three hours, waiting for the underground oven to finish cooking,

"Does it have a name?" Marion asked me.

I shrugged and hoped Ben would keep his mouth shut. He blurted out, "Dani's Song."

Sal smiled, my mother too; even my father seemed amused. Marion added to my embarrassment with, "You'll have to play it again when she gets back."

Dani searched for Jag with my grandmother and Jessie. After three days of scouring the hills surrounding Anaho Bay, we'd almost given up hope. Every few hours we took turns walking the length of the beach and calling his name.

"Music runs in your blood," Sal said before he turned to my father. "The other branch of your family tree."

"All I know is my grandfather played the piano and this was my grandmother's." I strummed a few chords and put my guitar back in its battered brown case, hoping to leave it there when Dani returned.

"Are you ever going to tell him?" my mother asked my father. He didn't reply.

"Tell me what? That my real name is Alex?"

He looked at my mother. I waited for him to say something. He didn't.

"Do I have a real name too?" Ben asked, sounding hopeful.

"Benjamin Aymar. We were going to call you..." My mother made him wait. "...Nicholas."

He made a face. Clearly, he disliked 'Nicholas' as much as 'Aymar.' Compared to 'Aymar,' 'Victor' was normal.

"Not Nicholai?" Sal asked.

My father took off his sunglasses. His right eye was bloodshot and surrounded by bruises. "He won't be safer if he knows everything."

"The more you know, the safer you are," I said under my breath.

My father looked like I'd kicked him.

Tony nodded with authority. "He certainly won't be less safe."

"Nowhere is safe," Sal said pointedly. "Isn't it time they knew the truth?"

"They don't need to know everything, John,." As always, my mother was the voice of reason.

My father made me uneasy while he stared at the sea. I had a bad feeling that he wasn't turning his back on me as much as the truth was so terrible that he didn't want me to know.

"My father was Russian," he began. "When he wasn't composing, he played cello in the Leningrad Philharmonic. They visited Germany in '56. He met a language student there, from Oxford University. Four years later, when the Orchestra was in London, he defected and married her."

"You make it sound so unromantic," my mother chided. "They had two boys, Peter and Nicholai, 11 months apart."

"Your parents named you after a Russian composer?" I asked.

"Your great grandfather started the tradition. I expect you to continue it."

If it was his idea of a joke, I wasn't amused.

Ben was amused. "I'm calling my son Igor."

He was tone deaf like my mother, yet he still knew Stravinsky. Tony slapped his thigh and gave Ben a 'high-five'.

Sal sat back, swilling wine in his glass. "You must have had an interesting childhood: growing up in London, learning other languages, surrounded by famous musicians?"

"We were constantly traveling so it was mostly a blur. I do remember when Segovia gave Victor's guitar to my mother. I'd just turned 12. It was the day before we moved to America." He looked at me approvingly. "She knew what she was doing when she left it to her first grandchild."

"After hearing Josh play just now, I'm sure your brother would agree," Sal said.

"You really have a brother?" Ben was as skeptical as I was.

My father merely nodded.

Sal waited until it was clear he wasn't going to elaborate. "They were both very talented. Peter was the better musician; I saw him conduct the New York Philharmonic. Tchaikovsky's *First Piano Concerto* was never better. Nicholai was the eldest. He worked for the FBI as an undercover agent. He was very good at it; maybe too good at it."

"Unfortunately." My father's tone made me hesitate to ask.

Ben barged right in. "What happened?"

"It was a few months before Josh turned four," my mother said when he didn't answer. "I was pregnant with you and trying to complete my internship, and…"

"You're really a doctor?" At the same time, Ben looked down the beach.

"She would've been a thoracic surgeon had she finished." My father was proud, no doubt about it.

Suddenly, Ben leaped to his feet. "They found Jag!"

Jessie and Dani waved frantically. Behind them, my grandmother carried Jag, taking no chance on him getting away again. When I looked back, my father and Sal were talking quietly. I didn't need to hear what they said to know we'd leave in the morning.

It was my turn to ask. "What happened?"

My mother answered again. "You spent the summer with your grandparents on Long Island."

"He doesn't need to know everything," my father butted in.

Tired of lies, I wanted to ask, 'Why not?' Some of it I could barely recall, like hot afternoons in the garden and my other grandmother teaching me strange sounding words. Twice a day, my grandfather taught me music. He was stern and sometimes impatient, yet he could also be gentle, like my father had been when I was in hospital.

"You were there the night their house caught on fire. He got there just in time to save you." She waited for him to say something. He didn't.

"Barkov started it." Like glimpses of a dream, most of it was just out of reach.

My father flinched. "You remember?"

"He was downstairs."

The house on Long Island was old, with a wide porch and a shingled turret on the corner, overlooking a bay. It had a circular staircase inside it, a playroom below, and my bedroom at the top. I'd used that stair on the night of the fire when I went downstairs to find Barkov creeping about.

"Your grandparents were in bed when the explosion happened. Your grandfather—his name was Alexander too; we think he tried to get to you…" My mother stopped and touched his arm. "It must have been awful."

"Your pajamas were on fire when I found you," my father said softly. "You were in terrible pain. I couldn't leave you alone. By the time the police arrived, the fire was out of control."

"You watched?"

He nodded slightly, not about to tell me what he'd seen.

"You made the right decision," my mother said, her voice no more than a whisper.

"Why did Barkov want to kill your parents?" Ben asked.

"He was after Victor. They got in the way. "He stared at me until I couldn't stand it. "Barkov tried again while you were in the hospital. It was obvious you had to disappear."

When he didn't continue, my mother said, "We left New York two days later. My mother came with us. You were her favorite. She gave up everything, her career, the rest of her family."

I looked up quickly. Later, I'd tell them about the old man in the sculpture garden, coughing as he shuffled down the path before the nurses discovered that he was missing.

My father finally turned away. "It was to send a message."

"What message?" I was tired of meaningless excuses. I guessed. "Because of the trial?"

"That was part of it." Sal was grim-faced. "Zagarovsky gets to the father by killing his eldest son."

"That's insane!"

My father nodded. "Very likely... It's also very effective."

I was about to ask, 'what did you do to him?' when Sal intervened.

"I was sure Zagarovsky would be here. Faro too. Maybe we'll run into them in Tahiti. I've got a score to settle with them."

"Did Zagarovsky kill Dante?" I was sure of the answer even though Sal didn't reply.

"Zagarovsky's been out of prison for 18 months," Tony said. "I'm surprised you lasted this long."

"Somehow they discovered we'd changed our names," my father said.

Right then, I decided never to tell him what Barkov said about my grandmother's photo in the paper. It wasn't her fault.

"Barkov traced us to Arcadia Park. He got the Masons by mistake," he went on. "We were lucky the *Spray* was finished."

Since I was four, I'd wondered why he built the *Spray*, why he wanted to sail around the world. It was who he was; however, it was more than that. He'd rebuilt our lives around Joshua Slocum.

"Your father read *Sailing Alone Around the World* to you too, didn't he?"

He smiled. "It was his favorite book. He used to say that music and sailing had a lot in common. We sailed on Long Island Sound every weekend until I went to college."

"What's our real name?" I asked. Not only were people not what they seemed, or what you wanted them to be; sometimes they weren't who they thought they were.

My father leaned closer. "We named you after my favorite composer; that's all you need to know."

I didn't understand. "So Dad, are you named after Tchaikovsky or Rimsky-Korsakov?"

After a moment, he began to laugh as if something pleased him deep down. "You and my brother are a lot alike, Alexander."

+ + +

With half of the voyage remaining, this isn't **THE END**. From French Polynesia, my father intended to follow Captain Slocum's route to Samoa, and then to Australia. From there, we'd sail across the Indian Ocean to Africa, and back to America. The Captain took three years, two months, and two days to sail around the world. My father's dream would take us as long.

A Preview of Chicken Too

Chicken Too

Neil Barry

Chapter 39 of *Chicken of the Sea* leaves Victor Joshua Walker's family reunited in the Marquesas Islands of French Polynesia, yet his father's paranoia is little changed. Two weeks later, the sun is a fireball on the horizon when Victor's grandmother thinks she sees a ship steaming towards them. A near collision leaves the *Spray* without an engine and drenched from bow to stern. They divert to Tahiti to make repairs, only to discover that Victor is still in danger. His father relocates to nearby Moorea, rebuilding the *Spray's* engine while the rest of the family stays at a resort hotel. What should have been welcome relief from cramped quarters in a luxurious tropical paradise, turns tragic.

With a $100,000 reward on Victor's head, each new port is a step closer to disaster. Despite murderous Russians and Filipino pirates, the Walker family, like the truth, remains just out of reach. Despite losing almost everything, Victor is never closer to his father than when they arrive in Australia. A breathtaking conclusion leaves Victor more confident, wiser, and with a family he never expected. With the mystery seemingly revealed, except for one question, and Zagarovsky taking a personal interest in Victor's demise, the family continues the journey into the final book, tentatively titled *Free Range Chicken*.

Chapter 1 of Chicken Too

I was fourteen when my father shaved off his beard. Since I was four, he'd had a mustache and a goatee, a bristly tuft on his chin that he dyed to look like the rest of his hair. A beard never belonged on his face, yet after two weeks of shaving, I still wasn't used to seeing him with soap and a razor, instead of trimming stray hairs with his manicure scissors.

"What are you looking at?" he demanded.

"What a nice day it is," I fixed my gaze on the peaceful Pacific Ocean behind him and tried not to smile. He looked ridiculous with a blob of foam on the tip of his nose.

He scowled at me, lather covering one cheek and streaks on the other. He made a few more strokes, put aside his razor, and wiped soap from his face. I quickly glanced down at my book. I was a heartbeat too slow.

"It won't be long before I'll have to teach you how to shave," he said, turning my head to the side.

I jerked away and dabbed foam from my chin. "It's not so difficult that I'll need instruction."

He hummed with Modest Mussorgsky's *Night on Bald Mountain*. I should have stayed in the cabin until 4:00 pm when my watch started. My little sister was less annoying.

He leaned over to check our speed. "We're making good time. Two weeks if this wind keeps up."

Under my breath, I said, "Good luck on that."

No sailor ever complained about trade winds. A steady breeze over the stern made for a pleasant voyage, easy sailing for our 38-foot yacht. My father built her from scratch the old fashioned way.

The *Spray* was far too small for six people and a cat, yet he was always quick to point out that small had advantages when it came time to put up the sails. The *Spray* was also slow, to which he countered his boat had an agreeable motion. It didn't. It wallowed through the long ocean swell, up and down, rolling from side to side. It was like living inside a washing machine day after day. I was lucky; I seldom got sea sick. My little sister and grandmother were constantly puking.

I turned back pages of Joshua Slocum's *Sailing Alone Around the World*, glimpses into the Captain's journey until I found what I wanted. "This part took him 29 days."

A month without setting foot on land! Sailing with the trade winds from behind was mind-numbing, yet vastly better than battling storms, or being becalmed.

"The wind hasn't changed in three days," he replied airily.

"It's the same time of year."

He dispatched my point and the possibility of fluky winds with a shrug. He was brushing his teeth when the wind veered south. Shortly, it expired. With feeble puffs, the *Spray* slowed to a crawl. I hated the thought of being cooped up a day longer than necessary.

"A temporary lull, right?"

He missed my sarcasm. "The wind will be back. A couple of hours, give or take."

Doubtless, our captain was right—astern, puffy clouds loomed on the horizon. However, prognostications of weather conditions based on cloud formations were as fraught with uncertainty as such ancient mariner sayings as 'Red sky at night, sailor's delight. Red sky in morning, sailor's warning.' Magnificent sunsets preceded some of our worst storms at night.

"Two weeks to Apia," he said, back to humming.

Apia, Samoa, where we were headed, was 1,250 miles west, two or three days on American expressways, rest stops and fast-food restaurants included. It didn't seem to bother my father that reefs dotted the course he'd mapped out. All around us, the sea was deep dark blue; however, atolls could appear without warning when the tips of volcanoes reached up from the depths. Usually, they didn't break the surface before coral took over. Captain Slocum wrote of the same stretch of ocean: 'coral reefs kept me company, or gave me no time to feel lonely.'

However, I was lonely. The gap between my father and me was as far as Apia. I had more in common with my brother, three years younger. Ben spent every spare moment reading his Encyclopedia Britannica, insisting it held the answers to all of life's questions. My sister and grandmother talked endlessly, making up for lost time. Whenever we went ashore, my mother collected postcards and travel brochures. At sea, she shunned the technology of the 21st century and documented our journey in scrapbooks with floral cloth covers. And me? I read novels from my father's collection of classics when I wasn't playing my guitar or doing school work by long distance.

Danielle, my closest friend, was 590 nautical miles astern in the Marquesas Islands. I'd known Dani for only twelve days, yet we'd become inseparable. I missed her even more than I missed her grandfather's stories.

"Sal must think Zagarovsky's in Tahiti," I said, hoping to steer the conversation in that direction.

Dani, her grandfather, Sal, and his wife, Marion, were headed to the Society Islands: Tahiti, Bora Bora, and Huahine. Sal hadn't said why they were going to Tahiti; however, everyone knew it was because of Zagarovsky.

"More likely he's back in New York selling crack. You'd think after twelve years, Sal would get over it."

"If someone killed my son…"

"Revenge is self-destructive." He always interrupted me.

He was about to lecture me on life's lessons when my brother came up from the cabin, lugging a Britannica volume. Ben occupied the opposite seat, choosing shade from the mainsail over sunburn and peace and quiet.

"Zagarovsky tried to kill me and you don't seem to care," I said, choosing persistence over common sense.

My father inclined his head as if he hadn't heard properly. After a few moments, he slowly nodded. "You think it's only luck that you're still alive?"

"I didn't mean it like that. You always say running away from your problems doesn't help."

He made me wait. It was never a good idea to confront him directly. "What makes you think we're running away?"

"Aren't we?"

"I've always wanted to sail around the world," Ben said quietly.

It was my father's dream, not shared by the rest of his family, to sail around the world. He said we'd be gone as long as Joshua Slocum—it took him three years, two months, and two days. God help us!

"We've seen the last of Zagarovsky's goons," my father declared. He hadn't heard Ben.

I didn't share his confidence. "What about Faro? Sal said nowhere is…"

He cut me off again. "I know what Sal said. If we report what happened to the police, we'll be cooling our heels for six months.

That's why we're getting as far away as possible. We should've left right away."

"He said Faro was even more dangerous..."

He glared at me so I skipped the rest of what Sal said about the need to be very careful. He also said running wasn't the solution. Zagarovsky would catch up eventually.

When I looked up again, he was watching me. "What?" I heard my voice break.

"Your eyes are just like your mom's."

"Mom's eyes are green."

"I meant my mother. Your grandmother. You're a lot like her."

"She had blue eyes, huh?"

"Ben looks more like my father," he said.

Ben put aside Volume XI. "What color were his eyes?"

"The same color as yours and mine. Brown."

Ben muttered what might have been 'no way,' his usual response when something aroused his interest and he couldn't explain it.' He picked up the pencil we used to record the *Spray*'s position, frowning as he scribbled on the scrap of paper that served as his bookmark.

"What color eyes did Grandma's husband have?" he asked.

My father pulled on his chin as if he expected to find a goatee. "The last time I saw Thom was before you were born. Ask your grandmother."

Ben went to find her, lugging his encyclopedia with him.

I took advantage. "Did I get anything else from your side of the family?"

"Your grandfather's love of music." He checked his watch. "You've got the wheel, Victor."

"We left him in the Marquesas, remember?"

"Good luck on that."

He'd used 'Victor' to annoy me, his way of letting me know he'd heard me earlier.

"I wasn't complaining," I said.

He ignored me. "No shipping channels to worry about until this evening. Keep an eye out for Caroline Atoll. Give us a call when we're closer."

He recorded our position, cast his gaze over the sails and rigging, and scanned the horizon. He always followed routine as if getting a step out of order would result in catastrophe.

"Aye, Captain."

"Pay attention. Just a mile off course could be a disaster in these waters, Victor."

I blocked my ears to the rest of his lecture and returned to my book. He knew I hated 'Victor,' yet he declined to call me "Joshua' like everyone else. After he'd gone to his cabin to nap, I occasionally looked up—no sign of civilization, no ships, no vapor trails all the way to the horizon. There were a few wispy clouds far astern, a reminder of where we'd come from.

+ + +

Unlike the rugged volcanic islands of the Marquesas, Caroline Atoll was flat and deserted, a skinny necklace of dozens of tiny sand islets and coral heads defining a half-a-mile wide lagoon. Scattered coconut trees burst through thick clumps of vegetation on the three largest islands. Everyone trooped on deck when I called them, even my father, rubbing sleep from his eyes. It was the first atoll we'd seen. For an hour, we sailed beside it, staying clear of reefs extending far into the sea.

Still unused to the ever-moving *Spray*, my grandmother preferred to sit in the rear of the cockpit. She crossed her legs, tilted down the brim of her sunhat, and folded her arms.

"Your boat rocks a lot, John." She grimaced, coughed twice, her expression rapidly approaching what my mother called 'squeamish.'

"Watching the horizon usually helps, Sarah."

She was already staring at the horizon. She gave a dissatisfied sigh. "It doesn't help."

"You're taking it remarkably well," my mother said. She meant my grandmother's house, burned to the ground, everything gone.

"It could have been worse. Even after all these years, I still have some things in storage."

My grandmother shifted her gaze from the horizon to my eight-year-old sister, my eleven-year-old brother, and me. Her gloominess struck a chord with me. I could think of nothing worse than losing my home.

"I was awfully sad when you left last year," she said

"We didn't have a choice," my father said. "You should've left with us."

"I'm here now." She didn't sound happy about it.

My grandmother's queasy face and near constant cough forewarned another bout of seasickness. It didn't stop her from helping Jessie arrange feathers on a square of plywood, scrounged from a dumpster in Hiva Oa, our first port of call in the Marquesas. They ranged from delicate colorful feathers from small tropical birds to straggly, long feathers from sea birds. My sister even had a huge albatross wing feather that someone had given her.

"Great Frigatebird!"

Jessie shouted it out, although the bird was impossible to miss—black with an eight-foot wingspan, and a long, forked tail. It soared close to the waves, veering away at the last moment.

Ben barely glanced up. *"Fregata minor."* With my grandmother's help, he'd mastered Latin pronunciation in two weeks. Now, she was teaching him Greek for good measure.

"They eat flying fish right out of the air." Jessie had my brother's enthusiasm for science.

"Because they can't land in water." Ben was the voice of authority on anything natural.

My grandmother glanced over the side as the bird swooped down over swirling water. She gulped air and swallowed, making a wry face. I hated the taste of bile even more than the actual throwing up.

"Try some of Jessie's ginger," my mother suggested, although it seldom worked for my sister.

"I'm fine." However, my grandmother grew paler with every wave. She handed me the pin jar. "Be a dear and help Jessie with her feathers." She looked nauseous. It had been two days since she'd been seasick. "I'm going to lie down for a while."

My mother and Ben went below too. My father watched Caroline Atoll disappear behind the waves. "About 30 miles to that shipping channel," he reminded me. "It shouldn't be a problem. It runs north-south, and it's not very busy."

"You have to pin both ends so they don't fall off," Jessie said as soon as he left. "I want the pins straight," she added after I bent the first pin.

"You want to do it?" I pulled out the pin and inserted another. There wasn't much room left on the board.

"It's loose." She wobbled the pin from side to side until it fell out.

"The wood's too tough." I tried again, pushing until the head of the pin hurt my thumb.

"Stop doing that," Jesse complained.

"Doing what?"

"You're doing that thing with your thumbs again, like they're broken."

"You want the pins pushed in or not?" I snapped.

"Mine don't do that." Jessie pressed her thumb pads together. Hers were straight. My thumbs bent back.

"Josh's got hitch-hiker thumbs," Ben called from the cabin. "Double jointed is recessive." He was studying seventh-grade science, two years ahead for his age. "No one else in this family has them. It proves he's adopted."

"Ben!" my mother barked.

I'd finished pushing in the rest of the pins, mostly straight, and returned to reading my book before my grandmother popped her head through the companionway. She inhaled deeply, savoring air laden with salt.

"It's so stuffy in the front room," she said. "I opened the skylight, but it's much nicer up here."

The 'skylight' was the forward hatch—she'd opened it all the way, breaking my father's seventh rule for safety at sea. However, the sea was so calm it wasn't worth worrying about.

"I think the sea air agrees with me." She handed me my history book. "Your mom says you have a big test tomorrow." She

328

leaned in to add, "I won't touch his sails, but if you tell me what to do, Alex, I'll be lookout and you can study."

Except for my grandmother, my real name was never used; and then it was quietly. It was as if my early years didn't exist. I grinned back at her and gave my version of my father's ten-points on keeping watch. "If it flies or swims, call Ben. If you see anything else, call him."

"What if I see a ship?"

"We're still 22 miles from the shipping lane, but if you see a ship, take a bearing on it."

"What on earth is a bearing?"

"A compass direction." I showed her how to sight over the compass. "If the bearing changes, we're not going to collide." As seafaring rules went, CBDR (constant bearing-decreasing range) was spot on, which was why my father said that not paying attention always preceded collision.

While my grandmother kept watch, I studied Russian history, a long march through wars, tyrants with impossible names, court intrigue, and social turmoil. The late afternoon sun grew steadily stronger, heating up the air under the awning until my clothes prickled. The wind was a hot humid breath that sucked out my energy. With no ships on the horizon and nothing else to do, I stretched out on the cockpit seat with my arm blocking the sun. My grandmother went below to see about dinner.

It seemed like only a minute later when she shook me awake. She pointed into the sunset and said quite calmly. "I'm not sure, but I think a ship is coming towards us."

Captain Joshua Slocum

Captain Joshua Slocum, 1844-1909. Century Magazine, September, 1899. US Library of Congress

Captain Joshua Slocum was the first person to sail alone around the world. Slocum departed Boston, Massachusetts on April 24, 1895. His voyage ended on June 27, 1898 at Newport, Rhode Island, more than three years and 46,000 miles later.

"The Spray's dimensions were, when finished, thirty-six feet nine inches long over all, fourteen feet two inches wide, and four feet two inches deep in the hold, her tonnage being nine tons net and twelve and seventy-one hundredths tons gross. Then the mast, a smart New Hampshire spruce, was fitted, and likewise all the small appurtenances necessary for a short cruise. Sails were bent, and away she flew with my friend Captain Pierce and me, across Buzzard's Bay on a trial trip – all right. The only thing that now worried my friends along the beach was, 'Will she pay?' The cost of my new vessel was $553.62 for materials, and thirteen months of my own labour."

Sailing Alone Around the World by Joshua Slocum.

"On July 1, however, after a rude gale, the wind came out nor'west and clear, propitious for a good run. On the following day, the head sea having gone down, I sailed from Yarmouth, and let go my last hold on America. The log of my first day on the Atlantic in the Spray reads briefly: '*9.30 a.m. sailed from Yarmouth. 4.30 p.m. passed Cape Sable; distance, three cables from the land. The sloop making eight knots. Fresh breeze N.W.*' Before the sun went down I was taking my supper of strawberries and tea in smooth water under the lee of the east-coast land, along which the Spray was now leisurely skirting."

Sailing Alone Around the World by Joshua Slocum.

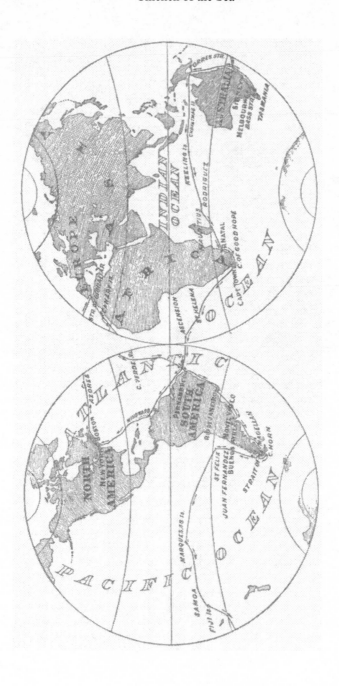

Captain Joshua Slocum's route, illustrated by Thomas Forgarty and George Varian in *Sailing Alone Around the World*, published by New York Century Co. in 1901.

The Walker Family's Spray

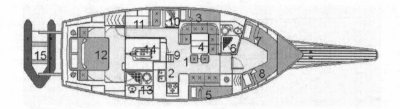

The *Spray*, modeled on Bruce Roberts-Goodson's Centennial Spray 38 ©, which is based on Slocum's *Spray*. Reproduced with permission.

1. Salon

2. Galley

3. Spare berth

4. Dining table

5. Jessie's berth

6. Head

7. Josh's berth

8. Ben's berth (Britannica under)

9. Companionway stairs

10. Chart table

11. Storage/workshop

12. Parents' cabin

13. Parents' head

14. Engine room

15. Squirt

Charts

Charts of the Walker family's journey are available at the author's website, neilbarrybooks.com. Go to 'Fact in Fiction', then click on 'Charts.' For example, one chart depicts the *Spray's* route, March 12-14, on the Intracoastal Waterway (ICW) in the vicinity of Beaufort, SC. It was created using open-source navigation software available from www.opencpn.org. Interested readers can follow the *Spray* by downloading Opencpn and obtaining charts from:

http://www.charts.noaa.gov/InteractiveCatalog/nrnc.shtml,

or use the online chart viewer;

www.nauticalcharts.noaa.gov/mcd/NOAAChartViewer.html.

For example, using the chart on the website, you will see that after leaving Charleston on March 11, the *Spray* negotiated St. Helena Sound into the Coosaw River, before turning to port into Parrot Creek. With the propeller tangled, the *Spray* was towed to Edding Creek. Two days later, the journey continued, with a stop at Beaufort for lunch in the park.

Another chart shows Victor Joshua's navigation exercise in the Bahamas. Print off the chart and try it for yourself.

A third chart shows the part of the around-the-world voyage covered by *Chicken of the Sea.*

Readers can also use GoogleEarth and Wikipedia to explore where the Walkers visited. Neilbarrybooks.com also links to YouTube videos on places visited by the Walkers (See Fact in Fiction-Interesting Places).

Glossary for sailing beginners

Abaft : a seldom used expression for near or towards the stern, often from a given reference point, such as 'abaft the beam', meaning back from the beam.

About : to change direction of the vessel by passing through the oncoming wind (tacking); e.g. to go about.

Adrift : not under sail or engine power, moving at the whim of the wind and sea.

Aft : towards the back or rear of the boat.

Aground : stuck on the ground, a mud bank, sand bar, or worse (rocks or coral).

Ahead : to go forward, or what is ahead of the vessel.

Aloft : anything above the deck and cabin, to go up the mast/into the rigging.

Anchor : a heavy metal 'claw' designed to grab hold of the sea floor and keep a boat from moving.

Anchorage : a place protected from wind and waves, with bottom conditions suitable for anchoring.

Apparent wind : combines both the true wind direction and the boat's speed and direction.

Astern : pass to the rear of a boat, as in to 'go astern', meaning to go behind the boat, or to leave astern.

Autopilot : a computer-controlled mechanical or hydraulic-powered device to steer the vessel. Often connected to a chart plotter.

Avast : To cease and desist. 'Avast there, mates,' if said with a pirate accent, means 'stop screwing around, guys.'

Backstay : the wire cable running from the back of the boat (stern) to the top of the mast.

Batten : a wood or fiberglass strip inserted through the leech of a sail, sometimes extending as far as the luff, to improve sail shape, support the leech, and prevent fluttering.

Beaufort Scale : a 0-12 scale of wind strengths (calm through hurricane) and identifying characteristics. For example, Force 6 is a strong breeze, 24-31 mph or 21 to 27 knots. Expect to see long waves with foamy crests and some spray.

Beam : the width of the boat, or a direction, as in 'off the beam' meaning perpendicular to the vessel. Replaces athwart.

Bearing : the direction to something, usually relative to the boat or a chart.

Bear away : to turn away from the current direction usually with respect to the direction of the wind, also 'bear off.'

Beating : to sail as close to the wind as possible.

Becalmed : when the vessel is motionless because of lack of wind.

Below : under the deck, as in 'to go below'.

Berth : a nautical bed, usually narrow, sometimes wet. The expression 'to give a wide berth' is not about a captain's generous berth allocation, but to avoid something (another vessel) by a wide margin. Also, berth refers to where a vessel is normally docked.

Bilge : the part where the side of the boat turns into the bottom of the boat, also the bottom of the boat where smelly water gathers.

Bimini : a sun cover of canvas stretched over the cockpit, and supported by a metal frame.

Binnacle : a stand or support for the ship's compass.

Bitter end : the last part of a line or anchor rode.

Boat hook : a sometimes-extensible pole with a hook in the end to catch things like mooring lines, pets, and hats when they drop in the water.

Bobstay : a wire running from the bow to the end of the bowsprit to relieve the load from the forestay.

Bollard : a hefty short post typically attached to the dock. Used to secure boats.

Boom : the stick attached near the bottom of the mast allowing the sail to pivot with the wind.

Boom vang : a system of ropes and pulleys, or a spring-loaded rod used to stop the boom from lifting up.

Bosun's chair : a canvas seat used to hoist crew up the mast to make repairs.

Bow : the front part of the boat.

Bowline : a temporary knot, easy to tie, and untie after being loaded. See http:// en.wikipedia.org/wiki/Bowline.

Bow line : the rope connecting the bow to the dock.

Bowsprit : the 'stick' extending from the bow, allowing the boat to carry more sail, not be confused with the anchor roller.

Bridge : the elevated position from which a boat is steered, or an overhead structure requiring care to go under.

Broach : when large waves and/or strong wind cause a vessel to lose control and turn sideways, often heeling dramatically, with a chance of rolling over.

Bulkhead : a vertical partition in the cabin providing stiffening/watertight compartments for the hull.

Buoy : a float used to mark a position or thing.

By and large : a common expression of nautical origin, meaning a vessel performs well going into the wind (by) and with the wind (large), so all possible points of sail.

Capsize : to turn the boat over by 90 degrees, or more. Not recommended!

Cast off : to let go mooring or dock lines so the boat is free to move.

Catamaran : a boat with two hulls side by side.

Chaffing wearing of lines against things causes them to fray and eventual fail. Prevented by chaffing gear, for example, covering the affected part with hose, canvas, or leather.

Chart : a map used on a boat, showing details of the coast and what is under the surface.

Chart plotter : an integrated computer and monitor that presents navigation charts and the vessel's location. Enables courses to be plotted as routes, or tracking of the vessel's movements.

Cleat : a fitting for preventing ropes from moving. For example, a dock cleat.

Clew : the corner of a sail furthest from the bow.

Close-hauled : to sail as close to the wind as possible. Requires hauling the sails in tightly.

Coach house : part of the cabin projecting above the deck, often with larger windows.

Cockpit : a somewhat protected area for sitting and steering, usually lower than the deck.

Come about : to change direction by passing through the wind.

Companionway : the entrance to the cabin, usually as stairs from the cockpit.

Constant bearing-decreasing range (CBDR) occurs when one vessel maintains a constant bearing relative to another vessel, while the distance between them (range) decreases. This is a collision course.

Course : the direction that is a boat is to be steered. Course over ground (COG) is the actual course after including the effect of wind, tide, and current.

Current : a flow of water from one area to another (not a tide, where the water flows back).

Cutter : a single-masted boat with two jibs. Also a fast motor boat often used by the Coastguard.

Davits : a small crane or spar used to lift things, such as a dinghy or outboard motor.

Dead ahead : directly in front.

Dead reckoning : is the process of using estimates of direction and distance traveled,and sightings of landmarks to determine a vessel's position.

Dinghy : a small open boat. Some dinghies can be inflated.

Dock : a place to tie up a boat for a period of time and walk on dry land, also a pier or wharf. To dock means to tie up at a dock.

Dodger : a see-through screen with a hood at the front of the cockpit to deflect wind and waves.

Draft : the minimum depth of water a boat requires in order to float.

Drogue or sea -anchor is a device towed through the water to slow down a vessel. Can be a parachute, a long length of rope, a large cone, or a series of small cones attached to a long line.

Fathom : six feet.

Fender : an inflated cushion between boats, or a boat and the dock to prevent damage to the hull.

Fiberglass :a durable, strong composite of polyester resin and layers of cloth made from glass fibers. Used for the vast majority of boats manufactured since the 1950s.

First rate : an expression derived from the top-of-the-line sailing warships (100 guns) from the 1600s through 1800s.

Flare : a pyrotechnic/firework, either hand-held or fired from a gun to draw attention to a vessel in distress.

Following sea : waves from astern, going in the same direction. Under certain conditions, the vessel can surf the wave, picking up considerable speed and a chance of losing control. Waves that overtake the boat can be especially dangerous if the wave is breaking.

Foot : the bottom of a sail.

Fore : forward or front, as in fore-deck (the deck between mast and bow), and fore-peak (the cabin squashed into the bow).

Forestay : the wire cable from the top of the mast to the front of the boat.

Forward : toward the front of the boat, as in "Go forward and drop the anchor."

Frames : ribs that form the hull's shape, typically used in wooden boats.

Furl : to reduce a sail's area. Jibs and genoas are typically wound around the forestay. In a similar fashion, mainsails may be furled inside/outside the mast, or inside the boom. The alternative is storing the mainsail along the boom by folding the sailcloth.

Gaff : an oblique stick attached near the top of the mast. Used to hold the top side of a four-sided sail, while allowing it to pivot with the wind direction. Also a pole with a sharp hook on the end to assist in bringing fish aboard.

Galley : the kitchen in a boat.

Genoa : a large, powerful jib overlapping the mainsail.

Gooseneck : a fitting connecting the mast and boom, allowing the boom to swivel.

Grounding : an ill-advised contact between the boat's hull or keel and the bottom (ground). Also used in lieu of 'bonding', a process of electrically connecting all metal (engine, thru-hulls, etc.) and the top of the mast to minimize damage in the event of a lightning strike.

Gunwale : the edge of the side of the boat and the deck.

Gybe : the process of changing course and/or repositioning the sails from one side of the boat to the other with the wind coming over the stern. A dangerous maneuver if the wind is blowing hard. Can occur accidentally if not paying attention.

Halyards : 'ropes' used to hoist and lower sails.

Hank : a metal or plastic hook/device to connect a sail to a mast track or forestay.

Hatch : an opening in the deck or cabin roof to allow light and fresh air to enter.

Head : the top corner of a sail, , to 'head up' is to sail closer to the wind or into the wind also a nautical toilet.

Heading : the direction the boat is going in.

Heave to : to stop the vessel by sheeting the jib to one side and locking the rudder in the opposing direction.

Heel : the vessel leans sideways, induced by the wind's sideways force on the sails.

Helm : the steering wheel, as in the command 'take the helm'.

Jackline : a continuous line running from the bow to the stern for crew to clip on to when moving about on deck. Essential when conditions are dangerous and/or there is a risk of falling overboard.

Jetty : a stone wall projecting from the shore to protect boats in a harbor. Also a quay.

Jib : a triangular sail in front of the mast, with one side usually connected to the forestay.

Jury rig : using whatever is at hand to make a temporary rig in the event of dismasting.

Keel : the very bottom of the boat, usually cast from lead. A sailing boat's keel functions to keep it upright.

Ketch : a vessel with two masts, the tallest one in front and a shorter one behind.

Knot : a speed equal to one nautical mile per hour (1.15 mph or 1.85 kilometers per hour).

Latitude : a geographic coordinate (distance) measured in degrees north or south (up to 90°) of the equator (0 degrees).

Lazy jacks : 'ropes' from the mast to the boom to keep a sail from falling to the side .

Leech : the aft or trailing edge of a sail.

Lee : the side sheltered from the wind, leeward is the direction away from the wind. A lee shore is on the side of the vessel opposite the wind. Being blown on to a lee shore during a storm is a good reason to be safely tied up at dock, or a long way offshore.

Life raft : an inflatable, usually covered raft used as a last resort when the vessel sinks.

Line (s) : there are no 'ropes' used on a boat. They are lines, unless specifically purposed as halyards, sheets, outhauls, downhauls, boom vangs, etc. Also see 'rode.'

Log : a record of a boat's operation with courses and events, also a device to measure speed.

Longitude : a geographic coordinate (distance) measured in degrees east (up to +180 degrees) or west (up to -180 degrees) of the Greenwich meridian (0 degrees).

Luff : the forward edge of a sail, also to head into the wind until the sails invert in shape and flap, sometimes very loudly.

Lying ahull : with sails removed, the vessel rides out a storm at the mercy of the sea while the crew cowers below.

Mainmast : the tallest mast.

Mainsail : the primary sail attached to the mainmast.

Mainsheet : line used to haul in the boom to adjust the sail's shape to wind conditions and direction.

Mizzen : (mast or sail) the mast or sail closest to the stern.

Mooring : attaching a boat to a sunken weight, or a dock.

Nautical mile : approximately one minute of latitude, or 6076 feet, 1.15 land miles, or 1.85 kilometers. Note that definitions of length vary. For example, the *American Practical Navigator* defines a sea mile as an "approximate mean value" of 6,080 feet; the length of a minute of arc along the meridian at latitude 48°."

Navigation : the process of way finding, from the current position to another position, conducting a boat from one place to another.

Oar : a rowing device connected to a dinghy and used to move it (not a paddle, which is used on a canoe).

Outboard : a detachable gasoline-powered motor mounted on the stern.

Painter : a line attached to the bow of a dinghy for tying up or towing.

Pier : a dock extending out from the shore.

Piling : a wood (or concrete/steel) pole driven into the bottom.

Pitch : the bow-to-stern up and down movement of the boat caused by waves.

Plane : when a boat lifts onto the surface of the water, rather than pushing through it. Most sailboats are displacement vessels, meaning they displace their weight in water and do not plane.

Port : the left side, identified with a red light at night. Also a harbor, a nautical destination.

Portlight : a waterproof window in the side of the cabin.

Pulpit : a safety railing at the bow, made of metal pipes.

Reaching : to sail with the wind off the beam, (ranging from 60 degrees to 160 degrees). A close reach has the wind forward of the beam, while a broad reach has the wind aft of the beam.

Reef : to reduce sail area by lowering the sail and tying up what is not used.

Rigging : the various lines, stays, and shrouds needed to support the mast and operate the sails.

Rode : the anchor rope or chain.

Roller reefing : used to reduce the sail area by winding it around the mast or boom.

Rudder : the board attached to the steering wheel or tiller which causes the boat to change course.

Run : to allow a line to move freely, also a direction of sail, such as running before the wind.

Running backstay : is an adjustable wire used to hold the mast from the rear, employed during severe wind conditions.

Safety harness : a harness made of webbing (or incorporated into a life jacket) enabling a crew member to be secured to the vessel during hazardous conditions.

Schooner : a sailing boat with two masts, the mainmast behind the first or foremast.

Scupper : a drain from the cockpit, or to enable water to leave the deck through the gunwale.

Sea anchor : see drogue.

Seat locker : a locker under the seats in the cockpit.

Seacock : a shut-off valve below the waterline; sometimes mistakenly called a thru-hull, which refers to a mushroom-shaped fitting penetrating the hull, and attached to a seacock.

Secure : to make fast.

Seasickness : motion sickness caused by the rocking action of the boat going through waves. The primary symptom is nausea, aka puking one's guts out.

Self-steering : a mechanical system of levers , gears, and wind vane to make course corrections via the rudder so that the vessel maintains a constant relationship to wind direction.

Sheets : 'ropes' used to control the angle and fullness of the sail, attached to the jib clew, the bottom corners of a spinnaker, or the end/middle of a boom.

Shroud : a wire connecting the top of the mast with the side of the boat. There may be several shrouds per side.

Slack : the opposite of secure, something not secured, to loosen. Also slack tide, when there is no water movement.

Sloop : a boat with a single mast, one jib, and a mainsail.

Spinnaker : a large, lightweight, usually colorful sail used when the wind is coming from astern to off the beam (perpendicular to the vessel).

Spring line : a line usually from the middle of the boat to a forward or aft dock cleat.

Stay : a supporting wire connecting the mast to the bow (forestay) or stern (backstay).

Staysail : a sail fixed to a stay, for example, a cutter rig has an outer jib and a smaller jib attached to an inner forestay.

Squall : a violent wind that arrives suddenly, often with rain.

SSB Radio : single-side band modulation radio, similar to Ham radio, used for medium to long-range marine communications with fixed channels and frequency selection. Range depends on environmental/atmospheric conditions.

Stanchions : metal pipes secured to the gunwale. holding lifelines to prevent crew from falling overboard.

Starboard : the right side of the boat, associated with green (e.g. navigation lights on the vessel and buoys).

Stern : the rear of the boat.

Stern line : a rope used to tie the rear of the boat to the dock.

Storm sails : very rugged, small sails (aka storm jib and trysail) used to replace larger sails in the event that severe winds make reefing or furling insufficient.

Stow : to put things in their proper place, not to be confused with 'Stow it', a rude expression comparable to 'shut up' or 'get over it.'

Tack : the bottom, forward corner of a sail; also changing direction when going into the wind.

Tide : a periodic rise and fall in water level caused by the gravitational pull of the sun and moon, and the rotation of the earth. Tides vary by location, ranging from a few inches in lakes to many feet.

Tiller : a handle attached to a rudder or outboard motor to enable steering.

Trim : the balance of a boat achieved by distributing the weight fore and aft. Also to adjust the shape of the sails for better performance.

VHF Radio : very high frequency two-way radio (marine application broadcasts in the 156.0 and 162.025 MHz range) with international-standard channels. For example, 16 is the hailing and distress channel. The range is 'line-of-sight' and varies depending on signal strength, antenna, environmental conditions, and obstructions. US Coastguard transmissions exceed 60 miles, while a typical sailboat range is between 10 and 30 miles.

Wake : the disturbance of water caused by a boat's movement.

Winch : a metal cylinder turned by ratcheting gears and a handle to give leverage, used to hoist or pull in the sails.

Windlass : a device for raising the anchor; may be electrically powered.

Windward : generally the direction the wind is coming from. For example, going to windward is to sail close-hauled.

Yawl : a two-masted vessel, the mizzen mast being much smaller and farther aft than that of a ketch.

About the Author

Neil Barry lives aboard his 50-foot sloop, *Imagine,* cruising the East Coast of the U.S., the Bahamas, and points south. Born in Sydney, Australia, he began sailing at 12 years old. While studying architecture in college, he graduated from 12-foot boats to crewing on racing yachts on Sydney Harbour and offshore.

In 1977, he took time off from sailing to attend graduate school, travel the world, raise a family, and build a career as an academic. His next boat arrived 13 years later, a 28-foot cutter that he finished from the bare-hull stage. He sailed with his family on a small man-made lake in Indiana for 17 years before the ocean called again.

Imagine at Hopetown, Elbow Cay in the Abacos, Bahamas, where the author is researching a forthcoming book. Copyright: Neil Barry

After 30 years as a professor, Neil Barry recognized the need for a new kind of novel, one that stimulates learning, while providing entertainment. His *Chicken of the Sea* trilogy combines real places, things, events, and situations with fictional people and an engrossing, believable plot. Readers can use today's digital technology to explore the 'real' world of Victor Joshua Walker, beginning by visiting neilbarrybooks.com.

The author brings the Ship's Log up to date, Bahamas. 2015. Copyright: Kathryn Ellis

43350590R00219

Made in the USA
Charleston, SC
25 June 2015